DISTANT
FRIENDS
Of
PELLAYA

By Eric Parkin

Who knows what tomorrow will bring?

A friend wrote that she looked forward to every new chapter. Thank you for such kind words, Katie.

I woke one morning and had the basics of the first part of this book thrust into my head. It didn't come from my imagination. I felt a warm breath of air at the base of my skull, and this story appeared in my mind. I can not dispute that it came from God because the story was suddenly there in my head. It seems odd that it is Science Fiction, but if you read on, you might understand.

For various reasons, I retired early from truck driving. The company I worked for went bankrupt, I was diagnosed with neck problems that made it painful to drive, and then COVID-19 struck. I decided to retire and then wondered what I would do with myself. When I woke up and inherited this book, I took that as a sign I was to write. I have been writing ever since.

The first part of this book is the outline I was given. I only had to flesh it in, and that was done in three months. The second part is all from my imagination and took another three months to complete. The editing of this book has taken me an additional two and a half years, because, and I admit, I didn't know what I was doing.

I thank God for his guidance and sending people and situations that inspired me to continue working to the end. There were quite a few.

EP Publishing

ISBN 979-8-9929362-1-6

Table of Contents

DISTANT FRIENDS OF PELLAYA

Chapter one
The Mental Abyss

He felt himself waking and opened his eyes to find himself in the darkness so black he couldn't see a thing. He wasn't waking from a deep sleep. He was emerging from nothingness into awareness. He imagined himself as a spirit that had just been born into existence, and a few things suggested that it was true. First, he didn't know who he was, where he was, or how he had come to be there, and thought a newborn spirit wouldn't know such things either. He also felt he was floating, and that too would suggest he was a newborn spirit floating in the dark. The last thing that had him convinced he was a spirit was that he felt comfortable and completely unafraid to have awoken in the darkness. It felt like he belonged here.

The darkness hung before his eyes like a black curtain and had such presence, he half expected to feel it flow around his arm when he reached into it. It didn't surprise him when he couldn't feel it, but he did question why he couldn't feel his arms moving. *Perhaps spirits can't feel themselves moving. We don't have physical bodies, so why would we feel movement?*

He agreed with himself that he had to be a newborn spirit, then immediately wondered why he felt like he should be somewhere else, doing something else. This was where he belonged, wasn't it? What was he going to do about it anyway? So far, he had been unable to move himself around in the darkness, and even if he could, where would he move to? He couldn't see a darn thing in this black pit. There was no variation in the black color at all, and not a speck of light anywhere.

He thought about this and was mildly concerned, but he was still confident that everything was as it should be. He wasn't going to let these concerns ruin the warm, easy feeling he had.

Suddenly, something flashed in his mind, and he saw strange creatures walking around him. It was confusing because they weren't in the dark with him, yet he could see them as clearly as could be. It was as if the creatures were being projected onto the black curtain in front of him.

The creatures themselves, though odd, didn't interest him as much as the fact that they were in the light. He couldn't see a thing where he was in the black pit, but these creatures were able to see everything because they were in the light. That made him long for light to come and push the darkness back. Maybe then he could understand where he was and what was happening to him.

Suddenly, one of the creatures was face to face with him, staring at him. It had a blank expression on its face, but it was so close, it was unnerving. He didn't like having this creature stare at him from so close.

He tried to look away, but wherever he turned, the images of the creature followed as if his eyes were the projectors. He had no choice but to see it whether he wanted to or not.

Then a strange thing happened, as if what had been happening wasn't strange enough. The creature looked away, picked something up, and stuck it in its mouth. It started moving the thing around rather quickly. White foam began forming around its mouth. What in the world was it doing?

Seeing this added to his already growing anxiety. He was trapped in the black pit, didn't know where he was, and had a strange creature staring at him while frothing at the mouth. His comfortable, easy feeling was leaving him.

He watched the creature, and suddenly knew the creature's name. This creature's name was John. How could he possibly know that?

Then another being, a female by the looks of it, came into the light and pushed her face against the side of John's face. As he watched this happen, he felt her warm breath on his ear. How could that be? She was whispering into John's ear, not his. How could he feel anything from her? He followed her with his eyes when she left the room. When he looked back at John, white foam was spilling from John's mouth, and he was laughing.

He watched John and remembered what John was laughing about. How could he remember that? And how could he feel her breath on his ear? Suddenly, he remembered the whole incident. *I'm John! That was my wife! I was looking at myself in the mirror brushing my teeth. She came in, kissed me on the cheek, and said something that cracked me up. I was laughing so hard I inhaled most of the toothpaste!* "That was a memory," he said aloud. "All these things I am seeing are memories. They're playing in my head like movies! I don't belong in this dark place. I'm supposed to be out there in the light someplace!"

It was now painfully clear that he wasn't a newborn spirit and didn't belong floating around in the dark. The comfortable, easy feeling he had had was gone. He was now terrified to be floating in total darkness, not knowing where or who he was. He didn't know how he had come to be here, so he had no idea how to get out of it.

He was starting to panic. He reached into the darkness, looking for anything, a door, a light switch, something to help him understand where he was. He tried to stand but had no way of knowing if he was or not. To make matters worse, he had a rapidly growing feeling he needed to get out of the darkness to where he belonged. He was certain his life depended on it.

"I have to get out of this… this…" he said, struggling for the words. *What has wiped my mind clean of all my memories? Was it something in this black pit? Where am I? Is it some Mental vacuum, or a Mental Abyss that somehow drained everything away from me? It's not just my memories that are gone. I don't know anything about myself or where I belong. What could take so much from me and leave me thinking I was a spirit?*

"I have to get out of here, but how?"

Unable to see, hear, or feel, he was trapped with no way out. His panic seemed to trigger something. *"I have to get out! I have to get out!"* kept playing over and over in his head, getting louder and stronger each time it replay. He felt like he was losing control of himself. Something else was taking over.

Terrified, he slipped into a full-blown panic. Not thinking, he started trying to swim up out of the darkness. He held his breath and hoped he was moving and would soon see light.

Suddenly, he was a young boy, floating three feet under water, looking up at the surface. He forgot all about the Mental Abyss and was completely at ease as he stared up at an amazing sight. The sunlight was hitting the ripples on the surface, and being carried away in all directions. It was quite a light show, and it fascinated him. To create more ripples, he pushed upward with his arms. For a moment, nothing happened. Then suddenly, the surface erupted, and the light show reached a new level.

The water was warm, and the light show above so fascinating, he didn't want it to end. His need to breathe told him it was time to head for the surface. He took one more second to look down around himself. It was pitch black! He had been so focused on that small area on the surface that he didn't realize how fast he was drifting deeper. He was so deep that sunlight wasn't reaching him. Only now did he realize how much trouble he was in.

He struck out, desperate to get to the surface. Almost immediately, his lungs began to convulse, trying to force him to suck in a lung full of water. He closed his eyes and concentrated on keeping himself from breathing. Suddenly, the convulsions stopped, but at that same moment, his strength left him. He was practically dead in the water from lack of oxygen. For a moment, he resigned himself to his drowning. Then, he exploded in one last desperate effort and clawed toward the surface. With great relief and surprise, he burst through the surface. Flailing his arms and sucking in volumes of air, he opened his eyes and stiffened. He wasn't in the water anymore. He was sitting in an odd little room. "What in the world is happening to me?" he asked.

A man was sleeping in the seat next to him on his right. The wall in front of them was very close and decorated with switches and gauges. The room was tiny. Just enough room for the two of them to sit, not much more.

Slowly lowering his arms from his struggle through the water, he studied the room. He didn't know, or more likely, couldn't remember this room or the man. He was sure the Mental Abyss had taken all that from him. All he knew about himself was his name and he was thankful to have remembered that.

He wasn't floating in the Abyss or in the water anymore, but he still felt like he was floating and that was confusing. He looked around and was most thankful for the light. He could see everything around him. As the surprise of waking in this room wore off, he became more aware of that sense of urgency. It was growing again. It was worse now than before. There was something he had to do or somewhere he needed to be, and it was important. But what was it?

He looked at the man next to him, thinking he might have answers to all the questions that filled his head. He reached out to wake the man and at that moment remembered his name. "Your name is Randy," he said aloud. Then he saw what Randy was wearing and that gave him Pause. He looked back at himself and was shocked to see he was also wearing a spacesuit. "Are we astronauts?" he asked. Each time he spoke, his voice seemed to shatter the silence. It was dead quiet and had been from the time he found himself in the Mental Abyss.

He looked back at Randy and was pleased that memories of him were creeping back into his head. He and Randy had been friends since grade school. He knew Randy's family and many of his friends very well. Carrol was Randy's wife. Angie was his wife's name, and he was very pleased to remember her name. The woman he saw whispering in his ear was beautiful, and he knew her to be smart and funny. It was soothing to remember the great love they had for each other. That memory made him want to be with her now more than ever.

It was all coming back now. He and Randy had lost track of each other, but eventually found themselves working together for…. "Holy crap! We work for NASA!" John said aloud. "This isn't a room! This is the lunar lander! I'm in the Lucky Lady! We were on a mission to the moon. Oh God no!" he said, lunging forward to look out the window on his side of the Lucky Lady. He had expected to see the moon's surface rushing toward him as the Lucky Lady crashed. He sat back with a sigh of relief.

He had remembered reaching up to throw a switch that would start the Lucky Lady down for a landing. Thankfully, he hadn't thrown that switch, and they weren't crashing. If he had pushed that switch, the Lucky Lady probably would have crashed or would have been about to.

John scratched his head. He remembered reaching up to push the switch, but everything after that was a blank. He didn't know what happened after that. At least now he had a good idea why he had felt such a sense of urgency. He needed to be here to pilot the Lucky Lady. That sense of urgency had left him, and he could relax a little. They were orbiting the moon like they were supposed to be, and he and the Lucky Lady seemed fine.

He sat with his eyes closed, trying to make sense of what had caused his black out. He remembered reaching up to push the switch, then… was in the Mental Abyss with his mind wiped clean. When he tried to swim out of the darkness, suddenly he was reliving a childhood experience where he had almost drowned. He wasn't just remembering it; he was there doing it as if it were the first time. Now he was back in the Lucky Lady. It was all so strange and made him quite confused. Thankfully, his memory was returning, but what caused him to lose it in the first place?

"What about the mission?" he asked himself. "Something caused Randy and I to black out. It could happen again. We need to scrub the mission until we know what happened, then we can return to the Mo……no! That wasn't the Moon! That was Earth!" he said, sitting up to the window again. He didn't want to be right, but he was. "How in the world did we get back to Earth?" he said, sitting back again. "This is impossible! We're supposed to be orbiting the Moon! How did we get here? What in the world is going on?"

"Randy, wake up!" John said, reaching out to wake Randy. John was in such a state that the gentle push he intended to give Randy could have shoved him out of his seat and across the room. If not for the seat belts, it would have.

Randy groaned. "I have to wake up! I shouldn't be sleeping; I have to wake up!" Then slowly turned to John. "Who are you? Why did you push me like that? I need to wake up!" he said again.

"Randy, it's me, John. Are you okay, buddy?"

"No, I'm not ok! I'm a skip in a record because of you. I have to wake up. I shouldn't be asleep. Why did you push me like that? You shouldn't have done that. You did something to me."

"Yeah, I'm sorry about that, Randy. I didn't mean to push you that hard, but I needed you to wake up," John said, noticing how peculiar Randy was acting. "Randy, we're not orbiting the Moon anymore. Something has gone wrong. I need you to help figure this out."

"What?" Randy said, thumping his head with his fist. "I have to wake up. Get out. Leave me, wake up!" Randy said and started pawing the air in front of him. "I need to wake up! I have to get out of here," he said, and turned to John. "This is your fault you son of a bitch! I'm trapped in here because of you! It's your fault!"

"Woe, Randy, what's going on. What's my fault? What are you talking about?" John asked.

"Stop! Stop! Stop!" Randy said, thumping his head again. "Damn you! You did this to me."

"Did What? Randy, what's the matter with you? Please calm yourself and tell me what's going on. I don't understand what you're talking about. I need you to calm down. You need to look out your window. We have a problem."

Randy yanked his head around and glanced out his window. It was obvious to John that Randy hadn't paid any attention to what he saw outside. Randy turned to John and snarled. "I'm a skip in a record because of you. You did this to me you son of a bitch."

"Randy, I don't know what you're talking about. I'm sorry I pushed you that hard if that's what your pissed about. I really didn't mean to. Randy, please calm down and look out your window. Something has gone wrong, and I need your help."

Randy looked out his window. When he turned back to John, he started yelling. "That's not the Moon down there, John. What have you done? Did you do this? Who do you think you are? Why are you doing all this?"

"Randy, what's the matter with you? I did not bring us here. I don't know how we got here. I didn't do this," John said, reaching out to take hold of Randy's arm, attempting to calm him. "Randy, please calm down."

Randy's face was red. Veins were sticking out on his forehead. He yanked his arm away from John. "Who do you think you are? You can't do this!" he yelled and threw a punch at John. Because of his seat belt, Randy's punch was awkward, and he completely missed John. Infuriated even more, he tried to lunge at John, pawing at him like a crazed animal.

John had no choice but to throw a punch of his own. He didn't miss. Randy's attitude changed immediately. "Oh my God," Randy said, staring at John. "John, I'm so sorry. I couldn't stop it. Something was controlling me. I can't believe I was doing that! John, what's happening?" he said. Randy's face said it all. He was embarrassed, humiliated, and wholly confused all at the same time. He looked down at the floor. "John, you won't believe what I've been going through."

John put a hand on Randy's shoulder. "I have a feeling I have a pretty good idea of what you've been going through. I have been on a very strange journey myself. I'm getting the impression your dealing with the same crap," John said, and with his hand still on Randy's shoulder, rocked him back a forth. "I'm just glad you're back with me. You scared the crap out of me."

Randy was visibly shaken. "I am so glad to be out of there and here with you. I am so sorry for what I said and did. I had no control over myself. There was more than one screw loose in my head. Man! I never want to feel like that again." Then he looked up at John. "Wait a minute. You went through something like this?"

"Oh yeah, you could say that," John said, nodding. "I was a newborn spirit blinded by darkness, then went for a swim, and finally ended up here," John said, rocking Randy again. "We should talk about all this later. Right now, I'm concerned about the Lucky Lady. I don't know what has happened or what she has been through. Did you see what's outside?"

"Yes, and I don't know what to make of it. How did we end up orbiting Earth?" Randy said, his heart pounding as if he had just run a race. "We fall asleep, I go berserk, and somehow, we end up back here orbiting Earth. I don't get it."

"I don't either. I don't even know where to start to figure it out," John said. He looked back at Randy. "You scared the hell out of me, buddy. Are you okay now? Has your memory returned?"

"Yes, I think so," Randy said, turning to John. "John, what happened to us?"

John shrugged. "I have no idea. I haven't had much time to think about it. I've been rather busy dealing with a crazy man,"

Randy nodded but said nothing. It was obvious he was embarrassed about his actions.

John glanced at his watch. "This can't be right. Randy, what time do you have on your Omega? I have 10:13."

Randy checked his watch. "I have the same time."

John looked lost. "That means it all happened in thirteen minutes?"

"What happened in Thirteen minutes?"

"Everything," John said. "From the time we fell asleep to now. It all happened in thirteen minutes. You remember that we were right on schedule, right?"

"Yeah, everything was going great."

John nodded. "It was 10 AM on the nose when I prepared to land, but both our watches say 10:13, and according to my watch, it's still the same day. That means only thirteen minutes have passed. All this," John said, waving his hand in the air. "Our falling asleep, our waking in the Mental Abyss, our waking here in the Lucky Lady, and our coming back to Earth, all happened in that thirteen minutes."

"That's impossible. You can't get from the Moon to the Earth in 13 Minutes," Randy said.

John cocked his head back. "Everything was fine. Then I reached up to push that switch, and the next thing I know, I'm waking up in the Mental Abyss."

"That's exactly what happened to me," Randy said. "I watched you reach up, then I was waking up in a black oblivion with no idea who or where I was."

"So apparently, we both blacked out at the exact same time. What could cause that?" John asked, then tried to answer the question. "What about a drop in oxygen. That could do it, couldn't it?"

"Yes, it could," Randy said, checking the gauges on the wall. "But nothing here indicates we had a problem. The Oxygen levels are good, and the air scrubbers seem to be doing their job. I suppose there could have been a temporary blockage in an Oxygen supply line somewhere, but even that would show on my read-out, and it doesn't. Besides, we wouldn't have blacked out instantly like we did. We would have felt tired before passing out, and I don't remember feeling tired. I was excited to be landing on the moon. This is, or was going to be, my second landing on the Moon. I can't imagine falling asleep at a time like that."

John nodded. "There's no way either of us would. Whatever happened to us must have happened very quickly. Everything was fine. We were here doing our jobs, then I was in the Mental Abyss. I assume that's where you were too, and I don't understand that."

"I don't know of anything in here that would cause us to black out like that," Randy said. "And nothing in here that could switch us off that quickly. Besides, even if we could explain why we passed out, what could explain our being here, orbiting Earth? I don't care how you slice it; you can't get from the Moon to Earth in 13 minutes. And since we were asleep, who or what was piloting the ship? So why did we black out, and what brought us back here?"

John shrugged. "Randy, we need to check out the Lucky Lady. I don't know what we have been through, but she has gone through it too. I'm concerned she might be damaged. Let's check her out and make sure she's okay, then try to contact Mission Control. It concerns me that we aren't hearing anything on the radio. There must be something wrong with our antenna."

"Yeah, let's get it done," Randy said.

Together, they went through their checklist. The antenna was there and in good working order. They had all the oxygen and fuel they were supposed to have, which added to their confusion. Somehow, the Lucky Lady had flown back to Earth without burning any fuel. If she had flown back to Earth under power, there would be far less fuel.

The only thing they found wrong was that their orbit was decaying. The Lucky Lady was slowly drifting down toward the Earth. Once they corrected that problem, John tried to contact Mission Control. "This is the Lucky Lady to Mission Control. Do you copy Control? Over." There was no response. "This is Lunar Lander 7 to Mission Control. Please, come in, Mission Control, we have a problem up here. We need to know what has happened. Do you copy?" Still, no response, and that was troubling because it was true that there should be some kind of chatter on the radio, but the radio was eerily quiet.

"Try raising Bruce," Randy suggested. Bruce was in the Lunar Orbiter waiting for them to return from the surface of the Moon. Bruce should have already contacted them. Why didn't he? "Man," Randy said, shaking his head. "What if he's dealing with the same crap we are? What if he woke up in your…, what did you call it? The Mental Abyss? What if he woke up in the Mental Abyss and can't get out?"

"That would be pretty bad. I hope he's okay," John said, raising the radio mic to his mouth.

Randy shuddered. "There's no one there to bring him out of it."

John clicked on the mic and tried to raise Bruce several times, but Bruce never responded. Unless Bruce was behind the Moon, he should have heard them and called back. John continued trying to raise someone on the radio until Randy started pawing at his shoulder. "What are you doing?" John said, a bit annoyed. He turned to find Randy with his face jammed in the window while pawing blindly back at John. "Randy, what is it? What do you want?"

Randy turned to face him. "John, have you looked down there, I mean, really looked? I don't recognize a damn thing down there. John, this can't be Earth"

John stared at Randy for a minute, then turned slowly and looked out his window. Randy was right. He couldn't see North or South America, Africa, Saudi Arabia, or Italy. He couldn't see any of the big areas that were so easily recognized. This was a big blue planet with white clouds, and the north pole was capped with ice, but that was where the similarities to Earth ended. He and Randy had merely glanced out their windows and assumed what they were seeing was Earth. Why would they think it was anything else? Now John could only stare at the planet in disbelief.

"Good God!" Randy said. "We're not even orbiting the Earth! John, how in the world could this be happening?"

John stared out at the planet, unable to accept what he was seeing. *This has to be Earth! How could it be anything else? Something must have happened. Yes! Maybe an Asteroid has hit the Earth. That would explain a lot.* He turned to Randy. "Could an Asteroid have caused all this? Maybe it grabbed hold of us, pulled us back to Earth, then hit the Earth and somehow changed the landscape?"

"In thirteen minutes?" Randy said. "There's no way that happened. The Asteroid you're talking about would have to be traveling extremely fast to get us back to Earth in thirteen minutes, and if its gravity were strong enough to grab hold of the Lucky Lady, it would have ripped her apart. We'd be in pieces floating around the moon. Besides, if something like that happened, we would see the smoke and fire from its collision with Earth. No, no Asteroid did this."

"What about a Rogue Planet?" John asked. "They exist, right? Maybe this is a Rogue Planet that came through, and we somehow got caught in its gravity. Is that possible?"

"You're grasping at straws, John. Don't you think someone would have seen something as big as this planet coming long before it got here and alerted everybody about it? Think about it. This planet would be right where our Moon should be. That means this planet would have collided with our Moon, and we would definitely see the destruction from that collision.

I don't know what happened, but the fact is, that's not our Earth down there. We are orbiting an alien world, John. I have no idea how it happened, but… well, here we are," Randy said.

"That means Mission Control isn't there either! We're alone up here!" John said, pushing back from his window. Then he sat forward again. "Randy, do you have any idea what might have happened here? Anything at all?"

"Not a thing," Randy said. "None of this makes any sense. If we hadn't fallen asleep, we might have seen what happened, but we did fall asleep, and that right there makes no sense. Who falls asleep while landing on the Moon? We would have to have Narcolepsy, and I guarantee we don't."

"What about a wormhole?" John asked. "Could we have traveled through a Wormhole?"

Randy shook his head. "A while ago, I would have said no. I mean, really … after all this time, suddenly there's a wormhole near the Moon? But now…" he said, letting his words hang in the air. "Now I look out my window and see the impossible. That shouldn't be there, and we shouldn't be here. So yes, I suppose it could have been a Wormhole or a time warp.

Something like that. How would we know? We were asleep. We woke up here without a clue of what happened. John, how are we going to find our way back?"

Randy's words sent a chill through bought of them. How could they get back when they didn't know how they had come to be there, or where Earth was? It was doubtful the Lucky Lady could make the trip even if they did know where Earth was.

They stared out their windows at the planet as the truth of their situation became clear. They were in big trouble, and the only way they would survive was to get down on this alien planet. At the moment, they didn't know how they would do that. They couldn't land the Lucky Lady. She was designed to land on the moon where the Gravity was much less. If they tried to land on this planet, they would burn up. One hope was that they would find Bruce, dock with the orbiter, and survive. But they didn't know where Bruce and the Orbiter were.

John sighed, knowing Bruce was out there somewhere, but where was he? Was he somewhere around this planet? If he were, and they could dock with the obiter and use the Return Capsule to land on this planet. If Bruce were still orbiting the Moon waiting for them to return, he would eventually have to give up and leave them behind. That would be very hard for anyone to do. John shook his head. There was nothing he could do for Bruce but wish him luck.

John's thoughts were interrupted by Randy talking to himself. Randy believed talking to himself helped him clarify his thoughts. It didn't matter if John was listening or not. "There's life down there. Do you see the green and brown colors? That's life. This planet has plant life on it, and since there is plant life, it's likely there is some insect or even animal life down there." Randy laughed. "The question of whether life exists beyond Earth has been answered, but who can we tell? Even if we could tell someone, where would we tell them to look for it? I haven't the foggiest idea where I am." Randy bobbed his head up and down and announced, "Yeah, we're screwed."

John wasn't part of the conversation, but he agreed. It seemed so unfair, and even abusive, that they had the answer humanity had sought for centuries, but had no one they could tell. He didn't say it out loud, but there was a good chance that that knowledge would die with them in the Lucky Lady, and that just seemed cruel.

John sighed, frustrated that they couldn't do anything to help themselves out of their situation. But then, Randy was supposed to be a genius. He might have ideas. "Randy, what can we do? What are our options?"

"Options!" Randy said incredulously, turning to face John. "John, are you kidding me? Options? What options do you think we have? We're stuck in this dammed Aluminum Taxi, floating around a strange planet. We don't know where we are, or where Earth is! Even if we knew where it was, we couldn't get there. The Lucky Lady wasn't designed for that kind of travel," he said, staring at John. Then he looked away and threw an arm up in the air. "Now, if you were contemplating suicide, we'd have plenty of options. We could let the Lucky Lady drift into the atmosphere and burn up. We'd be ashes long before we reached the surface, but the suicide would be successful. And just think! Our ashes would be spread around the planet at the same time. What a lovely thought, don't you think?" Randy said, and paused just long enough to glance at John. "There's no way we can get down there to land on this planet, and that, unfortunately, is our only option.

Options, Jesus John. Maybe you think we could land on a moon and grow crops or something. You know, become Lunar Farmers. Hmm, I haven't seen a moon. Have you ole buddy ole pal?"

Randy's words were thick with sarcasm, and he was managing to piss John off, but that didn't stop him. "Even if we did land on a Moon, which we could do, but then what? We have no food. Bruce has all the food in the Orbiter with him," Randy said, tossing his arms in the air, emphasizing his disgust. Then he turned to look squarely at John. "Oh, and here's a great little tidbit of news for you. Don't worry about the air scrubbers, they're working fine and will keep the air clean and fresh for us AS WE STARVE TO DEATH. I don't know about you, but I'm so happy to know that."

Randy paused for a moment again, gathering his thoughts. "Options! The only option we have is how we die, and we have plenty of options there. We could starve to death, which sounds like a whole lot of fun to me. Maybe we could open the door and slip out into space without helmets. Mm, not for me.

We could suffocate together when the Lucky Lady's batteries run dry. Oh wait!" Randy said, dramatically slapping his forehead. "We have those new Solar Wings recharging the batteries, so the batteries will continue working long after our expiration date has come and gone. Isn't it great that we'd be warm and fuzzy with plenty of light as we shrivel up like prunes and die! What more could you ask for?"

Randy rocked his head from side to side. "Well, there is that little black pill they gave us, telling us it was for the unexpected. I think our situation qualifies, don't you? I'd like to do the unexpected and give *them* a little black pill right now," he said under his breath. "Any way you look at it, the result is the same. We die! Do you like those options, John?"

John didn't answer. Instead, he sat waiting for Randy to finish his rant. He'd seen Randy like this before and knew it was Randy's way of dealing with his frustration. He didn't mean any harm. He was just pissed at the world.

"It seems to me," Randy said. "That everything meant to keep us alive is now only going to prolong our deaths. I will take the little black pill when the time comes, thank you very much, but why don't we have a meal before we go? What do you say, John, hmmm? Oh how could I forget; all the food is in the damn Lunar Orbiter with Bruce. I hope he gets fat! I hope he inflates like a balloon so he can't get out of the orbiter." Randy paused his rant again, and then shouted, "And where the Hell is Bruce anyway! Why isn't he sharing in our delightfully grand adventure?" Finally, Red-faced and thoroughly agitated, Randy ended his rant.

Scratching his head and grinning with amusement, John simply asked, "Are you done?"

Randy laughed a little and shook his head. "Okay, yeah, I'm losing it, and I don't need to be yelling at you. But John. I'm just so dammed angry and confused. What happened? How did we end up in this mess? The Mission was going so perfectly. You couldn't ask for it to go any better. All we had to do was land, do a little surveying, and head for home. So why are we sitting here staring death right square in the face? It pisses me off."

"I understand," John said. "And though you took a long time to say it, you're right, we don't have any options. I can't think of anything we can do but sit here and wait for … for whatever is going to happen to us. But Randy, you're the big brain on this Mission. I need you to stay calm and think of a way out of this. If there is a way out, you'll be the one to think of it, not me." John suddenly stiffened. "What about a Moon, is there any advantage in landing on one?"

Randy's answer was calmer but still laced with sarcasm. "Have you seen one?"

John grinned and pointed out Randy's window.

Randy leaned forward and saw two Moons visible in the distance. "Well, I'm sure we could land on one, but then what? We'd be in the same situation except we'd be sitting on the Moon. I can't see where a Moon would help. The only way out of our situation is to get down to the planet, and there is no way we can do that."

"Well," John said, pointing a thumb out his own window. "If a Moon could help, we'd have options."

Randy leaned over and looked out John's window. "Okay, it's three Moon? But that doesn't change a thing. The only way we survive this is by getting down to the planet, and there's no way we can do that. Face it, we're screwed."

John nodded. "And when you're wearing a spacesuit that's a pretty good screwing."

"Yeah," Randy said. "We deserve a place in the Guinness book of World Records for the worst screwing ever."

Both of them laughed uncomfortably. John picked up the radio and started calling for help. He had nothing else to do, and there was a chance Bruce or someone else would hear him. It was better than sitting there stewing.

Randy stared out at the planet, talking to himself again. "If there were intelligent life down there, they could come get us, but

I haven't seen anything that suggests there is intelligent life. Even if there was, they would have to know we were here and be advanced enough to come get us. That would be a miracle,"

Neither one said so, but a miracle was exactly what they were hoping for. It was all they had.

Randy shrugged and looked back at the planet. "Man, it would be great to see what's down there. Even if it is just plant life, I'd love to see it. Just imagine what insect or animal life could be walking around down there right now. And look at that atmosphere? It's so clear. This is a pristine world with alien life, and it's right there in front of us," Randy said, shaking his head. "

"You know what, Randy," John said. "With the kind of luck we're having, we'd get down there and that animal life you're so fond of would have teeth the size of Road Cones and love a good game of cat and mouse."

"Well, at least we'd be out of this Aluminum Taxi," Randy scoffed. "And down there, we mice could run for our lives. At least make it hard for them to get to the crunchy center."

"I'm sure we would," John said. "But here's something else for you to ponder. Say we manage to land and get eaten. Not only did we land, but we would land twice."

Randy laughed. "Well, it makes me happy to have that to look forward to."

John shrugged. "I was thinking Tyrannosaurus crap. What do you think?"

"Yes, I'm thinking a pile of crap too, John. One whopper of an experience," Randy said, turning back to his window. "Hey, look!" he yelled.

"What?"

"Look! There are lights down there!"

John looked and saw the light. They were heading into the dark side of the planet. "Is that a reflection?"

"No, that's not a reflection," Randy said, a smile growing on his face. "That, my dear friend, is intelligent life. Those are electric lights… Look, there are more lights. Those are cities, cities with electricity. This is fantastic!"

"I don't believe it," John said. "There is intelligent life down there. Randy, if they have electricity, maybe they have some sort of Radio. Can you adjust our radio to pull in a signal, like AM or FM?"

"I know I can," Randy said and started to adjust the radio.

"If you can, would you be able to patch into it and talk to them?"

"Yeah, I'm pretty sure of that too," Randy said. Then added, "But you realize they wouldn't understand a word we said."

"Yes, I know, but they would know we were here. It's worth a try."

After a few minutes, John asked, "Getting anything?"

"No, nothing yet, but there is a lot to go through."

"Keep trying," John said. "Our only hope of surviving this ordeal is to get rescued by these aliens. Obviously, no help is coming from Earth, and I haven't seen anything of Bruce and the Orbiter."

Randy suddenly shook his head in frustration. "I'd swear I was receiving a signal, but there's nothing there. This channel is noticeably quiet, and that can mean it's an active channel, but I'm not hearing anything."

"Are you sure the radio is working?" John asked.

"Yes. The radio is working fine. It's more like the channel is open, but no one is saying anything."

"Maybe nobody's home, or," John paused a moment. "Or maybe they hear us but don't know how to respond because of our language."

"That could be. I just don't know. Something doesn't seem right. I'd swear I was getting a signal."

"Well, keep working at it. Alien or not, I'd like to be rescued." John said.

"Oh, I know it," Randy said. "We need to attract their attention. Hey, wait a minute! What about the landing lights? Why don't we turn them on?"

"That's a good idea," John said. "They'll show well in the dark, but I wonder if they wouldn't be a greater signal flare during the day. Turn them on."

Randy turned on the lights and went back to the radio, but after hours of trying, he turned away from the radio. "It's useless. I'm not getting anything. All I hear is an odd emptiness. I don't know what else I can do." Randy left the radio on, just in case, but as the hours passed and the silence continued, their hopes faded. Their only hope was that the landing lights would attract some attention, and the aliens would rescue them. But it seemed reasonable to think that if the aliens didn't have radio technology, they wouldn't have the means to launch a craft into space either. Even if they saw the lights crossing their skies, they wouldn't be able to do anything about it. The situation for John and Randy was hopeless.

Randy looked out the window at the planet. " I sure wish we could get down there."

CHAPTER TWO
THE GRAY SPECK

Every time they orbited the planet; they saw the city lights. At first, it was exciting, but after being in orbit for 54 hours, making 35 orbits, the thrill had worn off. Their hope of being rescued had also vanished because several things about the planet, like the incredibly pristine atmosphere and the lack of radio, suggested this was an early civilization. These aliens wouldn't be advanced enough to rescue them, even if they knew they were there.

They had been crammed into the tiny confines of the Lucky Lady for far too long. They were bored, frustrated, and feeling helpless. To combat his boredom, Randy took to gathering information about the planet. He had timed how long it took the Lucky Lady to circle the planet, then determined how fast the Lucky Lady was traveling. Then, using the equipment onboard, he was able to learn their distance from the planet's surface, and had just now finished approximating the length of a day on this planet.

To amuse himself, *and irritate John*, he turned to John with a dopy supercilious look on his face. With a voice and attitude of English snobbery to match, announced, "It may interest you to know, my dear Johnny boy, that we are traveling at just over 23000 mph which is faster then if we were orbiting the Earth. This is significant information, as I will demonstrate to you in time. To be sure, my calculations are quite accurate. It may further interest you, that it takes a mere 105 minutes to circle this planet don't you know. If my equipment is working properly and my calculations are accurate, and I am certain they are, we are maintaining an orbit three hundred miles from the surface.

I cannot imagine that I should have to tell you, my dear Johnny Boy, that our speed, distance from the surface, and time it takes to complete an orbit all indicate that this planet is quite a bit larger than Earth. I should think that would be quite evident from looking out your window, but I have proven it scientifically, and you can rest assured my calculations are correct."

John gave Randy an amused look. "Well, thank you for that report, Professor Jack Cass," John said, taunting him. "We'll stop by your mailbox the next time around and get your Nobel Prize, what?" John added, mocking Randy's English accent.

Undaunted, Randy continued. "And a day on this planet is 28 hours, don't you know. Should you require any further information, I will make myself available to any requests you may have." Randy said, bowing slightly. He had completed his report and his act.

"I would request you be less of a Nut case," John said, laughing. This was one of the reasons he liked Randy so much. You never knew what he would do or say.

None of the information Randy had collected helped them in any way, but it gave Randy something to do, and both of them needed something to relieve their boredom and depression. The city lights on the planet had become little more than a carrot dangling in front of them. They could see the lights, but couldn't reach them. There was no way they could get to the surface, and being reminded of that every time they orbited the planet was painful.

The sunlit side of the planet was an unattainable carrot as well. They were crammed in the Lucky Lady, unable to move or stretch out, while down on the planet, in those wide-open spaces, they would be free to stretch out and walk around as freely as they pleased. They longed to be out of the Lucky Lady, but that, too, was a carrot always out of reach. It was certain that there was food and water on the planet, and that was something they needed. Randy's water supply had already run out. John still had a small amount, but they had no food at all. The food was in the Orbiter with Bruce.

These things were bothersome, but what made them most uncomfortable was that there were no bathroom facilities in the Lucky Lady. Their suits were designed to handle this problem for a short time, but it had been days now. They stank and were extremely uncomfortable. They cursed the designers of the Lunar Lander for not including a way for a body to relieve themselves. They knew the Lucky Lady had been designed to be an elevator, and that no one was meant to be in it for more than an hour. But that did nothing to relieve their discomfort or stop them from admonishing the designers.

They were trying to remain upbeat and joked around, but they couldn't avoid thinking about what was eventually going to happen. They were feeling miserable and very uncomfortable. The Lucky Lady was so small that all they could do was sit. There was no room to stretch out and relieve the tension in their limbs. Randy knew John was holding out for a miracle and respected him for that, but he was considering taking the Little Black Pill. He was reaching the limit of how much he could take. He would hold off for now, out of respect for John, but tomorrow he might not be willing to wait. For now, he would try to get some sleep and not think about it.

John was looking out his window, which he had been doing for quite a while. His neck and back were aching because of the position he had to hold his body, so he sat back to relax for a while. When he did, it dawned on him that he could be using the Lunar Landers landing camera to view the planet. The screen wasn't big, but he could sit back in comfort and view the planet. He turned it on and was pleased to see the Southern part of the planet displayed on the screen. They hadn't seen much of the Southern tier because of how the Lucky Lady was orbiting the planet. Now, with the camera, John was getting a good view of the southern parts of the planet's Southern Tier.

The Camera's Zoom proved its worth right away. John saw that what they thought was one massive continent extending around the belly of the planet was actually several continents strung close together. Narrow waterways ran between them, connecting the Northern and Southern Oceans. The camera didn't zoom in enough to show buildings or anything like that, but it brought the natural features of the land much closer. Seeing the continents lined up around the belly of the planet got John theorizing how the continents had formed. He imagined the gravitational pull of three moons on a rock planet before it cooled could have pulled the planet into this somewhat walnut shape. *Randy will tell me I'm wrong and give his own more sensible reason. I should slap him just for the fun of it,* John thought.

John was much more certain about his next theory. He believed the tidal pulls of three Moons and the sun would cause the Oceans to be very turbulent and dangerous. He could imagine the waters churning violently enough that the aliens weren't able to go on the surface. It seemed possible, even probable, that they had or someday would develop a submarine to go underwater and avoid the turbulent surface. John considered this and was pleased, even prideful of his analysis of the planet, but wanted to slap Randy before he had the chance to shoot down his ideas.

John was enjoying the new view on the screen. It was the same planet with the same basic view, but he appreciated the subtle changes in what he could see. Much of the Northern Ocean was no longer visible, and that was fine. He had seen all he cared to see of it. The southern hemisphere was all new, and that simple change was significant.

He was enjoying the different view, but something on the screen was distracting him. Without looking, he tried to brush it off. He was too busy looking for Islands in the Southern Ocean to be bothered by a hair on the screen. He had found a few Islands in the Northern Ocean, but so far hadn't found any in the Southern Ocean, but there was a lot more Ocean to look through.

Whatever was on the screen had moved farther onto the screen and had become so distracting that he couldn't ignore it any longer. He took a good look and was surprised to see that it wasn't a hair. It was something on the surface of the planet moving into view. It had to be huge to show up like this.

"What's this now?" he said aloud, leaning closer for a better look. It was a dirty gray in color and had a very well-defined curved edge. It was emerging from the right side of the screen as if someone was outside pushing a coin onto the lens of the camera. This thing had to be man-made. Alien made in this case. "What have you built?" he asked.

The outer edge of the coin looked solid, but inside, a gray mass was swirling around in all directions. He had no idea what the gray mass was, except that it was ugly in comparison to what lay around it. The landscape outside the coin was green and beautiful, but inside, it was an ugly mass of swirling gray… stuff. "What is that?" John asked as he reached out to wake Randy. "Randy, you better wake up and take a look at this."

Randy grunted but didn't wake.

John stared at the thing. The coin was a little more than halfway on the screen now, and he could see it was forming a perfect circle. He couldn't believe what he was seeing. This thing had to be a thousand miles in diameter. Large enough to cover half the United States, from Florida to New York.

John's mouth fell open when he realized this monstrosity reached the top of the Stratosphere or possibly the Mesosphere. It was so big he could see the slight curve at the top that followed the curvature of the planet. "What did you guys build?" John said loudly. "Randy, wake your ass up. Look at this," he said, giving Randy a push.

"What?" Randy said, sitting up in his seat.

John pointed to the screen. "Look. You're gonna love this."

"Wow! What's that?" Randy said, rubbing his eyes.

"It's huge!" John said.

"I can see that, but what is … Holy crap! It reaches up to the stratosphere!"

"We have yet another mystery!" John said. "Look at the edges of it. That's not a natural feature. It's too clean and sharp to be a natural feature. I've never seen anything in nature that forms a perfect circle like this. And look, you can see through it like it's a huge glass of fog sitting on the surface,"

"That's weird!" Randy said. "But that can't be fog. At least not any fog I know of. It looks more like a writhing mass of gray worms moving around in there. This is really strange! I can see it's not a storm. A storm doesn't act like that. The clouds are swirling all over the place instead of rotating like a storm cloud. From up here, this thing looks like a giant hockey puck lying on the surface," Randy said. "Another mystery we will never be able to solve. I'm really getting tired of all these mysteries."

They studied the Hockey Puck every time they circled the planet, and were able to watch an actual storm pass through it. The clouds in the storm never mixed with the gray crap inside the Hockey Puck. "What do you make of that?" John asked.

"I don't know," Randy said. "All I can think of is that there's a very strong magnetic field being generated down there. That could have that kind of effect. But it seems unlikely that they could create that kind of energy. I really don't know, I'm just guessing."

They studied it for quite a while, but eventually lost interest in it. It was just another mystery they couldn't explain. It was frustrating to see the Hockey puck and want to investigate it, but sit high above it unable to do anything but look at it.

Hours passed. Randy sat staring out his window, lost in thought. He was aware of the planet and its Moons, and a small gray speck clinging to the outside of his window, but in his head, he was miles away with his wife and kids. How he would like to be with them right now.

Randy had reached his limit and was about to take the little black pill that would end his suffering. He was cramped up, sore, hungry, smelling bad, and generally uncomfortable. He just wanted it to be over. There was no hope of rescue. No miracle was going to come out of the darkness and save them. They were only torturing themselves by staying alive, which was precisely why they had been given the black pill. He was sure John still had hopes of somehow surviving all this, but he had had enough and wasn't going to give John a chance to talk him out of it.

He reached into the shoulder pocket of his suit for the pill container, never taking his eyes from the window. He was thinking how much he would have liked to have seen what was down on the planet. It would be such a thrill to see it. He pictured himself making contact with the inhabitants. It was fun to think about, but not fun enough to stop him from doing what he was about to do.

As he fumbled for the pill, he noticed his faint reflection in the window. The 'gray speck' clinging to the window appeared to be on his cheek, and that reminded him of the beauty mark on his wife's face. He thought of her smile and some of the other looks she used to give him. Then thought of her, alone on earth without him, and that hurt. He loved his wife and kids very much, and it made him feel guilty to be giving up like this, but he had to do it.

He couldn't take it anymore. The pill would relieve him of his pain and guilt.

He went from tearing up to smiling, as he remembered his kids' antics and the games they played. He remembered how excited everyone had been while making plans for his return. His smile evaporated when he thought of them taking that vacation without him.

He studied the pill vile he held in his lap, wishing there was something he could do to get back to them. *I'm so sorry I can't be with you guys. I hope, I pray, all of you will be okay and can forgive me for not coming home.*

He cracked the seal on the pill vial and looked back to the speck on the window. It had a color and shape that reminded him of his Mother-in-law's gray hair. He thought how fortunate he was to have a Mother-in-law he loved. He loved her like he loved his own mother. They got along great together. He nearly laughed out loud, remembering the day he had teased Mama 2 relentlessly, and she had grabbed a broom and chased him around the house, cussing and laughing the whole time. His wife and kids had stood by cheering her on, "Get him, Granma! Get him good!" He had teased them about being traitors afterward.

He had a big grin on his face, remembering that day. It was one of those special days that the whole family would never forget. It had been a day when they had had so much fun together, everything else was forgotten.

He looked at the gray speck again, and it had moved. Now it reminded him of the gray 1968 Mustang he once owned. *Never should have sold that car.* "Wait a minute!" Randy said, pulling himself out of his daydream. The gray speck had moved! It wasn't clinging to the window; it was something far beyond it. He had been watching something move out there without realizing it. "It's getting larger!" he said loudly as he quietly slipped the pill vial back into his pocket.

John jumped in his seat. "What?"

"There's something out there," Randy said.

"What is it? Is it the Orbiter?" John asked.

"It's too far away. I can't tell," Randy said, "But I'm pretty sure something out there is moving."

"I'd really like it to be the Orbiter," John said, leaning over to look out Randy's window.

Randy cocked his head to one side. "It's too slow for an Asteroid. It could be they have a Satellite, or it's just a piece of rock caught in the planet's orbit," he said, then shook his head. "No, it can't be a piece of Rock if it's moving up away from the planet like that."

Randy's eyes widened as he realized what he had just said. If it were true and this thing was moving away from the planet, it could only mean one thing. This thing was under power, and someone was controlling it. Could it be Bruce in the Orbiter! They looked at each other and smiled. Whether it was Bruce or not, something was coming toward them, and that gave them hope they might yet survive this ordeal.

Randy turned back to the window with John eagerly looking over his shoulder. Randy was feeling guilty for what he had almost done to John. He would have left John alone in the Lucky Lady with his lifeless body. How could he do that to him? What had he been thinking? He knew John was still waiting for a miracle. *Was John's miracle now coming toward them?*

"Randy, I can't see. Tell me what you are seeing," John said.

"It's too far away for me to make out what it is, but I'm sure it's moving toward us."

John unbuckled his seat belt and let himself float up behind Randy so he could have a better view. "Any guess as to what it is?"

"It could be anything," Randy said. "Hell, when I first saw it, it reminded me of my mother-in-law."

"Your mother-in-law?" John chuckled. "Ok, Randy, I'm seeing counseling in your future. I really do."

They had hope again, and that improved their moods. Randy drew in a breath. "I hate to get my hopes up, but either it's Bruce in the Orbiter or it's something from the planet. Maybe a Satellite, or they heard us on the radio and have sent a ship."

John nodded. "Whatever that thing is, if it keeps coming up the way it is, it will pass close by us."

Randy moved his head, trying to get a better view of it. "John, what does it look like to you?"

John looked away for a second. "I don't want to get my hopes up either, but it looks like a ship. I don't think it's the Orbiter. It's very far away, so I could be wrong, but I'm seeing a ship that looks a bit like NASA's space shuttles."

"Then we are seeing the same thing. It looks like a space shuttle to me, too," Randy said.

John couldn't resist the opportunity to tease Randy. "Were you expecting a visit from your Mother-in-law, or can we rule that out?"

"Ha-ha. You are so incredibly funny, Johnny boy," Randy groaned.

John moved as close to Randy's window as he could. "It's staying with us, so it has to be moving in the same direction, and it looks like it's moving to a higher orbit."

"That's what I see, too. Could they really be coming to rescue us?" Randy said.

John shrugged. "It doesn't look like a rescue mission to me. They don't act like they are looking for anything, and they are so far below us, I doubt they could see us even if they knew we were here."

"Hmm," Randy moaned.

John hoped it was a ship, but if it turned out to be a satellite, Randy might be able to figure out how to use it to their advantage. If it were a ship, he and Randy wouldn't be the ones in control. Whoever was on that ship would be in control of everything.

Randy watched the thing turn just enough for the light to illuminate it in just the right spots. "John, it is a ship! I can see it now. I'm sorry to say it's not Bruce, but it is a ship, and they are moving up toward us! If they keep coming, they will pass right by us."

John moved behind Randy. "I see it! But there's no way they can see us unless they turn around or look out their back window, if they have one," John said. "It doesn't really look like they are looking for us. I doubt they have any idea we're here."

"Then we have to do something!" Randy said anxiously. "That's our chance to live, right there. What can we do?"

John picked up the radio mic. "Mayday, mayday, this is the Lucky Lady, does anyone hear us? Can anyone hear us?" He waited a moment and then tried again. "Look, you probably don't understand our language, but hear us. We are here. We need your help. Can you hear us? Please come back. Say something, say anything." He paused and looked at Randy, who was watching the ship for any indication that they had heard. Randy shook his head and motioned for John to continue trying. John called on the radio again and again, but there was no answer and no change from the ship.

"Damn!" John said in frustration. "You've got to have some form of communication to travel into space, don't you?"

John closed his eyes and said a silent prayer. *Lord, please help us. Make these guys see us.* He pictured the aliens coming to their rescue. Suddenly, he felt a twinge of pain in his head and nearly dropped the Mic. It was quick and only lasted a second, but it was a sharp pain, something he had never felt before.

"It's turning!" Randy shouted.

John opened his eyes and rubbed his head. He looked out Randy's window. The craft was turning very slowly back toward them. It turned completely around and was facing in their direction, but was too far below for anyone to see them.

"We've got to get in front of them," John said. Hastily, he flipped some switches, grabbed the control stick, and started the Lucky Lady down.

"John, what are you doing? It's too far down!" Randy warned. "John, this is not a good idea! We won't be able to get back up here!" Randy warned again, but John did not stop. "John, think about what you are doing. This will be a one-way trip if we go too close to the planet. John, you have to stop!"

John didn't say anything but brought the Lucky Lady to a stop. The alien craft was already turning away from them. "Look up here! We're up here!" John said desperately. He was watching their only hope of surviving turn away from them.

Randy reached over and gripped John's arm. "John, we can't go that far down. The Lucky Lady wouldn't have enough power or fuel to stop us and get us back up here. We would burn up."

John closed his eyes and again prayed that the aliens would not fly away and would see the Lucky Lady. In his mind, he pictured the alien ship turning completely around again with its nose lifted high so it would look straight at them. "Look up here!" he said through clenched teeth. Again, he felt a sharp pain in his head. It came quickly and faded away slowly.

Randy was waving his arms and yelling, "We're up here. Look up here!" knowing there was no way anyone in the craft would see or hear him. But he was as desperate as John and feared the aliens might fly off, leaving them behind. These aliens were their only hope. They were John's miracle. "What can we do? We have to do something!" Randy said.

Right at that moment, the alien ship started to move. "Hey, wait! Randy shouted and stuck his head back in the window. "They're moving again! Come on, guys. Turn around and see us!" Randy said.

"Randy," John said. "We don't have a choice. I'm going to drop down in front of them. It's our only chance. If we don't get their attention, we are going to die anyway."

"Wait, John! Look how the ship has changed position! If they keep turning like that, they will end up looking straight at us. When they are, I'll flash the lights to get their attention. We don't have to risk anything. Going down there might get us seen, but we would sail right passed them, unable to stop. They wouldn't be able to get to us in time. John, they're still moving up toward us, and the closer they get, the better it is for us. Let's wait and see, okay?"

John let go of the controls and leaned over to look out Randy's window. Both of them prayed they hadn't made a mistake by not flying the Lucky Lady down to them. They held their breath as they watched the ship continue to turn. Soon, it was turning back toward them with the nose of the ship high. Randy started flashing the lights on and off. The alien ship continued turning toward them. Then stopped looking straight at the Lucky Lady.

"They see us!" Randy shouted. "John, we're saved! They see us!" Randy was overjoyed, but then remembered they had no idea what these aliens might do to them. "Oh God, they see us!" he said in a much different tone.

Both of them were desperate to get out of the Lucky Lady, but were they going from the frying pan into the fire? They stared out at the alien craft, hoping for the best. Suddenly, the ship shot toward them at an incredible speed.

John gasped. "Holy crap that was fast. Our shuttle can't move like that. Nothing moves like that!"

"Nothing I know of," Randy agreed. "Look at the size of that thing. It's two times the size of our space shuttle. Now that it's closer, it doesn't look as much like our space shuttle as I thought. I don't see any wings or a tail. I don't even see anything that looks like engines."

John peered over Randy's shoulder. "That's a pretty big ship. Judging from the rows of windows, I'd say it has two levels. Look! There are markings on the side. Randy, what do you make of those?"

"Definitely not Earth markings. I have no idea what they are. Look! It's moving closer."

The Alien craft moved closer and circled them. The Aliens were inspecting the Lucky Lady. Then they stopped sitting broadside to her.

John moved back to his seat. "I can't keep looking over your shoulder like this. It's killing me. This Lunar Lander is so damn small you can't do anything but sit, but I want out of here so bad; I don't think I care what they do to us."

Randy rambled on a bit as he watched the ship. "Yeah, I know. It wasn't designed for comfort. It's an elevator. You get in, drop to the surface, and get out. No frills. No bells and whistles. That's NASA saving money, you know."

"Yeah, just let me know what your Mother-in-law is doing, ok. I need to rest my back and legs. God! If I could stretch out a little," John said, trying to stretch and relieve the cramps.

Randy kept watching the ship and finally saw movement. "Something's happening. Yeah, a door is opening."

John leaned over and watched as a large door slid back and a figure appeared in the doorway. It was a humanoid figure wearing a spacesuit very similar to the ones he and Randy were wearing.

"Well, they have two arms and legs," Randy said.

"That's a plus," John said.

"There's something else in the doorway. I can't make it out. It's too big to be a person," Randy said. "It's an alien riding a small craft. It looks like a four-wheeler without wheels."

The craft moved forward and circled the Lucky Lady. They were being inspected again. This craft, being so much smaller, circled only feet away. Then it stopped right outside Randy's window, and the rider floated off the space quad toward the window. Both men pulled back as the Alien approached Randy's window.

"Jesus! I hope a lot of that is spacesuit," Randy said, noticing how large this being was.

The Alien floated up toward the window, stopping several feet from it. Then he moved up to the window and looked in. John and Randy froze. What they saw was unnerving. The Alien had a fierce, almost evil look about him. As evil as he appeared, he did look human. But this human looked enraged to the point of wanting to rip your head off. From what they were seeing, he was big enough to do it. His large purple eyes added to the ferociousness of his appearance. Was he Human, or a beast? It could go either way.

The alien glared at Randy through the window. That glare seemed to cut deep, right to his soul. Randy sat frozen for long minutes as the Alien studied him. Then the Alien turned his hateful gaze on John.

Randy, now released from the grip of that glare, felt free to speak. "I feel like I was just dissected."

Now it was John's turn. "Did you have to call for help?" John asked.

"I never touched the radio. You're the screw-up here, not me," Randy said.

John suddenly went quiet. He was enduring the prolonged glare of the Alien. To Randy, it looked like a staring contest to see who would look away first. It was John who suddenly seemed to shrink away. He was holding his head and seemed to be cowering. That was something Randy didn't like seeing. John was the brave one, the Braun of the two men. John didn't rattle easily, so to see him shrink away from a mere look was disconcerting.

"John, are you okay?"

"Yeah, I'm fine,"

"You sure? You don't seem fine to me."

"I'm fine, but I can't …Can you see …?"

"See what?" Randy asked. Something wasn't right, and Randy knew it.

"I don't know. I saw, or heard …," John said. "Look, just forget it. I'm fine. Let's deal with this situation right now. I got a little confused for a moment, that's all. I'm okay."

John acted annoyed with Randy's concern for him, so Randy let it drop. They turned their attention back to the alien who had pulled back from the window. He appeared to be communicating with his ship. Then he looked back into the Lucky Lady and held up a hand to them. He was gesturing for them to stay put or to wait. Neither of them was sure what the alien's gesture meant, but both were a little surprised he had made the gesture at all. It somehow seemed in contrast to the persona of this being. He looked like he would tear you to pieces if he could get his hands on you, but here he was, seemingly concerned about them. It didn't fit.

John raised an arm, gesturing that he understood. The Alien nodded slightly and eyed John with what looked like suspicion, which was understandable. Two alien races were meeting for the first time. Who knew what was going to happen or what to expect from each other? Finally, the alien turned away from the window. Randy and John could still see the side of his face, and it looked like he was speaking.

"So, they do have some kind of communication," John said. "Maybe there is something wrong with our radio."

"Maybe, but I don't think so. I checked it out pretty well," Randy said.

A moment later, another figure appeared in the doorway of the alien ship and headed toward the Lucky Lady. It was another vehicle, larger than the space quad. This craft had Jaws on the front of it like those used on Earth to move heavy barrels around. This alien craft looked to be used in the same way, but these Jaws were much larger. They could reach completely around the Lucky Lady, and it looked like that was what these aliens intended to do.

"Oh no! Put on your helmet," John said. "They could crush the Lucky Lady if they do this! These walls aren't that strong!"

They regretted having to put their helmets on because of the stink inside their suits, but if the Aliens clamped the jaws onto the Lucky Lady, they could damage her, and air would escape. They had to do it.

Randy put on his helmet and looked up at the window. "Angry Man is back,"

John immediately got Angry Man's attention and tried to get him to understand that they couldn't clamp the jaws onto the Lucky Lady.

Angry Man glared at him and put up a hand.

"What does that mean?" John asked, then leaned toward the alien. "You can't do this. You will damage our ship. Do you understand?"

Angry Man put up a hand and moved away from the window.

"I don't think he understood," Randy said.

"I don't think so either. They're going to crush the Lucky Lady if they do this," John said. He glanced over at Randy and then right back out his window. "Randy, I need to say this: whatever happens from here on, I think you should keep that little black pill handy. We don't know what's going to happen or what kind of beings these Aliens are. If they are all like Angry Man, things could get rough."

"Oh, believe me," Randy said. "I take one look at Angry Man, and I think of that pill. He scares the hell out of me. I'm hoping these Aliens aren't in a dissecting mood."

"Here they come," John said, pointing out the window at the jaws. He couldn't see the driver and couldn't get his attention to stop him, but he saw the giant jaws move past his window and surround the Lucky Lady. He expected the jaws to close on the Lucky Lady, but instead, Angry Man and the forklift operator went to work using straps to secure the Lucky Lady between the jaws of the forklift. The Lucky lady was suspended harmlessly between the jaws like a fly in a spider web. It was a great relief for John and Randy, and it said a lot about the intelligence of these aliens. "I'll be," John said. "Somebody has good sense."

With the Lucky Lady secured, the pilot returned to the forklift and began pulling the Lucky Lady toward their ship.

"It sure seems like they know what they are doing, but leave your Helmet on just in case," John said.

"Yeah, let's hope they're as good with a Scalpel," Randy said.

"Keep that humor, Randy. It comforts me."

"What humor? I'm serious," Randy said, grinning.

The Forklift pulled the Lucky Lady inside the shuttle, and the Aliens secured the Lucky Lady to the floor. Then Angry Man was back in the window, holding up a hand to indicate they should stay put. Randy and John tightened their seat belts, knowing it would get rough when they entered the planet's Atmosphere.

When they looked up, Angry Man had gone, and no one else was around. John could see windows in the shuttle walls, but they were far away. They weren't going to be able to see what was happening outside.

Finally, they felt the slight tug as the Shuttle began to move. They couldn't see it happen, but they could feel every move the shuttle made. The shuttle had turned, moved in a straight line, and come to a stop. Now they felt themselves lifting out of their seats, indicating that the shuttle was moving straight down. They prepared themselves for the turbulence they would feel when the shuttle entered the atmosphere.

"Should be starting soon," John said.

"Ah huh," Randy grunted, gripping his seat straps.

The ride down seemed to go on forever, but so far it had been as smooth as anyone could imagine.

"Maybe they're not taking us to the Planet," Randy said. "Maybe they're taking us somewhere else, like a space station or one of the moons."

"Maybe," John said, looking to the nearest shuttle window. He caught a glimpse of clouds floating past. "No, we are heading down to the planet. We're entering the Atmosphere right now. Hang on," he said, gripping his seat belt tighter.

They prepared for something that never happened. They were amazed when they felt the shuttle land with hardly a bump. There had been no turbulence to speak of. Just a few bumps here and there, but nothing like what they had expected.

The shuttle had gone from space to the planet's surface, and it had been a slow, smooth ride down. The ship didn't fall from the sky, the way the Earth shuttle would. There had been no turbulence, no burning, and no rolling to a stop on landing. This ship's transition from space to atmospheric travel was flawless. That left Randy in awe of the Alien ship. "Whatever drives this ship must really be something. It would take a great deal of power to control a ship like this. Their technology must be incredible."

"Yeah, that's … Oh my God!" John groaned, letting his arms fall from his seat straps to his lap. "My arms weigh a ton! It feels like I have weights on them."

"Yeah. Remember, this planet is larger than Earth, so gravity is going to be stronger. I must admit, I wasn't expecting it to be this strong. This planet must have a greater density as well. It's going to take a while to get used to this," Randy said, straining to lift his arms over his head. With his arms over his head, he turned his head to look at John with a smart-ass look on his face and said, "You know…. if they don't dissect us first."

John ignored him as he released his seat belt and moved his arms around, exercising them. Strong or not, it felt good to be in gravity again, and it made them all the more eager to get out of the Lucky Lady, where they could finally stretch and move around. They were more anxious to get out of the ship than they were worried about what these giant aliens were going to do to them.

They waited for several minutes. Then they heard someone coming, and Angry Man pressed his face up to the window. He was wearing a different suit now. This one looked like a Bio-suit.

Angry Man's big head filled the window, but Randy was able to look past him and saw a large door on the side of the shuttle opening. Many more aliens dressed in bio-suits were standing just outside. When the door was opened high enough, they poured into the shuttle and went into action, erecting a tunnel that started from the shuttle door and came up to the hatch of the Lucky Lady. A vehicle drove up to the other end, and the tunnel was attached to it.

"They aren't taking any risks are they," Randy said.

"Nope. Doesn't look like it," John said.

When the work on the tunnel was finished, most of the aliens were outside the tunnel. Only three Aliens stood inside the tunnel facing the Lucky Lady. They stood at a distance for a moment, then started toward her.

"Here we go!" John said.

"Let me know if you see a scalpel," Randy said.

Two of the Aliens stopped back away from the Lucky Lady. They waited as the first Alien approached and looked in the window. It was Angry Man again.

"Damn if that guy doesn't look like he's ready to tear the Lucky Lady in two with his bare hands," John said.

"He sure does," Randy said.

Angry Man approached and knocked on the window and motioned for the men to come out.

"That would be our invitation," Randy said.

"You ready?" John asked.

"I am SO ready to get out of this Lander, but I'm not all that excited about meeting Angry Man," Randy said. Then, taking a deep breath, said, "Yes, open the hatch, and let's get on with it."

John struggled to open the hatch and crawl out. It was incredibly hard to get out of the Lucky Lady. He had been sitting there for days. His body was stiff and unwilling to move. The spacesuit was heavy and hard to move around in. Now, with the increase in gravity and the small opening of the Lucky Lady, getting out was painful and exhausting.

He made it through the hatch and climbed down the short ladder to the floor of the shuttle. With his back to Angry Man, he leaned against the ladder, out of breath, weak, and struggling against gravity. Just getting to the floor of the shuttle had taken maximum effort.

When he had regained some of his strength, he turned to face Angry Man and suddenly felt small. Angry Man towered over him. The beast had to be more than eight feet tall. He glared down at John, his purple eyes cutting into him. John stared up at him, fearing the worst. Suddenly, he felt a sharp pain in his head again. He didn't understand why, and he certainly didn't like it.

Then Angry Man's glare shifted to Randy as he got to the floor. Randy, out of breath and seeing stars, did not wait to catch his breath. He immediately turned to face Angry Man, and Randy, being Randy, raised his hand and in labored speech said, "Hey … dude. We come … in peace." Then his strength vanished, and he fell forward, but he never touched the floor. Angry Man stepped forward and caught him with one arm under his chest.

"Humf," Randy grunted as he fell on Angry Man's arm. It felt like he had fallen on a log. There was great strength and very little give in that arm. He grunted again as Angry Man lifted him into the air with one arm. The abrupt way Angry Man hoisted him made him worry that Angry Man was becoming violent. But then Angry Man set him on his feet with a gentleness that seemed out of place.

Randy hung in his suit, considering the amazing strength in those arms. Angry Man could throw him around like a rag doll if he chose to. Thankfully, he didn't do that. He held Randy for a while longer, steadying him, until Randy had summoned up enough strength to stand on his own. *Surprisingly gentle for such a murderous-looking beast.* Randy thought.

Angry Man stepped back and motioned for them to follow.

"John, help me," Randy said. "I have no strength. I can hardly move."

"I know," John said, taking hold of him, but John wasn't much better off, and the two of them struggled to move forward. Simply walking was unbelievably hard.

Angry Man turned and motioned to the other two Aliens in the tunnel. They moved past John and Randy and went straight to the Lucky Lady. Angry Man also moved passed them, but he turned and came up behind them, gripping their suits to help them along. Randy immediately felt Angry Man's power again. He did his best to keep up, but after several steps, his strength evaporated, and he slumped in his suit, having given all he had. He was hanging in his suit, being carried by Angry Man. All he and John could do was watch the waiting vehicle get closer as Angry Man carried them to it. Angry Man was carrying both of them, one in each hand, like an adult ushering two schoolboys to the principal's office. Their feet hardly touched the ground.

They reached the vehicle, which was quite similar to an Earth van. Bench seats ran the length of the van against both walls. Angry Man plucked Randy off the ground and placed him against the far wall of the Van. From his seat, Randy could see the Lucky Lady sitting inside the shuttle and the two Aliens inside her. *Air samples.* He thought. This seemed logical considering the precautions the Aliens were taking. *Air and radiation tests, perhaps.*

Then Randy watched as Angry Man lifted John into the van, placing him against the wall opposite him and next to the door. Then Angry Man closed the door.

"Man, that guy is strong!" John said. "Makes me feel like a rag doll in his hand."

"You're not kidding," Randy said, still gasping for breath. "That's exactly what I felt. He could toss me around like a rag doll. Strong!"

Soon, the van started moving, and they were on their way. The only windows in the Van were in the back doors. Through those, they could see vehicles following them and others passing them going in the opposite direction. Aliens, male and female, old and young, were walking on sidewalks beside the streets. Beyond the walkers were buildings of varied sizes and shapes. It was very much a scene from Earth.

John looked around the inside of the van. "Well, we're in a different vehicle at least, but we still can't stand up."

Randy looked at the ceiling and nodded. "Yep. But I haven't the strength to stand up anyway. I'm so weak, and the gravity is too strong."

John only nodded.

Soon, the van slowed and came to a stop. The door opened, and Angry Man stood inside another tunnel, motioning for them to get out. John groaned as he lifted himself off the seat and started for the door. Having to crouch down in the van made walking even harder. When he went to step out of the van, his legs buckled, and he fell out. Once again, Angry Man's arm came out and stopped his fall. The beast lifted him, then set him back on the ground. He held on to John a moment longer, steadying him, then helped him move out of the way so Randy could get out.

Randy sat looking out the door of the Van, not wanting to move. He was summoning up his strength for the attempt to get out of the Van. He was about to make a move when Angry Man reached in, grabbed him by the front of his suit, and pulled him out. So abrupt and forceful were Angry Man's actions that Randy feared the beast was losing patience with him. Then Randy found himself being placed on the sidewalk with such gentleness that it was confusing.

Randy stood in front of Angry Man, staring up at his face. *This beast has such incredible strength that anything he does would seem forceful to me. He looks like he wants to tear me to pieces, but then acts like he cares about my comfort. Who are you, Angry Man?* Randy thought as he stared up at him. Angry Man cocked his head to one side, obviously wondering what was going on in Randy's head. Then he motioned for Randy to move down the tunnel.

Randy looked away from Angry Man and saw John struggling to walk toward a door at the end of the tunnel. John looked like an old man struggling to put one foot in front of the other. Randy wasn't sure he would be able to do even that much. He tried to take a step, but his leg just shook. The heavy suit he was wearing didn't help matters. He tried again and was able to take a step. With great effort, he managed to take another step, and then suddenly, he was lifted into the air and carried. Once again, a great force had plucked him from the ground and was carrying him toward John. When they caught up to John, Angry Man grabbed John and carried them both to the door.

"Jesus, Randy! Don't piss him off!" John said.

Randy only groaned and watched the door get closer as he was carried to it.

Angry Man held the door open and helped them through. John found another door immediately to his right and a hallway to his left. Directly in front of him was another door, which Angry Man indicated he should go through. Angry Man helped them through, and the three of them stood in a large room.

A table with several chairs around it was right in front of them, and they couldn't miss seeing it. From here, the two men noticed different things. John noticed that the walls of this room were made of glass, and on the other side of the glass were many aliens looking in on them. *This is an observation room. They are going to study us. I don't think we'll have much privacy here.*

Randy noticed something different. "Beds! Oh man, a bed!" Randy said. "I hope we live to use them."

Angry Man moved past the men to a door in the back wall. He opened the door and stepped aside so the men could see.

"A bathroom? Oh my God, John, it's a bathroom!" Randy yelled.

"Is that a tub?" John asked, almost unable to contain his excitement.

Angry Man now made a gesture that seemed to be an invitation for the men to make themselves at home. Then he left them and entered the outer room. He barked out an apparent order, and the other aliens began pulling curtains to cover the windows. When they finished, only two windows were uncovered. One in the door leading into this room, and one at the center of the front wall. Through these windows, John watched the Aliens, including Angry Man, leave the building. He and Randy were suddenly alone. He stood trying to make sense of what was happening. Were the aliens coming back? What was going to happen next?

John turned his attention back to their room. It was a large room with a table and six chairs around it. Further in the room, there were a few larger cushioned chairs. The back wall had solid paneling except for the Bathroom door, which Randy was already struggling through. Randy had stripped off his suit and was heading for the bathtub.

Randy had already answered the question of whether the air was breathable or not, so John removed his helmet and took a breath. The air was good and clean, a great relief to his olfactory nerves.

John turned and struggled toward the uncovered window at the center of the front wall. There were tables and chairs out there, but no aliens that he could see. He moved back to the door and tried to open it. As expected, it was locked, and he was ok with that for now. He stood looking at the table and chairs. They were larger than chairs on Earth, no doubt because these Aliens were larger than man. From what he had observed, most of the adult aliens stood somewhere around seven feet tall. That was a foot taller than himself. Angry Man had to be at least eight and a half feet tall. He was much larger and taller than the other aliens around him. Angry Man was one big boy.

John left the door and went to the back wall of the room. He pushed on one of the panels, and it moved. He pushed it out of the way and found himself looking at what looked like a kitchen. He investigated and found it was true. There was a stove, refrigerator, and even a sink.

John turned and looked back into their room again. They had beds, chairs, a bathroom, and even a kitchen. These were things that would comfort them. Aside from Angry Man's appearance, he didn't feel they were in any danger from these Aliens. He looked again at the beds and lounge chairs. This was no prison or torture chamber. Nor was it a room they would be dissected in, as Randy feared. This room offered them comfort. John stood taking it all in and, suddenly felt less like a prisoner and more like he had been rescued. These aliens had rescued them and put them in quarantine.

Things could change. He didn't know if they were among friends or foes, but at the moment, he was thankful for the aliens getting them out of the Lucky Lady. He looked at the bathroom door and prayed he would get the chance to clean himself up before the aliens returned.

Less apprehensive, John stripped off his suit and walked around the room, continuing to look around. He just wanted to move around, get the blood flowing, and limber up his joints. He moved back to the back wall and found another much smaller Panel that slid to one side. When he pushed it back, he was surprised to find what looked like a TV. He found the power button and turned it on. Sure enough, aliens were moving around on the screen, and there was laughter. He had no idea what was being said, but it sure looked and sounded like a TV show. A funny one.

Randy finally came out of the bathroom feeling and smelling so much better. "I tried to hurry, but damn, that felt good," he said.

John wasted no time getting into the bathroom. The bath felt good. He had soap and towels, everything he needed. It was so much like Earth that he could easily have forgotten where he was. There was even a mirror that told him he needed a shave. John looked around and, sure enough, found an alien version of an electric razor.

Now, clean-shaven and feeling rather good, John wrapped a towel around himself. There was no way he was getting back into the spacesuit. Randy was already in one of the beds and sound asleep. John got into one of the beds, wondering if he should. What did the aliens have in mind for them? Would they be coming back soon, or would they be leaving them alone for a while?

He looked over at Randy, thinking there was no way he would fall asleep that fast. He definitely wanted to lie down and stretch out. Being in bed felt great and would no doubt do his body good. But how could he fall asleep as keyed up as he was? He was on a strange planet, in a strange room, and half expecting aliens to barge in to interrogate him at any minute.

Still, he sighed with pleasure as he lay back on the bed and covered himself up. He was clean and wonderfully comfortable. John stretched, which felt fantastic, and sent him drifting off to sleep. He didn't even notice the alien standing at the center window watching him.

CHAPTER THREE
LIEUTENANT BRANDEN WILSON

John woke feeling refreshed, and though he wasn't ready to run a race, he was anxious to get out of bed and learn where they were and who had them. Were they 'friends' or 'foes? Time will tell.

Swinging his legs out of bed, he was quickly reminded of the greater gravity of this planet. His muscles would need to grow to meet the greater demand on them. That wouldn't happen overnight, but it would happen. Right now, it felt good to stretch and move around. He was clean and well-rested. He and Randy were alive and out of the Lucky Lady. That alone was a cause to celebrate.

Sitting on the bed, he looked at the door leading into the room. Sunlight was pouring through the windows. It was daytime, but was it the same day or a different day? He had no idea how long he had slept.

He stood up beside the bed and was reminded that he was naked. He rewrapped the towel around himself and moved to the window in the center of the front wall. He was pleased to find that walking was much easier now that he had rested and wasn't wearing the heavy space suit. He reached the window and saw an Alien sitting at a table engrossed in reading. This Alien was much smaller than Angry Man and lacked the fierceness in his face. This one had a pleasant face and smiled at John as he got up and left the room. John was sure he had left to alert others that he was awake.

John followed him with his eyes. *Who will you bring back? Angry Man? Or more like you? Let's hope it's more like you.*

John made his way to the door. It was locked. He wondered what he would have done if he had found it unlocked. He decided he would have stayed in the room. He hadn't come to the door to escape. He just wanted to look outside.

Looking out, he saw that his field of vision was going to be quite limited. He was looking across a hallway to the outer door six feet away, and the window in the outer door was rather small, about two feet by three feet in size. This left him with a narrow view of what he could see. Most of what he saw was part of the building he was in.

He remembered Angry Man had led them to a door right at the inside corner of an L-shaped building. That explained why he was seeing the face of a building to his left. His room was in one leg of the building, right where it joined with the other arm of the L-shaped building.

A sidewalk ran from his doors to what had to be a road at the end of the building. Vehicles of all sizes were driving passed. People were also walking passed, so he guessed there was a sidewalk there as well. From what he was seeing, he could imagine that sidewalks formed a square around a courtyard with sidewalks crossing from corner to corner. The whole thing would form a square with an X in it. He remembered seeing something like that through the plastic tunnel.

John was pleased with his assessment and turned his attention to the aliens walking around in the courtyard. There were quite a few of these human-looking Aliens moving around out there. Old and young, short and tall, slim and fat. On average, these Aliens appeared taller and a little larger than humans, but none of them were as big or as fierce-looking as Angry Man.

Angry Man was a bruiser, and John knew, even with his military training, that he would never win a battle with him. Angry Man had lifted him off the ground and carried him with one arm. John shook his head as he did the math. He weighed 190 pounds, and his suit weighed an additional 130 Pounds. Randy was about the same. Angry Man had carried 320 pounds in each arm. A total of 640 pounds. There was no way he would win in a conflict against such a beast as Angry Man, and he hoped he wouldn't have to try.

John turned away from the doors and started back toward the table and chairs. *What kind of aliens are these, and what are they going to do with us? Will Angry Man be coming back to interrogate them?* Questions like these ran through his mind as he walked back and sat down at the table. His legs were already tired, and he needed to rest. As he sat there, he was very aware that his stomach hurt from a lack of food. It had been five days since he had eaten anything. There were water faucets in this room, and he wanted a drink, but that wasn't what he needed to stop his stomach from growling. He needed food and hoped these aliens could see to their needs and do it soon.

He stared at the top of the table, thinking how impossible their situation was. He had so many questions: What had happened to them? How did they end up here on this planet? Did these Aliens know what had happened? Did they know how to get them back? Would they help get them back? Would the Aliens continue to be friendly, or would things turn for the worse?

"Impossible," he said, shaking his head.

He looked up at Randy, who was still lying in bed, and at that same moment, heard someone at the door. He turned and found two Bio-suited Aliens entering the room. He stood up and stepped behind his chair as they walked toward him. Now, he would learn who had them.

"Randy, wake up. We have company." He said in a loud voice. "Randy, get up!"

Randy moaned and started to wake. Seeing what was happening, Randy attempted to jump out of bed and was also reminded of the greater gravity and the fact that he was naked. At the moment, he didn't care about his nakedness, he was more concerned about what was going to happen. This was no doubt going to be the first true interaction with the aliens. Tension now filled the air. He glanced around, expecting to see armed guards, but it was just these two.

Randy stood and watched the two Bio-suited Aliens approach John at the table. He could see through their face shields, and it appeared to him that one of them was female, the other male. He was happy to see that they didn't have the fierceness in their faces that Angry Man had. They weren't as large as Angry Man either, and those two observations helped him to relax a little. Not all these aliens were the murderous beasts Angry Man appeared to be. This male was much smaller than Angry Man, though he was very tall. He looked to be a little over seven feet tall, and the female was around six feet tall. Maybe six-foot 3 inches, Randy guessed.

The female was carrying a covered tray of something. The male was carrying what looked like clothes and a small briefcase. Seeing the clothing reminded Randy that he was naked, and having a female in the room made him rewrap the towel around himself.

The aliens set both the clothes and the tray on the table. The female stood by the table while the male took a seat. He motioned for John to sit down. John hesitated for a moment, then sat down. He could smell food in the air, and he suspected that's what was under the covered tray.

The Alien pushed the clothes toward John and gestured for him to look. John picked up a garment and inspected it. It was a pair of pants. Many of the Aliens here were wearing pants and shirts, so this wasn't a big surprise. These looked a little big, but they would be better than the towel and much better than getting back into his Spacesuit. He glanced to where he and Randy had left their Spacesuit and saw that they were gone. The Aliens had come in and taken them while they slept.

Then the male spoke to the female in their language, and the female left. John looked at the clothes again and found a shirt. He put the clothes on and sat back down.

"Thank you," he said to the Alien.

The Alien gave him a quizzical look and pushed the tray toward him. John uncovered it. It was food as he had hoped. It looked and smelled good. Randy sat down and eyed the alien as he picked up something that looked like meat. He held it for a moment and glanced at the Alien. The alien nodded, suggesting it was okay for him to eat it. Randy tasted the meat. It was good! And he was very hungry. "John, try this meat. It's delicious."

John ignored that and picked up something that looked like fruit and began to eat it. He was looking at the Alien the whole time. He was suspicious of him and wondered what was coming next. The food and clothing were appreciated, but what was the cost? What was going to happen now? Then suddenly the Alien spoke to him.

"American?"

John dropped his food and sat open-mouthed, staring at him. He shook his head. Had he heard that?

"Russian?" the Alien asked.

John shook his head again and looked at the Alien. Finally, John gathered his wits and answered. "Yeah... yes, American!" he stammered. "Yes, I am American. Do you understand English?"

The Alien raised his arms in a gesture for him to stop or to slow down. Then he pulled the little briefcase toward himself and opened it. He produced several pictures from it and placed one on the table in front of them. "Lieutenant Branden Wilson," he said, pointing to the picture. "American?"

Both men were shocked at what they were hearing. John asked him again if he understood English, but the Alien again raised a hand. No, it didn't appear he understood. Yet he was speaking English, saying "American" and "Lieutenant Branden Wilson." How did he know those names?

The Alien tapped the picture again and repeated his question with a little more force. "Lieutenant Branden Wilson. American?"

Both men leaned forward and studied the picture. They were looking at what looked to be an American pilot. The clothing he was wearing looked like he was from the WWII era.

Randy pointed at the picture. "Lieutenant Branden Wilson?" he asked the Alien.

"Yes, Lieutenant Branden Wilson… yes," the alien answered.

Randy picked up the picture and sat back, studying it.

"What is it, Randy? Does that mean something to you?" John asked.

"Yes. Not the picture of the man, but that name. I know that name from somewhere, but I can't remember."

The Alien placed another picture on the table. This picture was obviously of an American fighter plane from the WWII era. The plane was severely damaged and appeared to have crashed. Randy picked up this picture as well and held the two together. He looked at the Alien and asked, "How did you get these pictures?"

The Alien only gestured that he didn't understand. It became obvious he didn't know many more words than "American", "Russian", and "Lieutenant Branden Wilson". He seemed to understand "yes" and "no" as well, but nothing beyond that. The Alien did speak a little Russian to them and seemed to have a little better command of it, but again, he only knew a few words of it.

The Alien placed more pictures on the table. There was a picture of a man whom the Alien pointed at and said, "Russian." Another picture was of what looked like a Satellite that had crashed. There was a picture of the bow of a ship sticking out of a strange-looking fog. The name on the bow of the ship was so distorted by the fog it couldn't be read. The last two pictures shocked John and Randy. One picture was of a large, triangular-shaped craft hovering just feet above the ground. The last picture was of two little gray men standing in front of it.

"Jesus!" John said. "There's the proof we could never get."

"Close enough for me," Randy said. "I believed these guys existed before I saw this picture; now I am sure of it, and I'm sure some branch of our government knew all about them."

The pictures of the American pilot and the Russian showed men who were badly injured and were no doubt dying. The picture of the gray men showed beings that were standing up and very much alive.

"It just keeps getting weirder and weirder," John said.

The Alien closed the briefcase, leaving the pictures on the table. He pushed the food and clothing closer to the men and stood up as if to leave. Then he placed a hand on his chest. "Awth," he grunted with a slight bow. It certainly looked like he had sneezed.

"God bless you," Randy said.

Again, the Alien put a hand on his chest and said, "Awth", bowing a bit deeper. John understood he was giving his name.

John stood up and put a hand on his chest. "John," he said. Then, he held his hand out toward Randy and introduced him as well. "Randy." Randy stood up and bowed slightly. Awth tried to repeat their names and did a rather poor job of it, then turned and headed for the door. The first meeting was over.

John and Randy watched him leave, then huddled around the tray of food. They were very hungry, and the food tasted great. "Awth," John said, practicing the name between bites. "How does Awth know those names? Mm! You're right. This meat is good!"

Randy nodded and continued to eat. They wanted to dive in and eat their fill, but knew they should take it easy. The last thing they needed was to bind themselves up, and that could happen if they ate too much too quickly. They ate slowly and sparingly. Eventually, Randy moved back from the table and finally put on some clothes.

The clothing was similar to what they had on Earth. The Pants and shirts were made of a different material and were perhaps a little stiffer, but they were comfortable and better than wearing a towel. Not that that had mattered to Randy. He had stood in his birthday suit, in full view of the aliens, for quite a while.

Now, well-fed and clothed, they sat wondering what would happen next.

"How does Awth know those names: American and Russian? What in the world is happening here?" Randy asked.

"I don't know, but it gives me hope that maybe they know something about what's happened to us," John said, shaking his head. "I wish I had some answers. I mean, how did we end up here in the first place? Is it possible these aliens have something to do with our being here? Did they bring us here?" he asked, knowing Randy couldn't answer the questions any more than he could. "Well, at least they don't appear to be hostile toward us. I mean, I haven't seen a scalpel yet."

"Not yet," Randy said.

"What about this Lieutenant Wilkins or whoever? What does he mean to you?" John asked.

"Wilson," Randy corrected. "Lieutenant Branden Wilson,"

"Fine, Lieutenant Wilson. What does that name mean to you?"

"I don't know. I'm sure I have heard or read about him somewhere, but I can't place him. I am sure it was something he did during World War II. He was a hero or something, I can't remember. It will come to me eventually, I hope."

Randy thought for a moment. "You know…Awth had pictures of Lieutenant Wilson and his airplane. At least I assume it was his plane. He also had pictures of a Russian, the satellite, and pictures of the gray men and their ship. Do you see a connection between them?"

"There would be if it weren't for the gray men. All the other stuff must have come from Earth...just like we did." John said.

"Wait a minute, John. On many of our missions in space, you've seen some of the same things I have, and I'm pretty sure our government has been lying to us about their existence. Now we have proof," Randy said, holding the pictures of the gray men up for him to see. "Can you honestly say that these little guys didn't come from Earth? I think they may very well have. This picture proves they exist, and we can now figure they have been visiting Earth."

"Ok, I'll admit that. But what does that get us? Let's say we accept that everything came here from Earth; how does knowing that help us?"

"I don't know, but let's, for the moment, accept that everything is coming here from Earth. That tells us things are coming here from everywhere around the planet—the air, water, and space. For all we know, the Russian guy might have been standing in a parking lot somewhere in Russia. The American pilot was probably flying when he was taken. He could have been in Europe somewhere. The gray Aliens could have been anywhere. Maybe they were flying around in our skies, or up in space, who knows? For all we know, they might have landed on Earth and got taken."

"You forgot the ship in the fog. It looks like a ship from Earth to me," John said.

"Yeah, that ship. It looks like a cargo ship to me, too. I would think it was taken from somewhere in the Ocean."

John shrugged. "And we were taken from way out by the Moon, but what is all this telling us?"

"I think it's telling us…" Randy started to say, then changed his mind. "Oh hell, we haven't got a clue what's going on here. We're just spinning our wheels. We don't have anywhere near enough information to figure any of this out."

John nodded. "What I want to know is, was this intentional? Did these aliens bring us here, or was it accidental? No way of knowing, I guess. We need to learn their language. That's what it is telling us. We need to talk to Awth."

CHAPTER FOUR
TALLDA SHAYTS

Awth and the female alien named Nellaynan came in every morning, wearing Bio-Suits and bringing food and fresh clothes for them. They would sit, eat, and attempt to communicate with each other for hours. It was going to take time before they could talk to each other well enough to start getting the answers they wanted.

John and Randy were surprised when Nellaynan came into the room carrying games. She opened one and began placing game pieces on the table. "Stauto May Awk," she said, indicating the name of the game. It was obvious she expected them to play, but how could they? They couldn't read their language or understand her instructions.

Nellaynan did most of the playing until they began to understand how to play. This game had an arrow that you spun with your finger. Because of this, they learned the Alien numbers one through 10. They also learned words like 'go' and 'go back'. It was a child's game and a good place for them to start.

Awth and Nellaynan did much better at learning English than the men did at learning the alien language. Of the two men, it was John who was learning the Alien language faster, and that was a bit of a surprise. Randy was supposed to be "the bigger brain." Why wasn't he learning the language faster?

Randy didn't care that John seemed to pick up their language a little quicker, but he couldn't help but notice that at times, Awth and Nellaynan would be trying hard to make themselves understood with no luck. Then John would suddenly know what they were trying to communicate. It didn't happen all the time, but it happened enough that Randy noticed. John was an intelligent man, but this seemed to be more than intelligence.

What drew Randy's attention was that at the same moment John grasped what they were saying, he would suddenly seem fatigued or confused. Usually, he would put a hand to his head as if he had a headache. When Randy asked him about it, John admitted that he did have a headache and that the headaches had been happening lately, but he didn't think it was anything to worry about. When Randy pressed him for more, John said that he was fine and that it was probably due to his not eating for so long, or it was possibly the alien food that was affecting him.

Randy let it drop. It wasn't that big of a deal, but he couldn't completely accept John's explanation. John was making excuses, and his disorientation and confusion were indications that something was wrong. It could be the food or the environment, he didn't know, but he would keep an eye on him. His headaches and confusion didn't happen every day, but they happened enough to concern him. He would watch John and see if there really was a problem. It could just be a matter of stress. No matter how comfortable the aliens made them, they were on a strange planet far from home, unable to talk to the aliens, and didn't know if they would ever see home again. It was a very stressful situation.

On the day they had been rescued, Awth and Nellaynan had brought a tray of food and clothing for them. The next day, Nellaynan had come into the room and drawn blood from Awths' arm right in front of them. Then she motioned that she wanted to do the same to them. Once John and Randy understood what she wanted, they offered up their arms so she could draw blood from them. The aliens seemed very concerned about the transmission of disease, so this wasn't such an odd request. Randy would be the first to say that it was better than having them come at him with a scalpel.

On the third day, Nellaynan came into the room with the men's spacesuits on a cart. She was returning them after a good cleaning. Awth got the men to understand that they wanted to take pictures of them in these suits. This would help them document everything, just as they had done with Lieutenant Wilson, the Russian, and the gray men.

Today, Awth came into the room alone. Randy noticed John's disappointment that Nellaynan wasn't with him. Randy had already seen the growing attraction between John and Nellaynan.

Awth began with his usual greeting of, "Goood mor-rin-ning." Then, like any other day, he sat down and continued trying to break the communication gap. It was becoming clear that Awth and Nellaynan found it just as important to find a way to communicate as John and Randy did. It was a slow process and at times very frustrating, but they were making progress. They were beginning to understand simple communications, like "morning".

John wasn't sure they understood what "Good" meant, but he had had Nellaynan and Awth laughing hard while trying to teach them the difference between good and bad. His gestures and facial expressions got them laughing. Maybe that was enough for the day.

Today, Nellaynan entered the room about an hour after Awth. She spoke to Awth, and a big smile crossed Awth's face. He stood up and both he and Nellaynan took off their Bio-suits.

"Well, well," Randy said. "It looks like the Quarantine is over. I guess they didn't find anything to worry about."

"That's good to hear," John said, studying the aliens. This was the first time he had seen them without the suits. He tried to hide it, but he was most interested in Nellaynan.

Awth was thinner than he expected. The suit had covered both Awths' and Nellaynans' shapes very well. Nellaynan had a nice figure.

Without the face shield, Awths' green eyes shone brighter and took on new life. He was older than John had thought. His hair was a bit of a surprise, too. It was cut short and parted on one side. The more they looked at Awth and Nellaynan, the more they realized just how human they were. The most noticeable difference was the color and shape of their eyes. Awth's eyes were green, and Nellaynans were purple like Angry Man's. The upper eyelid seemed flatter across the top, while the bottom was more rounded. It gave them a slight reptilian look. It was that reptilian look that made Angry Man look so menacing, but on Nellaynan and Awth, it was appealing.

Another difference was their brow ridge. Awth and Nellaynan had elegant, slightly pronounced brow ridges, unlike Angry Man, whose brow was closer to a Cro-Magnon man's brow. The last truly noticeable difference was their teeth. The upper and lower incisors were slightly longer than Humans. Again, in the case of Angry Man, his teeth were longer. If he were covered in hair, he could pass for Bigfoot. He truly looked like a beast. Awth and Nellaynan did not.

Nellaynan, being female, was different in appearance. Her face was narrower than Awths' but had the same eye shape and brow ridge. She had long Blonde hair, which she pulled back and tied behind her head. She was slender but still large compared to Earth women. She stood eye-to-eye with John at six feet tall. John had admitted to Randy that he liked the look of her face and of her stature. He thought of her as an Amazon woman, big and beautiful.

Nellaynan and Awth had a very appealing quality about them, both physically and emotionally. They always seemed happy and upbeat. John and Randy had liked them from the beginning and liked them more now. Seeing them without the bio-suits meant a great deal. The suits represented a barrier. It signaled separation and even distrust. Without the suits, everything changed. They were more like friends.

Awth and Nellaynan put their bio-suits aside, sat down, and resumed the normal course of the day. Man, and alien, each struggling to learn the other's language. So far, there had been little progress. There was very little understanding between them, except on a very basic level, and that wasn't enough for John and Randy. They wanted their questions answered today not tomorrow. They had to accept that it was going to take time to truly understand each other on the level of understanding they needed. When that happened, maybe then they would finally start to get answers. Right now, it was a struggle.

This morning, Awth and Nellaynan had taken off their Bio-suits, signaling that the quarantine was over. Then the normal routine resumed, and they sat at the table struggling to communicate. Eventually, they pulled out a game and sat playing. The games were truly a great tool to learn from each other because they were learning facial expressions, hand gestures, and even what sounded like curse words. It was funny to hear Awth's apparent cursing's. He did it with such enthusiasm.

Awth usually left in the early afternoon, but today, before he left, he walked to the panels at the back wall. They heard the jingling of keys, and Awth slid several panels back, revealing windows in the wall. Everyone moved to the windows and looked out at what looked like an airport. But there was a huge difference in this airport. These ships were incredible. Most of them came straight down for a landing and straight up to take off. Most incredible to John and Randy was that these ships could stop and hover at any time. High up in the air or feet from the ground, it didn't matter. John stared out, thinking he would be spending a great deal of time at this window watching the ships come and go.

Awth spent considerable time trying to tell John and Randy something, but John and Randy weren't getting it. Awth pointed at the window and back at the door while speaking, but neither John nor Randy understood. Awth finally shrugged, and he and Nellaynan moved to the door. Again, Awth said something and swung the door back and forth, but John and Randy still didn't get it.

John watched them leave, and the door closed behind them. The quarantine was over, so would they still be held captive? He went to the door and tried it. Sure enough, it was unlocked. John moved through to the outer door and tried it. It too was unlocked. Was this a mistake? He doubted it. He believed Awth and Nellaynan meant to leave the doors unlocked, but he wasn't completely sure.

He looked out through the glass in the outer door. He half expected to see a guard or Angry Man glaring back at him. Aliens were walking around, but no one acted as a guard. He stepped out cautiously, thinking a guard might appear to stop him, but that didn't happen. None of the Aliens out here seemed at all concerned with him being there. They nodded to him in greeting as if he were one of them. They seemed completely unconcerned at having an Alien standing in their midst. This seemed odd to John.

But it sure felt good to be in the open air and sunshine for the first time in such a long time. He stood with his eyes closed, letting the sun's heat soak in. He breathed in the fresh, clean air laden with the odors of the outdoors. He couldn't help but smile, noticing a fragrance in the air that could be flowers, but he suspected it was perfume. Someone here might be wearing perfume. How much like Earth this place was, and how at home it made him feel.

Opening his eyes again, he noticed how bright and colorful all the plant life was. The colors of the flowers by the road and the leaves on the trees seemed so vibrant that they just popped out at him. The grass in the square before him was well-groomed, and the sidewalks were very clean. *Someone takes good care of the…"*

"We're not in Kansas anymore Toto," Randy said surprising the crap out of John. Randy had followed him out and was standing next to him.

"Jesus! I didn't hear you coming," John said."

"We're free to go wherever we wish, I guess," Randy said.

"Looks that way. It seemed odd that they left the doors open without saying a word. They just let us go."

"Yeah, that would be odd, but don't you think that's what they were trying to tell us before they left today? Who knows? We barely know what we are saying to each other most of the time," Randy said. Then, after thinking a moment added, "They certainly don't have anything to worry about from us anyway. Where are we going to go? What would we do? We know absolutely nothing about this place."

"Huh." John grunted, "That is a good point. We're pretty much prisoners of our circumstances here aren't we. Where would we go? What are we going to do, run and hide somewhere? Why would we do that? What do we have to hide from? We're well cared for here. We have food and water. They bring us clothes, and if we need it, medical care, I'm sure. We have nothing to run from. I can honestly say I haven't been in a situation like this since I was a child."

"Yeah, that's all true, but if I get the opportunity to get out of here and back home, whether they like it or not, I'll run for it," Randy said.

John grunted but said nothing. He was looking around the area in front of them. He had been right in his thinking that sidewalks crisscrossed the yard. Now he could see that sidewalks did indeed form a square around a very large yard. Sidewalks also ran from corner to corner of the square, forming an X inside the square. This created four triangles that were filled with grass lawns.

From inside the building, he had seen a road and a sidewalk at the end of the building. Now he could see there was a road and sidewalk at the end of the other arm of the building. The two roads met and formed an intersection at the opposite corner of the yard from him. Everything he had imagined was out there. John nodded, congratulating himself for being right.

The grass inside the four triangles was beautiful, and he wished his lawn at home looked that good. Flowers had been planted where the grass met the sidewalks, creating a second square of flowers just inside the sidewalk, broken only by the crisscrossing walkways. There was a Statue at the center of the square and park benches with people sitting on them. "Where are the picnic baskets?" John said, thinking of home.

Beyond the square and across the roads were many more buildings of different sizes and shapes. From high risers to plain old houses. From the look of it, he and Randy were in a small city or perhaps some military or scientific complex. Looking beyond the city structures, he saw tree-covered hills. Further out, he saw the snow-covered peaks of the Mountains.

Looking back at the grassy square, John noticed three female aliens sitting together on a bench. Three young children were playing nearby. Many Aliens were milling around and walking past him. Short people, fat people, old and young people, all going about their business. He caught the sweet-smelling scent again and was sure someone was wearing perfume. It was a scene from Earth.

The traffic on the roads also reminded him of home. Especially the dump trucks, because it was so easy to see that they were dump trucks. The one big difference was that all the vehicles appeared to be electric. He had not yet heard the rumbles of a gas or diesel engine. Only the whine of electric motors. The Van that brought them here had also been electric.

Seeing all this was pleasant, but at the same time painful for them. It reminded them of home, and home was a place they were sure they would never see again. How could they ever get home from here?

"I miss my wife," Randy said.

"Yeah, me too," John said, then grinned. "I miss your wife, too."

"Oh gosh, that is SO funny," Randy said, slapping his knee, purposely overacting. "And so original. What a cutup you are, John-boy."

"Oh, shut up," John said, laughing. They were both happy and in good moods because they were outside, and it felt so good to be free at last.

In the following weeks, they began to learn about their new home. They were free and could move about as they wished. John, much more than Randy, went out and mingled with the aliens often. He had even befriended three young aliens and their mothers who came to the square almost every day. Nada, a young girl, Gladin, and Glom, both young boys. They were very respectful and friendly toward him. All the aliens he dealt with seemed happy, caring, and respectful of everyone else.

Going out among them helped John learn more about their language, the people, and their culture. He learned that most, if not all, the equipment on this planet was electric. If he understood what the aliens were trying to say to him, they were telling him that this world had focused on electricity right from the start. They claimed that their God had given them knowledge of electricity.

Because he and Randy were free to go wherever they wanted, John took advantage of that and started walking into supermarkets and stores, restaurants, and other gathering places. He even waltzed into manufacturing plants and looked around. Not once was he ever asked to leave or thrown out on his ear. The aliens were always welcoming toward him, and he was glad of that because there was much to see and learn.

The place he liked looking around the most was the very same place where he and Randy were housed. That building, when translated, was called the Niglaie Air Carrier Center. Niglaie was the name of the city they were in. John had seen the airfield from the windows, but once they were free to go outside, he was quick to go around the building to see it up close. He liked to watch the airships take off and land. Standing beside the airfield, he could see it all. Ships would take off, going straight up into the air so high he couldn't see them anymore. They were incredible machines, and he hoped that someday he could go up in one.

Wandering around the way he did, John learned that the alien electric motors, generators, and batteries were far superior to anything he had seen on Earth. What powered everything was beyond his understanding, but he understood that the batteries charged faster and held that charge much longer than anything on Earth. The motors, generators, and batteries were all more advanced and much, much lighter in weight. He learned most of this through his own observations and not so much from talking with the aliens. He was always unsure what they were saying to him or what *he* was saying to them. He would occasionally get strange looks from the aliens he was talking to, followed by a smile and an understanding look.

During the morning sessions with Awth and Nellaynan, he and Randy learned about the planet and its people. The planet was called Pellaya. The continent they lived on was called Bayth, and the people called themselves Baythous. Baythous meant, "People of Bayth."

Awth and Nellaynan were doing their best to learn the English language and as much about Earth as they could. They were doing well at it, too. Enough so that Awth attempted to tell John and Randy what he could about Lieutenant Branden Wilson, the Russian, and the little gray men. He used English, Pellayen, hand gestures, drawings, and anything that helped him tell what he knew. It became apparent that he felt it very important that they talk about it.

Awth told them that Lieutenant Wilson, the Russian, the satellite, and the gray men had all come out of a place called Tallda Shayts. He placed a map on the table and showed them a very large blacked-out area. "This is Tallda Shayts," Awth said, pointing at the black area. "It has been there from our very beginning, yet we know nothing about it. Any of our people who have gone into it to explore never come back. Yet aliens, like your Lieutenant Wilson, the Russian, those you call the grays, and that satellite, all came out of it. The men died before we could learn anything from them." Awth looked straight at Randy. "You did not come out of Tallda Shayts. Why have you come here to us?"

Randy turned to John, "That must be what we saw from space! Remember the giant hockey puck? This must be it," Randy said.

"Yeah, I remember. This blacked-out area is where I remember it being," John said. He and Randy both turned back to Awth, hoping they were about to learn something to help them understand how they had come to be here.

Awth eyed them suspiciously. His question had gone unanswered, and it was answers to questions he wanted. But for the moment, he let it go and continued speaking, gesturing, and drawing. "We don't know what Tallda Shayts is. It looks like fog, but it isn't fog. It never lifts and never moves. It has been there as far back in recorded history as anyone knows. We believe it is a distortion of some kind, perhaps of time or space, we don't know. It is a very highly magnetic area which we can't explain. All we know for sure is that if you walk too far into it, you will vanish and never return to us. This is all I know, and I know that isn't much. We know nothing that helps explain what it is or why it is here."

"Sounds like a dangerous place," John said.

"You are safe unless you get too close. Then you vanish," Awth said.

"What about Lieutenant Wilson?" Randy asked. "You say he and the Russian came out of this Tallda Shayts; what can you tell me about them?"

Awth explained what he could about the people and things that had come out of Tallda Shayts. When he was done, Randy had a pretty good understanding of what Awth was trying to tell them. For the moment, Randy fell quiet and thought about all he had learned.

Lieutenant Branden Wilson, the Russian, the satellite, and the Gray's ship had all come to this planet out of this place called Tallda Shayts. It appeared most of these things, if not all, had come from Earth. Lieutenant Wilson and the Russian certainly did. The satellite in the picture had Russian lettering on it, so it also came from Earth orbit. The only real question was where the little gray men came from. The only answer Randy had was that since everything else came from Earth, the grays probably came from Earth as well.

After a few minutes, Randy asked Awth to explain how they found the American and the Russian. Awth told them that the Russian had crawled out, dragging his broken body. He was the first being ever to come out of Tallda Shayts, and that caused quite a stir. He had crawled out many years ago. The Little Gray Men were the second to come out of Tallda Shayts some years later. They stayed a short time and then left to find their home world. Lieutenant Wilson came next after the Grays. He crashed his plane at the edge of Tallda Shayts. Both he and the Russian had been severely injured and would die of their injuries. The 'Russian' had lived a little longer than Lieutenant Wilson, and that is why

Pellayens knew a little more Russian than English. They had had more time to learn more Russian, but he had only lived 5 days before he could no longer speak. His injuries were so bad that they could do nothing to save him.

"Because of you and John," Awth said. "We now know much more of your English,"

"Ah, huh," Randy said. "That makes sense. But what about the Grays and their ship?"

Awth nodded his head. "Yes. They flew out of Tallda Shayts many years ago. All these things happened before my time, but have been well documented. The grays spoke to us with their minds only. They never said a word with their mouths. They had such strong minds that they could move things with mental energy. They came out of Tallda Shayts, landed, and spoke to us for a brief time, then left again. All they told us was that they didn't understand what had happened to them. They had been near a planet, then were suddenly here. They didn't know how that happened, but they awoke inside Tallda Shayts."

"Did they say what planet they were near? Was it Earth?" Randy asked anxiously.

"No, they did not say," Awth said.

"Did they have an idea of where they were? Some idea of where Pellaya is in the universe?" Randy asked, hoping for clues as to where Pellaya was in relation to Earth. If he could learn where he was, he might get home someday.

"No. We tried to get more information from them, but it seemed to us they didn't want to tell us. All they said was that they couldn't see anything inside Tallda Shayts. They avoided our questions, and we believe our questions made them nervous and were the reason they left so quickly. When they left, those who spoke with them believed they were hiding something."

Randy grunted but seemed satisfied with the answers he had gotten. It had taken a lot of time and effort, but Awth had done well explaining what he knew. Unfortunately, there wasn't much he told them that helped to answer any of their questions. But now Randy understood there was a mystery on this planet and that he and John were now part of it.

Tallda Shayts had been there for thousands, perhaps millions, of years. But because of the nature of Tallda Shayts, even after all that time, the Pellayens still knew nothing about it. All they knew was that if you got too close, you would vanish, and that alien beings were coming out of it. They had no idea who they were or why they were coming.

Awth eyed John and Randy and finally repeated his question. "You did not come out of Tallda Shayts. Why have you come here, and how did you do it?"

John's eyes widened as he realized Awth was thinking he and Randy had *meant* to come to Pellaya. "Awth, we don't know. We were orbiting our Moon and somehow ended up here orbiting your planet. We ..." John said, pointing at himself and Randy, "thought you Pellayens might have brought us here. Did you bring us here?"

They watched Awth's shoulders sag. It was obvious his hopes had just been dashed to pieces. He had just learned that John and Randy had no more idea how they got here than the Pellayens did. He would get no new knowledge or understanding of anything from them. He lifted his eyes to them and shook his head. "No. We did not bring you here. We wouldn't know how to do that or where to bring you from. We do not know where your Earth is."

It was disheartening for all of them to learn they would not get the answers they had longed for. Getting answers was the main reason they struggled so hard to communicate, but now they understood none of them had the answers. They were all equally confused. No one knew how the men had come to be on Pellaya.

What they did learn was that they were all in it together. Something was happening between Earth and Pellaya. The pictures of Lieutenant Wilson and the Russian suggested that whatever it was, had been going on for a very long time. But what was going on? No one could answer that question. For now, maybe forever, Tallda Shayts would continue to be a mystery.

CHAPTER FIVE
SOMETHING IS WRONG WITH JOHN

The months passed quickly as John and Randy learned about their new planet. Randy resisted calling Pellaya his home. Earth was his home, and he wanted to get back to it. John was much more accepting of his fate and had become more integrated into Pellayen life. He wandered around the city, investigating everything. Lately, most of his time has been spent hanging around the Niglaie Air Carrier Center. This was Pellaya's version of NASA and a place where he felt most at home. Missions were planned and executed from here, and he could see it all happen.

The Niglaie Air Carrier Center was more of an airport than a launching area for missions into outer space. Ships came and went as often as airplanes did at an airport on Earth. Most ships carried Pellayens and cargo to and from other cities. But occasionally, a vessel was loaded with people and cargo and sent to one of the Moons or some other Planet. It didn't matter where the ships were going; they all launched from the same area and just as quickly. Any of these ships could fly off into space at any time, and this amazed John.

Missions into space were as easy to do as missions to other cities. The ship was loaded and told where to go, and it went; it was that simple. This made John laugh a bit. He and Randy could have landed on one of Pellaya's moons and been saved. The Pellayen had mining communities on all three moons. That was something he would harass Randy about.

John began to understand that the Pellayens weren't as interested in exploration as much as humans were. They would explore a new Moon or Planet as needed, and that didn't happen often. From what he had heard, there were only a few Pellayens in their history who had cared to go farther out to explore. One of them was gone for years, then returned saying he had found life on a planet in a nearby solar system. There was no intelligent life, but there was plant and animal life. Yet even with this discovery, no one went back. The need to go wasn't there.

John could only shake his head. If he had a ship as capable as a Pellayen ship, he would be out there exploring all the time. With a Pellayen ship, he could go anywhere in the solar system. He knew that if he never found a way home to Earth, and had to stay on Pellaya, he would find that planet when he was ready to spend the years necessary to do it.

He was thrilled when they invited him to go on a mission to one of the Moons. He saw firsthand just how incredible these Pellayen spacecraft were. They handled the same in space as they did in the air. They were fantastic machines, able to reach speeds far beyond anything Earth had. He felt like a little kid anticipating the arrival of a new longed-for toy when he was told he would one day be allowed to pilot one. He dreamed of owning one.

With a Pellayen ship, he could easily explore the planets around Pellaya. Then he thought of having a Pellayen ship to explore the Planets around Earth. What a thrill it would be to finally be able to travel to Mars, Jupiter, Saturn, and Neptune. How great it would be to fly to Jupiter, see all its moons, and look for life. With a Pellayen ship, that kind of exploration could really begin. He figured a Pellayen ship would be capable of flying into a gas giant like Jupiter. But because he was stranded on Pellaya, Jupiter was out of the question. He might someday be able to explore the planets around Pellaya, and that was something to look forward to.

Before he could do that, he had to become thoroughly versed in the workings of the craft. That included learning to read and speak the Pellayen language. He was doing well learning to speak it, but he had only just started to learn how to read it, and that was going to be very important when it came to piloting one of their ships and reading manuals.

John was falling in love with Pellaya and its people. He missed his wife and friends, but he was happy here. He had gained many friends on Pellaya, including three children, Nada, Gladen, and Glom, and their mothers, Shara, Azeela, and Nadeena. They came to the courtyard and sat on a bench while their children played, nearly every day. He knew them all, but the friendship didn't truly begin until the day John had walked into the courtyard and three squealing children ran passed him. Gladen wasn't watching where he was going and ran smack into John. Nada and Glom continued passed him and ran around the other end of the building.

Gladen looked up at John. "Sorry, Mister Baines," he said, just as they heard very heavy footfalls, thump, thump, thump, coming toward them. Gladen turned, shrieked, and tried to run away, but it was too late. The giant Angry Man scooped him up and began tickling him. How Gladen squealed.

John wasn't sure what to think until he looked at his mother on the bench. She was laughing right along with everyone else witnessing their play. Angry Man finally stopped torturing Gladen and looked around. His eyes fell on John. John stiffened, suddenly uneasy with having the fierce stare of such a large, angry man on him again. This was the first he had seen of Angry Man since being led into the building, and his fear of him hadn't changed.

Angry Man looked away, still holding Gladen, when Nada poked her head out from behind the building. It was obvious she wanted Angry Man to see her, and he did. He growled and ran after her, carrying Gladen, who continued laughing. Bartolos ran around the building out of sight, but the squeal that came next, told it all. He had caught Nada, and she was enduring the tickle torture.

John couldn't help but laugh. Everyone in the courtyard was laughing. Seeing this hadn't taken away his fear of Angry Man, but it did ease it a little. He walked to the Mothers and spoke to them as best he could. That day, the friendships started, and he would come to know them well. He liked Azeela, Gladen's mom. There was something special about her. He couldn't put his finger on what it was, but he liked being with her and talking to her.

It was different for Randy. He liked the people, too, but he refused to give up the hope of finding a way home. He spent a lot of time at observatories searching for Earth and trying to figure out how to get back to it. No one knew where Earth was, or where to look for it, but Randy looked almost every day. Nothing he saw looked familiar, and his prospects of finding Earth weren't good. It was a monumental task, but a task he wasn't willing to give up.

Though he didn't stop looking for Earth, he did start spending more time watching John. Something wasn't right about him. John would suddenly have a headache and seem confused for no reason, and it seemed to be getting worse. Randy had been seeing John's moments of confusion almost daily. John would look scared and confused, and later on, he would seem overly tired. Twice, Randy asked John about it, but John said he had a headache but was okay.

Randy didn't know what was happening, but he could see the effect it was having on John. John wasn't himself. He would suddenly clam up and withdraw into himself. It appeared to Randy that whatever was happening had John worried, confused, and afraid. He was much less confident and very withdrawn, yet he continued denying that anything was wrong.

This morning, Randy woke up with this on his mind. He looked for John, but John wasn't in the room. Randy dressed and walked out of their room into the square. He stepped just outside the door and saw John standing with a group of Pellayens talking. At that very moment, something happened that Randy had seen many times before. All the Pellayens suddenly stopped whatever they were doing and just stood silent, as if listening for something. At that same moment, he watched John slip into one of his fearful, confused states. John looked unable to cope with whatever was happening and abruptly left the Pellayens, heading back to their room. Without a word, John brushed passed him and went into the building. It was easy to see that John was upset.

Randy looked back at the Pellayens, who still acted as if they were listening to something. Randy closed his eyes and listened as hard as he could. He heard the wind, a few bird-like creatures, and vehicles on the road, but nothing out of the ordinary. Whatever caused the Pellayens to pause didn't bother him at all, but it had just become clear that it bothered John.

Then, suddenly, the Pellayens began moving and acting normally again. The "Event", whatever it was, was over, but Randy was sure it wasn't over for John. He would be distraught, trying to hide his problems and acting like nothing was wrong. Randy was more convinced than ever that something was wrong. He had noticed it was taking John longer and longer to recover from these episodes, and when he did, he seemed a little less like the John Baines he knew.

Randy stood outside, continuing to watch the Pellayens. He had seen them pause many times before, but this was the first time he had seen their "Pause event," and John's sudden confusion happened simultaneously. There had to be a connection between the two events. Something the Pellayens were doing was affecting John. He couldn't say what it was, but he was beginning to suspect telepathy was involved. What he could do about it, he didn't know.

Soon, Awth and Nellaynan arrived for their daily learning session, and they all went back inside. Later that day, when Awth and Nellaynan were leaving, Randy decided to walk out with them and talk to them about John. Once outside and away from John, he turned to Awth. "I am concerned about John. Something is wrong with him, but I don't know what. I have a suspicion, but I have no idea what to do about it."

"Yes, it has come to our attention that he is having difficulties," Awth said.

Randy was both surprised and comforted to learn that someone else saw that John was having problems. "So, you've seen him having these spells of his?"

"Yes. It appears he is having problems with our communication systems."

"Communication system?" Randy said. "No, Awth, I don't mean he can't understand your electronics. I mean, there is something that happens to John, and it is hurting him."

"Yes, I have been made aware of this. Randy, we Pellayens can speak with our minds. We are not masters at it like the little gray men, as you call them. Your Gray men don't need any help at all to make themselves heard," Awth said and was interrupted by Randy.

"No, Awth. I mean, there is something wrong with John. He is having a breakdown or something."

"Randy, listen to me," Awth said. "Nellaynan has made us aware of John's situation. I'm trying to explain. We Pellayens can speak to each other with our minds. We also broadcast thoughts around the world, but our minds aren't strong enough to do that without help. To broadcast thoughts around the world, we had to develop an amplifier that amplifies our thoughts. This is how we stay in touch with each other around the world and with our craft in space. Over the years, we have increased that technology so that the system is now very powerful. We believe John hears those communications, and that bothers him."

Randy shrugged. "I've never heard anything, and John has never said anything about it."

Awth shook his head. "You don't understand. It is the transmission of thought. You don't hear it with your ears. You hear it in your mind. We believe John is receiving those Thought Transmissions, and I doubt he would be able to make any sense of them. He might grasp a thought here and there, but for the most part, it would be energy entering his mind with no purpose. It must leave him confused and afraid for his sanity."

"Well! That's definitely not what I expected to hear you say!" Randy said.

Awth continued. "We need to talk to him, and we would have sooner, but after he told us how to find your ship, we assumed your race had Mental Ability."

"Wait a minute. I'm confused," Randy said. "What do you mean he told you how to find the ship? What ship?"

"Your Lucky Lady. John told us how to find you."

"What? I don't understand. I was with him the whole time. How did John tell you how to find the Lucky Lady?

Awth put up his hands to stop Randy from saying anything more. He thought for a moment and then began to speak. "The day they found you in the Lucky Lady, we had a ship going to Larros, one of our moons around Pellaya. Bartolos was on that ship and was the one who heard your language in his mind. He couldn't understand the language, but he heard it and could hear its urgency. Bartolos ordered his ship to slow down and waited for information from whoever was sending it. Eventually, Bartolos received a very clear image of his ship turning in a certain way, so he ordered his ship to turn just as he saw in his mind. He could feel the urgency in the message and believed it was a call for help. He looked for you but couldn't find you, so he waited.

Then he got the second image of his ship turning in a circle with its nose elevated and ordered his ship to do that. That's when they found you. If he hadn't heard John, they wouldn't have known you were there and wouldn't have found you."

"I can't believe this! You're telling me that John somehow spoke to this Bartolos with his mind and directed him to find us?" Randy said.

"Yes," Awth said. "By sending images to Bartolos, John showed Bartolos how to find you. This is also why all of us believed your species was able to speak with your minds. You communicated to us how to find you, but then, when Bartolos looked into your Lucky Lady, he found that both of you had closed your minds and no longer wanted to communicate. None of us understood why you would shut us out like that, but we believed you had your reasons for doing so, and that was your right. So, you see," Awth said in an apologetic tone. "Until lately, we thought you could speak with your minds but refused to do so for reasons of your own. Perhaps to keep your secrets.

I am sorry to say that it was only recently that we realized that John doesn't understand that he can speak to us mentally. We believe that he, and you, are unaware that you have this ability. Because John told us how to find the Lucky Lady, we believe it was an act of desperation on John's part. Sometimes, desperate thoughts can break free. Now that we understand John is unaware of what he is doing, we can understand how our thought broadcasts are causing him much discomfort. We certainly didn't know he was being hurt."

Randy nodded, remembering how John had reacted when Angry Man had looked in the Lucky Lady at him. He had cowered under Angry Man's glare. Now Randy could see why. Angry Man had been trying to communicate mentally with John, and John felt it in his head. John couldn't have known what was happening and was confused by it. It was also why Bartolos had glared at them the way he had. He was concentrating on communicating with them. It all fit together. Bartolos's intense glare and John's cowering and headache were caused by Bartolos's attempt to communicate with him.

"Wow! It all fits! So, does that mean you can read my mind?" Randy asked, feeling a little uneasy.

"No. You have not opened your mind to us," Awth said, shaking his head. "Think of it this way. If you don't open your mouth, you can't talk, and I can't hear you. It is the same when you speak with your mind. If you don't open your mind to me, I can't hear you. So no, I can't read your thoughts because you aren't open to me. None of us has heard anything from you, but we have heard things from John. Not very often, but we have heard things from him. He has sent more images to Nellaynan than anyone else. She is the one who first understood what was happening. She realizes John doesn't know we Pellayens have mental ability, or that he has it too. That makes him vulnerable to the thought broadcasts. The thought Broadcasts can cause his mind to open, so the broadcast floods into him. If he knew how to control his mind, he could shut the broadcasts out, but he is unaware of his ability, so he has no control at all."

"That sounds terrible," Randy said, shaking his head. Then he turned back to Awth. "John can't stop the thought broadcasts, but can he stop *you* from entering his mind?"

"If he knew of his ability, yes, of course he could. But Randy, he has no control over it. So sometimes we hear things from him, but most of the time his mind is closed to us, and we can't hear him. If John were in control of his ability, yes, he could keep us from hearing his thoughts."

Awth stopped for a minute and looked at Randy. "I assume this wasn't a problem for him on your Earth. I can imagine that, like you and John, most humans are unaware of their ability and never use it, so there was nothing for John to hear. Here on Pellaya, everyone has the ability and uses it, so there is plenty of opportunity for John to hear things. Do you understand?" Awth asked.

"Yes, I think I understand now. But why am I not affected in the same way?" Randy asked.

"I don't know. I'm sure you have the ability, but your ability might be dormant. Your ability is not working because you have never set it up and turned it on. It's like a computer or an unplugged light. If you don't plug it in, you can try to turn it on, but nothing is going to happen. You may not have plugged your mental ability in, but with training, I'm sure you could use your mind to speak with us."

"Okay, I think I understand now. Hmm. So you're saying the Pellayens, humans, and the Grays all have this ability. Even if it is at different levels?" Randy asked.

"Yes. The Grays are very strong. We believe they can read our minds any time they wish, even when we try to close our minds to them. We saw that kind of strength in them. So, you see," Awth continued. "We are limited in what we can do. Very few Pellayens could force John to open his mind. I know of one that could, and I believe that is what has to happen."

Nellaynan stepped forward. "John has sent thoughts to me more often than even you know, Awth," Nellaynan said. "I haven't told you because I saw in his mind that it would embarrass him. He has feelings toward me, and that makes him feel guilty. He loves his wife and feels he is betraying her. What he feels toward me, he won't say with his mouth, but fails to keep from my mind."

Randy looked at Nellaynan, feeling uneasy. From what he understood, John had been sending rather crude messages to Nellaynan without realizing it. "You have been getting messages from John?" he asked Nellaynan.

"Yes," she said.

"Does he owe you an apology?"

"No, but your thinking is correct. I know exactly what he thinks of me. His thoughts embarrass him. I am not embarrassed and need no apology," she said, nodding.

Randy closed his eyes and thought to himself, *Oh brother. I can imagine what he has told you.*

Randy shook his head, knowing that John had a very high opinion of Nellaynan. He thought she was beautiful and sexy. If John was sending messages of that nature to her, he owed her a very big apology.

When he opened his eyes, Nellaynan was standing close in front of him, looking at him with concern. "Randy, don't worry about what he has relayed to me. All Pellayens can see into another's mind. For us, it is a natural thing. There is very little that is hidden from one another. I open my mind completely to everyone. I would have it no other way. Everyone knows exactly who I am and what my desires are. If John's mind were open to me, he would know I feel the same toward him."

Yikes! Randy thought to himself. *Not sure I want to hear any more of this!*

Randy tried to imagine what it would be like to be completely open to everyone. "God. I don't think I could do that," he said.

"Not all Pellayen agree with being completely open," Awth said. "I hold much to myself. But I agree with Nellaynan's way of life, as more and more Pellayens do. It is a very healthy and clean way to be. You probably can't see how it removes so many problems. I would know if you were a threat to me. I would know if what you tell me is the truth or not, and yes, I would know if someone wanted to be with me or not. The questions go away, and knowing these things makes it easier to understand other people.

Even though I agree with Nellaynan, I am old and probably not as strong a person as she is. I hold on to the old ways. I am sure things change on your planet in the same way, don't they? That's what is happening here. The old beliefs are changing."

Randy nodded. "Yes, things do change that way on Earth," he said, looking up at Awth. "So, are you telling me that when John's mind is open, he receives all these thoughts at once?"

"No, I believe he is only receiving the stronger signals from our thought amplifier and possibly from the stronger minds among us. I want Bartolos to speak to him. Bartolos has the strongest mind of anyone I know."

Nellaynan nodded. "I don't know of anyone stronger or more knowledgeable about it than Bartolos Null."

Nellaynan took hold of Randy's arm. "Don't worry, Randy. John is in no danger. He probably does become confused when thoughts that are not his own enter his mind. I imagine it is scary for him. He may feel he's losing his mind. Now we know about it and can help him."

Randy thought a moment. "Couldn't one of you have told him what was happening? You say he was sending you messages, Nellaynan. Why didn't you tell him?"

"I tried to tell him, but I could not get him to understand. I do not have the words in your language, and he did not understand mine. I tried to speak directly to his mind, but because he doesn't even know he has the ability, it only confuses him. My mind is not strong enough to open his mind like the thought transmissions or Bartolos."

"Hmm," Randy grunted. He looked at Awth, who spoke up right away.

"I only just found out about it yesterday. I haven't had time to deal with it, and I needed time to think about it."

Randy nodded, "Well, I know now and can tell him about it."

"No. It would be best if you didn't do that," Awth said.

"Why not? Nellaynan said he was in no danger. Why not tell him?

Awth nodded. "He isn't in any real danger right now, but once he learns of his ability, there is a risk. Remember, he has no control over it, and this is a different world from your Earth, where no one uses their ability. Should he experiment and manage to open his mind, he could be flooded with all the thoughts of everyone around him. That could and no doubt would hurt him. It could drive him mad. This is a new situation for all of us, and we must be careful," Awth said. He thought a moment, then continued.

"Randy, we Pellayens are born with this ability and learn about it from birth. We must be taught about it and grow into it. Even so, it is a natural, normal part of our lives. Has it been a part of John's life?"

"No, it hasn't, and I see what you mean. He and I are new to a planet where everyone uses their mind like that. Yeah, I can see where that could really hurt him."

"Yes, it could be overwhelming for him," Awth agreed. "He most likely would not be able to control it. He needs to be taught about it and trained on how to protect himself."

"I understand. So, what do we do?" Randy asked.

"I believe we should have him talk to Bartolos. He has a powerful mind and will be able to show John how to close his mind, so he is no longer bothered by the Transmissions. Then we can train him."

"I understand," Randy said. "So, you think this Bartolos can help him?"

"Yes. Many of us could help John, but we should ask Bartolos. His abilities are greater than anyone I know, and he can do things I can not."

"Ok, let's do it then," Randy said. Though he agreed to have Bartolos talk with John, he hadn't missed Awth saying Bartolos had looked in the Lucky Lady at them. The only person who had looked in the Lucky Lady was the frightening creature they had been calling Angry Man. Angry Man had to be Bartolos and would be invited to help John. Randy wasn't eager to see Angry Man again, but if he could help John, that would be enough for Randy.

For now, Awth and Nellaynan went their separate ways, and Randy went back to his room. He told John that Awth and Nellaynan were coming to talk to him later, so he should stay around. He avoided answering John's questions about why they wanted to talk to him.

Later, Randy and John sat eating supper, waiting for Awth and Nellaynan. While eating, Randy looked at the picture of Lieutenant Branden Wilson. He would take the pictures out from time to time, hoping they would help him remember who Branden Wilson was. Today, he brought them out more as a way to avoid talking to John about the pending visit from Awth.

Randy picked up the picture of the damaged WWII fighter Plane and held it together with the picture of Lieutenant Wilson. Every time he looked at the pictures, he was certain there was something about him in history, but he couldn't think what that was.

Randy also had Tallda Shayts on his mind. *People go in and don't come back out. That's like the Bermuda Triangle on Earth.* Suddenly, it hit him.

John looked up just in time to see Randy frozen in place with the pictures pinched between the thumb and forefinger of one hand, while ready to shove a forkful of food into his mouth with the other. He was frozen with his eyes fixed on the picture.

"What is it?" John asked.

Randy put down his fork and gripped the pictures with both hands. "Wait a minute!" he said.

"What is it? Do you remember something?" John asked.

"Yes, I got it! I remember!" Randy said, still looking at the picture. "It's one of those weird stories about the Bermuda Triangle. I just remembered. This guy," Randy said, tapping the picture. "This Lieutenant Branden Wilson was on a mission that routed him through the Bermuda Triangle. John he was never heard from again."

"The Bermuda Triangle?" John asked, not quite getting the significance of it.

"Yes. Don't you see it, John? Lieutenant Branden Wilson disappeared in the Bermuda Triangle and ended up here on Pellaya! He came here, John! There must be a connection between the Bermuda Triangle and Tallda Shayts."

John sat up straight. "That's amazing!" he said.

Randy pointed at the pictures. "Do you see it? All these people, the Satellite, and the gray Aliens…. All of them must have come from Earth. I bet you all of them vanished from inside the Bermuda Triangle."

"No," John said. "I don't think the Satellite was in the Bermuda Triangle."

"No, I doubt that, too, but then neither were we. We were landing on the moon, and we ended up here. I'm willing to bet the Bermuda Triangle had something to do with it."

"That's a bit of a jump, but I agree it looks that way," John said.

"Damn!" Randy said. "This could be a way home! I need to talk to Awth and see this Tallda Shayts thing, whatever it is. Come to think of it, where is he? He should be here by now. He said this afternoon. It's evening now." Randy said, more anxious than ever to see Awth.

"I'm sure he will be along soon," John said. "Did he say what he wanted to talk to me about?"

"No. John, don't you see?" Randy said, avoiding having to answer the question. "This Tallda Shayts could be our way home."

"Yes. I see it. It's incredible!" John said.

Randy noticed John's lack of enthusiasm, and it didn't surprise him. John had been acting very subdued for the last several days. He was not himself at all.

Regardless of John's attitude, or lack thereof, they sat talking about this new discovery. Randy had just shown that Lieutenant Branden Wilson had flown into the Bermuda Triangle and come to Pellaya. The pictures of him on Pellaya proved it. There had to be a connection between Tallda Shayts and the Bermuda Triangle. This Force, whatever it was, had pulled Lieutenant Branden

Wilson, the Russian, the satellite, and the Grays here from Earth. That Force had also pulled him and John here from the Moon.

"And John, they were alive when they came to Pellaya. According to Awth, the Russian had fallen from a great height and been injured. Lieutenant Wilson had crashed his plane and been injured as well, but both had survived the trip from Earth to Tallda Shayts. The Gray Aliens had come out of Tallda Shayts without a scratch. No doubt because of their more advanced ship. So, it was possible to survive Tallda Shayts."

Randy could only hope that this phenomenon worked in the other direction, and anyone who entered Tallda Shayts would go to Earth. But if that were true, why had no one ever reported seeing anything that looked like a Pellayen? People claimed to see UFOs, little gray men, even sightings of Bigfoot, and many other odd creatures, but none of the descriptions described a Pellayen. Pellayens could easily be mistaken for humans, and they could easily blend in, but Randy felt that Pellayens would make themselves known.

The lack of evidence that the Pellayens who entered Tallda Shayts were going to Earth made entering Tallda Shayts a risky proposition. Who knew where they would end up or even if you went anywhere at all?

"But Randy…" John said. "You need to remember that the Bermuda Triangle is over the Ocean. Anyone who walks into Tallda Shayts and goes to the Triangle is going to end up in the Ocean. No one knew they were coming, so no one was looking for them. They would drown and never be found. So they could be going to Earth.

"Excellent point!" Randy said happily. "So that means we really might be able to get home! If we had a Pellayen ship, I bet we could survive the trip no matter where we ended up."

"Maybe, but we have no way of knowing what happens after entering Tallda Shayts. We might go to Earth, or we might go even farther from Earth. We could also die as soon as we entered Tallda Shayts. We don't know. I guess there's only one way to find out," John said.

Randy's head bobbed up and down. "Yeah, we would have to enter this Tallda Shayts."

John eyed Randy. "And you're thinking of doing it, aren't you?"

"Hell yes! I want to go home. I miss my wife and kids. If there's a chance I can get home, I'll take the risk." Randy said.

"Okay, then we need to find out what this Tallda Shayts thing is. That would be a good place to start," John said.

They sat quietly, lost in their thoughts and hopes that they might be going home. Their thoughts were interrupted when Awth and Nellaynan entered the room. Behind them, a huge Pellayen ducked his head down and entered the room. He was too tall for the doorway and almost too wide for it. They only knew one Pellayen that was that large. It was Angry Man.

Tension now filled the room. Angry Man's expression had not changed. He looked mean, nasty, and ready to kill. Without a suit on, the men got a good look at the size and condition of this being. He stood better than eight and a half feet tall and had very large, well-defined muscles. He was a menacing beast of a Pellayen.

He avoided looking at the men. He didn't stare at them like he had when they were in the Lucky Lady. This time he came into the room, moved aside the door, put his back to the wall, and looked away from them.

"You have seen Bartolos before," Awth said.

"Yes, we have!" John said.

"I know you have, and I can tell you are fearful of his size and the look on his face," Awth said.

"Yes. I'll admit I'm intimidated by him. Why have you brought him here?" John asked.

"His name is Bartolos, and he is here to help you. That is why all of us have come. Bartolos is the biggest and scariest Pellayen I have ever seen in my life, but he is not a threat to you. He is big, and that is threatening, but the fear comes from the expression on his face. He looks like he is going to kill you, but that is far from the truth. He was born with that expression. It is not an expression of his intentions or his feelings. It is the face he was born with. Poor Bartolos Null can do nothing to change it, and it gives the wrong impression.

John slowly straightened up and looked curiously at Awth. "I think I know what you're talking about, Awth. I saw something like this on Earth once. I met a man who looked like he was always laughing. He couldn't change his expression because, as you said, it was the face he was born with. So people assumed he was happy and very friendly all the time. I found out later he hated that. Is that what you're telling me?"

"Yes. That is it exactly," Awth said. "So you have no reason to fear him. He is here to help you, not hurt you. I will admit…"

Awth said, motioning Bartolos to come forward. "When I first met him, I was afraid of him, but there is no reason to fear him. Though I must say, it is wise not to anger him," Awth said with a gesture that he was teasing.

Awth introduced Bartolos and told them Bartolos didn't know their language, so they would have to speak Pellayen to him. Bartolos raised his hand and touched his fingertips to his forehead. Then, he turned his palm out and pushed his hand outward toward the men.

"What does that mean?" Randy asked. "I have seen it done many times before, but I still don't know what it means."

Awth grinned. "That's easy. Imagine that he has taken the thoughts from his head and pushed them toward you. He has given his thoughts to you. It is a Pellayen, let's say, special greeting."

"Ah! So if I could, if I had the ability, I could see his thoughts." Randy said.

"Yes. That's…" Awth stopped talking suddenly and turned his head to look at John. Awth just stood there as if listening to something. All the Pellayens were just standing there, and Randy knew it was a Thought Transmission. Quickly, he looked at John, and sure enough, John was having one of his episodes. He was holding his head with his eyes closed. His face was tensed up in emotion. John suddenly stepped toward Randy, seemingly out of desperation. He looked terrified and weak, as if he were about to collapse. This was the worst reaction Randy had ever seen, and he hated seeing John this way.

Knowing what John was dealing with, Randy stepped toward him, intending to help him, but Bartolos's big hand came out and stopped him. Then Bartolos placed his hands on John's shoulders. John balled up his fists and turned to defend himself, then immediately relaxed and lowered his arms back down to his side. It was obvious, even to Randy, that Bartolos had done something to disarm John. John stood staring up at Bartolos, appearing to be completely at ease. His expression was one of pleasant surprise.

"What's happening, Awth?" Randy asked anxiously.

Awth's response was very slow. It was obvious that he was still in that paused state, listening to the information being pumped into his head. He raised his hand, telling Randy that everything was ok. Then suddenly, the "pause" was over, and Awth responded normally. "I must apologize," Awth said. "This is not what we had planned. We asked them not to broadcast until we said it was okay. But this was important, so they tried to make it brief."

During the 'Pause', Awth had watched John's reaction to the Transmission. "As we suspected," Awth said. "John was affected by it. I felt John's fear and confusion because it was a very strong emotion. Bartolos did the right thing and shielded John from the thought transmissions. As you must have seen, that immediately eased John's mind. I am so glad Bartolos was here. I am not so sure I could have handled it so easily."

Randy looked back at John, who was still locked in a staring contest with Bartolos. "Is he ok?"

"Yes, he's fine. Bartolos is teaching him how to open and close his mind. John will now be able to defend himself against the unwanted invasions in his mind. You needn't worry. When Bartolos is finished with him, John will know what's been happening to him and how to keep it from happening again. He is in good hands. We will all work with John and help him learn to handle his abilities."

Randy watched John for a moment longer, then turned to Awth. "What was the transmission you heard, or saw, whatever happens?"

Awth nodded. "It was news about our world. People are claiming they are being taken from their homes by the Gray aliens. Apparently, the grays have found their way back to our planet and want something from us. We don't fully understand what is happening yet.

The reason they broadcast now against our wishes is because there has been an Earthquake to the East, and they are asking for voluntears to go help with the clean-up and rescue. A great deal of information is transmitted in what we call a thought capsule. I believe they used a Thought Capsule, thinking it would be easier on John. The opposite happened. John had such a strong reaction because he received an unusual amount of information that would have felt like an explosion in his head.

There was also an update about a ship we sent into Tallda Shayts. We still haven't heard from them, and the thought is that we have lost them."

"That does sound like a lot of info for such a short time," Randy said, then thought for a moment. "The Grays are taking people from your planet? We believed they were doing that on Earth, but never got proof it was happening."

"We know they are doing it here. It seems they are trying to hide that fact by causing our people to forget it happened, but our people do remember. They have also been seen taking people. Our ships are fast enough to catch up to them, but we can't do anything about it once we do, and for some reason, the Grays won't respond when we try to talk to them. We don't understand why they are doing this or what they want," Awth said.

Randy nodded, then changed the subject. "Awth, you said you sent a ship into this Tallda Shayts thing?"

"Yes, right after we found you and John, we sent a ship in."

"How long has it been since you sent it in?" Randy asked.

"About a year. We sent them in shortly after you arrived here. Your arrival gave us hope that the trip was survivable, so we sent a ship in."

"A year is a long time," Randy said. "How long can they survive on the ship?

"A very long time. They had supplies to last many years, so it's possible they are alive right now, but are lost."

"Awth, I've learned some things that make me want to see this Tallda Shayts. I need to see it and learn what it is."

Awth nodded. "We can do that if you wish."

Randy told Awth and Nellaynan what he had learned about Lieutenant Branden Wilson and the connection between Tallda Shayts and the Bermuda Triangle. "Now we know for a fact that Lieutenant Wilson came here to Pellaya. Awth, there has to be a connection between the Bermuda Triangle and Tallda Shayts. We have no way of knowing if it's just one way, but I'm willing to bet I can get back to Earth if I enter this Tallda Shayts," Randy said.

Awth's eyes widened as he listened. "That's amazing!" he said. "There has to be a connection between the two. Finally, we've learned something new about Tallda Shayts. This is the most information we have ever had about Tallda Shayts." Awth's excitement was obvious. He put his hands together and eyed Randy. "Randy, do you know what this means? Our people could have gone to Earth! As we speak, our people could be alive on Earth!"

Randy nodded. "Awth, there is no proof that the connection is two-way, but I want to find out. Is it possible your governing Council would give us a ship?"

"When they hear this, I am sure the council will agree to give you a ship. Randy, this is the most information we have ever had about Tallda Shayts, and I know the council will see this as an opportunity to learn more about it. It may take a little time, but I am sure you will get a ship. In the meantime, I will ask Bartolos to take us to Tallda Shayts tomorrow morning. Would that be good with you?"

"Absolutely," Randy agreed.

Now, having agreed on this, they all looked back at John. John and Bartolos were now standing side by side, looking back at them. Their mental communication had ended, and John looked like he had been relieved of a great burden. He had the goofiest look on his face that Randy had ever seen. The change in him was incredible. His mental conversation with Bartolos had done a lot for him, and Randy could only wonder what had taken place between them.

CHAPTER SIX
PREPARATIONS

The following morning, both men were in good spirits. Randy believed there was a real chance he could get home, and John had just learned he wasn't going crazy. He not only learned that he had Mental Ability, but now knew how to stop the mental energy from entering his head and causing him confusion and pain. Being free of these worries had just allowed him the best sleep he had had in a long time. He was feeling refreshed and ready to go. Randy, on the other hand, had been too excited to sleep. He couldn't stop thinking about Tallda Shayts and how it could take them home.

"How are you feeling?" he asked when John woke.

"I feel so much better. I gotta tell you, I thought I was going nuts."

"You had a pretty bad time with it, huh?" Randy asked.

"You bet I did," John said. "I didn't know what to think. I think I know what it would feel like to be possessed. I had a bad time all right. But Bartolos fixed me right up, and I am so thankful he did. I feel so much better now."

"So you're up for going to Tallda Shayts this morning?" Randy asked.

"Yes, of course I am. We need to see this thing and find out what it is."

Randy looked down at the cup of hot Mago he was stirring. "I'm not sure how to ask this … What was it like having Bartolos in your head?"

"Randy, it was something. It was such a relief, and it wasn't at all what you might think. Bartolos took hold of me, and I immediately felt like some kind of protective blanket had been thrown over me, my brain. My confusion was immediately gone, and I could think clearly again. Then I started receiving information, and I knew it was coming from him. Suddenly, I knew what Thought Transmissions were and that I had been receiving them. Bartolos told me it was the Thought Transmissions that were causing my confusion and pain. Until he told me about them, I had no idea what was happening to me. I thought I was going nuts!

Bartolos told me there was energy pouring into my head that I didn't know how to deal with. Then he showed me how to close my mind so the Transmissions couldn't get in, and Randy, that was an amazing thing. I could see and feel him manipulating my mental pathways. Suddenly, I knew how to open and close my mind. Then he explained to me that I had Mental Ability and that was why I was able to receive the Transmissions.

Randy, he did all that so quickly, and in such a way that it was soothing to me. I immediately wanted more, and he gave me more. He opened his mind to me and showed me who he was, and I tell you he is one compassionate man. I am no longer afraid of him and count him as a good and faithful friend. Randy, you asked what it was like to have him in my head; I enjoyed it and want more of it!"

"Wow!" Randy said. "Yesterday, I could see you were relieved, but now you sound like it was as good as sex."

John cocked his head to one side. "Well, I don't really like thinking that way, considering I was hanging with Bartolos, but yeah, it was great. Think about it. I was in trouble, and he stopped it. I had no idea I had Mental Ability, and now I do, and am thrilled about it. I understand I have never used this particular mental muscle before," John chuckled. "I didn't even know I had this muscle, let alone know how to use it."

"You sound more like the John I've known for so long," Randy said. "Well, that's not true either. You sound happier than I've ever seen you."

"Please allow me that," John said. "I am so relieved and happy. It feels like a huge weight has been lifted off my very soul. I feel free! When Bartolos pushed all that information into my head, I suddenly knew it was what I needed, and immediately craved more of it. Especially how to turn it off. My switch is off now, and I'm going to leave it off until I get more training. Bartolos warned me about opening my mind and not being able to close it. Randy, it was the most amazing thing I have ever experienced, and believe it or not, it was pleasurable. I am thrilled that I have this ability and want to learn more about it, and these Pellayens. Especially Bartolos. We have nothing to fear from him. He has no intention of hurting anyone and only wants to help us. He knows his appearance scares people, but he is not the monster he appears to be."

"That's good to know because he still scares the crap out of me," Randy said. "Oh, I just remembered something Nellaynan told me. You might want to say something to her about this. She heard many of the thoughts you had about her, and I know some of what you were thinking. You probably owe her an apology."

John nodded. "Bartolos told me about that and also told me that Nellaynan enjoyed the images she received and even felt the same way," John said, and couldn't resist a little dig. "Some guys got it and then there's you," John said and grinned.

"Ah, huh, John-boy is back," Randy joked. "But I am glad Bartolos fixed you up. It is good to have you back. Now we can get busy finding a way home. What do you say?"

"Yes," John said. "It will be a lot easier to think about that now that my head is free of Thought Transmissions."

Randy nodded.

They waited impatiently for Awth and Bartolos to come and take them to Tallda Shayts. Randy sat thinking about the Pellayen 'Thought Transmissions.' It seemed to him that the Pellayen communication system was rather inadequate for such advanced people. He admitted to himself that he didn't understand their system and was no doubt a poor judge of it, but somehow it did seem inadequate.

He turned to John, "How much do you know about the Pellayen communications? To me, it seems kinda backward."

John shook his head. "I just learned about it, so I'm no expert, but I can tell you from the little I do know that it is by no means backward. By comparison, it's *our* communication system that's backward. The two systems are completely incompatible, that's for sure.

"Hmm," Randy hummed. "Can we make some adjustments and make the two systems work together?"

"I don't think so. Knowing what I know now, I'd say they are two different animals. One is thought and the other is electronics."

"But doesn't the Pellayen system use electronics?" Randy asked.

"Yes, they do," John said. "And the electronic components are very much the same as ours, but their circuits are designed to amplify thoughts, not radio signals. Their electronics pull thoughts in and somehow amplify them. It has to be an entirely different kind of circuitry to do that. Those thoughts remain thoughts and don't become radio frequencies. Just as our radio will not translate into thought," John said, then snapped his fingers. "Randy, that's why you thought the channel was open but couldn't hear anyone when we were in the Lucky Lady! Do you remember? There was a signal, but it was their thoughts, not a radio frequency."

"Yeah, I was just thinking that myself," Randy said. "Okay, I understand the difference, but it still seems backward to me."

John nodded. "I know, and I understand why you are asking about it," John said, standing up, having heard Awth at the door. "We will need the radio equipment from the Lucky Lady aboard the Pellayen ship if they give us one. If they do, it won't be a problem to power up the radio from their power circuits."

Awth entered the room and asked if they were ready to go. Randy and John were more than ready. Tallda Shayts had become the most important thing in their lives.

John was happy to take the front seat next to Bartolos. He had lost all fear of Bartolos and wanted to learn more from him. It would have to be for short periods because that would be all his pained head could stand. On the other hand, Randy still had reservations about the giant and was pleased to sit in the back with Awth. He asked Awth about the council's decision to give them a ship. Awth nodded, knowing Randy would ask.

"I have spoken to the council, and they are as excited about it as I am. They will give you a ship, but it will take some time. You must understand, we have an opportunity to learn from your entering Tallda Shayts, but that window of opportunity is very small. Once you are gone, the chance of learning anything more is also gone. The counsel and I are searching for any other ways we can learn from this. For example. I heard you and John talking about the radio from the Lucky Lady. You will need to have your radio aboard the ship so you can contact someone on Earth. We also want to have a radio so we can be in contact with you as you enter Tallda Shayts. We lost contact with our people as soon as they entered Tallda Shayts. Your system might continue to work, and you can tell us what is happening to you.

Don't worry, Randy. You will get a ship once we have thought of every chance for discovery. I can't think of much more we can do besides the radio, but that is the reason for the delay. We need to give ourselves every opportunity to think of what we can do to learn from this."

"Okay, that is all good to hear, but what about the radio? Will it be a problem to connect our radio to the electronics on one of your ships?"

"No, there won't be any problem in doing that. Your electronics and ours are very much alike. It will be easy to power the radio and add it to the ship. But we are going to ask you to

116

help us build an Earth-style communication system so we can talk to you when you leave. Can you do that?"

"Wow! I understand why you want that, but you are asking an awful lot of me. I don't think I can do it. That is a very tall order," Randy said.

John looked back at them and told Randy that it could be done. "The Pellayen are quite familiar with electronics. All you have to do is show them how to build the radio equipment. Once it's built, all you have to do is supply power to it, and Pellaya has plenty of that. I am sure you could teach them how to do it and have a working system up and running in no time."

Awth nodded. "That is good to hear."

They continued for several more hours. As they crested a hill, Awth pointed out the front window at a massive gray cloud. "That is Tallda Shayts."

John leaned forward. "Awth, what are we looking at?"

"That is the very top of Tallda Shayts seen from many miles away. We won't come to the base of it for hours yet. That cloud will keep expanding on the horizon as we get closer. Eventually, it will be all we can see." And it was true. The longer they drove, the larger the cloud became and the more it blocked out what they could see.

"Good God!" John said in amazement. Tallda Shayts was far off in the distance and was already an enormous gray column reaching high into the sky.

"What in God's name is that thing?" Randy said. He was gripping the back of the front seat as he leaned forward to look. "I knew it was going to be big, but I didn't expect this. And we aren't even seeing all of it yet. I've never seen anything like it! How far from the base of it are we?"

Bartolos turned his head back toward him. "We are still many miles from it. We have to cross this valley and get over those mountains. From the top of the mountains, you will see most of it, but we still have to cross over some low hills before we see the base of it."

"I can't believe something like this exists. It's unbelievable," John said.

Randy turned to Awth. "Do you have any idea what it is?"

"No, we don't. We know what it isn't. It's not water vapor or gas. We do know there is a strong magnetic field being generated there, but we have no idea how or where."

"So I would think a Compass is useless near it?" Randy said.

"They are completely useless near Tallda Shayts," Awth said. "They spin and act very oddly.

"That happens in the Bermuda Triangle," John said. "And come to think of it, it happens most when you are in what they call the Magnetic Fog. I have flown through that fog, and my instruments have gone crazy, but that fog doesn't look anything like this. From here, Tallda Shayts looks solid."

Awth nodded. "From this distance, it does look solid, but when we get closer, you will see that it isn't. You will be able to see into it for a short distance."

They drove on for nearly two more hours, crossing the valley and climbing over the hills. Suddenly, Tallda Shayts loomed larger and more unbelievable than ever. All they could see was this massive gray wall that stretched as far as the eye could see in either direction. Tallda Shayts had become a huge gray curtain that hid the rest of the world from them.

Bartolos finally brought the car to a stop, and they all got out. Randy still had one foot inside the car as a Tendril of mist floated past him. He waved his hand through it, but nothing happened. The Tendril floated away unchanged. "That's weird," Randy said. "The air current should have dragged the mist along with it, but it didn't. What is this stuff? It certainly isn't fog."

He stepped out of the car and stood facing Tallda Shayts. What Awth said was true. Tallda Shayts wasn't solid. He could see into it for about two hundred feet before the false fog got so thick it became an impenetrable gray wall of swirling something.

In front of them, sticking out of the false fog, was the bow of the Earth ship. "This is strange," Randy said, studying the ship. He could see something was written on the bow, but it was impossible to read because of the fog. It was distorting everything.

Another misty tendril floated past him, and he put his hand in it. He kept expecting it to be water vapor and have his hand feel wet, but that didn't happen. Instead, he saw the tendril swirl around his hand close to the skin but not touching it. His hand felt fuzzy as if it were being hit with electricity. The Tendril floated away, and he looked back at Tallda Shayts. "These tendrils and Tallda Shayts have to be some kind of Electromagnetic anomaly. My own body's electricity is affecting it."

As he thought about that, he watched John walk up to a simple rope line closer to Tallda Shayts. The fog swirled around him in the same manner it had moved around his hand. Randy could only shake his head. "Will the weirdness ever end on this Planet?"

John stood at the rope line reading a sign that warned people not to go beyond the rope line or risk vanishing. Randy walked up beside him and noticed a series of different colored wooden stakes driven into the ground, leading deeper into Tallda Shayts. At a distance of around one hundred feet, the stakes ended.

He asked Awth about them, and Awth told him that the stakes had been driven into the ground by a man who had a disease that at the time was incurable. "He was in a lot of pain and knew his life was going to end soon. Instead of dying in bed, he wanted to walk into Tallda Shayts, driving stakes into the ground, hoping we would learn something from his sacrifice. He admitted that he hoped he might just make it to the ship and beyond to see what lay inside Tallda Shayts. He was near death and was going to do it whether we allowed it or not. So we gave him a drug he could use to end his life if he found himself in an unbearable situation, and let him go in."

Awth lifted his head a little. "He was an incredibly brave man, willing to sacrifice his life so we might learn just a bit more about Tallda Shayts. He walked; I should say limped in two steps, then drove in a stake. Then limped two more steps and drove in another stake. He did this until he vanished. His sacrifice showed us where the vanishing line is.

Hundreds of Pellayen came to watch him do this. They came hoping he would make it, at least as far as the ship. Everyone had come to give him their support and honor his bravery. All the onlookers saw him vanish after driving in the sixth stake and taking one last step forward."

"There are more than six stakes," Randy said. "I count twelve stakes,"

Awth nodded. "Yes. There are twelve stakes. What he did started something new. Walking into Tallda Shayts has become a phenomenon, an option to dying in a bed. They feel like they are contributing somehow, and there is always the possibility that they might just make it to the ship, Awth said, pointing to the stakes. "Notice that there are several different colored groups of stakes. The first six yellow stakes were his. The next four red stakes were from another man at a different time. The last two green stakes are from a third, a woman this time. All of them wanted to do this rather than die in a bed, hoping it would lead to us learning something more about Tallda Shayts. In every case, their dying wish was to see what lay beyond this curtain.

You can see other bundles of stakes lying on the ground. Those were left behind by people who vanished without getting the chance to drive a stake in. They set their bundles down, stepped forward, and vanished, leaving the stakes behind," Awth said, turning to face Randy. "Because of their sacrifices, we have learned that the Vanishing Line changes. It grows and shrinks. We have also learned that it grows and shrinks according to how close Pellaya is to the Sun. The closer Pellaya is to the sun, the farther out the vanishing line extends. Tallda Shayts also pulses in time with the alignment of the three moons. It grows and shrinks very quickly around the time the three moons are aligned."

Randy shrugged his shoulders, "What about the people who vanish. What happens to them?

"They vanish. We have no idea what happens to them?" Awth said with a shrug. "They are there one second, gone the next. No one has ever come back, so I can't tell you what happened to them. I can tell you a little about that ship," Awth offered, pointing at the bow of the ship.

Randy nodded for Awth to continue.

"Several people witnessed the whole thing. They saw the ship appear high above the ground, then fall. They saw a man falling with it. He was struggling with that," Awth said, pointing to a display case off to their left.

They walked over to it, and Randy saw a large canvas tarp inside. There was also a plaque which spoke of the man's fall to the ground and his later death.

"Is this the Russian you have pictures of, the one that crawled out of Tallda Shayts?" Randy asked.

"Yes," Awth said and pointed at the tarp. "They say he was tangled in these ropes as he fell. The Tarp caught the air and slowed his fall, but it wasn't enough to save his life."

"No. It wouldn't be," Randy said. "The tarp was way too heavy, and he was no doubt too close to the ground. It wouldn't have slowed his fall much at all."

Awth nodded and continued. "He was the first being ever to come out of Tallda Shayts, and it was a shock to us to learn that he was an alien from another world. Until that day, we had no idea this sort of thing could happen. He lived for seven days, but there were complications to his injuries, and we were unable to save him.

The gray aliens were the second beings to come out of Tallda Shayts several years later. Their ship wasn't damaged at all, and they suffered no injuries. They told us little about the inside of Tallda Shayts, claiming they couldn't see anything because of a dense fog. When you look at Tallda Shayts from out here, you can see how that could be true, but we know they were hiding something. We didn't know what at the time, but it looks like they knew they would return and start taking our people. That's what they were hiding. They must have seen something and known they would come back to abduct our people for their purposes.

Lieutenant Branden Wilson was next to come out. He was in his plane when it crashed. We were able to get him out of the craft, but he was too badly injured for us to save him. He didn't live for very long. Then what you call a Russian Satellite fell out of Tallda Shayts and crashed. We could see the Satellite, but it is too far in for us to get to it." Awth paused a moment to tell Randy they could go to that site and see the Satellite if they wanted, then continued.

"You and John are the last to come to us, but you didn't come out of Tallda Shayts. You are the first aliens to come to us, but not come out of Tallda Shayts. We hoped you had traveled here purposely to make contact with us. Unfortunately, you don't know how you came to be here, and that is exactly what the grays said. They had no idea how they got here. They said they were near a planet, which we can now assume was Earth, and then found themselves waking up inside Tallda Shayts. You have told us the same story, except you were near Earth's Moon. Everyone else came out of Tallda Shayts. You and John are the only ones who didn't come out of Tallda Shayts. It would seem that means something."

"Yes. We were orbiting our moon and found ourselves waking up in what John labeled the 'Mental Abyss.' We had no idea what happened and still don't," Randy said. "We hoped you would be able to tell us what was going on, but it turns out you are just as much in the dark about it all as we are. We found that very disappointing."

"As did I," Awth said, nodding. "When you arrived, we recognized that you were of the same race as Lieutenant Wilson and the Russian, who, by the way, brought a rather vicious disease with him, and that was why you were held in quarantine. We hoped you had planned to come to make contact with us. Now we know that isn't the case at all, but you being here has helped us to learn your language, and we are thrilled to learn of this connection between Tallda Shayts and Earth's Bermuda Triangle. It gives us great hope that we may finally be on the verge of learning what Tallda Shayts is. We know so little about it. Maybe that is about to change."

"Let's hope it is," Randy said. "There is no way to know what is going to happen, but if we enter Tallda Shayts and make it back to Earth, who knows what we will learn?"

They looked around the location of the ship's bow for a few more minutes, then loaded up and drove to Lieutenant Branden Wilson's crashed plane. Like the tarp, the Pellayens had enshrined the plane to preserve it. There was a plaque next to the plane on a stand. It told the story of Lieutenant Wilson's arrival and death.

There was another rope line and another set of stakes leading into Tallda Shayts, but nothing more of interest. Randy asked if there was anything else that they could see, and Awth said no. "In all the centuries Tallda Shayts had been here, this is all there is to see. Tallda Shayts keeps her secrets well," Awth said. With that, they headed back home.

For two days, Randy anxiously waited for word of when they would get a ship. Finally, word came that they would get a ship, but as Awth had suggested, they wanted Randy to help them build an Earth-style communication system. Awth surprised them when he told them the council had asked for and found two voluntears to go with John and Randy. The idea was that if they made it back to Earth and were able to learn how to get back to Pellaya, the two voluntears could make that trip home.

John understood their reasoning, but hated the possible outcome. "There is no reason for you to risk the lives of your people. I am willing to return if we can find a way to do it. If your voluntears came with us, the odds are pretty high that they would be trapped on Earth for the rest of their lives. If Tallda Shayts does send us back to Earth, I would already know I could get back to Earth by entering Tallda Shayts, so I wouldn't be risking a thing by returning to Pellaya. I would be risking very little, and don't forget, we don't know what's going to happen when we enter Tallda Shayts. We might go to Earth, or we could end up lost in space or possibly dead, so the fewer on the ship, the better. Don't risk the lives of your people. Let me return to you if a way can be found."

The council was pleased that John had volunteared to return to Pellaya. Even more pleased when they saw how serious John and Randy were about finding a way back to Pellaya. They were requesting all the information the Pellayens had about Tallda Shayts, its size, how and when it shrank and expanded, information about the lunar alignments, and all the dates and times of each event. Every little bit of information that might help them get back to Pellaya, they wanted. The last thing John asked for was Pellayen calendars, present and future, and several Pellayen clocks. With these, they should be able to project when Tallda Shayts was about to pulse, and when the moons were in alignment.

John and Randy already had a suspicion that the pulsing of Tallda Shayts might be the trigger that caused the vanishings from Earth. If they could keep track of when a pulse was coming and be in the Bermuda Triangle at that time, they might get sent back to Pellaya.

Finally, the council, John, and Randy were done with all the planning and discussion and ready to get to work. Randy's job was to work with Pellayens and build an Earth-style communication system. There was no way he could do it by himself, but the Pellayens were fully capable of building the system once they understood what they needed to do. Randy found that his real job was to get Pellayen's mind off the idea of building a better Thought Transmitter and on the idea of creating radio signals. Once he succeeded in doing that, the Pellayens were off and running.

The work on Radio progressed very quickly, because, to some degree, the Pellayens already knew how to build "Radio", but there had been no need for it. They believed their system was far superior to the electrical impulses of this Earth-style system. Randy didn't agree or disagree with their assessment, but he knew their system wasn't going to get the job done. So, they had to build and add this radio communication system to the ship and their space center system. It was the only way they would be able to talk to the ship when it left, and hopefully, in time, to Earth.

John's work was more physical and done much quicker. He helped in preparing the ship for a long flight. If they survived entering Tallda Shayts, there was no way of knowing where they might end up, or how long they would have to live on the ship. So they loaded food and water and all the supplies they would need to last for many years.

The ship was soon fully stocked and ready to go. All that was needed was to finish the radio system. That took months to complete, but the day came when all the work was finally completed. The ship was ready to go, and the radio system was up and running. All that was left was to set the day of departure, and there was no reason to delay.

John, Randy, Awth, Bartolos, and Nellaynan spent their last night together. They were all thinking the same things. In the morning, John and Randy were going to enter Tallda Shayts, and there was no doubt that it would be the last they would see of each other. Everyone hoped and prayed John and Randy would make it back to Earth and that someday John would return to Pellaya. The idea that there could be a Gateway between their two worlds was a thrilling concept for everyone. It opened up the possibilities of trade, the exchange of knowledge, and friendship.

Nellaynan was the only one who had reservations about John returning to Pellaya. John was returning to his wife, and if he succeeded, her relationship with him would change. It already had. Once John learned he might make it back to Earth, he began distancing himself from her, and it hurt. She knew he was doing it because of his loyalty to his wife and not to hurt her, but his devotion to his wife made her love him all the more.

They were all talking and joking for the last time. It was to be a long goodbye. It was a beautiful, warm Pellayen night, and there wasn't a cloud in the night sky. John and Nellaynan sat studying the stars, somewhat separated from the others. As they sat looking up into the night sky, John noticed something that seemed familiar. "It's funny, but those three stars look a lot like Orion's belt. That's a star constellation we see from Earth," he said to Nellaynan. He studied the three stars more closely. "Yeah, something's different, but it does look like Orion the Hunter's belt," he said. As he pointed out those stars, he found more stars in just the right places to form different parts of Orion the Hunter. But something was different about them.

Suddenly, John's eyes widened. "Oh my God! We are on the other side of Orion! We are incredibly far from Earth!"

"What?" Randy said, getting to his feet and hurrying toward John.

John pointed out Orion the Hunter to him, "But he's facing the wrong way!" he said.

Randy gasped. "Holy Crap! That really is Orion! We are looking at it from the other side. Good God! If this is true, we have to be thousands of light years from Earth! Somewhere on the other side of Orion is our Earth."

John and Randy stared at each other in disbelief. The distance they were talking about was immense and scared them. They questioned whether they should go ahead with their plans to enter Tallda Shayts.

Soon, Randy, who most wanted to get home, made the point that they had already made the trip once. There was no new and greater risk now than there had been a few minutes ago, so there was no reason to change their plans. John finally agreed. They would continue with their plans and launch the ship in the morning.

Randy looked around at everyone there. "What are the odds of everything being in just the right places for us to see Orion like this? It seems impossible to me."

John couldn't help but laugh a little. "If we do make it back to Earth and can tell about our little adventure, I think there is quite a bit that people will find impossible about our trip. I'm sure your mother-in-law will be quite surprised to learn of her involvement in our rescue."

"Oh, brother," Randy said, shaking his head. "I'd hoped you had forgotten that by now. Anyways," he said, getting to his feet. "It's getting late, and we're flying away in the morning. I am going in to try and get some sleep."

"Yeah, that sounds about right," John agreed. "It could be a very long day tomorrow."

Randy leaned back toward him so that only John could hear him. "And it could be our last."

Randy was the first one to wake in the morning. He was anxious to get started and go home. The ship was ready. The men were ready. It was time to go. Both men took time to say their final goodbyes. John was surprised when Nada, Gladen, and Glom, along with their mothers, came to say goodbye. He got a hug from all of them, but was most thankful for the hug he got from Gladen's mother Azeela. There really was something special about her that John couldn't put into words, but he loved having her near him.

Awth, Nellaynan, and Bartolos were the hardest to say goodbye to. They had been together the most. When it came to Bartolos, Randy's hand was almost too small to grip his. "Not going to forget you, big boy," Randy said, looking the two and a half feet up into Bartolos's face. Bartolos bowed a little and laughed. "God go with you," he said in his deep, gravelly voice. It surprised Randy to hear Bartolos speak of God. He hadn't heard any Pellayen mention God before.

Randy found it hard to say goodbye to all of them, but it was harder for John. He had great love for Awth and Bartolos and a greater love for Nellaynan. Bartolos had saved him from his madness and taught him about his new abilities. He had seen the beautiful being living in the brutish body that was Bartolos. What he saw made him love the big brute. He stood before Bartolos and made the 'special greeting.' Only he and Bartolos knew what passed between them.

Awth, too, had a place in John's heart. He was a kind-hearted, lovable old character who had eased their fears and at times made them laugh. John would miss him very much and said so in a mental message full of gratitude.

Then he turned to Nellaynan. Everyone knew they loved each other, and that saying goodbye was going to be hard. He hugged her and spoke to her with his mind. Nellaynan suddenly twisted away from him and walked away crying.

John watched her for a moment, then turned away. The pain on his face told how it hurt to leave her, but it was time to enter the ship and be on their way. John took his seat at the controls, while Randy took the seat next to him on his right. John moved the controls and lifted the ship a few feet off the ground. He turned the ship to look at their friends one last time. It hurt to see the pained expression on Nellaynan's face as he waved his last goodbye, then gripped the radio mic. "Neglay Space Center, this is John and Randy. We are ready to enter Tallda Shayts. Wish us luck, and I truly hope to see you again very soon," John said, never taking his eyes off Nellaynan.

"Be well, John and Randy. We're all hoping you make it back to your Earth. We are all set for you to enter Tallda Shayts when you are ready."

"Goodbye, and here we go," John said, starting the ship into Tallda Shayts. He moved the ship very slowly into the mist. Randy used the radio to relay what they were seeing and what was happening so the Pellayens could have a little more information about Tallda Shayts. The mist got thicker and thicker, then suddenly everything went black.

CHAPTER SEVEN
WHERE ARE WE NOW?

"Where am I?" John groaned. A man he didn't know was sleeping in the seat next to him. He reached out to wake him, but suddenly felt a twinge of fear. Something told him it was a bad idea to disturb him, so he pulled his arm back and sat trying to understand what was happening.

Soon, the man next to him woke looking just as disoriented and confused as John was. John shook his head. "I think we've done all this before. I'm sure of it," he said, turning to the man. "Randy? That's your name, isn't it?"

"I don't know, is it?" Randy said. "What's a Pellaya? It's in my head, but I don't know what it is, and who are you?"

It had happened again. Both of them had found themselves in the Mental Abyss, unable to remember their names or how they came to be there. This time was a little easier because Randy didn't go crazy, and John didn't relive his childhood experience of frantically swimming to the water's surface.

There was another difference this time. Right before he opened his eyes, John had heard a sound. It was somehow familiar to him, but he couldn't quite place it. He forgot all about it when he opened his eyes to find himself looking out a windshield at black space, with a man he didn't recognize sitting next to him.

He sat calmly, letting his memories return, filling in the blanks of his past. He had a big smile on his face when he remembered Pellaya and the people there. He groaned when he remembered the first time he found himself in the Mental Abyss.

"Well, it happened again," John said, sitting forward in his seat, still uncertain of where he was.

"Thank God I didn't go nuts this time," Randy said.

"Ah. You remember that, too, huh? I almost made the mistake of pushing you again."

"Bad idea, my friend. Bad idea," Randy said.

John cocked his head to one side and grinned. "Huh! I just realized that if I had pushed you, I would have had another opportunity to slap you. I'm sorry I missed out on that. Damn!"

"And I just remembered what a pain in the ass you are, John," Randy fired back.

It was all coming back to them. They remembered vanishing from the moon, living on Pellaya, entering Tallda Shayts, and coming to wherever they were now.

Randy scratched his head. "So, have you been awake long? Do you know where we are?"

"No," John said. "I'm just getting my wits about me, but I know this. We are not in the Bermuda Triangle or orbiting the Earth like we hoped. So, I have no idea where we are now. I think there's a Sun off to the left of us, but I'm not sure. I'll turn the ship and see what's around us."

"It would be nice to see Earth," Randy said.

"Yes, it would be nice to see Earth or your Mother-in-law's ship coming to take us home," John said, glancing sideways at Randy.

Randy shook his head. "Of all the things you had to remember."

John spun the shuttle slowly. There was a Sun some distance away, but was it Earth's Sun? They had no way of knowing. "I don't see anything to help us figure out where we are," John said. "It would be nice to see Jupiter or Saturn, anything that told us we were home."

Randy twisted in his seat a bit. "In hindsight... flying into Tallda Shayts may not have been the best idea," he said, half joking.

"Well, let's be thankful we're in a Pellayen shuttle and not the lucky lady," John said.

"You got that right," Randy said enthusiastically. "I wouldn't have come if we had to do this in the Lucky Lady. No way."

Suddenly, there was a loud "Beep." Then a voice came over the radio. "Ok, Jesse, they want an update on how you're doing up there." 'Beep.'

"That's it!" John said happily. "That's what I heard coming out of the Mental Abyss."

"Halleluiah, we're home!" Randy said, taking a deep breath.

Again, there was a beep on the radio. "I am finishing up right now, Control. Won't be but a few minutes more." Beep.

John and Randy cheered loudly and gave each other a High Five. That "Beep" was a very familiar sound, and they knew right away it was NASA. They also knew an Astronaut named Jesse, who had been new to the Astronauts' team several years ago.

These transmissions could have traveled several light years to get to them, but even if they were light years from Earth, they were in a Pellayen ship and would be able to make it home, even if it took years.

"Well, we are closer than we were, but how far from home are we? Randy, try to get the direction of their radio signal," John said, picking up the radio mic. "Mission control, this is... ahh…" he had to stop and think about how to present themselves. "This is the Lucky Lady calling Mission Control. Do you copy?" he said and turned to Randy. "Try to time the response if we get one."

"Already on it," Randy said. They were hoping for a quick response that would tell them they were close to Earth.

John waited a moment, then tried again. He was about to try again when they heard Jesse speak.

"Mission Control, the cover is on, and it's all buttoned up. We're all done up here. This mission is complete, over."

"Rodger. Get yourselves inside and head for home, boys. Job well done."

John jumped in again. "Mission Control, Mission Control, this is the Lucky Lady, do you copy Control? Over."

Both he and Randy sat leaning toward the radio, anxious to hear something from them.

"Control to Sarus 3. Jesse, repeat your last transmission. Part of it was distorted, or someone else is broadcasting on this frequency. Over."

"Rodger Control. I said we are at the hatch and going inside. I believe I heard someone else talking on this frequency also, over."

Randy jumped in his seat. "They heard us! And it didn't take long. We must be fairly close to Earth. We really are Home! That Sarus3 is the Service and repair craft they designed to be stationed and launched from the Moonbase. We must be hearing radio transmissions from another mission. John, they must be up here right now."

"I'd say so, but I'm hearing a delay in transmissions," John said. "How long did it take for them to respond? Did you get a direction?"

"Yeah, it came from off to our left toward the Sun."

Suddenly, an angry voice came over the radio. "Whoever is on this channel, this is a restricted frequency. You need to remove yourself from it or risk a heavy fine or worse. You must already know these rules, so this is your only warning! I advise you to remove yourself from this channel immediately! And your Joke about being the Lucky Lady isn't at all funny. Good men died in that incident, and we take your disrespect personally."

John knew that voice well and happily lifted the mic to speak to him. "Allen Janis, you are one ugly man when you're mad, but it is so good to hear your voice. Allen, it's John. This is John Baines and Randy Harrison; we have returned to haunt you. Damn, it's good to hear your voice. We have one hell of a story to tell you, but I'd like to tell it while standing on Earth," John said and quickly turned to Randy. "Are you timing the responses?"

"Yes, I am."

John and Randy waited for a response. It took two minutes, and an angry Allen Janis was back on the radio. "There is no way you could be who you say you are. Those two disappeared over a year ago and were in a Lunar Lander, so there is no way they could have survived this long. You were warned. If you keep talking, you can expect company very soon."

John was laughing as he responded. "Oh, by all means, send the Police out after us. I'll keep broadcasting so they can find us. I'd love to see them. But you'd better have them pull a tanker full of gas to get here. I believe they will find it's going to be a very long trip."

"You think this is funny, huh!" Allen growled. "Well, you just stay where you are and keep talking. Someone will be with you shortly!" That response took much less than a minute.

Allen started to say more, but stopped when someone else in the Control room started talking to him. John couldn't hear all that the other man said, but he heard enough to know that the man was telling Allen where the signal was coming from.

"What? You're kidding! Are you sure about that?" Allen said and clicked off his mic.

Shortly, Allen spoke again. "I don't know how you're doing this, but you can't be John and Randy. Those two vanished over a year ago."

"Yes, something did happen to us, but we're back now. Allen, it's me, John Baines. I know it's hard to believe, but we are back, and we have quite a story to tell. We'll gladly tell that story, but we would rather tell it while standing on Earth. Can you help us out here? We want to come home."

"John? ……. It sure sounds like you, but how in the world could that be possible? Look, if this is some sick joke, you can bet your ass you're going to be sorry."

"Allen," John said, laughing. "It's really us. We're back from the dead. We were as good as dead, but Aliens saved us, and before you say anything, I know that's going to be hard to swallow, but it's the truth. Aliens saved us."

"Man, I want to believe you, but this is too incredible," Allen said.

John and Randy could hear others from Mission Control becoming excited and talking about what was happening.

"Allen, has anyone except me ever called Mary the Earthquake Queen?" John asked. John used to tease Mary, Allen's wife, about her sneezes shaking the world.

"No, no one," Allen said. "John? Is it really you? What happened to you guys? I went to your funerals and everything."

It had become hard to hear Allen because the people around him were cheering. "Allen, we'll tell you everything, but can you first tell us where we are here? We can't see Earth. We're blind out here and want to come home."

"All right, John, keep talking so we can get a better fix on where you are. Sing a song or something so we can triangulate your location. It will take a little time because it appears you're pretty far out there. There is a slight delay in your transmissions. John, I still can't believe it's you. You've been lost for 17 months. Where the hell have you been?"

"A planet called Pellaya, if you can believe it. It's a long story, Allen, and it will blow your mind when we tell it. I'll keep transmitting, but I don't want to tell the story now. I'd much rather tell it while standing with you on Earth. Can you hurry the process along so we can come home? It's been a long time, and I want to see my wife. Besides, Randy is driving me nuts."

"Hello Randy!" Allen said joyfully. "Let me be the first to welcome you guys home. I still can't believe it's you, and if this is a prank… Well, I won't be happy."

"Believe it, Allen. It's us. We can't see Earth, but we have the general direction of where it is. You have to be around here somewhere."

"Right, keep talking and I'll let you know when we have a better idea of where you are," Allen said, and went quiet.

John rambled on about nothing for some time, then asked, "I'm running out of things to say, Allen. Do you have anything yet?

"Yes. You guys are out there!' Allen said. "They're telling me your transmission appears to be coming from the other side of the sun from us. John, you guys are about 160 million miles away. I'm sure Randy could tell you, that places you somewhere near Earth's orbital path on the other side of the Sun. This is unbelievable! John, if this is true, the sun will start blocking our signal soon. We're going to lose contact with you," Allen said and clicked off.

"Rodger. Allen, make sure they do their best to pinpoint our exact location. Randy and I believe, that information could be of great importance. Do you copy that? That information could be crucial."

"Rodger that, John. We'll do our best to mark your location. John, you're already starting to break up."

"Yes, I hear it. Let me know when you have it," John said.

Allen finally told them on a very staticky radio that they had marked their location as best they could. Then the radio went dead. The Sun had blocked the signal.

Randy flipped down his sun visor and looked toward the sun. "So they are on the other side of that," he said, twisting up his face. "We're 160 million miles from Earth. That does put us in the Earth's orbital path. In six months, the Earth will be right where we are now."

"Well, we aren't going to wait for it," John said.

Randy continued to ramble on, talking to himself as he often did. "The Earth travels at 66000 mph, the fastest any Earth ship can travel is between 25000 and 30000 mph. John, we can't catch the Earth unless this ship goes faster than 66000 mph. Even if it does, we should go around the sun in the opposite direction. That way, the Earth will be traveling toward us rather than away from us."

John nodded. "Yeah, that makes sense, but Randy, I think you're in for a big surprise. If my figuring was right when I converted Pellayen distances to miles, this ship can fly at speeds up to 222 thousand miles per hour. We could chase the Earth down if we wanted."

Randy shook his head. "222000 mph? If you're right, we could be on top of Earth in…ah, … in about one month. I'm having a hard time believing that."

"You'll see," John said and began moving the shuttle. "I'm having a hard time believing you never went up in a Pellayen ship and learned this for yourself."

"Oh, I did, but we never left the atmosphere or tried to set a speed record."

John increased the speed slowly so G-forces wouldn't splatter them all over the back wall of the cock pit area. As the ship moved faster and faster, Randy was surprised to find he could see they were moving. That was something he wouldn't be able to do if he were in an Earth ship. In an Earth ship, you had to be much closer to something like the Earth or a space station to see any kind of movement. At the moment, they were in the middle of nowhere with nothing around them, yet he could see movement. "Amazing! You're right. I am surprised. This ship really caaaa … Look out!" Randy yelled and attempted to duck out of the way of something shooting toward them. They were moving so fast; they had almost run into something before John could react. "Man! That scared the crap out of me!" Randy said, sitting back up in his seat. "What did we almost hit?"

"I don't know," John said, slowing the ship and turning it around so they could look behind them. "Holy Crap!" he said.

"I don't believe it," Randy said, with the same Awe. "That's a Pellayen ship."

"It sure is. It looks like it's adrift," John said. John maneuvered closer to the ship and circled it. There was a big piece of the bottom of the ship missing.

"It looks like something hit it," John said. "And right where the engines are. I can almost guarantee their engines are out. What are they doing here?"

"John, don't you remember? Awth told us they sent a ship into Tallda Shayts shortly after we landed on Pellaya?" Randy said. "This has to be that ship."

"I guess you're right. This has to be them," John said. "Awth also said they had equipped the ship with enough supplies to last years. They could be alive in there."

"Even with damage like that?" Randy asked.

"Yes. The engines have little to do with the other systems in the ship. As long as the main power is up and running, life support and everything else could still be working. As long as they could seal off the damaged area, they could be alive."

John maneuvered to the front of the other ship and saw lights on inside. "Well, there you go. They have power, but I don't see anyone in there." He switched on the Pellayen communication system and tried to raise anyone who might still be alive. He tried several more times but got nothing but a headache.

"Randy, I'll suit up and take a space quad over there to check it out. You stay here and man the ship."

"Will their communication system amplify my thoughts?" Randy asked.

"Huh! That is a good question. Never thought about that. Try it if you wish; maybe it will work for you. I'm pretty sure you won't be able to hear them, but they might hear you," John said. "Ok, I'm going over. Stay on our radio with me as well," John said, and left the cockpit.

John was soon outside on a space quad and moving up to the alien ship. He moved up to the windshield and looked in. He saw indicator lights flashing on some of the consoles, and knew flashing lights were a bad thing. It was no surprise that lights were flashing on the engine maintenance console. The damage to that area of the ship looked pretty bad. A second consul had flashing lights, but he wasn't sure what system they pertained to. He had to get even closer.

John left the quad and floated to the window for a better look. He could see the consuls much more clearly now. It was the communication console. Their Communications were out as well. Whether Randy could or couldn't transmit his thoughts didn't matter. No one was going to hear him on that system. "Randy, their communication system is damaged, so don't waste your time trying to talk to them. I suppose this is the reason they never contacted Pellaya."

"John, we know Pellaya is on the other side of Orion from here. Even if they had sent out a message, that message wouldn't get to Pellaya for several hundred years from now. So it wouldn't make much difference if the radio worked or not."

"True enough," John said, turning his attention back to the Pellayen ship. He looked for any sign that someone was alive inside, but couldn't see anything. One thing was certain. With the engines gone and communications out, if they were still alive, they would be in bad shape.

John was about to return to the Quad when he saw a Pellayen float through the ship to a console where he picked up a magnetic clipboard. The Pellayen floated there, studying the clipboard with his left side toward John. Suddenly, he stiffened and slowly turned his head to look straight at John. His eyes widened, and the clipboard floated away from his hands. He stared open-mouthed at John, surprised to find someone looking in on him.

John placed his gloved fingers on his helmet, then turned his hand palm out and pushed his hand toward the Pellayen. The Pellayen blinked and pulled his head back, surprised to see the "Special Greeting" being given to him by what appeared to be an Alien. He blinked and shook his head again, then refocused on John.

John opened his mind and tried to move his thoughts to this Pellayen. He hoped this Pellayen's mind was strong enough to see how weak his mental strength was and help him relay information. It didn't take long, and John could feel the Alien doing just that.

John focused on one thought to send and told the Pellayen he was there to help. Immediately, he heard the Pellayen language in his head, asking him to go to the side door of the ship. Then he saw an image of that door emerging in his mind, and when he opened his eyes, he saw the Pellayen motioning for him to go around to the side door. John couldn't help but be impressed. The Pellayen had just invited him inside in three different ways and in about as many seconds. He grinned. Though it hurt his head, he liked his new mental gift.

John moved back to the quad while talking to Randy. "There is a survivor in there. I'm going inside to talk to him. You mind the fort."

"Rodger," Randy said.

John climbed back on the Quad. As he did, he saw more survivors floating into the cockpit area. "Randy, there are three of them in the ship now. I believe Awth said there were three, didn't he?"

"Yes. So they all survived," Randy said.

John moved the Spacequad to the side of the ship and saw a door opening. He flew inside and landed near the Airlock. He looked up and saw the face of a Pellayen looking back at him through the small round window in the chamber door. The Pellayen motioned for him to enter the chamber as he backed out of it, closing the inner door behind him. When John got the "Enter" signal, he opened the door and entered the chamber. He was no stranger to this procedure, having done it a few times in Pellayen space.

With the chamber pressurized, he was free to enter the ship's living area. He floated inside and found three anxious Pellayens waiting for him. When he removed his helmet, their faces showed their surprise. When he greeted them in their language, they were even more surprised. The three of them moved in closer to John, anxious to talk to him.

John was afraid to open his mind to them, fearing the thoughts and questions of the three of them would overwhelm him, so he kept his mind closed. He spoke to them verbally and asked that only one of them speak to his mind. He told them he wasn't strong enough mentally to deal with more than one, but he wanted to communicate mentally so they would know immediately what was happening.

The Pellayens were all staring at him, studying him, but not saying anything. He was a surprise to them, and they were experiencing many different emotions. Surprise, fear, suspicion, and hope were probably a few of them.

The Pellayens spoke to each other, then one of them stepped forward. "I am Tellgus," he said, then pointed out the other two. "This is Awntoon and Fallgonan. You may communicate with me."

John nodded and opened his mind. As usual, the communication only took a few seconds, and a wealth of information was passed between them. Tellgus nodded as he received the whole story of what John and Randy had been through, and how they had come to be here now.

John had also received the Pellayens' story and knew they had fallen into the same Mental Abyss he and Randy had. Unfortunately, something hit the ship, which woke them all up before the Mental Abyss was ready to let go of them, and the three of them went a little crazy. Tellgus was the first to get out of the Abyss, only to find he had to deal with the other two.

Once they were themselves again, they found that the engine, communication, and a few other systems had been damaged by whatever hit the ship. They managed to repair a few systems and were close to repairing the communication system, but the engine was beyond repair.

John groaned when he learned they had been floating in this same spot for more than a year. The Earth had been nearby when they first arrived, but it had continued on its way to go around the sun. It came back later only to pass by once more. It was now behind the sun again. They were emotionally and physically sick of being trapped on the ship.

Without the engine, they were continually drifting toward the Sun and had to use a Spacequad to pull the ship back a safe distance from it. They had tried to pull their ship into an orbit around Earth using the Spacequad, which nearly ended in disaster. One Spacequad was too underpowered to keep control of a ship this size. They nearly lost their ship to the gravitational pull of the planet. There had been three quads on the ship, and with all three of them, they might have been able to do it, but whatever hit the ship had damaged one beyond repair, and the other was nowhere to be found.

John knew how they felt when he learned they had seen lights and other signs of intelligent life on the planet. They even saw ships in space, but couldn't raise them on their communication system or with Mental Ability. They could only hope to be spotted and rescued by its inhabitants. Unlike John and Randy, these aliens never came to their rescue.

Their last resort was to send someone down on a Spacequad, hoping to get help, but they feared the rider wouldn't be able to return, and the two left aboard the ship would die as the ship was pulled into the sun. All they could do was try to fix the engine.

John suddenly ended the Mental link. His head was now throbbing. Tellgus's mind wasn't as strong as Bartolos's, and this connection with Tellgus was a real strain on him. He asked Tellgus to continue using the Pellayen language, which he did.

"When you appeared outside our ship, I thought you were from the Planet you call Earth. Then you gave the Special Greeting, and I noticed the Spacequad, so I thought you had come after us from Pellaya, but you haven't.

I also saw that you have been through a lot yourself. I am glad you have made it back to your home. You are from Earth, aren't you?"

"Yes, I am from this planet, and yes, we have been to Pellaya and back. It has been quite an adventure. Awth told us that they had sent a ship into Tallda Shayts, but we never expected to find you here. I am glad we did."

Tellgus and the other Pellayens were moved at the mention of Awth. Tellgus smiled. "We are very pleased you have found us. We are sick of being on this ship. It is good to have new people to talk to and great to have you able to speak Pellayen. You can tell us what is happening on Pellaya."

"I can do that, but right now, I have a Pellayen ship out there that is fully stocked and in perfect working order. Why don't we get you on board and head for Earth?"

"That sounds good," Tellgus said. "Just to be doing something other than trying to fix our ship will be a great thing."

The Pellayens gathered what belongings they wanted and moved to John's ship. They made it known they hoped there was a way to save their damaged ship, and John told them he would do everything he could to save it. With that being understood, the Pellayens were suddenly eager to get to Earth and get their feet on solid ground.

It was no surprise that the Pellayens were at home on John's ship. The only real difference in their ships was that John's ship was smaller. It was still very large compared to the Earth shuttles, but small beside Tellgus's ship.

Because of their Mental Ability, John and the Pellayens were completely at ease with each other. Randy was the only one who felt a little awkward around the new faces, but it was a mild case of nerves and would pass quickly. He remembered Awth telling him about their Mental Ability, saying, "You would know if I were a threat to you." Randy didn't have the ability, so he would have to suffer through getting to know the Pellayens the old-fashioned way. It was just a matter of time.

John sat down at the controls and slowly increased the ship to full speed. They were finally on their way home to Earth. Randy was once again impressed with how fast the ship could move. If John was right and the ship could travel at 222000 mph, it would take about 45 days to meet up with Earth. Randy was pleased to hear that, but as far as he was concerned, they couldn't get there fast enough to suit him.

They had been flying for about five minutes when Tellgus stepped up beside John. "You were taught to fly near Pellaya?" He asked.

"Yes."

"Then you were never taught about Sperneckeens Stitton Tod?"

"Sperna… what?" John asked.

"Sperneckeens Stitten Tod," Tellgus said, pointing to a small door on the left side of the control panel in front of John. "You will go much faster if you use it."

John looked over and saw a small door in the control panel. He pushed it, and a small control panel folded out.

"You will go much faster if you use that," Tellgus said. "That is Sperneckeens Stitton Tod."

"Ok, but I don't understand what 'Sperna whata plots' is or how to use it. So you better take control of the ship."

Tellgus took John's seat while explaining that "Spernecky" was the name of the Pellayen who discovered the engine, and Neckeens meant energy. They combined Spernecky's name with Neckeens and you have Sperneckeens.

"Using this," Tellgus continued. "We will move as fast as energy."

"Jesus!" Randy said. "The speed of energy is the speed of light. Is he talking about the speed of light, John? I think he's saying we can travel at the speed of light."

Tellgus engaged the Sperneckeens Stitton Tod, and instantly they were screaming through space at an incredible speed.

"SHIIIIIT!" Randy yelled, pushing himself back into his seat. John, too, grabbed the back of Tellgus's seat with a death grip fully expecting to fly back against the wall. But they felt nothing. They had accelerated in an instant to light speed with no G-forces at all. G-forces should have plastered him all over the back wall.

Tellgus laughed a little, then explained that they believed this Drive caused a shell to form around the ship. That shell contained the ship and the space around it. The shell was flying through space, not the ship. The ship was sitting still in the space contained inside the shell, so the ship was not affected. Which meant, no G-forces.

John flinched. "You mean you're flying the shell right now?"

Tellgus nodded. "It's not quite that simple, but yes, that's what we believe."

Randy was listening while looking out the windshield. He was fascinated by what he had just heard and what he was seeing. Light particles of an image were stationary in front of the windshield. A picture was flying along in front of them. "This is incredible!" he yelled very loudly as if trying to be heard over a crowd.

"Randy! Why are you yelling?" John said, laughing.

"I don't know!" Randy yelled back. He was smiling ear to ear, truly enjoying the ride. "This is fantastic!" he said, still yelling. Then in a little more normal volume apologized for yelling. "Sorry about that. It was just such a surprise. I wasn't ready for that."

All of them watched as they rounded the Sun like a fast car rounding a curve. Soon, they saw the Earth coming toward them very quickly.

"This is so freaking incredible!" Randy yelled again. A big grin on his face.

"Welcome to Earth," John said to Tellgus.

It was no wonder Randy was yelling. It was truly an amazing experience to be flying along *with* the light, and able to see its parts right beside and in front of them. Randy understood that each tiny particle of light was a slightly different hue because it was one tiny piece of the larger puzzle. All the light atoms made up the whole picture of what a man standing on Earth would see, and that amazed him. He wondered what their ship, being part of that picture, would look like. It was mind-blowing to think they were among those particles rushing toward Earth, and would arrive there in seconds, not days; this was something to yell about.

As they neared Earth, Tellgus turned off the Sperneckeens Stitton Tod, and the ship slowed to the last set speed of 222000 miles per hour. Tellgus warned that they always had to return to the last set speed, or they would experience the G-forces, and if the difference was great enough, they could be killed. Then he stood and gave control of the ship back to John.

"That was incredible," John said, taking his seat. "I will remember Sperneckeens Stitton Tod, but I think I'd like to call it light speed or Energy Drive from now on. Your Pellayen name is a mouthful."

"Not for a Pellayen," Tellgus said, taking a seat behind John.

John settled in behind the controls and told Randy to get on the radio and tell Mission Control what was happening. "It would be a shame to come all this way just to get shot down by somebody thinking we were attacking or something. Let them know I plan to land at Mission Control Center in Houston."

Randy picked up the radio mic. "Mission Control, we are here much earlier than we thought. That will take some explaining, and we will also have to explain the three aliens we have onboard. For now, know that we do have aliens aboard and that they are friends, not foes. They are no threat to anyone. I need to make that clear. They are here as friends and should be treated that way."

"You didn't mention any Aliens before. Don't you think that is dammed important for us to know?"

"Of course, it is Allen, but there was no way we could tell you until now. We were traveling at light speed, so any radio message we sent would have arrived at the same time we did. Look, Allen, we can argue about this later. Right now we are here and coming down to land. Just know we have three Aliens on board and that they are no threat to anyone. We will explain everything, but it is a long story, and we are coming in to land right now. So keep everybody calm and cool about the aliens. Okay?"

"We will do what we can, Randy. And Randy, it's good to hear your voice. Welcome home."

"How are my wife and kids? Am I still married to Carol?" Randy asked.

Allen didn't answer immediately. When he did, he said they should talk about these things after they landed. This answer created suspicion. Something was wrong. One or perhaps both of their wives might have remarried. Or something worse. Something might have happened to one of them. Randy's thoughts jumped to his sons. What if something had happened to one of them?

"Stop thinking about it," John said. "They are probably just fine, so stop worrying about it. We will know soon enough." John said, but he had heard the tone in Allen's voice and wondered why. He was concerned about his wife Angie, but at that moment, he was more worried about the Pellayens. How would they be treated? Would Mankind be as considerate and trusting of the Pellayens as the Pellayens had been of him and Randy? John had real doubts.

"Tellgus, my people don't have mental ability and won't be able to see that you are not a threat. This could create problems for you. Hopefully, they will heed our words and treat you with the same respect your people gave me and Randy, but I have doubts. I know they will be interested in this ship, and no doubt, try to take it from you. Don't let them. This is your ship now, and I think you should stay with the ship after we land. At least until we see how they respond to you. I'll do what I can to help you, but if it comes to it, take the ship and run. There is nothing they can do to stop you. Do you understand?"

Tellgus understood and was pleased that John was giving him the ship, but it alarmed him that John had such suspicions about his own people. This sort of thing didn't happen on Pellaya.

John opened his mind to Tellgus so he would see the distrust, suspicion, prejudices, hatred, and the wars that came with his people. "Do you see it now?" John asked, rubbing his temples.

"Yes. I saw, but I also saw how good and kind they can be," Tellgus said. "I see this in you and Randy."

"Yes, but your people saved us, and except for concerns of diseases, they did so without the least bit of suspicion. I don't know how my people will respond to you. I have good reason to be worried for you. I thought you should know this and be prepared for it.

Tellgus nodded his understanding.

"Once we are on the ground, the ship is yours," John said. "This ship can outrun anything Earth has, so you will be safe here."

"Understood," Tellgus said.

"If you guys are done, can we go home now?" Randy asked impatiently.

"Yes. This is long overdue. Let's go home," John said and started the ship down.

Some of the people on the ground were aware of what was happening and were coming out of the buildings to see if a ship was landing or if the whole thing was a hoax. Others had no idea what was happening, and seeing an alien craft dropping out of the sky to land was causing quite a stir. Some of them ran into buildings to report what was happening, but most stood watching the ship move lower to the ground. They grouped together in clusters and watched the ship land right in front of them.

For those aware of what was happening, seeing an alien ship descend was proof that this was no hoax. John and Randy had to be onboard, and that meant three aliens were onboard as well.

It was only an hour or so ago that Mission Control had first heard John on the radio, and thinking it could be a Hoax, had tried to keep the news from spreading. But the word had gotten out and was spreading fast. Randy had only told Mission Control about the aliens a few minutes ago, so that news was just starting to spread, but it too was spreading fast.

From what they could see from the ship, the media hadn't arrived yet, but they were sure to come. Military personnel were already unloading from trucks and helicopters and taking up positions around the ship. Thankfully, it looked like they were positioning themselves to keep people away from the ship, which gave John hope that they were here for crowd control and not to point guns at the Pellayens.

A large crowd was already forming around the ship, and more were sure to come. This was the story of the century, and everyone wanted to be there to see it all happen. The Military was keeping everyone away except for a smaller group of NASA employees and officials who stood nearer the ship. This group appeared to be there to greet John, Randy, and the Pellayens. John was pleased to see this. He much preferred that NASA greet the Pellayens rather than a Military escort.

John turned away from the windshield and looked back at the Pellayens. He was shocked to see that they were struggling against gravity. He hadn't thought about them being thrust back into gravity after being in space for sixteen months. Their muscles had weakened to the point that they could barely move. Their breathing seemed labored, but it didn't look like an emergency just yet, but it was something that needed to be dealt with very quickly. He hated to see them suffering. They had already suffered so much, for so long, in an uncomfortable situation.

"I hadn't thought of this," John said.

"Me either," Randy said. "What do we do?"

"They're going to need medical care. Damn, we're going to have to take them off the ship," John said.

John stood and turned to the Pellayens. "The ship is yours, but it doesn't look like you should stay with it. You need medical attention."

Tellgus nodded as he labored to speak. "And we do want to get off this ship and on solid ground. John, look down by your right knee. There is a little door there that opens a small compartment. In there, you will find a Remote Key. I can control the ship with it and keep the ship safe." This was another thing John didn't know about the ship.

John slipped the remote key into his pocket. "I will hang on to this for now. It will be safer with me until you are in better shape."

Randy stood and moved to the door, anxious to get off the ship. When he looked back, John was speaking to Tellgus in his newfound mental way. He wondered what they were saying, but really didn't care. All he could think of was getting off this ship and returning to his life on Earth. "Can we go now, please!" he said.

"Yes, let's go," John said, moving toward the door. "Don't worry," he said to the Pellayens. "We will get you out of here. We will take you to our infirmary as soon as we can. Just sit still. I'll get help as soon as I can. Ok, let's go," John said, turning to Randy. John opened the cockpit door and extended the ramp. As he stepped into the doorway, those witnessing his return began to cheer. They did the same when Randy stepped into the doorway.

"It's him! It's really him! Oh my God, it's him!" came a loud, clear voice from the crowd. John moved aside when Carol, Randy's wife, ran past him and threw herself on Randy. She was delighted to see her man alive and well.

John stopped just off the ramp, looking for his wife, Angie. Someone had called Randy's wife; they must have called his, but where was she? He was already suspicious. Now, his suspicions grew. He scanned the crowd for her, but she was nowhere in sight. He did spot someone he was delighted to see. It was Bruce! Bruce was here, alive, and well. He had survived, and that was a great relief. He and Randy had wondered what happened to him, but here he was, alive and walking toward him.

"Dammed good to see you, John. Glad you could make it, but you are just a bit late to the party."

"You have no idea how good it is to see you, Bruce. We didn't know what happened to you after…whatever happened to us. But here you are, and man, it is good to see you!"

"I heard you have Aliens on board with you?" Bruce asked quietly. "I assume they are friendly. Are they the Grays?"

"No, they are much more like us, almost human and definitely friends. Their people saved our lives. We owe them a great deal. Bruce, there are three of them inside, and they need medical care. Can you get some people to help get them into the infirmary?"

"Sure, John, I'll take care of that. Will you be there to help us?" Bruce asked.

"Yes, I speak their language, so I want to be there. Don't worry about them, they are good people. You have nothing to worry about. Get to it, would you," John urged.

"I'll get right on it. I can't wait to hear *this* story," Bruce said. Bruce started to leave, then turned back to John. "You know, I was watching you guys. You were there, and then you were gone. You vanished right in front of me. You winked out of my sight, and that was it. You left me there to take the long ride home all by myself. I suppose you think I should forgive you for that."

John laughed a bit. "Well, I'm sure sorry about that, Bruce, but on the other hand, you left me alone, crammed in the Lucky Lady with Randy for days. I suppose you think I should forgive you for that?"

Bruce grinned as he turned to walk away. Seeing Randy, he shook his hand and spoke to him briefly, then left to do as John had asked.

John turned back to the cheering crowd, looking for Angie, but the greeting committee pressing in on him was all he could see. Suddenly, Allen was in front of him, shaking his hand and welcoming him home. "I couldn't believe it was you, but here you are. It's impossible, but here you are. It is great to see you. You, too, Randy. So dam good to see you guys."

When the opportunity came, John asked, "Allen. Where is my wife?"

Allen's expression changed slowly. "I know, no one has told you. Prepare yourself, John. The news isn't good."

"Just tell me, Allen. Where is my wife?"

"John, I want you to know it hurt her deeply when you didn't come home."

"Dammit Allen. Where is my wife? Stop messing around and tell me."

"John, she is no longer with us," Allen said. "She was at the wrong place at the wrong time. There was a Terrorist attack. She was one of the casualties."

"Angie is dead?"

"Yes. I'm sorry, John. Not a great welcome home, I know."

The news hit John like a ton of bricks. Angie was the main reason he came back to Earth. Learning that somebody had murdered her over a difference in religious beliefs infuriated him. He couldn't understand how people could choose the murder of the innocent to represent their god. "Yeah. A great welcome home," he said with venomous sarcasm.

"I'm very sorry, John," Randy said. "I'll help with Tellgus and the others. You take whatever time you need. I'll see to the Pellayens."

Randy left to help get the Pellayens out of the ship and into the infirmary. This went surprisingly well, but what was more surprising was the way the Military and politicians received the Pellayens. They were abnormally trusting and respectful of them and had great concern for their health. They were given immediate medical attention, and the Pellayens appreciated being in beds as much as John and Randy had when they landed on Pellaya. Their recovery was going to take a while longer than John and Randy's, but it would return.

When the Pellayens were squared away, John and Randy were asked to speak to a rather large group of people anxiously waiting to know what happened to them. Knowing what John was going through, Randy said he would take care of it, but John checked his emotions and took his place behind the podium and began to speak.

All eyes widened, and mouths fell open, as he told them how they woke up orbiting a strange planet. They were in awe as he told about Lieutenant Branden Wilson and Tallda Shayts. They were very interested when he talked about the Pellayen ship. NASA's scientists could not help but start asking questions about Sperneckeens Stitton Tod.

"We were traveling at Light Speed," John said. "We flew 160 million miles in a matter of seconds. I know you will have many questions about the Sperneckeens' drive engine, but remember this: the Energy Drive was discovered accidentally. The Pellayens use it but don't understand much about it. So if they say they don't know, they don't."

John and Randy answered many questions and had to retell parts of their story before the debriefing was over. Eventually, John and Randy were free to go their way.

Randy asked John to come home with him and be with his family, but John refused. He wanted to sit with the Pellayens and be there to interpret their needs. They were weak, and all three of them fell asleep quite quickly, which reminded him of how quickly he had drifted off to sleep and how good it had felt. John was happy to stay with them and return the good deed that Awth and Nellaynan had done for him.

This wasn't the only reason John stayed with them. He was hurting over the loss of his wife, and didn't want to go home to an empty house. Being close to the Pellayens somehow eased his pain.

CHAPTER EIGHT
HOME AGAIN HOME AGAIN

Not in a million years would John have guessed the Pellayens would be treated so well. Perhaps it was because they looked so much like humans that they were treated as valued guests, but John was sure it was because they were so likable and forthcoming when asked questions. They were given good homes, a very handsome bankroll, and citizenship in the United States. They were free to come and go as they pleased. At least as free as any other citizen.

Scientists worldwide came to them eager to learn what they could about Pellayen engines. They discovered some of the materials the Pellayens used to build the engines didn't exist on Earth, and that was disappointing. It didn't mean they couldn't build the engines; it just meant it would be more difficult, take more time, and the engines would be much, much larger and heavier than what the Pellayens could build.

The biggest surprise for John was that no one tried to take the ship from them. The Pellayens were so willing to tell everything they knew that there was no reason to risk harsh feelings. The Pellayens allowed scientists to inspect the engines.

Pellayen engine technology was of great interest to everyone. Not as many were interested in the Pellayen communication system. John told them he had Mental Ability, and then told them that the Pellayens believed all humanity had it, but it was dormant.

When word of this got out, suddenly everyone claimed to have the ability and thought they could hear someone else's thoughts. Fights broke out because of their ignorance. John and the Pellayens could easily see that most of them were fooling themselves, and did not have Mental Ability. They were relying on intuition and looking for fifteen minutes of fame, but some actually had Mental Ability. It was weak, and like John, they didn't know they had it, so they had no control over it.

Pellayen Electronics was another Pellayen technology of great interest. It was already known that a Pellayen wire was made of materials not found on Earth, but after studying the wire, they found it to be much better at conducting electricity than Gold or any superconductor. Amazingly, it also amplified the current because the material had so many free electrons. This was one reason the electric motors and generators were so much stronger and physically lighter. To the average person, this meant very little, but to a Scientist or an engineer, it meant a great deal, and they longed for these materials.

Two other elements that the Pellayens used that didn't exist on Earth were used in much the same way as plastic on Earth. These metals were used for everything from kitchen utensils to Automobile parts and building construction. The clear tunnels John and Randy had walked through when leaving the Lucky Lady, and being escorted into there room, was made of it. It was stronger, lighter, and much more durable than metal on Earth, and it didn't rust. Scientists craved it.

While the scientific community was drooling over Pellayen technology, the media eagerly sought John, Randy, and the Pellayens to get them on their TV and Radio shows or in their papers and magazines. They had become celebrities whether they wanted it or not. The world wanted to know everything about what happened to John and Randy and everything about the Pellayens and their world.

Tellgus, Awntoon, John, and Randy weren't interested in interviews, but Fallgonan liked being interviewed and accepted every invitation. Randy called him an Interlocutor who was taking the pressure off the rest of them. John called him a Ham.

Of the two men, it was John the media sought the most. They wanted to know all about his Mental Abilities. They asked questions like, 'Was he able to communicate with any other humans?' and 'Was he able to read minds?' Randy had once asked Awth these same questions. Now, they were being asked of John, and it was just as hard for John to explain as it had been for Awth.

Having mental ability while back on Earth was an eye-opener for him. "Now I understand why the Pellayens thought I could communicate with my mind. Sometimes I hear someone say something and try to talk back to them, but they don't talk back. I am fortunate to know they haven't opened their mind to me, and are unaware of their ability. Bartolos, Awth, and Nellaynan didn't know that about me and must have thought me rude, to put it gently."

John, the Pellayens, and their technology was big news, but the one thing that nearly everybody wanted to know about was Spernecky's Energy Drive. Even the general public understood the value of the Pellayen engines. Deep space exploration would be greatly enhanced with Pellayen engines. The idea of traveling at light speed ignited everyone's imagination. No place in the solar system would be out of reach. It was a no-brainer that Mars would be the first to be explored. Certainly, Jupiter and Saturn would be next.

It was apparent that Earth would benefit greatly from a relationship with Pellaya. This made finding a way back to Pellaya a priority. John, Randy, the Pellayens, and many of Earth's top scientists began trying to unravel the mystery behind the connection between Tallda Shayts and the Bermuda Triangle. Dr. Robert Pedgley was chosen as the lead scientist to head up the investigation, but in no time, Dr. Pedgley was deferring to John and the Pellayens. John, Randy, and Tellgus took the lead.

Under their leadership, they began exploring the Bermuda Triangle aggressively. Scientists were on ships, in the air, and under the water, looking for answers. Many people were now in the triangle daily, and because they were, reports of "Magnetic Fog" increased. John and the Pellayens had seen it repeatedly and reported that it was similar to the fog in Tallda Shayts but wasn't anywhere near as dense.

The fog, and the fact that navigation systems on planes and ships would go haywire, were the only things of significance they had discovered. So far, no one had vanished.

John and Tellgus turned their attention to the area of space where they had appeared in Earth's orbital path. This "Area of Interest," or AoI, as they began to call it, needed to be studied as well.

Now, tests were being done in both areas. Buoys fashioned with cameras, microphones, and sensors of all kinds were floating in the Triangle and AoI. None of the tests or sensory information had any impact until they noticed that the Magnetic Energy in both the Triangle and AoI was increasing, and doing so simultaneously. The question was Why?

John had been taking the Pellayen ship to check on the damaged Pellayen ship once a week. Now he was bringing scientists with him daily. The scientists did their thing, while John saw to the safety of the other Pellayen ship. That ship was too valuable to lose, and he would tow it back away from the Sun when needed.

Towing the ship was a dangerous job. Much too dangerous to attempt towing it all the way back to Earth. Too many things could go wrong, and the result would no doubt be that both ships ended up damaged. John planned to wait until the Earth was closer before trying to tow it into an orbit around Earth. Once it was in orbit around the Earth, it would be much easier to protect. Once they had an engine to put in it, they could land it and repair the body of the ship. The work to build an engine for it had already begun.

They were attempting to build a new engine for it using the materials available on Earth. The old engine was beyond repair, but thankfully, some of the major components that contained the 'Two Element' conductors could be reused. In some places, they would have to make do with copper or gold conductors. The engine would be very heavy and larger than a Pellayen engine, but it would work.

The Pellayens helped in any way they could. They had a full plate with everything they were involved in. They were a sensation on TV and radio, and were always being asked to be interviewed or to sponsor some new product of some sort. They also needed to be on-hand and sometimes hands-on when it came to the building of the new engine. The largest amount of their time was spent studying the "Area of Interest" and the Bermuda Triangle.

It was John and Tellgus who discovered that the Earth's Moon had been very close to AoI at the time of John and Randy's disappearance. They discovered that Lieutenant Branden Wilson had also gone missing when the Earth was close to AoI. As they continued to investigate, they found that almost all the disappearances had occurred when the Earth was at or near AoI.

John and Randy had had a theory that it was the pulsing of Tallda Shayts that triggered the events leading to the vanishings, and though it was still a viable theory, it was beginning to weaken. More attention was being given to what was happening as the Earth got closer to AoI. Magnetic energies were continuing to rise in both the Triangle and AoI. They began to speculate that Earth's proximity to AoI could be the trigger that activated the Bermuda Triangle and sent the unfortunates to Pellaya.

It was becoming clear that just as there was a connection between AoI and Tallda Shayts, there was also a connection between AoI and the Bermuda Triangle. Somehow, they were all linked together.

It was Awntoon who suggested that the disappearances in the Bermuda Triangle were secondary events. The main event was what took place in AoI. AoI was the key, not the Bermuda Triangle. The disappearances in the Triangle and other areas on Earth were reactions to whatever was happening in AoI. There was no concrete evidence of this, but Awntoon believed he was right.

John was intrigued. He and Tellgus dug into the information they had in the ship's computer regarding the pulsing, shrinking, and expanding of Tallda Shayts. They found a correlation between the pulsing of Tallda Shayts and Earth's proximity to AoI. A new theory emerged, that when the Earth was closest to AoI, and the Magnetic Energy was at its highest, Tallda Shayts would pulse, and bingo, someone was going to Pellaya.

When they looked at John and Randy's disappearance, they found that the Earth and the Moon had been directly in line with AoI. This could have created a stronger magnetic field and triggered their disappearance. But as they continued the investigation, they discovered that two of Pellaya's Moons were directly over and aligned with Tallda Shayts at the same time the Earth and its Moon were aligned with AoI.

They realized AoI could be the gateway. At the time of John and Randy's disappearance, the Earth and its Moon had been aligned with AoI, while on the other side, AoI, Pellaya, and its Moons were aligned with AoI through Tallda Shayts. They were all lined up in a row on either side of that doorway. The Magnetic field could have been immense at that time. The records also told them there had been an unusually strong pulse from Tallda Shayts at that time. This could have caused a door to open, and John and Randy started their "Grand Adventure."

John was becoming very hopeful. "This means if we can figure out how to generate a strong enough Magnetic Field, we could trigger the event ourselves. We could get back home!"

Tellgus gave John a knowing look. " 'WE' could get back home? Have you decided then? You wish to return to Pellaya?"

"Yes. I want to go back to Pellaya. I am more at home there than I have ever been here on Earth." John said, with Nellaynan on his mind.

"I see," Tellgus said, sounding surprised. "You are thinking of Nellaynan. She is a treasure, but would you leave your Earth for her?"

"Yes, but not just for her," John said, nodding his head. "I liked living on Pellaya. and want to learn more about its people. I want to learn more about my Mental Ability, and I can best do that on Pellaya. Yes, I want to go back to Pellaya."

"Then that is where you shall go," Tellgus said. "That is, if any of us can get there. If we can, you are most welcome to come with us if that is truly what you wish."

"It is," John said.

That evening, John and the Pellayens were relaxing at Randy's house after a long day playing poker. As they sat playing, Randy asked John if he was sure about his plans to go back to Pellaya. "It's not like you have to. I know you told the counsel you would, but we have Tellgus, Awntoon, and Fallgonan here now. You don't have to be the one to take the ship back. Do you really want to go back to Pellaya?"

"Yes. I do. And why not? Say I went back, then changed my mind. All I have to do is fly into Tallda Shayts, and I'd be back here in AoI. We know we can get back here by entering Tallda Shayts. It's been done twice now. Tellgus came through, and so did we. It's getting back to Pellaya that's still uncertain."

"Yeah, that's true," Randy said. "Have you figured out how to do that yet?"

Tellgus spoke up. "We believe we have. You haven't been around for quite a while. Where have you been?" Tellgus asked Randy.

"No, and I make no apologies for that. I have been on an extended vacation with my family. A vacation I thought was never going to happen." Randy said and grinned at Tellgus. "Try as you might, you are not going to make me feel guilty for taking my family to the Bahamas."

Tellgus smiled and continued. "We have discovered that as the Earth nears AoI, the Magnetic field is intensifying between the Earth and AoI. We have come to believe that as the Magnetic field grows, it will trigger the doorway. We believe if we are there at that time, we will go back to Pellaya."

Randy nodded. "But wouldn't that mean this gateway was triggered every year at the same time?"

"We don't think so," John said. "For one thing, the Earth and Moon might not line up with AoI the same way for thousands of years. So we don't think the Magnetic field being generated each year is strong enough to trigger the anomaly. Something else has to happen to trigger it. We have considered that it could be the alignment of the moon and the other planets that adds the extra strength needed, but we don't know."

"So you're not sure that the gateway will be triggered this time either, right?" Randy asked.

Tellgus held up a hand. "That's true. If we left everything to do as it normally would, it may not trigger the event. But we think we can make it work."

"Really," Randy said doubtfully. "How in the world do you plan to do that?"

"We might be able to trigger the event using Spernecky's Energy Drive Engine. If it is true that a strong Magnetic Energy triggers the event, Spernecky's Energy Drive could work. Spernecky's Energy Drive is a very strong Magnetic Energy field confined in what we call 'Spernecky's Sphere'. Inside this sphere, the Magnetic energy created has a strength very near that of our Sun. We think we can expose that Energy to AoI and trigger the event. All we have to do is…" Tellgus looked to John for help.

"All we have to do is rev the engine," John said. "It's like doing burnouts in a car. The engine is revving, but the car isn't moving. That's what we have to do right in AoI."

"And you know how to do that?" Randy asked.

Tellgus nodded. "Awntoon and Fallgonan believe we can. They are much more knowledgeable about it than I am, and they say we can. If we do it when the Earth is close to AoI, it is possible that we could trigger the Event. I have to add that there is evidence that some other form of energy is created inside Spernecky's sphere along with the Magnetic energy, but we don't know what it is. That same energy exists in Tallda Shayts, but we don't know how to study it. As you well know, it is dangerous to mess around with Tallda Shayts."

"I see," Randy said. "So you intend to add the magnetic field, and this other form of energy from Spernecky's sphere to the natural magnetic energy being created between the Earth and AoI," Randy said. "That sounds like it could work. So, when do you plan to do this?"

"Very soon," John said. "Time is running out. The Earth is very near AoI, so we have prepared our ship and are ready to leave. We want to have the other ship repaired before we go, so it can be used to observe us when we try to trigger the Gate. A new engine is being installed right now. When that work is finished, we can land the ship and repair the body. Once that's done, we will be ready to leave."

"I want to be on that ship and watch what happens," Randy said.

John grinned. "You already volunteared to pilot that ship, Randy. Aside from me, you are the only one who knows how. Bruce will be there, but he can't read Pellayen and is unfamiliar with the controls, so you're it. Thanks for voluntearing."

"Huh!" Randy grunted. "I must have used my Mental Ability when I volunteared because I don't remember doing that," Randy said. "I'm happy I'll be there to see you off. It could be a long time before I see any of you again."

"If this works, we could be back at any time. We can return through Tallda Shayts anytime we want," Tellgus said. "And coming back to bug you is something I will look forward to."

"As would I," Randy said.

CHAPTER NINE

STEPPING THROUGH A DOORWAY

The new engine was finally installed in the damaged ship and flown down to Earth. Tellgus gave the ship, as a gift, to the United States and NASA. They repaired the damaged Hull and flew it into space to test it. Now it was ready for the big day. Earth was entering the heart of AoI, so the Magnetic Energy would be reaching its peak. It was time to find out if there was a gate and if the Pellayen ship could open it.

John, Tellgus, Awntoon, and Fallgonan loaded onto their ship, while Randy, Bruce, Allen, and several dignitaries loaded onto the second ship, which had been renamed the 'Tataro.' "Tataro" being a Pellayen adage meaning 'Lasting Friendship'.

The two ships lifted off and headed toward the Area of Interest. John moved his ship into the area they believed was the heart of AoI. Randy flew the Tataro to a position far from John. They feared they could get dragged along with John to wherever he was going, if anywhere.

Tellgus pulled down a small panel on the wall and started to adjust the engine so it would produce power, but not move the ship. John stood by him to learn what he was doing."

Tellgus nodded. "These two switches will disconnect the drive function. The engine will generate a lot of Magnetic energy inside Spernecky's sphere, but won't move the ship. This switch sets it up, so the Energy Drive won't start until you push the controls forward. Once you do that, hopefully, we will open the gate and go home.

"Okay then. I guess we are all set. Let's get to it," John said.

Tellgus had created helmets out of the same compounds used to make Spernecky's sphere. That compound blocked magnetic energy, which they had begun to believe was causing them to fall into the Mental Abyss. They hoped the helmets would stop or limit the degaussing of their brains and keep them from falling into the Mental Abyss.

John and Tellgus were going to wear the helmets while Awntoon and Fallgonan would go without. If John and Tellgus remained awake and Awntoon and Fallgonan fell into the Abyss, it would be obvious that the helmets worked, and they could avoid that discomfort in the future.

John put on his helmet and groaned loudly. It was time for him to switch radio channels to speak to an anxiously waiting public. Cameras had been set up in his ship and also in the Tataro, so the whole thing could be broadcast to the world. He wasn't thrilled with having to do it and didn't care much for the words they had written for him, but he would do it.

He switched to the appropriate channel and started his little speech. "This is Captain John Baines. I am with Tellgus, Awntoon, and Fallgonan. As you well know, we are aboard the Pellayen ship, Sanghoe, and about to attempt opening a Gate to another world. If the Gate exists, and we can open it, we hope to be transported back to Pellaya. Say a prayer for our success and wish us a safe journey. This could be a new era for all of Mankind and the Pellayen people. With God's help, I will see you again."

John finished his public address and looked at Tellgus. "How did I do?"

Tellgus smiled. "Randy's mother-in-law couldn't have done better."

John laughed, then called out to the Tataro. "We're all set here, Randy. Wish us luck and try to stay out of trouble while I'm gone."

"Rodger, and good luck, guys. Hope to see you again soon," Randy said.

"Enjoy the show," John said, and prepared to start the countdown. "Randy, I don't know about you, but I find it funny that I'm actually hoping to disappear this time."

"Look at it from my point of view," Randy said. "I'm hoping you disappear too. No hard feelings, buddy."

John laughed and began the countdown. "Five, four, three, two, one." He pushed the controls forward.

"SHIT!" John yelled.

"AGMA!" Tellgus yelled at the same moment.

They were suddenly hanging upside down with all their weight thrust into the shoulder harnesses. If not for the seat straps, they would have landed head-first on the ceiling of the ship. "We're in gravity!" Tellgus said loudly.

"We're upside down!" John yelled just as loudly, struggling against his seat belt. "What happened?"

"Look!" Tellgus said, pointing out the windshield. John looked and saw nothing but a gray swirling mass against the windshield. They had jumped from Earth space to what had to be the gray fog of Tallda Shayts and a lot of gravity.

"Tellgus, I can't right the ship with the controls set as they are. Can you get to the panel?"

"I'm going to have to. The ship won't move unless I do."

Tellgus carefully released his seat belt and held on to it as he eased himself down onto the ceiling. "Hey, it worked!" he said.

"What worked?" John asked.

"You and I are still awake. Look at Awntoon and Fallgonan. They are waking up. They must have fallen into the Abyss."

John looked back to see the two of them waking up. "Oh boy. That's not good. You had better hurry. Randy didn't react well when I woke him up before the Abyss was ready to let him go."

"Neither did we," Tellgus said, moving to the panel to adjust the engine. "Whatever hit our ship woke us up, and that put us into a strange mental loop that took considerable time to get out of."

John nodded. "I had to slap Randy to get him out of it."

Tellgus stood to readjust the engine. He had to turn off Sperneckeens Energy Drive to do it. As soon as he did, the ship filled with gray fog. The air around him suddenly felt charged with electricity. The fog was so thick he couldn't see the panel in front of him. "Newnas Tasksssss" he hissed in anger.

"What just happened?" John said. "I can't see a blasted thing. Tellgus, what happened?"

Tellgus grunted and felt for the panel. "I turned off the engine, and the fog came in." He felt for the panel, trying to make the changes from memory. The panel was also upside down, making it even harder.

From somewhere in the fog, Awntoon and Fallgonan were moving and beginning to say some strange things. It was obvious they were locked in that strange mental loop. Things were going to get a little crazy.

"How are you doing, Tellgus?" John anxiously. "It's about to get weird in here!"

"I got it," Tellgus said, turning the engine back on. The fog in the cabin cleared rapidly. "Okay," Tellgus said. "So something about the engine keeps the fog out of the ship. That's good to know. You can right the ship now."

John righted the ship while listening to Awntoon and Fallgonan get louder and crazier. Fallgonan started yelling about being upside down and about to crash, and something about his need to get out of 'this thing!'

Awntoon was yelling about something that made no sense at all. It sounded as if he had become trapped in a strange and disjointed dream. Both of them were out of their minds.

Tellgus and John had to resort to slapping and shaking them to get them out of it. Awntoon and Fallgonan were thankful for being slapped out of the Mental Abyss. When they had calmed down, they talked about what they had experienced.

Fallgonan had it easy. He believed he was upside down and about to crash into an object in the gray fog of space. Awntoon, on the other hand, was in a world of trouble. He, in his mind, was in several places at once. He was on Pellaya arguing with his wife, and at the same time on Earth in front of TV cameras in an interview. Cameras were also pointing at his angry wife, who was hanging upside down, which made him incredibly angry at her. She shouldn't be hanging upside down like that. His mind was in all sorts of chaos, and he was pissed about that too!

When they had calmed down, John shook his head. "Well, it's pretty obvious that if you wake a person before the Mental

Abyss is done with them, you lock their minds on whatever they were thinking. Awntoon, I don't even want to try to understand what you were thinking," John joked. "Anyway, now we know the helmets work and we can avoid this in the future," John said, "By the way, Tellgus, what does 'Newnas Tasks' mean? I know 'Task' means trick, but I don't know 'Newnas.'"

Tellgus sat back down in his seat and stared out into the gray mass. "Newnas is the name of the Evil One. All Pellayen believe in what *you* call God. But there is one that fights against him, and his name is Newnas. You are right, 'Tasks' means tricks in your language. I hiss at the end to emphasize my displeasure with him."

"Huh," John said. "Satan's Tricksssssss. I find that interesting and fitting. It feels like someone has been messing with me right from the very start of this Grand Adventure."

John turned back to the windshield. "Do you see anything?"

"Not a thing!" Tellgus said. "I never dreamed I would see the inside of Tallda Shayts if this *is* Tallda Shayts."

"It has to be," Fallgonan said. "And she's still keeping her secrets."

Tellgus nodded. "John, I suggest you fly high up so we can get above anything that might be in here. Take it slow and easy."

John moved the ship straight upward. Gravity told them they were upright, but there was no way to know if they were level to the ground. If they were tipped downward toward the ground even a little bit, they would eventually run into the ground. They had to move very slowly and carefully until they had a better idea of where they were.

"We could fly up into space," Fallgonan said. "We would be able to see where we were going."

Tellgus nodded. "We could, but you know no one flies up there anymore. Ships have crashed after flying over Tallda Shayts. I think we should stay low and work our way out of here."

They all agreed, so they crept along in the fog for hours. The fog was so thick it crawled across the windshield like mud. Awntoon and Fallgonan left their seats and moved up closer to the windshield, hoping they would be able to see a little better, but still couldn't see through the sludge.

After a few more hours, John heard Awntoon and Fallgonan mumbling back and forth. Then Awntoon turned and spoke to him. "We think we see something, but we don't know. It's just a shadow, or a darker area, but it could be something."

John tipped the ship forward to get a better look. It was a slightly darker shade of gray, but it didn't appear to be moving. "That could be something," John said and started the ship down toward it.

"There must be something there," Tellgus said.

Awntoon turned to John again, "This stuff on the windshield is so thick, I would think whatever that is, is just outside the windshield, but I can't see where we are getting any closer to it."

"Newnas Tasksssss," John hissed. "Who knows what's in this soup? This Tallda Shayts is already proving to be a very strange place. That shadow could be anything."

They all kept an eye on the darkened area, but nothing was changing. They appeared to be just as far away from it as they had been when they first saw it. Then suddenly, the ship slipped out of the fog, into the ground.

"I never saw it coming!" John said.

"None of us did! It happened too fast," Tellgus said, then quickly pointed outside. "Look! What happened to the fog?"

Awntoon and Fallgonan still stood at the windshield. "We're inside a bubble!" Fallgonan said. "We're inside a glass dome, with that fog sliding all over the outside of it."

John and Tellgus moved forward for a better look, and it was true. Inside the dome, the air was as clear as could be, but outside the dome, the gray sludge continued to slide around on the outside of the dome. "This is very strange," John said. Then he caught sight of something that made him feel a little sick. An airplane and a large container ship were half inside the bubble with them. The ship looked very old, like a wooden clipper ship. There was another ship lying on the ground that looked like a spaceship. "Is that one of yours?" John asked.

"No," Tellgus said. "I have never seen a ship like that before. I have no idea where it came from. It's not one from Earth?"

"No. We don't have anything like that. Unfortunately, that is just another mystery," John said. Then he noticed the skeletal remains. Some were animals, and some were human or Pellayen. It was not a pleasant sight.

"Let's get out of here," John said after a few minutes. "This is a graveyard."

"I hope we can get out," Tellgus said. 'It would be just like Tallda Shayts to trap us here."

John pulled on the controls, and the ship started upward. Soon, they were facing a wall of sludge. It looked so solid and impenetrable that he feared it would damage the ship. John nudged the ship into it very carefully, expecting to hit the wall, but the ship flew through without a problem. Once again, they were in the fog and couldn't see a thing. John moved the ship upward until he was convinced he was high enough to avoid any hills or Mountains that might be inside. Then he started forward again.

They flew on for two more hours, and finally, the sludge began to thin.

"We must be nearing the edge of it," Fallgonan said.

"I hope so. This is hard work flying in this soup," John said.

Then all of them noticed another dark spot to their right. This one seemed darker than the first one, so John headed toward it. This time, they could see they were getting closer to it. Slowly, the rear end of a very large Cargo Ship took shape.

"Can you believe it?" Fallgonan said. "That's the ship we've all seen sticking out of Tallda Shayts." He shook his head. "I would love to stop and explore it."

John hesitated a moment. "That is a tempting idea, but we need to keep moving. Who knows what Tallda Shayts will do to us if we start wandering around out there? If all goes well, we could come back some other time. In fact, we need to. There is a ship in here that none of us knows where it came from, but right now I just want to make sure we can get out of here," John said.

They all looked out the windshield. It was like looking out of a smoke-filled room through a dirty glass window, but they could see the landscape beyond the gray curtain. They were almost out of Tallda Shayts.

John started to move the ship a little faster until he noticed the name on the bow of the derelict ship. "U.S.S. Cyclops? I'll be darned!" John said. "This ship was one of the first ships known to have vanished in the Bermuda Triangle, but I thought they found her at the bottom of the Ocean. Well, there she is, another victim of Tallda Shayts."

"Newnas Tasksssss," John said, enjoying his new Pellayen phrase. They were all very happy to be leaving Tallda Shayts, but none of them would celebrate until they were sure Tallda Shayts had let them go.

They passed the bow of the Cargo ship, and John pushed the controls far forward, and the ship sped away. They were finally out of Tallda Shayts. He stopped and turned the ship around to look back. "We made it! We made it back to Pellaya," he said. "I had my doubts we would ever be able to do this, but here we are!"

Tellgus, Awntoon, and Fallgonan cheered loudly as they looked back at Tallda Shayts, remembering what they had been through and how impossible it all seemed.

John watched them and could imagine they were looking far beyond Tallda Shayts to a time when they first entered the fog and found themselves in Earth space. At some point, they must have felt they would never see home again. When they were watching the Earth come and go, they must have been thinking the same thing he and Randy had thought when they were stuck orbiting Pellaya. They would die, and no one would know they had ever been there. Now they were back, and John knew how good that felt, too.

John smiled and turned the ship toward the Niglaie Air Carrier Center. "You know," he said with a brief pause. "This is the ship I left in. I'm sure they will recognize it and think I am returning. They won't be expecting you three to walk down the ramp. Why don't you guys keep your thoughts in your heads so we can surprise them? I would love to see their faces when they see you step off the ship."

Tellgus agreed. They would refrain from contacting anyone mentally and let their return be a surprise.

John flew on and soon saw the grassy square he was so familiar with. Ships weren't supposed to land there, so of course, this was where he intended to land. It would draw a lot of attention. He purposely made unnecessary maneuvers and false landings just to draw attention, and it was working.

People in the square stepped out of the way and stared up, pointing at the ship and calling to others. John saw the three Pellayen women sitting on their bench with Nada, Glayden, and Glom playing nearby. Others were running into the building, no doubt reporting that John had returned.

People were coming out of the Space Center and other nearby buildings to see what was happening. Awth came out of the door, wiping his hands on a cloth and looking up at John's ship with great expectations. Bartolos came out of the same door and stood towering over the others like a God. He, too, looked … less angry than usual.

Many Pellayens inside the Space Center were coming to the windows to see what was going on. John was pleased to see so many he knew and loved, but he found himself looking for someone in particular. He finally found Nellaynan looking out a second-story window.

John let the ship settle to the ground and shut down the engines. He grinned. "This is going to be fun to watch."

"We are home! Let's get off this ship!" Tellgus said happily, and all of them stood up and moved to the door. The three of them stood side by side as Tellgus opened the door. For a moment, there was silence as the crowd realized who they were seeing. Then everyone erupted with cheers and moved forward to greet them. The three of them walked off the ship into the throng of cheerful people welcoming them home. They were engulfed by overjoyed family and friends.

John moved toward the door. They wouldn't be expecting him to walk off the ship now that Tellgus, Awntoon, and Fallgonan had appeared at the door. They would recognize the ship as the one he and Randy had left in, but since Tellgus and the others were here, why would he return?

He stepped into the doorway expecting to be greeted, but not the reaction he got. So many of them seemed overjoyed to see him. Nada, Gladen, and Glom ran to him and hugged him. John hadn't realized how much they cared about him until now. Bartolos too hurried toward him and gripped him by the shoulders. "Welcome back, my friend. I was surprised to see you when I saw Tellgus, Awntoon, and Fallgonan standing at the door. I thought you would have stayed on Earth, but here you are, and I am glad.

You were missed." Bartolos said. He was gripping John's shoulder a little too hard, and John squirmed and had to remind Bartolos of his strength.

Before John could say anything more, Awth stood in front of him, extending his hand. "It is so good to see you, but *why* am I seeing you? I assume you made it back to Earth and found Tellgus and the others there. You could have stayed on Earth and let them come back here."

"Yeah, I could have stayed, but I knew *you* would need my help to run things around here, so I came back. I found these guys hanging around my planet, causing problems, so I decided to bring them back for you. You should keep better track of them from now on."

"Ah huh," Awth groaned and smiled. "You will have to tell that story to us. But for now…" Awth said and pointed behind John.

John turned to see Nellaynan coming toward him. He could see she was holding herself back from running to him. He understood why. As far as she knew, he was a married man and might even have Angie with him.

John walked to her, and they stood talking. Awth watched Nellaynan suddenly act concerned, and John's shoulders slumped. Awth looked to Tellgus and received a mental message that John's wife had been killed. It was apparent that John had just told Nellaynan, and that saddened them both. The next time Awth looked at them, they were in an embrace. John would admit later that she had hugged the stuffing out of him. That had made it hard for him to follow through with his plans to fly into Tallda Shayts and go back to Earth right away. He wanted to prove that the whole trip could be done one more time before the Earth moved too far away from AoI. He would let Earth know he had made it back to Pellaya, and that there was a gateway between the two worlds. He was quite surprised when Tellgus volunteared to go with him.

✳✳✳✳✳✳✳✳✳✳✳✳✳✳✳✳✳✳✳✳✳✳✳✳✳

Randy had watched John move the ship into position. Then, in the blink of an eye, the ship, John, and the Pellayens winked out of sight. He sat with his mouth open, amazed at what he had just witnessed.

Bruce wasn't quite as surprised. He pushed back in his seat in a dramatic display. "Yep! Seen that before," he said, turning to Randy. "But this time I won't be traveling 240,000 miles by myself."

Randy and Bruce stared at the space John's ship had occupied a moment before. Randy bowed slightly. "Goodbye, my friend. I hope you make it back to Pellaya and I get the chance to see you again."

Bruce took a deep breath. "Ok. now what? You know, Mission Control is anxious to get this ship back. I'll let them know we're heading back."

He turned to use the radio, but Randy reached out and gripped his shoulder. "Hold on a minute, Bruce. We are in a Pellayen ship, and could go anywhere. Do you really just want to take it back? Right now we have an opportunity we might not get again."

Bruce thought for a moment, then smiled. Randy smiled and, still looking at Bruce, called out to the others in a loud voice. "Anyone up for a trip to the Moon before we go home?"

Bruce's smile broadened. "Yeah! That's a great idea. Let's go take a look."

Some of the others worried about the risks, but Randy quickly put their concerns to rest. "Haven't you seen how easy this thing flies? There is no risk. We can go, circle the Moon, see the dark side, and land wherever we want. Are you telling me you want to pass up an opportunity like that?"

"No! Come on, let's go!" Allen said. He, like many of the others, never dreamed they would get the chance to go into space, let alone go to the Moon. There was no way any of them wanted to pass up the chance to visit the Moon.

"Ok, let's go," Randy said and started the ship toward the Moon. The ship shot toward the Moon at such a speed that the Moon grew very quickly in the windshield. This impressed everyone onboard. Randy enjoyed showing them how fast and agile the ship was. He circled the Moon, then brought the ship to a stop on the dark side, very close to the surface. Every face was glued to a window, and most of them were taking pictures. Just being there was a claim to fame, and they wanted to record the moment.

Randy held the ship mere feet from the Moon's surface, then, with lights blazing, flew the ship down into a crater. "With this ship," Randy said. "You decide where you want to go, and you go."

To prove the point, Randy took the ship back to the sunny side of the Moon and landed close to the new space station. It struck him that surveying this area had been their mission the day he and John had vanished. He never got the chance to walk on the Moon that second time. Now was his chance. "This ship has been supplied with Space Suits for each of you in the unlikely case of an emergency," he said loudly. "Why don't we use those suits to take a stroll on the Moon. That will be something for you to remember."

Bruce and Allen were the first to speak up, "Yeah! Let's go!" Bruce said, and "You bet your ass!" was Allen's contribution.

This was the opportunity of a lifetime, and they would never get another chance to do it. All of them suited up and left the ship. They walked around the ship and even went into the new station. They were living the dream of a lifetime. The Pellayen ship was such an amazing vehicle, they could go anywhere and be there in a short amount of time. That made it easy to ignore, stall, and lie to Mission Control about where they were and what they were doing. None of them were ready to go home just yet.

Their visit to the Moon station was a surprise to those already living inside. They didn't know anyone was coming, but they enjoyed being visited like this. Still, they were happy when the visitors left. There were too many of them for the size of the station.

When everyone was back on the ship, Randy still wanted to explore, but Mission Control was becoming increasingly impatient about their new ship. Randy managed to appease them by suggesting that there were some rather important people onboard who wanted to explore a little longer. He had his doubts that it would work, but they agreed to give them a little more time. Randy was going to take the time, whether they allowed it or not, but it was nice to have their permission.

"I could really show you something if I knew how to do it," Randy said. "This ship can travel at light speed, and that is an amazing experience. Unfortunately, I never learned how to do it, and I don't think Bruce knows either, do you?"

Bruce shook his head. "I think everyone who knows how to do it is on Pellaya."

Randy nodded. "So, you'll just have to be happy with 222,000 MPH, but even at that speed, we could be on Mars in about an hour."

"The heck with Mission Control, let's go!" Allen said. "What can they do about it? It's not like they can send a ship up after us."

Bruce nodded. "I'd love to go to Mars. Let's go. Where is Mars right now?"

Randy's shoulders slumped. He didn't know where Mars was, and it turned out no one knew which direction to go to find it. That was disappointing, but it didn't end his desire to explore. He lifted off the Moon and shot out into space. Eventually, he turned the ship and looked back at the Earth. The Earth was very small, and no one but Randy had ever seen it from so far away. Not even Bruce had been this far away from Earth. He had only been as far as the Moon.

Next, Randy flew back to Earth and circled it a few times. His passengers were thrilled, especially when Randy circled the Earth from pole to pole. They were most impressed with Antarctica.

They were having a great time flying around, but now Mission Control was demanding that they return the ship. Randy sighed. He could hear the anger in their voice and realized he could face repercussions if he didn't comply. He started the ship back, but stopped when he heard Bruce.

"There's something out there. I think it's a ship!"

"It is a ship!" Allen said. "And it looks like it's heading to Earth."

This got Randy's attention. What ship could be out here heading toward Earth? He turned the ship toward it and soon saw it was John's ship! "Ah oh! Something must have happened," he said. He grabbed the radio. "How about it, John. Do you copy?"

"Randy? That you? Where are you?" John said.

"We just spotted you. If you look off to your right, you should see us."

"Ah, we see you now. I thought you would be back on Earth by now."

Randy grinned. "We decided to take a walk on the Moon, you know, take a little tour before we have to give the ship back. What are you doing back here? Did you make it to Pellaya?"

"Yes, we did. We went right into Tallda Shayts. I wanted to come back right away and let everyone know that I made it to Pellaya, and prove it a second time before the Earth moved too far away. There is a path between the two worlds. I was going to report to Mission Control, then go right back."

"Mission Control will be thrilled to hear that," Randy said. "Why don't you let me tell them? Maybe they won't be so mad at us for keeping their ship so long."

"Making trouble as usual, I see," John said. "Can you believe Tellgus volunteared to come back with me? You would think the last thing he would want to do was risk leaving home again, but here he is."

"Rodger that, and welcome back, Tellgus. So what's your plan now, John?"

"Since you're here, you can report what you've seen, and Tellgus and I will go right back through the Gate. You can watch it again. Sound good?"

"Sounds good, but you have to tell me, did you have any problems getting back to Pellaya? What happened?"

"As we suspected, we ended up in Tallda Shayts. It was weird. The helmets worked, and we were awake through the whole thing. But we never saw what happened. We were here, then we were there, just like that. Don't ask me how that is possible, I haven't a clue.

The only problem we had was that we were suddenly hanging upside down inside Tallda Shayts. Try to imagine what that was like, suddenly being upside down in Pellaya's gravity. Then there was that blasted Fog in Tallda Shayts. It was so thick it looked like it was crawling across the windshield.

Look, Randy, every minute the Earth moves away from AoI, the magnetic field grows weaker, and our chances of getting back grow less. We need to go now before we get trapped here. Tellgus is getting anxious about that. I'll try to get back to you at another time and give a better report."

"Understood. You take care, buddy. Good luck."

Randy followed John back to AoI and watched them vanish again. This time, they could be more certain that John and Tellgus had returned to Pellaya. Randy chuckled, thinking of John and Tellgus hanging upside down in Tallda Shayts at that moment.

Bruce grinned, thinking the same thing as he reached for the radio mic. He was eager to inform Mission Control of what had just happened. "Yes! He came back. No, he has gone back to Pellaya. Yes, he's proved it. There is a gateway to Pellaya."

As thrilled as they were to hear this news, Mission Control wanted their ship back. "So, are you guys done playing around up there? Do you think maybe you could bring our ship back now?"

Randy nodded that he would return the ship to Earth, and Bruce passed the word on. As they flew toward Earth, Bruce asked, "Do you think John will be happy living on Pellaya? I mean, all his family and friends are here. Why would he want to leave everything behind like this?"

Randy nodded. "Yeah, I understand why you would think that way. I still wonder about that too, but I was on Pellaya with him and can tell you it is different than Earth. The Pellayens have that mental ability, and that seems to make a big difference. I don't have that ability, so I don't understand it, but John does and was anxious to go back. He was pissed that his wife was murdered over a difference in religious beliefs. He couldn't understand how someone could kill other people in the name of their god, and saw that as an example of mankind.

Pellayens aren't like that. They help each other and do what they can to make everyone around them safe and comfortable. John loved that about them. He has also fallen in love with a Pellayen woman, and I know he was anxious to see her."

Randy turned to face Bruce. "Do I think John will be happy living on Pellaya? I absolutely do. I believe he is where he needs to be right now. I feel honored to call myself a friend to the Pellayens, and Bruce, if you knew what I know, you would know John will be happy on Pellaya."

CHAPTER TEN
A GREAT LOSS

John and Tellgus did indeed find themselves hanging upside down in Tallda Shayts once again. It was a little easier this time, having done it once already. John righted the ship and moved it out of the fog. Once out of Tallda Shayts, he flew back to Niglaie Air Carrier Center and landed in the proper area this time.

They were finally home, and this time, they would stay. It didn't take long, and they were in the company of Awth, Nellaynan, Bartolos, and so many others that they knew and loved. So many came that John felt all Pellaya had turned out to welcome them back. It was a good feeling.

When the fanfare died and he was left to himself, John went back to the room at the Niglaie Air Carrier Center. It seemed empty without Randy there pestering him. He sat down and reflected on the day he and Randy were brought to this room. He shook his head and almost laughed when he thought of Randy standing naked when Awth and Nellaynan entered the room that first time. Randy hadn't cared at all.

At that time, he and Randy had wanted nothing more than to get back home to Earth, but now, he had come to Pellaya to stay and be a citizen of Pellaya.

He stood and walked to the back windows, looking out at the Niglaie Air Carrier Center. *That's where my future is, right there in that airport.* He shook his head. *But this is no airport. This is a spaceport, and those are spaceships, not planes. If I had one of these ships, I would be out there in space all the time.*

His thoughts were interrupted by Nellaynan coming to the door. John had already told her of his wife's death and his desire to live on Pellaya. Now, he opened his mind to her to let her see the confusion he was feeling. He had loved his wife dearly, but he had also fallen in love with Nellaynan. This made him feel guilty for wanting a relationship with her so soon after Angie's death.

She smiled and let her thoughts flow back to him. John suddenly knew the truth, that she loved him and would wait for him to be ready. That simple joining of their minds had already made him feel much better about their situation. The sharing of such true thoughts and feelings had already brought them closer together and shortened the time John would need to be ready for the next step. They both knew it wouldn't be long, but for today, they would go their separate ways.

In the morning, John was awakened by a commotion outside. He got up and walked out into the square. A ship had landed there, and a crowd of Pellayens turned to face him as he walked out. "Okay, what's going on here?" John said.

"It's yours," Awth said from behind him. John hadn't seen Awth standing beside the door when he came out. "The administration is giving you a ship. You can come and go as you please. It was believed you might want to return to Earth occasionally."

John didn't quite know what to say and stumbled with his words. "I…Your….why… Really!" he finally said.

"Yes. They are giving you a ship, and we are hoping you will act as a go-between from Pellaya to Earth for us."

"You want me to act as an Ambassador for Pellaya?" John asked.

"If that is what you call it, yes," Awth said. "But that can wait. Right now, I think you should get dressed. It wouldn't look right, you, excepting this gift in your pajamas."

John looked at himself and laughed. He was only wearing the bottoms.

John was thrilled and honored to receive such a gift and liked the idea of being the Pellayen Ambassador. He could go back to Earth whenever he wanted. He'd have to juggle the time to come back to Pellaya, but he could manage that.

With this ship, he could explore the Moons and other planets in Pellaya's solar system. Then he realized he could go back to Earth and explore Saturn, Jupiter, and Mars. With a Pellayen ship, this was all doable. This was truly a tremendous gift, and he was grateful for it.

For the next several months, John found the time between other duties to explore the Pellayen Moons. Later, he made the time to go farther out and visit some of the other planets in this solar system. Like Earth's solar system, there were gas giants and rock planets here. It was thrilling to be able to go to the planets, land, and get out to explore them. One was a giant snowball, which he thought could have life under the Ice. Two others were rock planets, more like what he believed Mars would be. He didn't find life on either of those, but then, he didn't look for life. He just walked around enjoying being able to do it.

He became an expert at flying his new ship and would often talk to other pilots to gain more understanding of the ship and its systems. One day, while talking to a fellow pilot, he was told about a Pellayen who had discovered a planet with plant and animal life on it. The planet was in a solar system that was considered nearby by Universe standards, but even at lightspeed, it would take three years to get there. Still, John thought he might someday try to find that planet.

When he thought about taking trips to that planet or the planets around Earth, he usually imagined Randy being by his side. Somehow, it seemed right that Randy was there. He could go to Earth, pick Randy up, then fly off to Mars, Jupiter, or Saturn, wherever they cared to go. The problem was his getting back to Pellaya. Getting to Earth was as easy as flying into Tallda Shayts. Getting back to Pellaya was the problem. He would have to wait for Earth to return to AoI. That could take months, depending on where the Earth was at the time.

John didn't have any plans on doing any traveling right away. He was happy on Pellaya and didn't want to leave his friends or Nellaynan. He and Nellaynan had already gone through 'The Bonding,' which was the Pellayen form of Marriage. He now lived with Nellaynan in her house and was very happy with his new life. He had no intention of leaving it any time soon.

From the Bonding, John learned of the Pellayen God. He had no idea the Pellayens had such faith until that marriage. He had never seen a Church or noticed anyone praying. Now, after the Bonding, he understood what he called 'Church' had been going on all around him all the time. On Pellaya, the Church was a meeting of the minds in what he called a Mental Temple. There was no building where they worshiped. They gathered in their minds to praise God, and that could happen anywhere and at any time. It was their Mental Ability that allowed them to gather like this. He hoped to learn more about this and eventually join in these meetings of the minds when his mind was strong enough. He had learned a lot, and his mind was stronger, but he had a long way to go.

John believed in God and wanted to learn more about their religious life, but right now, he needed to work with the Pellayens to understand what was happening between Tallda Shayts and AoI. They knew the gate on Earth's side could be opened with strong Magnetic Energy. They had proved that twice now. The Pellayens believed Spernecky's Energy drive generated more than enough energy to open the gate without the need for Earth to be near AoI. Inside Spernecky's Energy Engine was a Magnetic Collector called 'Spernecky's sphere'. Inside the sphere, magnetic energy was produced and reflected on itself, which caused the magnetic strength to grow even more. That level of magnetic energy was extremely high and could not escape because of the compound the sphere was made of. It kept that energy from leaking out, so it added more energy to itself. If they could expose that energy to AoI, they were sure it would release enough energy to open the gate.

This seemed to be a fairly easy task, but there was a problem. Sperneckeens Energy Drive 'Light Speed' wouldn't work if Spernecky's sphere was opened to allow the energy out. They had to figure out how to maintain the spheres' integrity when they wanted to use Spernecky's Energy Drive.

They considered adding a second engine to the ship just to open the gate. The second engine would certainly work and wouldn't take up much room because the engines were quite small. However, Fallgonan offered an idea that eliminated the need for a second engine. He suggested making two spheres, one larger and one smaller. The smaller sphere would fit inside the larger sphere. Both spheres would have openings in them. The inner sphere will be stationary, while the larger outer sphere will have to be free to rotate. When the outer sphere rotated so the two openings aligned, the Magnetic energy would be released into AoI. To use the Energy Drive, all they would have to do is rotate the sphere to the closed position, and the Energy Drive will work properly. Everyone liked the idea and agreed to start working on it right away. Fallgonan was the hero of the hour.

Because John would be the one going back and forth to Earth the most, it made sense to put the first new engine on his ship. If he tested it and it worked, there was no problem. If he tested it and it didn't work, it still wouldn't matter because he was at his original home. He would be trapped on Earth for six months until the Earth was near AoI again. Then he could return.

If the new engine worked, he would be able to travel back and forth at any time he wished. He was very happy to have the new engine placed on his ship.

To test the engine, they wanted the Earth as far from AoI as possible. Having the Earth on the other side of the Sun from AoI would be a true test of the engine's ability to open the gate. If he could open the gate with the Earth that far away, they could be sure it worked.

They knew the Earth was still fairly close to AoI at this point, which gave them time to build two of the new gate-opening engines. One was installed in John's ship. The other was loaded into the cargo area of John's ship along with one old-style engine. He was to deliver those two engines to the humans.

Finally, the day came when everything was ready, and they believed the Earth would be on the other side of the sun from AoI. The time to test the engine was now.

John kissed Nellaynan, put on his helmet, and boarded the ship. He moved the ship high and then flew into Tallda Shayts. He was immediately back in Earth space at the Gate. The helmet had worked again, and he had seen the transition. It was seamless. He had been in Tallda Shayts, then instantly in Earth space as if stepping through a doorway. It was impossible, yet it had happened.

John looked around and saw no sign of Earth. It had to be on the other side of the sun from him. He was anxious to test the new engine, but first needed to deliver the two engines gifted to Earth.

He slipped the ship into light speed and headed around the sun to Earth. "Mission control, this is John Baines coming back to you from Pellaya. I have returned bearing gifts. I want to land; do you copy, Mission Control?"

"John Baines? Yes, Captain, I copy." It was Allen, and he sounded anxious. "Do not land, John. I repeat. Do not land! We've been hit with a plague, and it's bad. It's already killed a lot of people. Do not land. Do you copy?"

"I copy Allen. What Plague? What's going on?" John asked.

"John, it's bad. People are dying every day from it. If you get it, there's no saving you. It is highly contagious. Go back to Pellaya if you can. Can you get back?" Allen asked.

"I'm not sure. I'm here to test a new engine that we hope will open the gate. Now, even if it works, I'm not sure I want to go back. Is there something I can do to help?"

"No, there is nothing you can do. Go back to Pellaya if you can. People are hiding in their homes. Schools and businesses are closed. People are going hungry because there is no food in the stores anymore. Don't land. Don't risk taking this back to Pellaya."

"Jeez, Allen, why are you even there? Why aren't you home with your family?"

"We have the Moon base to consider. There are people up there, and we are not sure what to do with them."

"Are they infected?"

"Not so far. We have to wait to see if they get it. It could have been taken up there a few days ago. We don't know."

"How many are there? I could get them and take them back to Pellaya." John said.

"Quite a few, but don't risk it. There is a possibility they could be carrying it. They have enough food and water to last about a month. After that, we don't know. I don't know if anyone will be around to help them in a month."

"I'll be here," John said, "and I have a lot of food onboard that I could drop off at the Moon Base. I could leave it without making contact with them. If they don't get sick, I can take them to Pellaya."

"John, Randy, and Bruce are up there."

"Oh, man! What about their families?"

"So far, from what we know, they are ok. But this bug is so contagious and stays around so long, it's hard to avoid it."

Well… I don't know what to say. This is hard to hear. What about you? How are you doing?"

"Everyone here is living in a bio-suit. No one is taking chances. We've had Plagues before, but not like this one. This one is worse than anything the world has ever seen."

"Where did it come from?" John asked.

"That's just it. It seemed to start everywhere at the same time. The United States, Mexico, Japan, China, Russia, Africa, and Europe all started reporting it at the same time. It hit the whole world all at once."

"Okay, I'm not going to land, but what about the people on the Moon? What do I do there?"

"Go home to Pellaya if you can. You can come back later. We will know more then."

"Ok. I guess that's best. I came to test a new engine design that we hope will open the gate. If it works, it means I can open the gate at any time. I can come back and check on you often."

"That would be great. No one is sure we can survive this. Their talking about it being an extinction-level event."

"Good God! Okay, I will check on you as often as I can. I'll go back and talk to the medical teams on Pellaya, maybe they can help. I'm not sure, but I think they cured Cancer. Their knowledge of disease is incredible. They may be able to help."

"Make it happen, John. The sooner the better," Allen said. "They have slowed the spread of it a little, but everyone has to be in a Bio-suit 24/7. We can't live like this, and you have to open the suit to eat and crap. When you do, you run the risk of being infected. They don't know how you contract the disease yet, but they are working on it."

"Ok. I'm going back to the gate. If you don't hear from me, you can assume I made it back to Pellaya. I will come back as soon as I can. Take care of yourself, Allen."

John hurried back to AoI, more anxious than ever to have the new engine open the gate. He had to get back and talk to Awth about this. He moved up to the Area of Interest, turned on the Energy drive, and threw the new lever that stopped the ship from moving. Then pushed the controls forward and rotated Spernecky's sphere to open.

"Damn it!" John said, finding himself hanging upside down in Tallda Shayts. "This has to end. Next time I do this, I'm flipping the ship over first. Maybe then I'll end up upright in Tallda Shayts!"

John righted the ship and looked into the fog. The new engine design had worked, and the gate had opened, but something was different. He could see! The Fog was pushed away from the ship. He was in a giant bubble in the middle of the fog. He pulled the controls back to the neutral position, and the fog instantly closed around the ship. "Ok. What's going on here?" he said aloud. He pushed the controls forward again, and the fog shot back away from the ship. "So apparently, the Magnetic energy, or that unknown energy created in Spernecky's Sphere, pushes the fog back. That's interesting, but I don't have time to mess around. I have to get to Awth," he said, closing the sphere and starting the ship moving.

When he emerged from Tallda Shayts, he was in an area he was unfamiliar with. He skirted around Tallda Shayts until he found Lieutenant Wilson's crashed plane. Now he knew where he was and quickly flew off to land at Niglaie Air Carrier Center. He landed and ran into the space center to Awth's office.

"It appears the new engine worked!" Awth said, with a smile. His smile disappeared when he saw the state John was in. "John, what's wrong? What are you doing back so soon? I thought you were going to be gone longer than this. Did something go wrong?"

"Yes. The new engine opened the gate, but I couldn't land Awth. Earth has been hit with the Plague. It sounds pretty bad and is killing a lot of people. I came back hoping the Doctors here could help."

"A plague?" Awth said. "Of course, the Pellayen Doctors will help if they can. You need to talk to Bartolos's wife, Gullaynianna. She is the top mind in the medical field."

"Where is she now?" John asked.

Awth escorted John to Gullaynianna. John hurried to tell her the situation and asked if they could help.

"Yes of course. We will do all we can to help. I will get my team together and discuss this. We will come up with a plan on how to best proceed. In the meantime, will you take one of my doctors back to Earth so she can learn as much as she can about the plague? Do not land. Let her talk to them on your radio. Would she be able to talk to one of your Earth doctors on the radio?"

"Yes. That can be arranged. Send her to my ship and we will leave immediately."

John thanked her and went back to his ship. When the Pellayen doctor arrived, they left for Earth.

Gullaynianna called an emergency meeting of medical professionals and explained what was happening. They all knew they would have to go to Earth, but how could they do it safely so they wouldn't bring the disease back to Pellaya?

One of Gullaynianna's colleagues, Breathall, offered a simple plan of converting one of the larger special occasion ships into a hospital ship. "There are two of them, and both are just sitting there, not being used. Turn one of those into a hospital ship and fly it into orbit around Earth. We can work from there, and if we get the disease, we stay away from Pellaya until we have a cure." It was a good plan and was quickly accepted.

The hospital ship could house thousands of people, but because of the danger, only a limited number of Doctors, Chemists, and Specialists were chosen to go. Fifty nurses were also allowed to go.

Changes to the ship began immediately. Seats and tables were removed to make room for sealed rooms and all sorts of X-ray machines, MRIs, and diagnostic equipment. They had just finished building a new engine that they planned to place in a different ship, but plans had changed. The new engine was large enough to handle the Hospital ship, so it was installed in it instead.

John and Doctor Faris returned from Earth with the information Gullaynianna had asked for. It was the worst plague ever to hit Earth. Hundreds of thousands of people were already dead, and many more were dying. The first symptom seemed to be a mild cold, but the patient would become overly tired and seemed to fade into death quietly.

"There are no obvious outward signs of the disease, such as vomiting, coughing, skin rash, or lesions," Doctor Faris said. "The victims drift away rather peacefully. But they all dye, and that doesn't sound right to me."

"No, it doesn't," Gullaynianna agreed. "What about the patients? How do they feel? Do they complain of feeling nauseous or have pain?"

"No. It is as I have told you. Except for a Head Cold, they feel okay. They just grow tired and die. There doesn't appear to be any pain or irritation of any sort other than a stuffed-up nose."

Gullaynianna shook her head. "That is very strange. Is this disease airborne?"

"They aren't sure. I was told they don't know how it's being transmitted. They suspect it's airborne but still haven't isolated the pathogen causing the problem. It sounded to me like they were guessing about it all. I know it has them baffled."

"Do they know where it first broke out?" Gullaynianna asked.

"No. They claim it broke out all over the world at the same time. There is no way to determine where the first case started."

Gullaynianna shook her head again. "Something doesn't add up. We will just have to go and investigate this for ourselves."

****

The massive hospital ship flew across the sky and into Tallda Shayts. John followed in his ship. Both ships were suddenly in Earth space. John led the hospital ship to Earth and contacted Mission Control. Allen was still there complaining about having to live in a Bio-suit. John told him that they had come with a hospital ship and were ready to help. "The Doctors need a few patients to begin their examinations, but want to limit contact with people, so would you see to it that someone gets a few patients ready to be picked up? I'll be doing the transporting, so tell me where to go to get them.

"Rodger, I'll see to that right away."

John landed his ship inside the hospital ship and went to talk to Gullaynianna. His ship had been outfitted with a sterilization chamber, and Gullaynianna gave him instructions on how and when to use it. "Don't sterilize the patients. Sterilizing the patients would destroy evidence of the disease. Sterilize the chamber after we have taken the patients from the ship. Do not enter the chamber yourself. If, for some reason, you do, sterilize yourself before going back into your ship. Once we get our first patients, you're going to have to stay away from us. When you transport me or any member of my team, we must never enter the main area of your ship."

John nodded, and Gullaynianna left him to do what she needed to. John only had to wait for Allen to respond and tell him where the patients were. After several hours, Allen radioed up that they had three patients ready to go. John gathered Gullaynianna and her team, and they flew down to get them.

Gullaynianna and two of her team went into the chamber to help with the loading. When the patients were loaded, Gullaynianna stood looking through the little window in the chamber door at John. They stared at each other, knowing the danger Gullaynianna and her team were now in. John put a hand on the window. "You take care of yourself, Gail. See that you don't get sick. Bartolos and I won't forgive you if you do."

Gullaynianna smiled back at him and placed her hand on the glass against his. "Don't worry. We know how to handle situations like this," she said, then stepped back from the door. From here on, John could have no contact with any of them until this was over. There would always be something between them when they met.

John couldn't go to Earth, couldn't go to the Moon, and couldn't go to Pellaya. He could remain in his ship or go to the crew area of the hospital ship. It would be safe to go there because the crew wasn't allowed in the hospital area of the ship, and no one from the hospital area was allowed into the crew's area. John was thankful he could go there to be with other people.

After delivering the patients, John found himself with nothing to do. He moved his ship closer to the Moon and talked to Randy and Bruce on the radio. He had been advised not to leave his ship, but he could at least land and see them through windows.

It was good to talk to them and see that they were both fine. No one on the Moon had it, and it appeared they weren't going to get it. John considered taking them to Pellaya, but Gullaynianna told him, "Not yet. We need to wait a little longer and see what develops."

Because of those restrictions, John found himself alone in space most of the time. He would occasionally go to the Crew Area of the hospital ship, but most of his time was spent flying around Earth. He was seeing an unusually quiet Earth. People were moving about, but there were so few of them and every one of them was wearing a bio suit. It appeared most people were hiding in their homes or wherever they had taken refuge. Highways were almost empty of cars and trucks. It was an apocalyptic sight.

The massive hospital ship hovered in the sky above Atlanta Georgia, inspiring wonder in all who saw her. They had moved the Pellayen Megastructure into a lower atmosphere to take advantage of gravity, allowing the doctors to work more efficiently.

Two of the first three patients John delivered had already died, and John needed to bring more to replace them. Bringing patients and transporting Gullaynianna and the CDC doctors to and from the hospital ship was keeping him fairly busy. It also kept him informed. He overheard Doctors talking and learned how impressed they were with the Pellayens' knowledge and technology. They didn't know what some of the equipment was, but when they saw the results of its use, they were amazed.

From Gullaynianna and the CDC doctors, he learned that their effort to cure the disease wasn't going well. "We don't understand," Gullaynianna admitted. "It appears to be a simple upper respiratory infection, which we can cure, but the patient continues to weaken and die. There are several peculiar things about this disease. It survives much too long on outside surfaces, and is on everything, and everywhere. Weirdest of all, it appears to be multiplying even outside the host body. That shouldn't be possible. We don't know what it is feeding on?" Gullaynianna said, raising her hands in frustration. "We know the pathogen, and we know how to cure it, but this strain has mutated into something that, at the moment, has baffled us.

John didn't like what he was hearing. "Gail, I have landed this ship on Earth many times. Is it contaminated?"

Gullaynianna nodded. "Yes. There is no doubt that when you land on Earth, the outside of your ship becomes contaminated. I have taken samples from the outside of your ship several times and found it, but something about your ship is killing the germ. I have tested the outside of the hospital ship, and it too is killing the germ. We were surprised to find the germ on the Hospital Ship because it had never landed. That indicates that this disease is airborne and possibly coming from space. It's out there, everywhere in the atmosphere." Gullaynianna said, turning to John. "Right now, I believe your ship is clean, but I can't tell you why. It appears the germ can survive in space, and may even have come from there, so taking your ship into space isn't what's killing the germ."

John shook his head. "I don't like not knowing when my ship is carrying germs that could kill me. Gail, would it help to bring your team aboard my ship to study this thing?"

"Yes, it would make things easier.

It didn't take Gullaynianna long to discover that something about Sperneckeens' Engines was killing the Pathogen. She didn't believe it was the magnetic energy that was killing the Germs. It was that other unknown energy that the engine produced that was doing it. The Pellayens had suspected there was something else being produced in the engines for a long time. It was a different form of energy that they still couldn't prove was there, and certainly didn't understand.

Gullaynianna wasn't interested in explaining what this new energy was. She was only interested in what was killing the disease, and it definitely had something to do with the engines. When the engine was turned off, the Germs lived. As soon as the engines were turned on, the Germs died. There was nothing else that could be killing the Germ. It had to be that unknown energy being produced by the engines.

Hearing this eased John's mind considerably, but he still preferred to stay away from Earth as much as possible. When he wasn't needed to transport patients or the doctors, he spent his time flying around in space, staying away from the germs.

He was enjoying a little trip around Earth when he spotted a strange ship leaving Earth's Atmosphere. This ship was too big and oddly designed to be anything from Earth, and it didn't appear to be Pellayen.

Puzzled, John radioed down to Mission Control. "Mission Control, this is John Baines. Is anyone listening?"

It took a few minutes and a few attempts, but someone did answer. The voice was unfamiliar.

"Where's Allen?" John asked.

"Allen has the bug. My Name is Jason. How can I help you, Captain?"

"How bad is Allen? Is he going to make it?"

"No one survives this dammed disease. His whole family has gotten it now. John, there is hardly anyone left here at Mission Control. We need a miracle, or we're all going to die."

John didn't know what to say. He knew it was true. Millions had already died, and millions more were sick. The situation was bad.

"What was it you needed, John?" Jason asked.

"I saw a ship up here that I don't recognize. Has NASA built a ship with a Pellayen engine in it?"

"No. So far, they're having trouble just getting an engine built. They are nowhere near getting a ship ready to fly. Why do you ask?"

"I saw a ship up here, and I know it's not Pellayen. I thought maybe you guys had built something."

"No. They're close, I guess, but not yet."

"Jason! I completely forgot I have two Sperneckeens engines onboard my ship that I was supposed to give to you guys. I need to get them down to you so you can get them into some kind of craft. Find out where I should take them, would you?"

"I'll do that, Captain. Was there something else?"

"Yes! I'm concerned about the ship I saw. Jason, do you know anything at all about whose ship this might have been?"

"No, I haven't heard anything, and I haven't seen anything on radar. But then we are so shorthanded down here, I'm surprised we see anything at all. There may be something up there, but no one noticed. I'm not seeing anything right now."

"Well, I need to get these engines down to you. Let me know where to take them."

"Rodger, I will get on that right now."

While he waited, John started his ship down into Earth's atmosphere, preparing to deliver the engines. He was surprised to hear a different voice on the radio talking to him.

"Captain Baines, this is General Andrews, do you copy?"

"Yes, General, I read you loud and clear."

"Captain Baines, I am head of the Military Space Force here at Wright-Patterson. We picked up your conversation with Mission Control, and right now could use your help. We *have* been seeing things on radar, and at this moment are seeing a bogie on our screens. You have a ship that can get there and investigate. Will you do that for us?"

"Yes, General, but I need a little more information on where to look. I don't have radar or any way to find them."

"John, I have you flying above Texas at the moment. You need to move toward Georgia. That is where we see the Bogie."

John turned his ship and shot toward Georgia. "General, why aren't you using the Tataro? Is it broken down?"

"The Tataro is on the Moon, and until now, there have been orders not to use it for fear of contamination. Gullaynianna has just told us that the engine will kill the germs, so the ship can be used without concern. She also said that enough time has passed to prove that no one on the moon is going to get sick. Because of that, I have asked Randy and Bruce to investigate this with you. They will meet you there."

"Understood," John said.

John scanned space looking for the bogey but couldn't find it. "General, I will need a little more information on where to look. Where is the bogey now?"

"The Bogie is more toward Florida. Does that help?" the General said.

"It should," John said and turned his ship to look a bit further south. "Okay, I see something, General, but it's a long way off. I imagine it will turn out to be the ship I saw earlier, but I have to get closer to be sure."

"We suspect it's a ship as well, but whose ship. That's what we want to know. John, I just got word that Bruce and Randy are approaching your position. They will join you shortly."

"Rodger that," John said, speeding toward the object. "It is a ship, General. I know it's not a Pellayen ship, so either it's from Earth, or we have a new alien presence."

"No country on Earth has managed to get a ship with a Pellayen engine built yet. We are much closer to getting one finished than anyone else, but no country has built one yet. It must be a new threat. Be careful, John."

John approached the ship from behind so he wouldn't be detected. The ship was much bigger than his own, about the size of a Navy destroyer. "General Andrews, do you copy?"

"Go ahead, Captain."

"General, I'm alongside the ship, but it's kind of hard to describe. It's not like anything I've seen before. There are no markings on it that I can see. It's almost as big as the hospital ship, but it's oddly shaped like a flying saucer stretched out. I suggest ….Oh shit!"

The alien ship had suddenly spun to face him so fast that it should have killed anyone inside. He was now looking through the windshield of the craft at Alien beings. "General. They're not human, and they're not the Grays. I've only seen pictures of Aliens, so I don't have much to go on, but I have never seen anything like these guys before. They make me think of insects. At the moment, we are engaged in a staring contest. Wait! Something's happening. Something is coming out of the ship. It looks …. It's a weapon!"

John moved his ship back away from them, trying to keep his ship out of their sight. A bolt of yellow fire shot passed him. They had fired on him. John pulled back harder on his controls, moving his ship farther back and to one side just as another yellow bolt of energy flashed passed. He dropped his ship down to get under them, but they were suddenly in front of him and firing. Every time he moved, they were there, firing at him. It was as if they were anticipating his moves.

He had no weapons to fight with. All he could think to do was get the Energy Drive turned on and hope he could outrun them, but he needed time to do that, and they weren't giving him that time. He was in trouble. If he turned around, he wouldn't be able to see what they were doing, and wouldn't know how to move his ship to avoid getting hit. He had to keep backing away from them, constantly dodging their Yellow Fire that trailed after him with every move he made. He threw the control stick to one side and down, just as another bolt of yellow shot above him. He pulled up and to the left on the controls, but they were there, shooting at him, forcing him to move again. He had his hands full and couldn't take even a second to turn on the Energy Drive.

The ship creaked from the maneuvers he was making. He was stressing his ship to its limits and still couldn't shake them. Their ship was moving in ways he couldn't. He would see them fire, and react, only to find them in front of him again and have to react again. If it weren't for his seat belt, he would have been thrown out of his seat. His ship was complaining, and he was tiring. He couldn't keep this up. His ship was so outclassed by theirs that it was clear he was going to get hit. He had to do something.

Thinking quickly, John pulled back hard on the stick, which flipped the ship up on its back, then commanded it to move down, which, now being upside down, sent his ship higher about the aliens. His plan worked. His actions confused the aliens. They were shooting in the wrong spot, giving him a chance to turn on his Energy drive.

He got it turned on, slammed the controls forward. Suddenly, an electric shock surged through his body. Everything slowed down, and he felt his life leaving him. He had been hit! His last desperate thought was of *Gullaynianna!*

****

"No, no, no! No damn it! No!" Randy shouted in horror, seeing John's ship disintegrate. He and Bruce had watched it all happen. They stared at what little was left of John's ship. Small pieces of debris were floating away in all directions.

"No," Randy said again. He had just witnessed the murder of the best friend he had ever had. He had watched John fly his ship like a madman. Saw the alien ship move with incredible agility and shoot at John again and again. He saw John's ship flip on its back and fly high, and witnessed the aliens shoot in the wrong spot. Then the aliens fired again, and he saw the yellow fire shoot toward John's ship and John's ship disintegrate. Randy sank in his seat. He couldn't believe what had just happened. He had just lost a man he had known all his life. He loved John and couldn't believe he had just been killed.

Bruce brought their ship to a stop and began to retreat away from the Aliens. There was no point in going on. Like John, they had no weapons. All they would do was get themselves killed if they approached the aliens. The Alien craft had to have anti-inertia generators or something of that nature to maneuver like that. They were far outclassed. They had watched John do things with his ship that shouldn't be done, and he had still gotten hit. The Alien ship was just too much for them. John didn't have a chance, and neither would they.

Bruce headed back to the Moon, turning his ship every so often to make sure the Aliens weren't following. He was relieved to see they had gone back to whatever they were doing. Neither he nor Randy spoke a word. They were stunned and hurt. A good friend of theirs had just been viciously attacked and killed by an alien race. Both of them had revenge on their mind, but were helpless to do anything about it, and that added to their hurt.

CHAPTER ELEVEN
GONE FOREVER

The Radar tech slumped in his seat. "They got him, Sir."

"What do you mean, Private?" General Andrews barked. "They got who?"

"Sir, the aliens just destroyed John's ship. You saw the dogfight on the screen, now John's blip has vanished. That means he is no longer there. His ship was destroyed, Sir."

"Damn!" General Andrews said, turning to his aide. "Get Randy and Bruce on the horn. I need to find out what happened up there," he said, then turned back to the Radar tech. "Where is the Alien ship now?"

"It went back to where it was and is now moving toward the center of the States."

General Andrews slammed his fist on the counter. "Who are they, and what are they doing here?"

"General, I have Randy on the radio."

General Andrews snatched the mic from his aide. "Randy, did you see what happened up there? Did we lose Captain Baines?

"Yes, General, I'm sorry to say John was killed. His ship was destroyed."

"Tell me what happened. Give me every detail. I need to know what we are up against," the general growled.

"We saw John trying to get away from the aliens, but their ship was just too agile. They have to have antigravity or something to move the way they were. John didn't have a chance. They hit him, and his ship disintegrated. There is nothing left of it."

"Damn," the General grunted. "What weapons are they using, Missiles, bullets, what?"

"Some kind of energy blasts. It looked like bolts of yellow fire."

"Are you sure John's ship was destroyed?"

"Yes, General. I saw it happen. John's ship was destroyed. There is no way he survived."

"That is a great loss. We needed John and that ship. Randy, I can't order you, but with John gone, we need your help. You can speak Pellayen, correct?"

"Yes, General, I do."

"Will you step in and take John's place working with Gullaynianna and her team?"

"I will, General."

"Good. I also need you and Bruce to patrol the area around Earth as well. We need to learn what these aliens are up to. You have the only ship that can do that now. Will you do this?"

Yes, General, we will, and if I had the weaponry to do it, I would blast them out of existence!"

"Well, you don't have the weaponry, so stay away from them. Run like hell if you have to. Don't let that ship get damaged. We need it now more than ever."

"Understood," Randy said.

"Randy, someone needs to tell Gullaynianna about John. She would probably prefer to hear the news from a friend. Are you willing to do this?"

"I will take care of it, General. I had already planned to do just that."

Randy dreaded having to tell Gullaynianna. She would be hurting as much as he was, but it was right that he was the one to tell her.

Randy thought of Nellaynan, Awth, and Bartolos. They would have to be told as well, but they were on Pellaya. The only way to contact them was to go to Pellaya. The Tataro had an old-style engine that had to have the Earth near AoI to open the Gate, and he didn't know how to open the gate anyway.

As much as he dreaded telling her, he decided to go to her with the bad news right away. While he was aboard the hospital ship, he would ask the captain, Captain Laysee, how to open the gate. He would use this as a chance to familiarize himself with his new role as John's replacement. Randy closed his eyes and groaned. He hated thinking of himself as John's replacement.

On the Hospital ship, he met a crew member who took him to a room where he could talk to Gullaynianna through a glass window. When Gullaynianna came into the room, it was easy to see that she had been crying. Randy didn't want to assume she had already heard about John, so he had to be careful. She could be crying for a patient or for some other reason.

They greeted each other and sat down. Gullaynianna looked up at Randy through the glass, "How did it happen?" she said, tearing up.

"What have you heard?" Randy asked, gauging what she knew.

"He reached out to me, Randy! I felt him die!" she said and began to sob.

"What do you mean? Do you mean John reached out to you with his mind?" he asked.

Gullaynianna said nothing but nodded. After a moment, she calmed herself and asked again, "How did it happen? How did he die?"

Randy tried to hide the tear that rolled down his face. "John was sent to investigate an alien ship flying around Earth. They attacked him. He never had a chance. Gullaynianna, I believe his death was quick, and he didn't suffer."

Gullaynianna again only nodded. Randy wanted to hold her and share their grief, but that was impossible because of the glass. After a few minutes, Gullaynianna asked Randy if he was taking over for John and if he would take her where she needed to go. She was genuinely pleased when he said that he was. After a moment, Gullaynianna spoke again. "What happened to the Alien ship? Was it damaged?"

"No, it wasn't damaged. They went back to what they were doing."

"What were they doing?" Gullaynianna asked.

"We don't know. John was trying to discover that when they attacked him. We don't know why they are here or why they attacked him. I've already heard people suggesting it could have been a mistake, but that's not what I saw. I saw a deliberate attack with no interest in peace at all." Randy growled.

Gullaynianna wiped her eyes again and looked up at Randy mournfully. "Thank you for coming, Randy. I will be needing you soon to take me down to the CDC."

Randy nodded. "I will be happy to take you wherever you want, and Gullaynianna …I'm very sorry for your…. *OUR* loss. It is a great loss."

Gullaynianna stood up, smiled at him, and started to walk away. Randy called after her and asked if he could bring everyone from the Moon base to the hospital ship. "They've been living in low gravity for a long time. Getting back to Earth's gravity would do them good," he said.

Gullaynianna kept her back to him but cocked her head back slightly. "No one is sick?"

"No, and it has been a long time. I think it's time to end their quarantine."

"Yes. Bring them to the crew's quarters. That would be fine," she said and started to leave. She stopped suddenly. With her back still to Randy, she stiffened and just stood there. Then she turned her head slightly. "You, your people, don't know who these aliens are?" she asked.

Randy shook his head. "Not a clue. We've never seen them before."

Gullaynianna turned her body a little more toward Randy. "What *was* the Alien ship doing?" She was no longer crying and seemed very serious.

"They were just drifting through the atmosphere. I couldn't see that they were doing anything at all."

She stood thinking for a moment, then turned all the way around to face Randy. "Can you get me near one of those ships without being seen?"

Randy could see the concern on her face. "It would be risky, but I think so. Why?" Randy asked.

"It's this alien ship. No one from Earth knows who they are?"

"No," Randy said. "They are something new to us."

"Randy, I need to get near that ship. Can you do that?"

"The General won't like it, and we would have to stay far away from them, but yes. I could do that. When?"

"Is the alien ship still there right now?" she asked.

"It was."

"Then I want to go immediately," Gullaynianna said. "I will meet you at your ship as soon as possible."

Randy couldn't help but notice Gullaynianna's excitement. She was onto something. He didn't know what she was thinking, but if Gullaynianna wanted to do this, he would help her.

After a thorough sterilization, Gullaynianna met him, and they took off to find the alien ship. They found it still moving high above the United States. Gullaynianna asked him to get underneath it. Randy stayed low to the ground and then started up toward the bottom of the alien ship. "This is close enough," Gullaynianna said. "Hold the ship here. I'm going to get what I need and come back. Randy, I will have to stay in the back of the ship from now on."

"Gullaynianna, what are you going to do?" Randy asked.

"Just hold the ship here. I will be back," Gullaynianna said and left.

While he waited, Randy studied the Alien ship. Something about it was different. He couldn't say what, but this didn't look like the same ship. Was it the color or the shape? He couldn't tell, but something was different. Suddenly, Gullaynianna yelled at him from the back of the ship. "Now, take me down to the ground. Anywhere on the ground."

Gullaynianna's yelling through the ship seemed odd to Randy until he remembered that Pellayen ships weren't equipped with intercoms. Pellayens had an intercom system called Mental Ability. *Hmm, it does come in handy.*

Randy flew the ship down and landed on a grassy field. Gullaynianna yelled that she was going out and that he should turn the ship off. He soon saw her outside in a bio-suit. *What is she up to?* Randy thought.

He watched Gullaynianna hurry back inside the ship and, from the sterilization chamber, yell, "Get me back to the hospital ship." She seemed very excited about something. He asked her about it, but she pressed him to get her back to the hospital ship.

Randy did as she asked. When they arrived, Gullaynianna spoke quickly. "Randy, I'm sorry, but I might be on to something. I don't know yet. I need to get these samples to the lab, but if I am right, I may need you soon."

Randy nodded. "Do I have time to get the people from the Moon station and bring them here?"

"Yes, of course. Go get them. Randy, feel free to do what you need, but please be on hand. I don't know how long it will take to get the answers I need, but if I'm right…." She paused and looked at the floor. "Randy, if I'm right, I may have found the cause of the Plague."

They stared at each other. This was incredible news, and cause for joy, but both of them were swimming in sorrow at the loss of a dear friend. Gullaynianna suddenly put her hand on the window, and a tear ran down her cheek. "Randy," Was all she said.

Randy saw the hurt on her face and knew she was thinking of John. He placed his hand on the glass against hers and nodded that he understood and shared her pain. Then Gullaynianna turned and quickly left his ship. Randy stared at the door she had gone through. "Good luck and God's speed, Gullaynianna. Do a good job for us."

Randy flew out to the Moon to collect the people from the Moon base to bring them back to the hospital ship. He was sure they would be more comfortable there, and he wasn't wrong. They were all pleased to be in gravity again.

Randy found himself having to help the humans settle aboard the hospital ship because he was the only one who spoke Pellayen. The job naturally fell to him, so he asked Bruce to take the ship and do as General Andrews had asked. "Look for Alien ships. Find out what they are doing, but don't get caught."

Bruce immediately spotted an alien craft drifting over Asia. To his surprise, he spotted another above Europe and another over Africa. Randy had told him he thought there might be more than one ship, and it was true. Eventually, the three ships came together, and as a group, flew over the United States. He followed them and was shocked when they joined with three more alien craft already there.

Bruce was suddenly on edge. The Hospital Ship was directly below these aliens, and they were advancing toward it. He tried to warn the Hospital Ship, but even though they had installed a radio system on the Hospital Ship, no one understood what he was saying, and he couldn't speak very well in Pellayen. He could only hold his breath and watch the six alien ships approach the Hospital Ship. He sighed in relief when he saw them turn and flash away from Earth, leaving the Hospital ship untouched.

It was obvious that something had to be done. The Hospital Ship was vulnerable to attack. "General, it's pretty simple. Move the hospital ship back to Pellaya, where it will be safe from attack. With their new engine, they can travel back and forth any time they wish. If they don't land on Pellaya, they won't contaminate their own people."

General Andrews, Captain Laysee, and Gullaynianna all agreed that the hospital ship should be moved back to Pellayen space. General Andrews asked Randy to go back with them to ask for help. "Ask for ships, engines, anything they can offer that will help. The Earth is helpless against these Aliens. If they attack, we can do little to stop them."

Randy agreed to go, but wanted himself and Bruce to be taught how to open the gate with the old engines before he left. They would no doubt need to know these things in the near future. The old-style engine in Tataro was more complicated to set up than the new engines. Still, in a few hours, the lessons were over, and Randy was back on the bridge of the hospital ship, ready to leave. He was looking forward to going back to Pellaya. Like John, he liked the Pellayen people and looked forward to seeing Awth, Bartolos, and Nellaynan again. He didn't like what he would have to tell them, and Nellaynan was sure to ask, but he was happy to be going back.

He stood on the bridge of the Hospital Ship, remembering what John had told him about being upside down in Tallda Shayts every time he went through the gate. It would be particularly bad if it happened to the Hospital Ship. Everything not tied down, the equipment, tools, and the patients, would be thrown onto the ceiling. He told Captain Laysee that John had planned to orient his ship to the south pole of Earth in the hopes that he would end up upright in Tallda Shayts.

Captain Laysee agreed to do as John had intended and turn his ship so that the top of it was oriented toward the south pole of Earth. He also gave instructions for everything to be tied down. Randy was about to tell Captain Laysee about the Mental Abyss, but Captain Laysee already knew about the loss of memory and the craziness that could result. "John warned us about the Mental Abyss," he said while producing two helmets coated with Spernecky's compound and handing one to Randy. Then with a bit of a laugh, and speaking loudly for all to hear, "John also said, 'Do not push Randy unless you want a crazy man throwing punches at you. You will see a nut case going crazy, and you don't want to see that!"

Randy felt slightly embarrassed, but also enjoyed the humor. "Ok. John has been telling stories, I see. Very funny."

But Captain Laysee wasn't quite finished. As he put his helmet on, he casually asked, "How is your mother-in-law these days? Will she be visiting us today?" Everyone laughed, and Randy couldn't help but guffaw. The only thing he didn't like was that these things reminded him of John and how much he missed him.

Thankfully, being involved in getting the hospital ship ready to go through the gate helped him forget about John for a while. When all was ready, they reached the Area of Interest, and Captain Laysee rotated Spernecky's sphere to open. Immediately, they saw something they had never seen before. A stream of gray energy shot out from the ship and merged with the space in front of them. Then a window full of swirling gray fog appeared, and suddenly they were in Tallda Shayts, and right side up! "It worked," Randy said. "At least we don't have to deal with being upside down anymore."

When Randy looked out the windshield, he wasn't surprised to see that the fog was being pushed back. John had told him that the energy field pouring from Spernecky's sphere had done that. The Hospital Ship was inside a large bubble. The air inside the bubble was clear, but where the bubble ended, the gray sludge crawled across the surface. Randy shook his head. "It looks like a monster searching for a way to get inside."

John had also said that he had been afraid to move the ship with Spernecky's Sphere open. Captain Laysee Informed Randy that it was true that the Energy Drive wouldn't work with the Sphere open, but they didn't need the Energy Drive. They could leave it open so they could see the ground, and use the lesser engine to move the ship.

Randy nodded and looked out the windshield. He was shocked to see a plane, an old car, and a spaceship that none of them recognized lying on the ground. Captain Laysee couldn't help himself and flew the ship around this strange ship, trying to figure out where it had come from. It wasn't Pellayen, nor was it from Earth. They couldn't get out and investigate for fear of bringing the Plague to Pellaya, so Captain Laysee flew on.

This was the first time any of them had seen the inside of Tallda Shayts, so nearly everyone except the patients had their faces to a window. This was a big deal, and since the Hospital Ship couldn't land and no one would be allowed to leave the ship, they could take the time to look around inside Tallda Shayts.

Most of what they saw was derelict ships and planes from Earth lying in heaps on the ground. But there were a few more surprises. Nothing beat the one Randy recognized right away. He spotted it off near the edge of the bubble and asked that they go closer to it. It was a rebuilt Canary yellow Biplane, perfectly intact, with the name 'Sparrowhawk' written on it. Randy was amazed. The plane had belonged to Ashley Hellens, who disappeared while flying inside the Bermuda Triangle. Naturally, everyone believed she had fallen prey to the Triangle. "Well, it turns out they were right," Randy said.

An even bigger surprise was that the Sparrowhawk looked to be in perfect condition. Somehow, Ashley Hellens had managed to land the plane in the fog of Tallda Shayts. "Maybe she had landed in a bubble where the air was clear," Randy said. It seemed unlikely that she could have landed in the incredibly thick fog. "And why, after you landed, didn't you walk out of Tallda Shayts?"

Randy stared at the plane, thinking he would never know what happened. One thing was clear. If she had landed her plane in this fog, she was a much better pilot than anyone gave her credit for. In the future, they could stop and investigate mysteries like this. Maybe someday they would know what happened to Ashley, but right now, no one could leave the ship.

Though they couldn't leave the ship, it was incredibly satisfying for them just to see what lay beyond that great, impenetrable gray curtain of fog.

****

John had been killed, and Randy was on Pellaya, so that left Bruce and two Pellayens, Jacqualla and Kalaynin, in possession of the Tataro. Bruce had learned how to fly the Tataro but not well enough to keep from getting killed by the aliens, so one of the Pellayens was always onboard with him, teaching him all about the controls and how to better control the ship. He, like Randy and John, found he liked the Pellayens a great deal. He liked Jacqualla, the female, the most. She was a lot of fun to be with, and that made time with her something to look forward to. Kalaynin, a male, was more reserved but still easy to be with.

Eventually, Bruce learned enough that he felt confident to take the ship and spy on the aliens by himself. This meant they could watch the aliens in three shifts, but that didn't last long. General Andrews ordered the surveillance stopped after several close calls with the aliens. They needed that ship and didn't want the aliens to discover the Moonbase by following them back to the Moon.

The Tataro was hidden when it wasn't being used. Most of what Bruce was doing was shuttling important people to and from meetings about saving the planet. Presidents, Prime Ministers,

Kings, and Queens, all going to meetings on how to save the planet, and yet he couldn't see where anything was being done.

They had tried to contact the aliens a few times, but the aliens never answered the radio, and they weren't ready to make another attempt to contact them by flying a ship up to them. All the aliens were doing was flying around in Earth space, and as long as that was all they were doing, everything was ok.

It wasn't at all okay with Bruce. He was frustrated with the lack of action from governments. He wanted revenge for John's murder, and he wanted to be part of that revenge. He wanted something done about the Plague, but it seemed to him that nothing was being done there either. He had already lost friends and was worrying himself to death about his family, who were still on Earth. He wanted to get them and bring them up to live with him on the Moon base, but was told the risk of contamination was too great.

It seemed to him that all anyone was doing was talking about it, while the aliens had control of Earth space, and a Plague ravaged its people. It frustrated him to no end and made him less willing to adhere to their wishes. At the moment, he was shuttling a load of scientists and engineers to yet another meeting where nothing would get done. He decided he was going to get his family up to the moonbase whether they liked it or not, and he was going to find out what was happening at these meetings.

When he was dropping this group of people off, he put on a Bio-suit and joined a group going into the meeting. He fooled security, which was surprisingly sparse, and got inside. Now he would see what his leaders were doing about their situations.

It was as he expected. It began with the usual BS. Members, thanking members, and angling to gain political points. Finally, someone began to speak directly about the Alien threat, but what Bruce heard made his temper flare. Part of what angered him was the way the speaker spoke. He acted so proud of his eloquence and seemed to enjoy hearing himself speak, but he wasn't saying anything worth hearing.

"If the Pellayens do supply us with ships, we have been assured that we can arm those ships. However, the question remains as to what we would arm those ships with. It has been suggested, and I believe it is true, that they would best be armed with rocket-propelled ordnance. That would work very well in space, but is that all we have? I am told that putting big guns on those ships wouldn't work because when fired, the ship would move backward almost as much as the bullet would move forward. I believe our Sonic Weapons could help disorient the enemy and …." On and on it went.

Bruce listened until he couldn't stand it any longer. This blowhard knew nothing of what he was talking about, and those who listened weren't any better. He stood up and shouted at them, "You have been meeting for weeks, and this is what you are *still* talking about? For God's Sake, we could be attacked at any minute, and you still haven't done a thing about it! It has become obvious to me that you don't know what you are talking about," He said, turning to the speaker. "You say you can't use big guns, but you could! A big gun on a Pellayen ship would work very well. You obviously don't understand how a Pellayen engine works. As long as the engines are on, a Pellayen ship attaches itself to the space around it. It would not move backward when you fired the gun, and because you are in space, the projectile would fly straight and true. In space, there is no gravity to effect the projectile. Then you show your ignorance by suggesting that Sonic Weapons would work. Sound waves don't travel in space. That weapon would be totally useless," Bruce shook his head. "You have had a Pellayen ship for a long time, and you still don't understand how it works. You!" he said, pointing at the speaker. "You say 'Rockets will work well on Pellayen ships. Well, get them on there then! What are you waiting for? The Aliens could attack at any moment, and we are defenseless. You have a Pellayen ship. Arm it for crying out loud and get more Pellayen engines built. What good is my flying around watching the Aliens every day? We know they're there. The question is, when are you going to do something about it?"

He sat down expecting to be thrown out of the meeting, and the speaker stared at him with indignation, but the others started asking him questions. "How big of a gun could the ship handle, in your opinion? How much weight can the ship carry?" They knew nothing about the ship, and that amazed Bruce even more.

Then the questions became about his health and his abilities as a pilot. That's when he realized he was about to lose the Tataro. They were about to take the ship from him and give it to a younger pilot who was more experienced in aerial warfare. He was going to be stranded on Earth and forced to wear a bio-suit 24/7. He didn't like the idea, but at least he would be with his family.

When he left the meeting, he was met outside by General Andrews' aide, who told him his family had been taken to the

Hospital. All of them had contracted the disease. Suddenly, nothing else mattered to Bruce. Not even their taking the ship from him. He hurried to be with his family.

Days later, while sitting in the hospital with his family, Bruce got the news he was expecting. They had taken the ship from him and given it to Major Theodore Thomas Benet, a Top Gun flying Ace. What he didn't expect was to be praised by the deliverer of the message for yelling at them during the meeting. "It lit a fire under them and got them to make decisions. They're going to Arm the ship, then fly it up to meet the aliens face to face. We are finally going to learn once and for all why they are here and if there can be peace."

Bruce could only shake his head and continue holding his wife's hand. With his family so close to death, nothing else mattered. He sat for days watching his family grow weaker, knowing they would soon be leaving him. His thoughts were for his family only, so he was unaware of anything happening outside the hospital. He didn't know Randy and Gullaynianna had returned to Earth Space with the Pellayen hospital ship and two large cargo ships in tow.

Randy and Gullaynianna were quick to contact Earth to call for an emergency meeting of the United Nations. "It is urgent that Gullaynianna speak to as many heads of countries as possible and as soon as possible."

The session was scheduled for that afternoon, and Gullaynianna stood in front of the representatives with Randy at her side as an interpreter. "Ladies and gentlemen, I can tell you are surprised to see me stand before you without a bio-suit. I am pleased to say I can do so because we have found the cure for your Plague."

This brought on an explosion of cheering and applause. So many had died, and so many more were now sick with the disease. To hear that a cure had been found was the best news they could get.

Gullaynianna raised her arms to quiet them. "There are things I need to tell you, so please quiet down. This plague you are facing is not a true plague at all. We believe it has been created by the aliens circling your planet and is being dumped into your atmosphere." She again had to quiet them. "I do not have 100% proof, but I do have the evidence that strongly suggests they are responsible for it. I took an air sample from close under one of their ships. I found the highest concentration of germs there. Then I took samples from the ground directly beneath their ship and found that the germs there were spread much thinner. I don't know if it is intentional, but the evidence suggests it is.

I found the same Pathogens in every location I checked, and the evidence strongly suggests they are spreading the germ. If they are doing it intentionally, there can be no other reason for doing this except to cause sickness and death. When I finish, you will understand why I say they intend to rid the Earth of the human population."

Gullaynianna definitely had their attention now. The room was very quiet as they waited for her to continue. "The germ you are fighting is no more than a Rhinovirus. Your Doctors knew this, and together we discovered that it has been expertly modified to survive longer and even reproduce outside of the host body. In other words, the Virus is growing as it sits on any surface outside the body. It is on the streets, the sidewalks, the trees, the grass, the roof of your house, and at this moment growing on the Bio-suits you are wearing."

Everyone began squirming in their seats. Gullaynianna raised her hands. "Don't worry. This is not what is causing the deaths of your people. This virus is no more than a delivery system for the Toxin we found embedded inside the Pathogen itself. It is this Toxin that kills. Understand what I am saying to you. You are being poisoned in a way that makes it appear as a disease. They wanted us to believe it was a plague."

Again, everyone squirmed in their seat and began shouting questions. Gullaynianna ignored the questions and continued to explain her findings. "The Rhinovirus had been engineered to accept the Toxin as part of itself. When the Virus multiplies, amazingly, the Toxic protein multiplies right along with it. The Virus is nothing more than the host for the Toxin. The Virus feeds on your bodies, and the Toxin feeds on the virus. It is amazing medical technology and rivals Pellayen's technology, but we understand it now and can stop it.

You should understand that this Toxin already exists in your body, creating the protein. These aliens must have been studying you for some time to realize you were already poisoning yourselves. You have been contaminating your body by using plastics to contain your food. Those toxins leach into your food from the plastic then you ingest them. The aliens found a way to make it multiply inside the body and slowly poison the host. That's why no one feels much more than a cold. The rhinovirus is the only thing that's truly visible to Doctors, while the Toxin continues to grow undetected. The point is, these Aliens are using your body chemistry against you and have disguised it as a terrible Plague."

The room was eerily quiet. All eyes were on Gullaynianna, and she could see the questions in their faces. "Yes," she said. "We have developed the antidote for the Toxin, which has a long-term effect of causing what you call Cancer. We Pellayens are quite adept at manipulating genes ourselves and can cure that Cancer. We can end this Plague and save those who are sick." The room erupted in cheers and congratulations.

She quieted them once more. "We have brought a fairly large supply of the Antidote with us. It is by no means enough to cure everyone, but we have prepared packets with all the information you will need to manufacture the Antidote for yourselves. Everyone will need to continue taking the Antidote until the poison has been removed from your planet, and yes, we know how to do that as well."

Gullaynianna was finished with her presentation. "I wish you all well. My team and I will remain here to help as much as possible, but for now, I must go. I leave you with Randy, who has information of a different nature that I am sure you will be happy to hear. Thank you."

With that, Gullaynianna left the room, leaving Randy to address the assembly. Randy explained the presence of the Cargo ships. He was pleased to tell them that the Pellayens had sent pallets of pill-form Antidote as well as 35 Pellayen ships and 982 engines. "There are also many tons of Pellayen wire and electronic components. The second Cargo ship is carrying thousands of tons of food, and there will be more coming until the Earth can start producing it for itself again.

Of the thirty-five ships, only seven have the new gate-opening engines, but I am sure you are pleased to get whatever the Pellayens were willing to give."

After Randy had finished relaying all his information and could finally go his way, he was tired to the bone. He hadn't slept in days, and his body was letting him know it was time to rest. He was ready for a good night's sleep.

Many Pellayens had come to Earth aboard the hospital ship to go to John's memorial service, which Randy was supposed to set up. Services like this would now be possible because of the Antidote, but they had to be careful. If people started going about without Bio-suits, the Aliens would see this and know their poison was no longer working. The aliens would certainly go to the next step and invade the Earth. Earth was in no way ready to defend itself against such technologically advanced beings. Their only hope was to keep the aliens thinking the poison was working, to keep them from attacking, and give Earth time to get prepared.

They went to great lengths to fool the aliens. Nothing about the cure was broadcast in the open where the aliens might hear. People were sent door to door to quietly administer the Antidote, and inform everyone what was at stake and why they must continue wearing the Bio-suits. So intent were they on fooling the aliens that they continued to fill the airways with fake stories of thousands of tragic deaths each day due to the disease.

Meanwhile, the thirty-five ships sent from Pellaya were being Armed. The Tataro was the first Armed with a large 105mm gun, sixteen rockets, and a Gatling gun. The Tataro had gone from being unprotected to being a flying fortress.

When all was ready, Major Teddy Benet and a limited number of gunners were to fly up to one of the alien ships and attempt contact with them. Every Government around the world hoped War could be avoided, and the reason was obvious. This was a War they could not win.

Bruce still sat in the hospital, unaware of what was happening outside. He had been told they were taking the ship from him, which was no surprise, and it even pleased him. The job had fallen to a younger, more experienced flyer. He had seen how the Alien ship could maneuver and didn't feel he was the right man for the job. Besides, he wasn't about to leave his family. His wife was almost gone, and his two children weren't doing much better. They hardly ever woke up.

He had tears in his eyes as he held his wife's hand. His entire family was about to leave him, and he was at his lowest. Suddenly, Gullaynianna rushed into the room and approached his wife without saying a word to him. He was surprised to see Gullaynianna back from Pellaya and more surprised that she wasn't wearing a bio suit. She injected something into the I.V. tube and turned to Bruce. Using broken English, she said, "She be OK. Antidote," she said, holding up the syringe. As soon as she had heard about his family, she had rushed to find them and inject them with the Antidote.

Bruce got to his feet, looked down at his wife, then back at Gullaynianna. "You found the cure?"

Gullaynianna smiled brightly. "She be ok. They all be ok."

Bruce stared at her, unwilling or unable to believe what she was saying. "You found the cure? They will live?"

Gullaynianna smiled again and pointed to herself. "No Bio-suit. No need. Your wife, kid, be okay. See better day, ah two."

Bruce moved around the bed with tears running down his cheeks and hugged Gullaynianna tightly. He was so relieved and overjoyed to hear that his family, perhaps minutes from death, would live. Still holding Gullaynianna, he reached down and took hold of his wife's hand. It was lifeless and made him wonder if Gullaynianna had come in time, but she assured him that the poison was already being neutralized. "Bruce, she live."

Bruce had sat there hour after hour, day after day, and hadn't known that the hospital ship had returned or that a cure had been found. Now, Gullaynianna was here telling him, not only would *his* family survive, but everyone who got the antidote was going to live. The Plague was over. The cure was 100% effective, but the poison had done some damage. Their bodies would have to heal, but they would heal.

Bruce couldn't hold back his relief and thankfulness. He sat down with a smile on his face while tears flooded down his cheeks. That's when he noticed Randy standing in the doorway, smiling in on them.

Randy nodded at him. "They are going to live, Bruce. Gullaynianna and her team have saved our bacon. But we aren't out of the woods yet. We still have to deal with these damned aliens that did this to us."

****

Major Teddy Benet loaded into the Pellayen ship with two gunners and headed out to find an alien ship. His mission was to attempt contact and learn what the Aliens' intentions were. Earth was giving a peaceful resolution every possible chance, but peace didn't seem likely.

He flew into space and spotted one of their ships right away. He headed toward it, reporting his movements to General Andrews. "I'm coming up behind them now. It's moving forward slowly. I can't see anything falling from the bottom of it, but I don't doubt they are dumping their poison on us. What do you want me to do?"

"They won't or can't answer the radio, so all we can do is get in front of them to get their attention. Be ready, Major. We all expect them to attack, but there doesn't seem to be any other way to communicate with them, and we have to know the truth once and for all."

"Rodger," Teddy said. "If I see that weapon coming out, I'm out of here."

Teddy moved in front of them and saw four Aliens looking back at him. He turned on the Energy drive to be ready to run for it, then raised a hand in greeting. The aliens looked at him curiously. A fifth Alien moved forward to look at him, and then it looked as if they all started laughing at him.

Then he saw the weapon coming out from under the chin of their ship. He pushed the controls forward and shot away from them. He saw yellow bolts of fire shoot off into space beside him. They had fired on him. The answer was clear. There would be no peace.

Far out in space, Teddy stopped and looked back. The Aliens weren't following him. They were right where they had been, dumping poison on planet Earth. These Aliens weren't the least bit concerned about his being there.

"General, as soon as they saw me, they fired on me. There's no way they want peace. They are clearly hostile, and they didn't seem the least bit concerned about my being there. Earth had better get prepared for War, and do it fast. The speed of my ship doesn't seem to threaten them at all. I can't believe they haven't already attacked. What do you want me to do?"

"Come back here. There's nothing we can do until we have more ships ready to go, and we don't want to provoke them into attacking until we are ready. We can't engage them with one ship. But at least we know for sure what their intentions are. Bring that ship home, Major."

CHAPTER TWELVE
RANDY'S UNTOLD STORY

The Aliens continued dumping their poison on Earth, while the people continued doing their best to fool the aliens into thinking their poison was working. Anytime anyone was outside, they were wearing Bio-suits, and the airways were alive with chatter of how terrible the Plague was, and the inability of the doctors to find the cure. Humanity was unified in a way never seen before because they all knew the stakes were high.

The Antidote was being manufactured and distributed as quickly as they could. People had stopped dying and were getting better. This was the calm before the storm, and a good time for people to honor their dead. It was a good time to have John's Memorial service.

The hospital ship landed to allow Pellayen friends to walk off the ship into a large tent erected to hide everyone from prying Alien eyes. John's friends had already gathered in the tent and watched the Pellayens filter out of the hospital ship to join them.

The first three Pellayens out of the ship were those most comfortable among the humans. Tellgus, Awntoon, and Fallgonan strolled down the ramp with confidence, eager to join their new human friends.

Randy sat watching the Pellayens exit the ship. Some he knew and some he didn't. He was happy to see Awth and Nellaynan walk out and into the crowd. Awth looked ok, but Nellaynan looked uneasy, and that was understandable. She probably wasn't feeling her best and might fear the attention she would get, especially if they were to learn the secret she and Randy knew.

Suddenly, the crowd went quiet. Randy looked up to see Angry Man and his wife, Gullaynianna, walking out of the ship. The Pellayen monster towered over everyone, and the ever-present look on his face had everyone on edge. Randy knew this would happen. To this day, he still had a twinge of fear when he looked at Bartolos.

Bartolos and Gullaynianna sat down with him and his family. Awth, Tellgus, and Nellaynan were also sitting with his little group. When they started talking Pellayen to each other, this drew the attention of the humans. Few Humans had learned Pellayen while many Pellayens had learned English. The Pellayens were pleased to talk with John's human friends in English.

Groups of humans and Pellayens formed and dissolved as people mingled. Many stories were told of John's antics, and many of those tales caused laughter to erupt. John could be funny, but he would be the first to admit he could also be stupid.

It was easy to understand why Randy's little group was growing. Bartolos was sitting at his table. People were curious about him. No one had ever seen anything like him. His size was something to admire, and the fierce look on his face caught everyone's attention. Bartolos's presence pulled them in like flies to molasses. They wanted to know this mountain of a Pellayen.

Randy told a few stories of his adventures on Pellaya. Bartolos chimed in with his deep gravelly voice, to tell the story of when John and Randy had climbed out of the Lucky Lady. "John climbed down the ladder and stood with his back to me," he said.

"It was obvious to me he was catching his breath. I could see he was having difficulty. Then Randy came down the ladder and turned to face me right away. He turned around and said, 'Hello. I come in peace.' Then I saw his eyes cross, and he fell to the floor." Laughter erupted, which drew in more people to the group.

Tellgus told the story John had relayed to him about Randy's Mother-in-law coming to save him. Randy's mother-in-law was sitting at the table and couldn't help but laugh, then added, "If I had known he was up there, I would have left him there!"

Laughing, Randy blurted out, "Man, I'm really beginning to wish I hadn't told John about your involvement in this, Mama 2," he said. He looked at his Mother-in-Law and smiled. He knew how lucky he was that all his family had survived the plague. Allen and his family hadn't been so lucky. All of them had passed on before the antidote came.

When Randy was asked what happened when he went back to Pellaya to ask for help. He shrugged and told a very short version of what had happened. Nellaynan, Bartolos, Awth, Gullaynianna, and Tellgus all looked at Randy, knowing what he had left out and why he chose to do so. Some of it was very personal for him.

He had told them the hospital ship had gone through the Pellayen gate and arrived in Tallda Shayts right side up. He told them about the new engine design clearing the fog away so they could see, and that Captain Laysee had suggested renaming the Air Carrier Center. He finished by telling them that Awth already knew what had happened to John and that Earth needed help before Randy got to him.

The whole story was that they landed at the Air Carrier Center, where Captain Laysee told Randy, "John called this the 'Niglaie Spaceport'. I think I will suggest that we rename it the John Baines Air Carrier Center in his honor."

"I like the idea," Randy said. "I think Nellaynan will like …" Randy started to say, but couldn't finish his statement. He had just reminded himself that he was here, partly, to tell everyone of John's death. He wasn't looking forward to telling any of them, particularly Nellaynan.

He decided to go talk to Awth first and ask Awth to talk to the council about help from Pellaya. That would get the ball rolling on this important issue, then he could spend as much time as he needed with Nellaynan.

Randy made his way off the ship and walked up to Awth's office. He found Awth leaning against a wall with a tear in his eye. Randy approached him, wondering why, but soon realized Awth was listening to the Mental Transmissions informing him of John's death. Awth gripped Randy's shoulders. "I am so sorry to hear about John. It is bitter news."

Awth had been listening to that transmission, which meant everyone was hearing it and knew about John. "Oh no! Nellaynan!" Randy said. "Oh, that poor woman!"

"Randy, don't worry. It is our way," Awth said. "In time, she will be ok. We will help her."

"But Awth, it is such a horrible way to learn of your husband's death!"

"Is there a better way?" Awth asked. "Do you think there is a way to tell someone this kind of news that would make the pain any less?"

Randy wanted to argue the point, but found it hard to do so. "No, I don't suppose there is."

Awth nodded in certainty. "It is our way, and we will lessen her pain. Haven't the Transmissions also lessened your discomfort? You don't have to be the one to break the news to her. Hasn't that eased your mind?"

Randy hated admitting that it did. "But what about Nellaynan? Who was there to comfort her when she heard the news?"

Awth shook his head. "In the instant she learned of his death, so did everyone around her. Anyone around her will join with her. It is our way. You don't know what I mean when I say Join, and don't let it concern you. I believe we can teach you so you can understand, but at a later time. Just know Nellaynan is well cared for."

Randy stared at the floor, thinking of Mental Ability, and remembered a phrase he had heard Pellayens say many times. *Nothing hidden, no lies, no secrets.* In many cases, he could see how this would be a good thing, but in this case, it seemed harsh. He felt bad for Nellaynan finding out this way.

Then he thought about what Awth had just said. *We can teach you so you can understand.* For a moment, he questioned what Awth had meant by that.

Randy suddenly felt Awth take him by the elbow. "Come, the council has already gathered to talk about what we can do to help you. We need to go there." It surprised Randy how quickly things were happening. He realized later it shouldn't have. This was Pellaya, and the thought transmissions had no doubt informed everyone of John's death and Earth's need for help. No doubt everyone had known before the ship had landed. He was sure all Pellaya knew Earth was facing a war they were unprepared for. *'Nothing hidden, no secrets, no lies'.*

As Randy and Awth entered the council chamber, they heard the council elder say, "It is agreed. We will supply what ships and engines we can spare to Earth. The vote was unanimous."

Randy was happy to hear this, but was also a little puzzled. Last he knew, Awth was a member of this body, and the Elder had said the vote was unanimous. Awth hadn't voted. "Awth, are you still a member here?"

"Yes, I am."

"But you didn't vote?"

"Yes, I did."

"When? I have been with you right from the … never mind." Randy said, realizing he had already forgotten how things happened on Pellaya.

Awth smiled and tapped the side of his head. "I radioed it in."

Randy laughed. Awth tapping his head and saying, 'I radioed it in,' was quite humorous.

Awth was grinning as he looked up at Randy. "Why don't you go visit Nellaynan. I don't think you are needed here after all, and it will take us some time to formalize a way forward. Nellaynan is no doubt at her home. You know where that is, don't you?"

"Yes, of course I do, and thank you, Awth, for everything."

Randy left Awth and went straight to Nellaynan. She was alone and crying when she greeted him. She hugged him and sat down on the sofa. Randy stood looking at her, wondering what he should say and do. She was in tears, wringing her hands, and generally not doing well. She was hurting, the kind of pain that made physical pain go unnoticed.

Randy sat down beside her and pulled her close. "Nellaynan, I can't express how sorry I am for you," he said. Nellaynan turned her body toward his. He hugged her tighter. "I'm so sorry." He said, and sat rocking her back and forth, letting her cry.

Nellaynan spoke very softly. "Why did it have to happen? Why did he have to die? Why?"

Randy knew exactly how she felt. He was asking the same question. He didn't say anything, but sat quietly rocking her. There was nothing he could say to ease her pain. Her next words shocked him. "Randy, I'm carrying his child!"

Randy stiffened. "What! That's good news, isn't it?" he asked, uncertain of how it was affecting her.

Nellaynan only nodded that it was, and Randy knew it increased the hurt she felt for losing the father of her child. "Did John know?" he asked.

Nellaynan cried a little harder and said no, she had intended to tell him when he came home. "Now I will never get the chance," she said, turning her face into Randy's shoulder as her sobs deepened. Randy could only let her cry and hold her tighter.

Soon after, Randy heard someone at the door, and Bartolos walked into the room. Nellaynan sprang at him with the agility of a cat and wrapped her arms around him. "Help me, please!" she pleaded.

Bartolos scooped her up into his arms like a father cradling his child. Nellaynan all but disappeared under his massive arms. Randy sat feeling a little hurt at being abandoned so quickly, but he understood, or thought he did.

For Randy, it was a bit much to see this grown woman being held like a child. At the same time, he was deeply touched by what he was seeing. There was a closeness between Nellaynan and Bartolos that he had never seen before. He had to remind himself that this was Pellaya, and things happened differently here. As if to drive that point home, Bartolos began to cry hard enough that it embarrassed Randy to see it.

Bartolos managed to say between sobs, "Others are coming. They will come soon."

Randy felt awkward and out of place watching this giant Pellayen carry on this way. This was something men on Earth didn't like others to see them do. He didn't like seeing Bartolos do it, and was afraid he too was about to break into tears. He wanted to run from the house so no one would see him crying. Seeing these two crying had him on the edge of balling his head off.

Losing John was a tremendous loss. They had grown up together and were more like brothers than friends. He loved John, and losing him was a deep wound. As he watched Nellaynan and Bartolos, he thought how much John was loved by so many others, both human and Pellayens.

Bartolos looked at him, "Yes, he was."

Randy stiffened and stared back at Bartolos. How could Bartolos have heard him? Maybe Bartolos was responding to something Nellaynan said, but why was Bartolos looking at him when he said it?

Bartolos spoke again. "It appears your Mental Ability is active after all."

"Did you hear my thoughts?" Randy asked.

"Yes. You have very strong emotions about John, and I heard them. What came through to me was very weak, but I heard it."

Randy couldn't believe Bartolos had heard his thoughts, and now Nellaynan was reaching out from under Bartolos's arms, calling to him. "Come, Randy. Join with us."

This bothered him. It was one thing to hold Nellaynan. It was something else to join a group hug with a blubbering Bartolos. Randy found himself stepping back away from them, unwilling to give in to this Love fest. It was too weird for him, and he didn't want to be part of it. It made him a little sick to his stomach just to see it.

Bartolos looked at him again. "There is no shame in this, Human."

Randy didn't understand what that meant. He was being asked to join in something he didn't understand and something that went against his human nature. He wanted to help Nellaynan, but not like this. Bartolos had just told him he had Mental Ability, but he wasn't aware of it and didn't know how it would help in this situation.

Randy jumped as a man brushed passed him and joined the grieving with Bartolos and Nellaynan. He never heard the man enter and hardly noticed him as he walked passed. He watched the new arrival join with them and begin to cry, and again he felt embarrassed by what he was seeing.

Randy stepped back as another woman brushed passed him to join the Group Hug. She didn't join the group right away, but stood away from them with her head lowered. Then, suddenly hurried toward them as if being pulled in by some unseen force. It was the same with the man who had joined them. *There's something very strange going on here,* Randy thought.

Seeing these people clinging to each other and crying seemed very odd and made him uncomfortable. Lovey-Dovey Love fests like this were frowned on by most men from Earth, and Randy was one of them. It embarrassed him and he started to turn to walk away, but Bartolos cocked his head to one side and repeated, "There is no shame in this, Human."

Then Nellaynan called to him. "Help me, Randy, and let us help you."

Randy was starting to believe those who had joined were taking some of Nellaynans' pain onto themselves. If that were true, he would have liked to be part of it and help ease Nellaynans' sorrows, but he was struggling with his social conditioning from Earth that deemed this sort of thing weird, sick, and perhaps gay, and he didn't want any part of that.

He took a few steps back, then turned and walked out the door. He just couldn't let himself join in that weirdness. Yet even as he walked away, he felt he was betraying his best friend's wife. Nellaynan was a woman he cared for very much. How could he walk away from her after she asked him to help?

He was growing angry with himself. He had not only betrayed Nellaynan but himself as well. What difference did it make if he had Mental Ability or not? He wanted to be there for Nellaynan. Why couldn't he have said to hell with his disquieting emotions and at least stayed there to lend his support? Bartolos's words came back to him. *There is no shame in this Human.* "No!" Randy growled. "Not on Pellaya, maybe. On Pellaya, it's nothing hidden, no secrets, no lies. On Earth, it's all secret, all hidden and …all lies."

He kept walking away, disgusted with himself for doing so. Even now, he wanted to run back and join them, but he kept on walking, betraying himself and those he loved.

He walked to the room he and John had stayed in. The room had been cleaned and reorganized, but everything was still there. The room seemed empty without John there. Feeling the loss of John and his displeasure with himself for leaving Nellaynan, Randy couldn't stop himself. He burst into tears.

After a few minutes, he regained control of himself. He stood up and put his hand on the lounge chair John used to sit in. "Man, I miss you, buddy. I could use you around here right now. Things don't seem right at all without you. I'm sorry, but I think I hurt your wife and insulted your friend Bartolos. I feel like I'm making a mess of things. I have betrayed all of them, and now myself. I feel so small and ashamed. Why couldn't I join them? It doesn't matter if I have Mental Ability. I wanted to join them. Why didn't I?

Randy sighed and rocked his head around. "I know you found something here, buddy. I know it made you very happy. I fear I may have just run from it. I don't know. God, I wish I could talk to you." Randy lowered his head and stared at the floor.

He stood for a moment longer, then wiped his eyes, turned away from the chair, and found Gullaynianna standing by the door. Randy hadn't heard her come in and was sure she had heard every word he said. He was now quite embarrassed.

"I am sorry, Randy. I didn't mean to intrude. I didn't want to interrupt your prayer."

"Prayer? I wasn't praying. I just felt the need to talk to… well, I needed to talk to John, I guess."

Gullaynianna nodded, "I understand. I want to talk to him, too."

Randy found it hard to look at her after his weak moment.

Gullaynianna nodded and spoke. "Awth is looking for you. He wanted me to ask you to go with him to meet the Chenowa."

"The Chenowa? Who or what are the Chenowa?" Randy asked.

"I'm sorry. I forget that you don't know about the Alien threat that has come to Pellaya, and I forget that you can't hear the thought transmissions," Gullaynianna said. "The Chenowa are what you call the little gray men. They came here several months ago and have been abducting our people and taking them aboard their ships."

Randy moved closer to her. "Awth told me something about that. I didn't know they were called Chenowa. They were doing that on Earth, but we never had proof."

"Well, we know it's happening here, and we want it stopped. They take our people against their will and won't tell us why.

They won't talk to us. Awth wants to fly up to meet them and see if he can get them talking."

"And Awths wants *me*? Why me?" Randy asked.

"Because you and John have known about them longer than us. You may know something that will help us get through to them."

"Hmm, I doubt that very much, but if Awth wants me there, I will go with him. Where is he now?"

"Awth is on his ship, waiting on the field near the Cargo ship."

"I'll go right away," Randy said and started to leave the room, but Gullaynianna touched his arm as he passed her.

"Randy, you have nothing to be embarrassed or ashamed of. You have done nothing wrong. Bartolos and Nellaynan love you just as much as before. You shouldn't worry about any of it," she said.

Randy only nodded and left.

He found Awth and Tellgus waiting for him. They were still waiting for Bartolos. Randy wasn't sure why he was there, but it was easy to understand why Bartolos was coming. According to Awth, Bartolos was perhaps the most important one to have on the ship.

When Bartolos arrived, Tellgus flew the ship into space. As they flew, Awth told Randy that a Chenowa ship had been spotted a few minutes ago. This was what he had been waiting for. The Chenowa weren't responding to radio or their mental hails, so the only way to get their attention was to fly up and get in their way.

Randy shook his head. The last time this was tried, John died. "Let's hope it works out better this time," Randy said.

"These aren't the same aliens," Awth said. "These are the ones you call the grays. I have never heard anyone say they were hostile, and they haven't taken any hostile action toward us. They are simply taking our people, and we want it to stop, or at least get them to tell us why they are doing it. We did make contact with them some time ago, but all they do is tell us to go away. Since then, they will not respond at all. Any ship we send up to meet them comes back without making contact. The Chenowa use their mental strength to make the pilot turn back. We are hoping Bartolos's mind is strong enough to help us fight against their will."

Randy nodded. He had heard it many times, 'Bartolos has the strongest mind and knows more about using it than anyone else', so it made sense to have him aboard. Randy still didn't understand why he was there. He brought nothing to the party.

Tellgus spotted the Chenowa ship and flew in front of it. They could see one Chenowa inside looking back at them. Awth began probing his mind, but just as before, the Chenowa ignored him and closed his mind up tight so Awth could not get in. Then the Chenowa moved his ship away. Tellgus followed him. The Chenowa moved away faster this time, and again Tellgus followed and planted his ship right in front of him.

Finally, the Chenowa opened his mind and allowed Awth to speak. "Can't we sit down and talk? Why do you do this to us?" he asked.

The answer was the same as it had been before. "We need no meeting, and we do this because we need to," the Chenowa said.

"Why do you need to? Why can't we talk this over? Let us live in peace."

"We are at peace. We mean you no harm," the Chenowa said.

Awth suddenly felt thoughts being pushed into his head. "Everything is ok. You have no reason for concern. Go back home. We are at peace. There is no need for a meeting."

Tellgus suddenly turned the ship back toward Pellaya.

"Tellgus what are you doing. Tellgus!" Bartolos said.

Awth began to mumble. "We are at peace. Everything is ok. We can go home now."

Bartolos got out of his seat and physically removed Tellgus from the pilot seat. "Randy! Take the ship!" he ordered.

Randy took the pilot's seat. "Where do you want to go?"

"Back up to the Chenowa ship. We are not done here, and we are NOT at peace!" Bartolos said in a voice that made Randy tremble. Angry Man was angry!

It was clear even to Randy that the Chenowa had taken control of Tellgus and Awth's minds and now feared his own vulnerability. He had no defense against this Chenowa and was sure the Chenowa would easily take control of him. It didn't take long, and he heard the alien speaking in his head. "Take your ship back home. There is no problem here. We are at peace". Randy could feel the Chenowa making him believe it was all true and that he needed to go back down to the planet.

Suddenly, the Chenowa's influence on his mind was gone. He looked at Bartolos and saw him sitting with his eyes closed, leaning forward, and gripping the armrest of his seat. His concentration was intense. Randy watched his grip tighten on the armrests of his seat, and Bartolos's jaw tightened. Suddenly, both armrests cracked under Bartolos's great strength. Bartolos began to groan. Then he was growling, and Randy could tell he was in a mental battle with the Chenowa. From the way it looked, Bartolos was losing.

Suddenly, Bartolos opened his eyes and screamed in rage. "Then take it ALL!!!!"

****

Randy opened his eyes and found himself sitting in one of the two back seats of the cockpit. He had been removed from the pilot seat. Awth and Tellgus were standing over him, looking concerned. Awth leaned in closer. "Randy, are you okay?"

"What happened?" Randy asked.

"You passed out. We all passed out," Awth said. "Well, all but Bartolos."

"You ok?" Tellgus asked.

Randy sat up in his seat. "Yeah, I think so. What happened?"

"We aren't sure. Awth and I are fine, but we don't know about Bartolos. He's just sitting there staring out the windshield."

Randy looked out the windshield and saw the Chenowa ship still facing them. "What about the Chenowa?"

Awth turned his head and looked at the ship. "He's just sitting there. I'm not sensing anything from him anymore. He's not blocking me, but I can't find his mind. I think Bartolos did something to him."

Randy looked at Bartolos in the seat ahead of him and to the right. He couldn't see Bartolos's face, but he could see that he still sat leaning forward, gripping his armrests. He looked stiff as a board. "What's wrong with him?"

"I don't know," Awth said. "I have never seen this before. I can only hope he will be ok." Awth turned to Tellgus. "Tellgus, take us home. There is nothing more we can do here."

Tellgus took the ship back to the Air Carrier Center and landed. Randy stood up and walked in front of Bartolos. He was surprised to see the look of shock and surprise on Bartolos's face. His eyes and mouth were wide open, and his expression fixed.

Randy spoke to him and attempted to shake him, but that was like trying to shake a large boulder.

Randy straightened up and looked at Awth. "Have we lost our big man? What do you think happened to him?"

Awth shrugged. "I don't know what happened. Time will tell if we have lost him or not. I only know his mental outburst was strong enough to cause us all to black out, and I think it did something to the Chenowa. Bartolos may have hurt himself in the process. We have to hope he comes back to us and can tell us what happened. We need to get him to our hospital, maybe they can do something for him."

"Not… necess…sasss…sssary," Bartolos mumbled.

Surprised, everyone moved in front of him, hoping he was back with them, but he still looked much the same. Bartolos was still somewhere else.

Bartolos spoke very slowly. "I … have … all … Toc's … mind," Bartolos said.

"Toc? Is he the Chenowa we spoke to?" Awth asked.

Bartolos nodded almost imperceptibly and closed his eyes. Awth considered what Bartolos had said. *I have all Toc's mind.* Something had happened between Toc and Bartolos, that was obvious, but what? How did Bartolos get all Toc's mind? What did he mean by that?

"I … need… time. Be… O…K," Bartolos said, and leaned back in his seat.

Awth looked a little confused. "Well, at least he's moving and talking to us, but I don't know what he is dealing with. I don't know how to help him."

"What do we do now?" Tellgus asked. "We'll need more help if we are going to take him to the hospital."

"No… I …stay," Bartolos said.

"Tellgus, Bartolos wants to stay here, and I tend to trust his decision," Awth said. "You and I should go assemble the council and let them know what has happened. Randy, will you stay with Bartolos?"

"Of course," Randy said. "I will stay and let you know if something changes or things get worse."

Randy sat close to Bartolos, watching him for any sign of his coming back to them. An Hour passed. "Bartolos, what's happening?" Randy asked. "What can I do for you?"

Bartolos only shook his head. He wanted nothing.

It was growing dark outside when Bartolos finally spoke. "Randy, help me get home."

"Help you. How can I help you? You are way too heavy for me to carry. I'll get some help."

"No. I can …walk. Need you…ti …to guide me," Bartolos said and slowly stood up.

"Bartolos, shouldn't you go to the hospital. You need help…"

"No, ... getting…better…Mind is…overflowing. Be ok. Home…please," Bartolos said.

Randy took the giant's arm and started to lead him home. Randy was surprised by the way Bartolos was moving. "Have you gone blind?"

"No. Mind…over…flowing," Bartolos said.

Randy thought he understood. There was nothing wrong with his eyes; Bartolos was mind blind. He couldn't see through the clutter in his head.

Randy led him home and took him to a large, comfortable-looking chair. Bartolos asked Randy to get Gullaynianna. As he opened the door to leave, Bartolos called out to him. "Randy don't worry. I am feeling better. I can ex….splain soon. I w…will be ok." Randy didn't say anything, just hurried off to find Gullaynianna.

He found Gullaynianna already hurrying home. Bartolos was still sitting in the chair, staring at the floor, when they entered the room. He looked up at them and nodded. "I will be alright now. Thank you for helping me, Randy," he said without a skip or stutter. He was sounding more like himself again.

After a few hours, Bartolos assured Randy that he was okay and there was no need for him to stay. It took a while longer, but Randy finally felt it was okay to leave, so he headed back to his room. He stopped by the Cargo ships to see how the loading was going and was pleased to find they had already loaded a good number of engines. He counted twenty-six engines and three Ships so far. This would make the people of Earth very happy.

Benta, the Pellayen in charge of loading the ships, came to him eager to tell him that they were still looking for more ships and engines to give to the humans. "We will continue loading the ships through the night. We hope to finish loading sometime tomorrow."

Randy couldn't help but yawn as he thanked Benta. He had gone without sleep for several days and was very tired. He was happy to be going home and planned to sleep just as long as he wanted. He was getting ready to get into bed when a Pellayen came to the door. She told him Bartolos was back on his feet and was asking for Randy to return. "We are gathering to hear him tell what happened when he talked to the Chenowa."

Randy thanked her, redressed, and headed to Bartolos's.

As soon as he saw Nellaynan, he felt guilty. He couldn't help but feel he had let her down. It was hard to look her in the eye. After all, he had run from her after she had asked him for help. He didn't think he could forgive himself for that. How could she forgive him?

So many people were holding on to her, caring for her. Whatever was happening in this 'Joining' had to be working because she seemed so much calmer. He even heard her laugh at one point.

Then Bartolos was standing in front of him, and he felt his guilt again. He had betrayed him, too. But he saw nothing from

Bartolos that indicated any bad feelings or disappointment. Bartolos put a hand on Randy's back and gently pushed him forward. "Thank you for coming. I want to tell you what happened up there, why I was the way I was," he said. Then he spoke louder to everyone there. "I think everyone is here, so let me start from the beginning."

Bartolos seemed to be his old self again, except that occasionally he would slur a word or two. "I saw that the Chenowa was influencing Tellgus and Awth. Tellgus was taking us back to Pellaya, and you, Awth, were convinced that all was well, that we were at peace. It angered me, and I decided I would try to deal with them myself. I removed Tellgus from the Pilot seat and asked Randy to pilot the ship so I could try to talk to them. When I found his mind, Toc became aggressive and started fighting with me. I found myself in a mental battle with someone much stronger than I. I could feel his anger and contempt. I realized I didn't stand a chance against him, and I guess I slipped into rage when Toc started laughing at me. He was laughing because he found me so weak. He was just toying with me.

What happened was that Toc tried to disarm me by taking my mind from me. He was very strong, and I was losing my mind to him. He would have succeeded, but he laughed at me, and that made me angrier than I think I have ever been. I was so angry I didn't care, and thought if he wanted my mind, I would give it all to him. Not only did I help him take my mind; I shoved it at him with all my strength. That surprised him, and he started pushing everything back at me, at the very moment I changed my mind and started pulling everything back with all the strength I could summon. Do you understand? In an instant, we switch positions. Now I was pulling my mind back, and he was pushing it back to me. It happened so quickly and with such force that his mind came into me. In an instant, my head was overflowing with everything Toc had in his head. It was too much for me to handle. I had a very hard time dealing with all that had been pushed into my head. I didn't think I was going to survive it. Then I saw a way to deal with it and slowly began absorbing what I had gotten from him. I had to sort through his thoughts and find places for them. It was hard at first. I was trying to put things in the wrong place, and that made things worse. Eventually, I understood what I had to do, and that is when I started to clear my mind. I'm still sorting things out, but it is much easier now. Some of what I received from Toc, I don't yet understand, but I can file it away to study later."

Bartolos put a hand on Randy's shoulder. "That's why I needed you to guide me to my house. My eyes were seeing, but my mind couldn't process it. I couldn't even remember how to get home. I was mentally blinded by all I had gotten from Toc. I can now function on my own.

"Ah ha. That is what I thought was going on," Randy said. "I could see it in the way you were acting."

"When it first happened, I was in trouble. There was no way I could process so much information. My head was hurting. Then I found I could section off part of my brain and take the information in smaller doses. If I hadn't learned that, I think I would be a vegetable. I'm still processing a lot of that information. As I do, I am learning about Toc and the Chenowa."

Awth leaned in closer. "I am glad it happened that way, and that you are here, able to talk to us. So, what have you learned . about the Chenowa? Have you learned anything that can help us deal with them?"

"I know why they are here, and when they discovered us," Bartolos said. "They discovered us long ago when they flew out of Tallda Shayts that first time. They realized right away that we Pellayens were a better match for what they needed. That is why they left Earth and came to Pellaya. They need genetic material and certain chemicals, and enzymes from us in order to save their species. They were getting it from the Humans, now it's us."

"Do you mean they are no longer interested in Earth?" Randy asked.

"Yes. They have abandoned Earth and come here." Bartolos shook his head. "The Chenowa are desperate. Their race is dying a very slow death. They have to constantly keep restoring their genetic pool to restore the health of the newborn and adults as well. They are losing the battle, and that is why they are so desperate and unwilling even to talk to us. They don't have time to waste, but I see their biggest problem is that they are a very proud people. They won't talk to us because of their pride and arrogance."

Bartolos bowed his head slightly. "Toc didn't like what he had to do, but it was necessary. He felt he had to ignore his empathy toward us, or he wouldn't get the job done. They don't like what they are doing, and feel sorry for the way they are handling things, but it is their only course of action."

"Still, what they are doing is wrong," Randy said.

"And they agree, but their young are being born with more and more incapacitating mutations. Each new generation is increasingly unable to care for itself, and the older generations are less and less capable of caring for them. They know their race is dying and have become desperate to save themselves."

"Hmm," Randy grunted. "If their so caring about what they're doing to us, why couldn't they just ask us for help? That seems like a more caring approach than stealing people."

"They have asked for help from other races and have been turned down. Even we Pellayen's are resisting them right now. Of course, we didn't understand their situation, but now that we know, I'm sure we will help them if we can. That means we have to get them to talk to us."

"Yeah, I can understand that, but I still don't like what they are doing or what they were doing to my people on Earth," Randy said.

"Randy, I have some other information that probably won't improve your view of the Chenowa," Bartolos said. "I know the name of the aliens around your planet, and why they are there. They are called the Itchaian's, and they came to your planet after the Chenowa left. They wouldn't approach Earth as long as the Chenowa were there, but once they left, the Itchaian were free to move in. Toc knew of the Itchaian and sensed they were hostile toward Earth. Toc also sensed growing fear in the Itchaians. He didn't know why."

"Okay, but what do they want? Why are they there?" Randy asked.

"I can't answer that because Toc didn't know. He knew they were after something, but didn't know what."

Bartolos answered all the questions he could until everyone was satisfied, then everyone turned their attention to Nellaynan. She was another reason many of them had come. They wanted to help ease Nellaynan's pain. Bartolos once again cradled her in his arms like a child. The others gathered around, placing their hands on Bartolos and Nellaynan. Soon, it was one big group love fest.

Randy stood alone, looking at them and feeling out of place. He hadn't come for this and didn't understand what they were doing. It did seem that whatever they were doing was helping Nellaynan, and that made him want to join with them, but all that hugging and crying was a real turn-off for him. He backed away toward the door and turned to leave.

"Randy, wait," Awth called after him. Awth left the group and walked up to him. "You were knocked unconscious when Bartolos battled the Chenowa, and Bartolos has told me he heard your feelings toward John. That tells us you have Mental Ability. You are unaware of it and haven't used it, so it is very weak, but with our help, I think you could join us in the grieving. Are you at all interested in trying?"

"Yes. I am Awth, but it's all the hugging, kissing, and crying that has me heading for the door. On Earth, something like this is frowned on. It makes me feel embarrassed."

Awth grinned. "No one is kissing, and they aren't hugging. They are drawn to each other in a way that looks like they are hugging. Randy, you don't understand what's happening here. Look at Bartolos and how he holds Nellaynan like a child. His body has the strength to do that. The others can only cling to her, but they are not hugging or kissing.

Randy, you won't understand unless you join with us. That's the only way you will truly understand. Come, take Nellaynan's hand. Do just that much. If you still feel the same after that, you are free to go, but I would guess you won't want to."

"Awth, I admit I am intrigued, and I would most definitely like to help Nellaynan. I care a great deal for her. She is…was my best friend's wife. Of course, I would like to help her. But how can I? I haven't a clue as to how to do it."

Awth raised his arm toward all the Pellayens in the room. "We can all help you. Trust me. Come, take Nellaynan's hand."

Randy gave in and stepped forward to take Nellaynan's hand. "Now close your eyes and seek Nellaynans mind," Awth coached. "Just do as I say and try to empty your mind and open it to Nellaynan. Think of nothing but Nellaynan and her pain. We are helping you."

Randy felt stupid doing it, but tried to focus his mental energy on Nellaynan. *This is ridiculous*, he thought.

"No," Awth said. "Think only of Nellaynan."

Randy couldn't help but be surprised that Awth had heard his thoughts. Something was happening. He focused again on Nellaynan and sawt to comfort her. He could feel himself becoming free as if he were growing weightless. Awth's voice was growing more and more distant. Then, in his mind, he saw a rock with water pouring on it. The water poured down and began to erode the rock. Somehow, he knew *he* was the rock, and the water pouring on it was the help he was getting from the others. The rock washed away, and suddenly he was standing in a different reality. Awth, Nellaynan, and all the Pellayens looked different. It was as if he were seeing their souls. Nellaynan's soul was crying out, and he felt her sorrow. All of them were crying out in sadness for John's passing, and happy to be sharing their grief. There was joy and sadness.

Randy could feel he was being helped. He was urged to reach out with his mind to Nellaynan. He saw her smile and knew she was opening herself up to him. Suddenly, he was filled with her pain and also her tremendous joy that so many others had come to help her. He felt it all!

Then he felt his own sadness being pulled from him, being replaced with love and understanding. These people cared, and cared with all their heart. It was amazing!

"Ahh! God!" Randy said, grabbing his head. He had just been yanked back to the Physical world with a splitting headache. "That didn't take long," he said, rubbing his temples. He was surprised to find himself with his arms around the people nearest him. Somehow, he had become part of the group hug without knowing it. His arms had been wrapped tightly around two Pellayens.

He stepped back, still rubbing his head. It was the worst headache he had ever had. It felt like an ax was splitting his head open. Through the pain, he looked at the group. None of them were crying anymore. They all seemed very happy. Even Nellaynan was smiling and happy, almost as if she had forgotten all about John. He knew she hadn't and was still hurting, but she was being helped. A moment ago, he had been one of the ones helping her, and that made him feel good. It had only been for a short time, but he had been in there helping.

He stepped back away from them, holding his head. The group hug that he had found so distasteful was now all he wanted to do. Awth was right. He didn't want to leave. He wished his head could take the strain, so he could stay in there with them.

What he had just experienced felt like the truest expression of Love he had ever known. It was pure and complete! Bartolos's words echoed in his head. "There is no shame in this human."

Randy suddenly understood that John had gone through something like this with no one to explain what was happening to him. Without Awth coaching him, he wouldn't have known what was happening, and it would have been very confusing. Add in the splitting headache, and there was great reason to be concerned. He felt sorry for John and what he had gone through all alone. At the same time, he was glad John had had the chance to understand his own Mental Ability before the end came. Now it was Randy who had the headache, but he understood what was happening. He had had help to deal with it. It was his first taste of the Pellayen way, and he liked it!

A big smile crossed his face as he thought about what had happened during the joining. Nellaynan had had a giant smile on her face when she had taken his hand. He had felt his love for her and her love for him. He felt Bartolos's love for him and even his love for Bartolos. "There is no shame in this, Human," Randy said aloud.

Randy suddenly realized that he had, at some point, been crying. Like all the others, their bodies were crying, while in that mental world, their spirit bodies were joyous. He didn't fully understand all of this, and it didn't matter. He understood that there was a difference between the physical body and the spiritual body. It seemed one was destined to live in sorrow while the other lived in joy. That part of it made sense to him.

Randy stood there holding his head with a big smile on his face. The pain was becoming less, and he was happy about that. He looked up to find Bartolos standing in front of him. He too had a smile on his face, though to anyone who didn't know him, he was growling. Randy nodded his head and stated, "There is no shame in this…Bartolos."

"Not one bit," Bartolos said, with a laugh. "It is a thing to be celebrated, not cursed."

Randy reached out and touched Bartolos's arm. "I felt you helping me. You destroyed the rock, didn't you?"

Bartolos nodded. "I helped, but it was you who let the rock break apart and allowed yourself to join with us. That was you letting go of your fear and letting me and the others guide you into the Joining. You do have mental ability. I am sure all humans have it, but you never use it."

"I never have," Randy said, holding his head. "Will I be able to join on my own now?"

"No. This was your first time, and you had a lot of help. We will help you again if you wish to return to the joining, but I warn you not to go crazy doing it. It's all new to you, and you could hurt yourself. Take it easy. We learn about our Mental Ability throughout our lives. You won't learn it overnight."

Randy made a big show of holding his head. "I completely understand that. My head is still throbbing. But I do want to return." Bartolos nodded and told him, "One or two more times, but for short periods. The people in the grieving process will know you are returning and help you, but I need to stress the point that you take it easy. Don't hurt yourself."

The Grieving went on for quite a while longer. With Bartolos's help, Randy returned to the joining twice more, but only for short periods. His head wouldn't allow him to go longer. He had a constant headache that got worse when he returned to the grieving, but it was such an incredible experience he endured the pain to be able to join with Nellaynan and the others again.

After the last joining, he felt so tired and wobbly that he knew it was time to quit. He sat looking at the group, knowing they had lessened his pain and sorrow over the loss of John. He felt lucky to be here and experience this.

As he sat nursing his pained head, he thought of John and how he had gone through some of the same things, and his love and admiration of John grew all the more. It hurt to know they would never be able to share these experiences. John was gone, but he was happy to have known him at all.

Randy smiled as he looked at the group hug. He was grateful that he and John had been pulled to Pellaya so long ago. These were great people, and he cared for them more and more all the time. The joining had let him see who these people really were. Bartolos, the angry beast on the outside, was full of love and compassion on the inside. Randy felt privileged to have seen his soul and knew why John had befriended him.

Randy was tired and in pain, but didn't want to leave. He sat watching the group, feeling blessed to be part of it. Some of their physical bodies were still crying, and some weren't. But they still clung to each other, and Randy wished he could be in there with them, but his newfound mental muscle had had enough. He had to quit, and Bartolos had said so the last time he left the grieving. So he sat watching them, feeling enlightened. *"There is so much more to life beyond the physical."*

After a while, Gullaynianna and Bartolos broke from the joining and walked over to him. They were leaving, but told him he was welcome to stay as long as he liked. "No," he said, standing up. "I think I will leave with you. It's already morning and I am so tired. I need to get some sleep."

He started to leave with them but found himself in Nellaynan's arms. She hugged the stuffing out of him. It was an embrace Randy would not soon forget. He had joined with her, and the bond between them had been greatly enriched. He felt the same toward Gullaynianna, Bartolos, and all the others who were involved in the joining. He had a new and special bond with every one of them and knew John had had the same blessing.

He felt good when he left. He still had a headache, but he was happy as he walked back to the Air Carrier Center. On the way, he was met by the Pellayen named Benta, who told him they had finished loading the engines and ships, and were now loading other supplies. "We have thirty-five ships, and nine hundred eighty-two engines loaded for you. Most of the engines and ships have the old engine design."

"Eight hundred engines? That's great!" Randy said. "Earth will be very pleased to get these. I can't thank you enough. How long before you're finished loading?"

"We will finish loading the ships in a few hours. I have already informed Awth and Gullaynianna. I am sure you want to get it back to Earth as soon as possible."

Randy suddenly felt hurried. He had to get some sleep before they left. Yawning, he left and hurried back to his room. He was imagining how comfortable it would feel to crawl into a nice warm bed and drift off into beautiful sleep.

Nope! It wasn't going to happen. Tellgus came to the door. "How is your head?" he asked. Randy nodded and said he was ok. Tellgus opened the door and walked inside. "Nellaynan was very pleased that you joined with us. It was very thoughtful of you to do so."

Randy nodded. "I didn't know what to expect. I was pretty apprehensive at first, but in the end, it was all my pleasure. I have never in my life experienced anything like that. It was amazing. I felt good! I feel good!" he emphasized. "It made me happy knowing I was helping Nellaynan deal with her sorrow, and my pain was lessened. I could feel you share my pain. That was the greatest feeling, but my sadness has returned," Randy said.

"That is the way it works," Tellgus said, sitting down at the table. "You should feel a little less hurt for the loss of John, but when you leave the joining, no one is sharing your pain. You are left to deal with it alone."

Randy nodded. "Yeah, I felt that."

Tellgus looked up at Randy. "During the joining, you learned that we have a God, didn't you?"

"Yes, I did, and I have to say that was a bit of a surprise. I didn't know you had religion. I have never seen a church anywhere."

"That's because we don't have what you call churches. We gather wherever and whenever we wish. We gather to worship all the time. You just didn't know we were doing it. Even the Joining you were involved in last night was church for us. You must have heard 'Adonai' being praised during the Joining? We were there to help each other with their suffering, yes, but we were also praising our maker for giving us the ability to do so. You must have felt that?" Tellgus asked.

"Yes, I sensed something like that. I learned during the Joining that you had a God and believed very strongly in him. I felt you had a genuine love for him."

Tellgus turned his head slightly and looked at Randy quizzically. "You don't recognize the name then, 'Adonai'?"

Randy shrugged. "No, I don't think so. Should I? I mean that's your God and I know nothing about him."

Tellgus shrugged in response. "John recognized the name right away. It is one of the names given to your God on Earth. Do you understand? We have the same God named Adonai."

Randy shrugged again. "Like I said, I haven't been much for believing in God. I don't think I have ever been in a church except for weddings and such. I've never opened a Bible either."

"John did believe," Tellgus said. "He told us the story of Adonai sending his son to be among you. Adonai did the same thing here on Pellaya, but our story is different. He praised us for our faithfulness and lived among us for many years. We knew who he was and loved him. Then one day, in the sight of everyone, he moved back through the invisible curtain and went back to heaven. He still speaks to us from beyond and is still happy with us. It will shock you to learn that the Chenowa also have the same God, but they are rejecting him because they believe he is letting their race die. They are angry with him. Bartolos learned all this from Toc.

Our Lord had already told us that other people existed in the Universe, but until now we didn't know them. Now we know of you, the Chenowa, and the Itchaian's. We know there are more. Many more."

Randy nodded. "I have never been much of a believer, but after joining and talking to you, I'm seeing things in a new light. This God of yours … ours, is everywhere. He's here on Pellaya and Earth and wherever the Chenowa comes from. I do need to take this more seriously and take another look at it."

"It is good to hear you say that," Tellgus said, shifting in his chair. "This is not what I came to talk to you about. Awth asked me to get you and bring you to the cargo ship. Will you come?"

"Of course I will. Why didn't you say so earlier?"

"Awth asked me to take my time, but I think we can go now. Let's go," Tellgus said and motioned for Randy to follow him.

They walked back to the cargo ship and were greeted by a rather large group of Pellayens. Awth stepped forward and greeted Randy with a smile. "Welcome, Randy. We have been waiting for you. The council has agreed to honor you as we did with John. We are giving you a ship. It occurs to us that you may very well be traveling back and forth between our planets quite a bit. SO, you should have a good ship to do it in. This brand-new ship is yours. A gift from us to you," Awth said, stepping aside to reveal the ship.

Randy stood, not knowing what to say. They had done the same thing for John, and now it was his turn, and like John, he didn't know what to say.

There was a short ceremony in which Randy was handed what could be considered the keys to the ship. Then, almost everyone except Awth left and went about their business. Awth stayed behind to show Randy the ship. It even had a new smell to it that amused Randy. Awth finished showing him the ship and turned to another subject. "Many of John's friends on Pellaya would like to meet John's friends on Earth. Would that be possible?"

"I think that is a great idea. The only thing is I don't know what is happening on Earth. If the Aliens haven't attacked, we should be able to hold a Celebration of Life ceremony for John. Would your people be willing to travel to Earth?"

"Yes. Could you set it up for us?" Awth asked.

Randy said he could and would. Awth nodded. "There is one more thing. It was suggested that we rename the Niglaie Air Carrier Center the 'John Baines Air Carrier Center', and the council has agreed. What do you think of that?"

Randy smiled. "I like it. I like it a lot. I can see why you would call it that. Thank you and thank the council for everything for me."

Awth and Randy left the ship and went their separate ways. Randy headed back to his room for a much-needed sleep. He reached the outer door and gripped the handle. "Sleep. All I want is some sleep," he said aloud.

Again, it wasn't to be so. A voice came to him from behind. "Randy, can you take me to Earth? It's important." He turned and found Gullaynianna and a few of her team standing there. "We have discovered what is happening on Earth. We have the cure to the Plague."

Randy stiffened. "You found the cure? Of course, I will take you. I was just given a ship. I can take you in that."

"That would be good," Gullaynianna said.

When they got back to the Air Carrier Center, they learned the Cargo ships were loaded and ready to go, but Gullaynianna wanted to wait a few more minutes until the last several pallets of supplies had been loaded. They were pallets she had asked for and seemed important to her.

A great number of people had already boarded the hospital ship, all wanting to go to John's memorial. The last of them had just entered the ship, so four ships lifted off and headed toward Tallda Shayts. Two Cargo ships, Randy's new ship with Gullaynianna aboard, and the Hospital ship. Together they entered Tallda Shayts and appeared in Earth's space. Randy led them to Earth, then hurried to coordinate a meeting with the United Nations, where Gullaynianna told the world they had found the cure to the Plague.

****

Despite Randy's untold story, the memorial service was a success, and everyone had a good time. Most of them went home feeling they had finally, sadly, said goodbye to John. Not having his body left them feeling, or perhaps hoping, that John could somehow still be alive, but most accepted that John was gone. Gullaynianna had felt him die, and they trusted her. Randy and Bruce had seen John's ship get hit by the bolt of energy, then fade away, leaving only a small amount of debris.

They didn't have his body, but they unveiled his burial stone, which had a picture of John, Randy, Tellgus, Fallgonan, and Awntoon, all standing by John's Pellayen ship when they had found their way back to Earth. The same picture was added to a Plaque that was to be hung in the Smithsonian Museum to remember his story.

There were still tears, both Human and Pellayen, because John was so well-liked, but he was gone now, and life had to go on. Nellaynan and the other Pellayens all went home to Pellaya. Randy would soon follow them back to Pellaya because he wanted to learn more about this mental ability. He had joined in a Grieving and enjoyed it immensely. His opinion of it had changed dramatically, and he wanted to know more. The only place he was going to learn about it was on Pellaya. He was surprised when his wife and kids not only agreed to spend their two-week vacation on Pellaya, but were anxious to go.

He hadn't realized what a thrill it would be for them to travel into space, go through the gate, and into Tallda Shayts. Randy had forgotten the thrill he felt finding himself on an alien planet and living among Alien beings. His family wanted to experience that same feeling.

Randy's real surprise came when his son Josh started having trouble with the Thought Transmissions. He saw the same things happening to Josh that he had seen happening to John. He asked Bartolos to help Josh, and the next thing you know, Josh came away from the meeting with Bartolos much more at ease and with a big, happy grin on his face. A new world had just been opened for him, and he now had the biggest, most interesting friend any kid could want.

Randy was a little envious of Josh. Josh seemed to have a knack for using his mental ability, whereas Randy struggled with it. He was learning, but it didn't come as easily for him as it did for Josh. At times, Josh would hear thoughts from Randy that Randy didn't intend to send, and at first, it was a problem. Later, when Randy learned to control his Ability better, it was no longer a point of contention. Bartolos assured them that the closeness they would gain through the Mental Ability would cause them to laugh about their difficulty later in life. It would bring them even closer together.

When it came time to return to Earth, none of them wanted to go. They liked living on Pellaya. His wife Carol had additional reasons for not wanting to return. She worried about the coming war and what would happen to her family. She wanted to stay on Pellaya where they were happy and safe, but she also knew Randy couldn't do that. He would be needed, and he would want to do his part. They had to go back.

When they got back to Earth, they learned that the Aliens hadn't been seen for many days. This was causing concern. Their absence from Earth space could mean they had learned the poison was no longer working and were preparing to invade. People were on edge, certain that War was about to begin, and there was nothing Earth could do to stop them.

CHAPTER THIRTEEN
SO FAR AWAY

The pain in his head and body was unbearable. He opened his eyes and then slammed them shut again. The light hurt his eyes. In the brief moment his eyes were open, he had seen the two clocks above the windshield. One Pellayen and the other Earth time. From what he could recollect, it had only been a few minutes since the aliens had shot at him. He had been passed out all that time, but it wasn't the time that bothered him. He had seen that his ship was traveling at light speed away from Earth.

The ship had to be stopped. It was speeding away from Earth at 186000 miles per second, taking him far from Earth in a direction he didn't know. He would be lost in space if he didn't stop the ship. With no one at the controls, it could slam into something. He reached for the controls and felt himself drifting back into unconsciousness. With his eyes closed, and only half aware of what he was doing, he felt for the controls to pull them back and stop the ship. That simple movement caused more pain to shoot through his body, and he blacked out.

John opened his eyes again, and things were very different. The pain he had felt the first time was much less, but good lord, he felt sick to his stomach and weaker than he had ever felt in his life. Why? He hadn't felt this way when he first woke up. When he tried to move, his body wouldn't cooperate. His arms were unresponsive and sluggish when they did respond.

He opened his eyes, groaned, and closed his eyes again, hating what he had seen. The ship was still flying away from Earth at Light speed. *I must have passed out before I could pull back on the controls*, he thought. But now he felt physically incapable of doing it. That confused him. What had happened between then and now? What had made him so weak and sick?

His stomach threatened to expel anything that was in it, his joints ached, his head hurt, and he believed he was running a fever.

He sat with his eyes closed, thinking of all that had happened to him. The Aliens had been shooting at him just as he slammed the controls forward to go into light speed. Then the pain hit him, and he died. He had died, and he remembered it very well.

He was surprised to remember the Satellite that had drifted between him and the Alien ship just as they fired on him. That Satellite had been hit by the yellow bolt of energy, which had saved his ship. The Satellite had exploded, but it must have taken enough energy from the yellow fire to save his ship, but not enough to save him.

But I did die. I left my body and floated above myself. I was looking down at my body. Then he remembered being pulled out of the ship into darkness. There were other people and animals there with him. Most of them were moving right along with him toward a brilliant light. Others seemed afraid to go forward.

He wanted to pass it off as a dream, but knew it was no dream. He had died and gone to Heaven, where he met Jesus, his wife Angie, and others he knew to have died before him. All of it was crystal clear in his mind. Angie had been allowed to show him around heaven, where he saw and felt amazing things. Everything there was alive and seemed to be singing. Even the grass was alive and singing praises to God. He didn't want to step on it for fear of damaging it. The flowers produced a ringing sound that was beautiful and soothing. There were buildings all made of what looked like crystal. Those buildings housed people happily going about their business. No one did anything they didn't want to. If you wanted to work, you worked. If you didn't, you did as you wanted.

There was an amazing Library there with books you didn't have to read. They released their knowledge right into his mind when he opened them. It had been a wonderful place, and he never thought of leaving it until Jesus came to him and asked him to go back to his life on Earth. He immediately said 'No' and he meant it with all his heart. Then Jesus told him that if he stayed, he would not complete his mission, and many others wouldn't be able to complete their missions because he wasn't there to help them. He needed to go back to help them with their missions.

Reluctantly, he agreed to return. That's when Jesus said something to him he didn't understand. "Your body will need food and water. I will tend to your needs." That was it, but what did that mean? John imagined it had to do with the living water mentioned in the bible, which pertained to the word of God. Before he could ask, Jesus sent him back with a wave of his hand. Now he sat in his ship with caked blood on his nose and face, sickness in his stomach, and incredible weakness. Why hadn't he stayed in Heaven?

He looked at the clocks above the windshield, expecting to see the date of January 3rd. The day the Aliens shot him. He was shocked to see February 12th showing below the clock. He had been unconscious and flying away from Earth at light speed for more than a month! He was incredibly far from Earth! How would he ever find his way back home?

I'm okay. I'm in a Pellayen ship and have plenty of food. He thought, trying to calm himself. *Why would they send me back only to die out here in space? I must be able to make it back somehow. Good lord, I haven't moved or eaten in over a month!* Now he knew why he felt so bad. He was starving to death.

Suddenly, the words Jesus had spoken to him filled his mind. "Your body will need food and water. I will tend to your needs." It made sense now. He hadn't drunk any water or eaten anything in over a month! That should have been the end of him. It became apparent God had performed a miracle and tended to his need for food and water. John was amazed and thankful, yet wished God had done things differently so he didn't have to feel so bad.

Believing he had experienced a miracle and feeling God was with him, helped him stay calm. Now, if he could get control of his ship, he would be all right. He struggled to lift his arms and, thanks to zero gravity, was able to pull back on the ship's controls. Nothing happened. The ship wasn't responding.

He let his arms fall back in his lap and sighed. What did he need to do to get control of the ship? *Turn off the engine.* But how was he going to do that? He could barely move.

He sat thinking. *I need food! I have to eat and regain my strength, but what am I going to do about the ship? No! I have to get my strength back first, then worry about the ship. Eat! I need to eat and get my strength back.*

John unbuckled his seat straps and let himself float up out of the seat. Nauseated, weak, and in pain, John propelled himself down the hallway. He used his fingers to push against the wall to keep himself moving because nothing else wanted to move. His arms and legs were useless.

There was plenty of food in the galley, but he figured he should start slowly with liquids. The Pellayens had a drink he liked very much. It was full of Vitamins and nutrients. That's what he needed now. It took a lot of effort and time to retrieve the liquid and get some into his body, but he managed to do it.

The drink upset his stomach even more than it already was, but he kept it down. At this point, all he wanted was to lie down on a bed in gravity, but that wasn't going to happen. He would have to settle for strapping himself into a sleeper berth.

He took a few more of the drinks and slowly made his way down the hall. Using his fingers again, he kept himself moving toward the bunk. If not for Zero gravity, he never would have made it.

When he got to the sleeper berth, he tried not to think of the ship speeding away from Earth at light speed. In the condition he was in, there was nothing he could do about it. Worrying about it would only keep him from sleeping. He did his best to put it out of his mind. The ship would have to sail along uncontrolled until he felt better. As he tried to rest, he prayed the ship wouldn't hit anything. *Just get some rest and eat for now. Don't let yourself worry about stopping the ship or getting home.*

He slept a little, and each time he woke from his sleep, he drank more of the health drink. This went on for days. Nursing himself back to health was taking a long time, and as he lay there, he knew he had to get out of the bunk and move around. As hard as it would be for him to do, he needed exercise. He had sat unconscious in the pilot seat for more than a month, and he had lost track of how long he had been in the bunk. If he didn't push himself, he would die out here. No one was coming to help him.

Keeping the body strong in space was hard enough. Building his strength back meant a lot more work, but if he wanted to live, he had to do it.

He worked hard at it, and his workouts were helping. He woke from a sleep one day, and felt better, so he tried his first meal of solid food. It was solid but soft. The last thing he needed was to bind himself up. When it came to food, the name of the game was slow and easy. He was no doctor, but he thought that was the right thing to do.

Finally, he woke feeling noticeably better. Still far from feeling great, he was heading in the right direction, so he continued following his doctor's instructions. Get plenty of rest, eat easily digested foods, and get a lot of exercise.

The day came when he woke, feeling less like a starving dog that had been hit by a car, and more like he could do something. His arms and legs were starting to cooperate, and his mind seemed more alert and ready to deal with things. He grabbed more food from the galley and floated down the hall to the pilot seat, where he sat eating and thinking. He had to figure out how he was going to get the ship stopped and headed back home.

At times, he found it very hard to stay calm when he thought about how long he had been traveling away from Earth. It had been over two months now that he had been traveling at 186000 miles per second. That was a mighty far distance. It was going to take an awful lot of luck to find his way back to Earth.

He found himself feeling happy he had died and gone to heaven because it gave him 'Faith'. Faith in God, yes, but also faith that he was sent back to live, not die. The Lord's plan must have been that he make it back to Earth. He had to have faith that he could.

He pieced together a plan and started memorizing the stars he saw in the windshield. The brighter ones formed the shape of a 4. Hopefully, he could get control of the ship, turn it around so that 4 was behind him, and head for home. If he could do that, he would at least be headed in the right direction. But it wasn't lost on him, that being so far away, there was no way he would sail straight back to Earth. He could only hope he could get closer and somehow find his way.

First, he had to get control of the ship. He thought about that, and the answer seemed obvious. *Get up and turn the engine off.* With some effort, he floated back to the engine control panel and eventually managed to switch off the engines. Nothing changed. He was still racing through space at light speed.

He floated back through the ship, looking for damage, and found it in the engine room. A very large char mark stained the metal walls. This had to be where the yellow fire had hit his ship. Thankfully, the wall was only charred. The metal was weakened but still intact. *The yellow fire must have burned something out in the engine.* He couldn't see anything wrong, but he didn't understand much about the engine, and had no idea what to look for beyond burned wires.

Behind him were the heavy double doors that led into the cargo area. He looked through the thick glass. There was no damage out there that he could see. Then his eyes fell on the two Pellayen engines he was supposed to have delivered to Earth. He had forgotten about them and was glad he hadn't had the chance to deliver them. He could use one to replace the old engine. Maybe that would lead to his getting control of the ship. He didn't know what else to do.

As he started to turn from the window, he spotted the space quad. He could use that to help him move the engines. He moved back from the window and sighed. He at least had a plan, but was still too tired and weak to do anything about it. Just turning the engine off had taxed him. The ship would have to sail on a little longer.

He moved back to the pilot's seat and continued memorizing the stars before him. He drew a map of them and hung it near the controls. He ate a little and slept a lot. Finally, he felt rested enough to go to the back window of the ship. He hoped for a miracle that he would see Earth, but knew he was too far out in space to see that. It was possible he could see the Sun, and he was right.

Most of the lights he saw were very bright, and he figured they were Galaxies, but nestled in the middle of them, directly behind the ship, was a very dim light. It had to be the Sun, his home. Seeing it gave him hope that he could get back there. He stayed by the window, studying the Stars and drawing another map. If all went well, he would soon be looking at them through the front windshield. He would be headed home. He just stared at that dim light, longing to head back toward it. Then, finally, he moved back to the front of the ship.

He ate, exercised, and rested for many more days until he finally felt able to tackle the job of changing the engines. Some of his strength had returned, and he felt pretty good. That meant it was time to replace the old engine and get this ship stopped!

He knew nothing about Pellayen engines except that they were bolted to a metal plate, which was then slid onto 4 studs that stuck up from the floor of the ship. Each stud fitted through a hole in the mounting plate, one in each corner, and was tightened with a large 3-inch nut.

The engine itself was way beyond his understanding, but changing one out looked to be fairly easy. The engine was small compared to the Jet engines he was used to. This one was about four feet high and five feet long. He believed he would be able to maneuver it around in zero gravity. There wasn't much attached to the engine; one long adjustable rod, two smaller linkages, and a fair amount of wiring. That was it.

He nodded and moved toward the engines. All he had to do was take the nuts off the four studs, and the engine would be free. He planned to leave the wires attached as long as he could. His memory had never been all that good, and this was no time to forget how things went back together, so he would leave the wires attached until the last.

From a toolbox on the wall, John took out the big wrench that fit the 3-inch nuts and went to work. He was sweating and breathing hard before he had the first nut off. He was exhausted and had to rest after he got the second nut off. To give himself a little break, he floated over to the space quad, unstrapped it from the floor, and moved it up to one of the new engines. He strapped the engine to the front of the space quad and moved it closer to the old engine. He sat on the quad to rest a moment longer, then propelled himself off the quad toward the old engine.

That was his first mistake. He had pushed off the quad with his legs, which propelled the space quad backward. It slammed into the doorpost. This was a big ship, but that collision was enough to start it tumbling end over end. It wasn't fast, but if it got any worse, he wouldn't be able to complete his work. He had to be more careful.

He turned and saw that the quad was drifting up toward the ceiling. He pushed off the floor, got on top of the quad, and started it back down to the floor. He was about to make his second mistake. He didn't pay enough attention to the fact that the floor of the ship was now moving up toward him as he was moving down toward it. It hit hard and sent the quad up into the ceiling. It bounced and slammed into the door jams again. He got control of the quad and kept it from hitting anything more, but the damage was done. Now, not only was the ship tumbling, but it was also rolling. He had made a mess of things and was in more trouble than ever.

If he left the space quad, it would bang around like a ball in a box, but if he didn't leave the space quad, how would he get the engines changed? He was forced to stay on the quad to keep it from hitting anything else. He had to figure something out.

His eyes fell on the holes in the mounting plate of the engine he had strapped to the front of the quad. He looked at the studs sticking through the mounting plate of the old engine. There was enough of the stud sticking through the mounting plate that he could put the new mounting plate on top of the old plate and still get the nuts on.

It wasn't where the new engine belonged, but if he could get the studs through the holes, he could get control of his situation. Since the engine was strapped to the quad, he would have the quad under control as well. But could he do it? The ship tumbling and turning would make it hard to get the studs to pop up through the mounting plate.

He moved the quad forward and lowered the plate down toward the studs. Everything was moving and shifting in all directions. He had to make the space quad move in the same way. That took some time, but he did get the two moving together.

Still, it was nearly impossible to get things to cooperate. He took a deep breath and backed away, intending a fresh start, but one of the studs popped through the hole. What luck!

Quickly, he climbed off the quad and got on top of the engine. Pushing against the ceiling, he pushed the engine down so the stud came all the way through. Quickly, he reached into the toolbox, retrieved one of the nuts, and started it on the stud. It went on with no problem.

If he could push the engine to one side, the second stud might come through, and he would have two studs holding the new engine in place. He pushed the engine to one side, wondering what he would do if the stud popped through the mounting plate. The old engine would still be in the place where the new engine had to be.

The second stud popped through, and he got the nut on, but this wasn't where the engine belonged. Somehow, he needed to unbolt both engines, move the old engine out of the way, and put the new engine in its place. That was going to he hard to do with the ship tumbling like it was. He was going to have to figure out how to get that done, but for now, he continued to secure the engine to the floor of his ship. Because the quad was strapped to the engine, the quad was kept from floating free as well.

Now came the hard part. Tightening the nuts down. This tapped into his energy reserves. When he finished, he was exhausted and wanted to stop, but the quad was flopping up and down, banging against the floor, causing the ship to tumble and turn even more. He had to stop it.

He floated past the quad into the cargo area. The floor, walls, and ceiling were constantly coming at him as he moved through the ship. Grabbing two straps from the Cargo area, he returned to the quad and started strapping it down to the floor. The ratchet straps made it easy for him to pull the quad tight to the floor, but the ship was tumbling and rolling quite badly now.

With the ship tumbling the way it was, there was no way he could remove the old engine, then replace it with a new one. He had to leave both engines where they were. Unbolting the engines from the floor would only make things worse. He had no choice but to run new wiring to the new engine and hope it would work. From what he knew about Pellayen engines, he thought it possible.

If he left everything connected to the old engine, he could use extra wire to jump from the connection on the old engine to the same terminal on the new engine. This would help him make sure he was making the right connections. It would be a total Cob Job, but it would get the job done. Hopefully, that would be enough.

When he got down to doing the job, he found out just how hard this job was going to be. The tumbling and rolling of the ship tended to throw his body away from the engine. He was holding on to the engine with his left hand while doing the work with his right. The work was hard enough with both hands. He was doing it with one.

John growled, "This is like working on a car rolling backward downhill with the wheels turned to the left! How am I going to get this done?"

The engine was constantly trying to throw him off, but he clung to it like a bull rider. The exertion tired him out, and he was thrown off many times, but he went back at it, again and again. Finally, he finished the job. The last wire was in place, and he had cobbled two linkages together so they would work.

He was very happy to be able to let go of the bucking bronco. He was sweating badly, out of breath, and not feeling well as he floated down the ever-moving hallway toward the front of the ship.

He reached the control room and grabbed hold of the engine control console, which was bucking worse than the engine had been. He clung to it with a death grip until his body began to move in concert with the console. He still had to hang on, but he could at least wipe the sweat from his face.

As he reached to turn the engine back on, he prayed it would stop the ship and give him back control. He paused, realizing he could be thrown forward when the engine started. He could be thrown forward with enough force to kill him. He didn't know what would happen, but he had no choice.

He grabbed the control console, closed his eyes, and threw the switches. Nothing happened. He opened his eyes. "Ah! Thank God!" he said, letting go of the control console, to float forward to the Cockpit area. "Yes!" he said, seeing that the ship was no longer tumbling and had come to a complete stop.

John hugged the back of the pilot seat, happy to have stopped the ship, but he was exhausted, sick to his stomach, and feeling he would pass out at any minute. As much as he wanted to find out if he truly had control of the ship, he floated back down the hallway to his sleeper berth and strapped himself in. He had to rest. Everything else would have to wait.

He woke feeling much better! He figured all the exertion from messing with the engines must have done him good. He looked at his watch. He had been asleep for 12 hours. Obviously, he had needed a good long sleep. Now, he was hungry, and food was first on his mind. It felt good to feel hungry and not sick to his stomach. *I must be getting better.*

The meal was the best he'd had in a long time. It felt good to be hungry and have the meal satisfy that hunger. After devouring the meal, he strapped himself into the pilot seat and reached for the control levers. It was time to find out if he had control of the ship. As soon as he touched the controls, the ship shuddered. This had never happened before. When he looked out the windshield, he saw that the ship was slowly rotating to the left. He let go of the controls, and the ship stopped. He gripped the controls, and again, the ship shuddered and started moving.

He moved the control to the right, and the ship spun around faster than ever before. G-forces should have thrown him hard against the seat belts, but he felt no G-force whatsoever. He moved the controls again, and again the ship spun quickly, and without G-forces. The ship had never responded this quickly and certainly had never done so without G-forces. Something had changed, but it appeared to be a good change. If this ship had operated like this when he ran from the Aliens, he might never have been hit.

He shrugged and very gently eased forward pressure onto the controls. The ship moved forward in a way he was more used to. He eased back on the controls, and the ship stopped and moved backward. It was clear he had control of the ship, but the controls were ultra-sensitive.

But why were there no G-forces? Normally, there were no G-forces when the Energy Drive was turned on. He looked down at the little panel by his left knee and was surprised to see the Energy Drive was turned on. That suggested another problem. The ship should have gone to light speed as soon as he moved the controls, but it didn't.

"Crap! Light speed must not be working," he groaned.

It was in his mind to go back and finish changing out the engines. That might get everything back to normal, but he was anxious to find the stars that pointed the way home. The ship had tumbled wildly, so he had no idea where the stars he had mapped out were. The '4' pattern the ship had been flying towards for so long would be the easiest to find, so he looked for that.

He turned the ship a little and studied the stars. Turned it a little more and looked again. He worked like this for several hours. Finally, he spotted it. It was almost upside down, but he was sure he had found it. He rotated the ship, and slowly the '4' turned upright. He had it. Now he knew Earth was somewhere behind him. All he had to do was turn the ship around, and he would point in the general direction of home.

He placed the map of the stars from what had been behind him, near the controls, and started turning the ship. He smiled, seeing the cluster of stars he was looking for come into view. He couldn't see the dim light at the center that he presumed was the Sun, but that didn't bother him. He knew the ship had traveled so far from it that it couldn't be seen anymore. It was still there in the middle of the cluster of stars. All he had to do was head for it, and eventually, the Sun would appear again.

He was sure he was pointed toward home. Anxious to get started toward it, he pushed the controls forward. Light Speed wasn't working, but that didn't matter. He was heading home! He would finish changing the engines later. Flying home at 222000 mph would take a very long time, but for now, he just wanted to start toward home.

He pushed the controls further forward, and things seemed to move toward him. He kept easing the controls forward, and suddenly, light particles became stationary around him. He was shocked. The ship had accelerated from a standstill to light speed by pushing forward on the controls. It shouldn't be happening this way.

He pulled back on the controls, and the ship slowed. He pushed them forward again, and the ship jumped to light speed. Amazed, he pressed the controls farther forward. Now he was screaming passed the light particles outside. He was traveling faster than light! "Good Lord, what has happened?" he said. It bothered him that things weren't working as they should, but he couldn't help but be happy about it. The faster the ship traveled, the sooner he would get home.

He eased the controls farther forward, and the view in the windshield became very bizarre. He was looking down a lighted tunnel. Directly in front of the ship, the view was clear, but looking a bit to the side, everything was a blur of light. It truly looked like he was traveling through an illuminated tunnel.

"I must have hooked something up wrong or maybe that bolt of energy changed something," he said, taking his eyes from the windshield. "But, I don't want to fix it. I'm traveling faster than light. Why would I want to change that?"

He looked back at the windshield and realized he had inadvertently let the controls move back, which caused the ship to slow down, and he hadn't felt it happen. "Amazing!" he said and let go of the controls. The ship stopped instantly, and he didn't feel a thing. He pushed the controls forward hard, and the ship almost instantly was flying faster than light again. "I don't know what happened to change the way this ship handles, but I like it. I'm not touching those engines. I'm going home!" he said. He shook his head and smiled, "Oh no. I'm talking to myself like Randy. I am in more trouble than I thought."

John sat holding the controls all the way forward for an hour, hoping he would soon see the light of the Sun appear in the middle of the cluster of stars. He had no idea how far from the Sun he was or how long it would take to get back. He knew he had been flying away from Earth at light speed for more than three months, so it was a no-brainer that he had a very, very, long way to go.

He didn't want to sit holding the controls forward hour after hour, so he got wire from the cargo area and wired up the controls so they would stay where he wanted them. When he finished, he was rather proud of his makeshift cruise control system. He kept an eye on the windshield to be sure the ship stayed on course, but now he was free to move around, get food, and exercise. Occasionally, he had to make adjustments and bring the star cluster back in front of him, but for the most part, his wired-up cob job was working.

When he found himself getting tired, he brought the ship to a stop. He wasn't about to risk losing sight of the star cluster while he slept. He was sure the ship would sit motionless, facing the star cluster while he slept.

When he woke again, he hurried to the windshield to check and found the Star Cluster was still framed in the windshield, right as he had left it. He reconnected his makeshift cruise control and left the controls to grab breakfast from the galley. Bringing it back to the pilot seat, he sat eating and staring down through the lighted tunnel. He didn't care that he couldn't see anything beyond the sides of the tunnel. It only matters that he saw the Star Cluster he believed was home.

Day after day, he woke up, set the cruise control, ate, got some exercise, and flew on until he was too tired to go further. When he woke, it started all over again. It wasn't much of an existence, but it was all he had. He thought of Nellaynan, Bartolos, and Awth often. He missed them all badly and hated the thought of Nellaynan thinking he was dead and the pain that would cause her. Thankfully, he was heading her way and hoped to be able to show her he was alive soon.

One good thing was that he was feeling better every day. All the pain and nausea were gone. The bad thing was that he was bored out of his mind. He had nothing to do but stare down the tunnel, thinking of Nellaynan, and look for the Sun every day.

Digging around the ship, he found a maintenance manual for the engine and sat reading it. It was in Pellayen, which made it hard to read, but that also made it interesting. He needed to learn more of the Pellayen language anyway.

He sat reading it for the third day when shadows began flashing on the windshield. He looked up. "Shiiiittt!" he yelled, throwing his arms up in front of his face. Immediately, he dropped them and reached for the controls. "Damn it!" he shouted and threw his arms back up in front of him.

He lowered his arms and quickly brought the ship to a stop. "What the hell just happened?" He had just slammed into two asteroids. He was traveling so fast; he had no time to react except to throw his arms up. It was over as soon as he saw it. But there was no crash, banging, or jerking of the ship. Nothing had happened.

Had he missed the Asteroid somehow? "Impossible!" John said. "I was already hitting them. There is no way I missed them. What happened? Did I go through them?"

He moved through the ship to the back window and looked out. A debris field of small rocks was floating toward the back of the ship. It was obvious! He had smashed through two asteroids, and pieces of them were now floating toward him. "But I never felt a thing. How is this possible?"

He watched the rock drift closer to his ship, and he let them come. If he had just blasted through Asteroids, a few small rocks wouldn't hurt anything. The rocks got closer, then suddenly hit some unseen force that stopped the rocks cold or sent them off in different directions.

John pulled back from the window and stared at the floor. "A shield?" he said after a moment. "Have I got some kind of shield around my ship now? How? When?" John shook his head in amusement. "My God, my life has certainly gotten interesting. I vanish and go to Pellaya. Find my way back to Earth, then back to Pellaya. Married an alien woman. Get shot by Aliens. Visit heaven. Get lost in space. Go faster than light. And now it appears my ship has a shield around it. My ship has become a Juggernaut. What's next?"

He moved back to the pilot's seat and risked turning the ship around to get a better look at what was behind him. Believing his ship was protected, he edged the ship into some of the larger rocks and watched them break up and move away. It was true. He did have a force field or shield around the ship.

"Faster than light speed, lack of G-forces, and now a shield around my ship? It all must be happening because of my cobbled-up engine," John said. He smiled, thinking every bit of what his ship could do was a good thing. He had nothing to complain about and no reason to change a thing.

His next thought was of the Asteroids. Where did they come from? Usually, Asteroids were orbiting something. Were these Asteroids free-floating through space, or were they orbiting a Sun? If so, what Sun could they possibly be circling?

He turned the ship and saw more Asteroids, and there were a lot of them. He was in the middle of an Asteroid belt, and from its orbital curve, they were orbiting something off to his left. He turned the ship to look and saw the faint glow of a Sun far away. What Sun could this be? He was following what he thought was Earth's Sun. What Solar System was this then?

He turned the ship back to the cluster of Stars he had been following. It appeared they were still very far away. If he was heading in the right direction to find Earth's Sun, the one now to his left had to be Earth's Sun. The cluster of Stars he was following had to be galaxies. The light in the center, had to be a galaxy so far away that its light was dim. "That can't be my Sun," he said, turning back to the sun on his left. "This one has to be my home."

He sat staring at it, thinking about what to do. Slowly, he put it all together. When the Aliens shot him, his ship had been pointed up out of the Galactic plane. That helped explain why he hadn't hit anything while flying away from Earth for three months. There was less to hit above the Galactic plane. When he got the ship turned around, the ship was traveling faster than light, which caused the lighted tunnel to form. Because of it, he never saw the Asteroid belt coming. He had also been reading and not watching what was happening outside.

His eyes widened as he stared at this new Sun. "I must be in the Kuiper Belt, he said. The Sun was a tiny speck of light far off in the distance. "I almost missed you!" John said, amazed. He closed his eyes. "Lord, you gave me that cluster of Stars to follow, didn't you?" he said, shaking his head. "You made sure I found my way back. I thank you for that."

Going to heaven had given him great reverence and respect for God. The Pellayens had a hand in that, but seeing Jesus proved the point for him. God was real and was helping him get home. The cluster of stars he had been following was his Star of Bethlehem, showing him the way to Earth, his manger.

John wasn't sure he was looking at Earth's Sun, but it made the most sense. He gripped the controls and started his ship toward what he hoped was home.

As he flew, he recounted everything that had happened to him. The aliens shooting at him. A Satellite crossing between them just in time to take the hit and save his ship. His ship flying in a direction that limited his chances of hitting anything. His mistaking a dim Galaxy for Earth's sun which led him back to what he hoped was the Kuiper Belt. He had smashed through at least two Asteroids and not been damaged because his ship had a protective shield around it. Was it all a coincidence? He didn't think so. God was protecting him; that's what he believed. He believed God's hands were all over his situation and were helping him find his way back home to Earth. "And then back to Nellaynan," he said.

He flew out of the Asteroids without worry because of the shield. With the Asteroid belt behind him, he started looking for any of the outer planets. He hoped he would spot one of the larger outer planets so he would know he was on the right track.

It didn't take long, and Saturn loomed large in the windshield. It was amazing to see Saturn in all its splendor, but more than that, seeing Saturn meant he was on the right track and heading home.

He passed Saturn, knowing he was the first to see it with his own eyes. There were tons of pictures, but nothing compared to seeing it like this. Saturn was a magnificent sight. As much as he wanted to stay and investigate, he was anxious to get home. He pressed on, pushing his ship faster.

Soon, he was blasting through the Asteroid belt, and suddenly, he was in the inner solar system. Earth was here somewhere. He circled the sun and found Mars. Soon after, he spotted Earth. "YAHOO!" he shouted and sped toward it. What a relief. He had done the impossible and made it home. He wore a big happy grin as he closed in on Earth and headed toward the Pellayen gate. "I'm coming, Nellaynan," he said.

He headed toward the Pellayen Gate, but his attention was drawn to Earth. He was seeing flashes of light there. Something was happening. As he got closer, he realized the flashes were explosions, and he was flying into a War Zone!

He recognized some of the ships as the same design that had shot at him. The others had to be from Earth. "What? A Submarine? In Space!" he said, shocked to see Submarines flying in space above Earth. There were many of them along with Pellayen ships, and many he didn't recognize.

He looked on at the fighting, not sure what to do. Earth was obviously under attack. He thought to join the fighting, but had no weapons, and couldn't be sure who was who. He could assume the submarines were from Earth, and he knew the Pellayen ships, but many of the others were a question.

He continued to the Pellayen gate, intending to head home to his wife. There, he might learn what was happening to Earth.

As he neared the gate, he saw something that made his blood run cold. A Pellayen ship was moving into the battle area, and he knew the ship. It was Awth's ship. In front of Awth's ship was one of the aliens' ships. Its weapon was out and firing at Awth. The Aliens were attacking Awth!

"This is not happening!" John shouted angrily and, without thinking, slammed the controls forward, sending his ship straight toward the alien ship faster than light. "You're just another Asteroid!" he growled, slamming into it.

CHAPTER FOURTEEN
A DOOMED RACE

Bartolos flew Awths' ship into Tallda Shayts and came through the Pellayen gate. They had no idea the invasion the Humans feared had begun just minutes earlier. He, Awth, Tellgus, Fallgonan, and Awntoon had come to visit with Randy and his family. Bartolos was noticing all the activity around Earth and started slowing the ship. It didn't take them long to figure out that the long-expected war had begun, and they were flying into a battle zone.

He turned his head, intending to speak to Awth, just as a bolt of pale-yellow energy hit their ship. None of them saw it coming until it was too late. All they had time to do was duck for cover. When they opened their eyes, they were happy to see the ship was still in one piece. But when Bartolos tried to maneuver the ship, nothing happened. The ship's engine was dead, but the ship was still drifting closer to the battle.

"I don't see anyone who would be shooting at us," Awth said. "I assume what hit us was intended for someone else. It must have lost a lot of its energy before hitting us."

Bartolos nodded. "But it left us with no power, and we are drifting into the War. We have to get this ship stopped."

Awntoon and Fallgonan immediately jumped up to find the problem. Awth, Tellgus, and Bartolos stood staring out the window, watching the battle get closer. Bartolos studied the alien ships. "Those are Itchaian' ships. I know them because Toc knew them," Bartolos said.

"Did Toc know what they wanted?" Awth asked.

"Earth! They want the planet Earth. That is all Toc knew about that. He didn't know why. He only knew the Itchaian would stay away as long as the Chenowa were around. That didn't stop the Chenowa from leaving Earth behind. It seems they have little regard for Earth," Bartolos said.

Their attention was suddenly drawn to something coming into view at the left edge of the windshield. An Itchaian' ship was crossing their path, moving quite slowly.

"Awntoon, Fallgonan, we need that engine, **now**!" Awth shouted. "We need to stop this ship somehow!" he said, turning to Tellgus and sending him a mental picture. Tellgus immediately headed for the cargo bay and the space quad. He left the Quad anchored to the floor and used it to slow the ship. The Quad's engine was small, but given enough time, it would eventually bring the larger ship to a stop. But could it stop them before the Itchaian 'saw them?

Bartolos and Awth groaned when they saw the Itchaian' ship stop directly in front of them. It was still a considerable distance away, but Awth's ship was moving forward at a pretty good clip. If these Itchaian didn't move, Awth's ship would collide with them. There was no way the space quad could stop Awth's ship in time to avoid the collision.

As if taunting them, the Itchaian' ship slowly turned to face them. It was obvious they had been spotted. Suddenly, the Itchaian' ship shot forward and stopped right in front of them. Bartolos and Awth watched helplessly as the Itchaian weapon turned to point at them. With no power or weapons, they were completely at the mercy of these Itchaian's.

Awths' ship continued to drift forward, and was soon close enough that they could see five Itchaian inside. It looked like they were laughing. The Itchaian 'ship started to back away, keeping pace with them, while their laughter continued.

Bartolos and Awth attempted to communicate mentally, but couldn't understand their language. Bartolos pieced things together from the images and emotions he was receiving from them. On the surface of their minds, they knew Awth's ship was a drift and were taking pleasure in tormenting everyone aboard. They were taunting them by backing away with their weapon pointed at them, knowing there was nothing they could do about it.

Bartolos felt their cruelty and need to harm humans. What he didn't understand was 'why.' Deeper in their minds, he saw their hatred for what they were doing. They were ashamed of it, yet felt great pressure to continue doing it.

He delved deeper into their minds, deeper than he had ever gone into anyone's mind before. He saw their innermost feelings. Each of these Itchaian hid their empathy for the humans, as if it were a terrible thing. Several of them were privately hoping the war with the humans would fail and the Itchaian would be driven back. Privately, they felt great sorrow for what they were doing (the war), and had already done (the poisoning).

This confused Bartolos. If they felt this way, why were they continuing to do it? He felt their desire to stop the war and even help the humans, but he also felt their fear of what would happen if they did. Something was driving them to continue acting as if they hated the Humans and that their hatred was justified. Each one of them was going to great lengths to hide their true feelings from the others. No one could be allowed to see how they felt.

Bartolos was surprised that none of the five Itchaian were offering any resistance to his entering their minds. Then it dawned on him that they were completely unaware of his presence in their heads. It was as if he had entered their minds through a secret back door. He was viewing their unguarded thoughts and emotions without them knowing it. He had never been able to do anything like this before. It was clear Toc had given him far more than he had realized. He was thrilled to learn the level of mental power he had gained.

His sudden exhilaration over this new ability sent a wave of mental energy out from him and into the minds of the Itchaian's. Suddenly, all the Itchaian knew he was in their heads, viewing their secrets!

Instantly, they panicked and tried to close their minds to him, but couldn't. That surprised Bartolos as much as it did them. He was in their heads, and they couldn't shut him out. Bartolos saw that they were shocked to find him in their heads, but that wasn't why they were panicking. Their true feeling toward humans had just been found out. They were desperate to keep that truth secret. Bartolos was surprised that none of them knew the others felt the same way. The others could never learn their secret!

Immediately, the Itchaian thought to blast Awth's ship to pieces, and Bartolos heard their thoughts. "They're going to fire on us!" Bartolos yelled, reaching for the ship controls. He had forgotten the ship was adrift with no engine.

Quickly, he reached into the Itchaian's' minds and found the one in control of the weapon. Bartolos did as a Chenowa would do, and told him everything was all right. *You shouldn't fire the weapon. We are at Pease. Take your ship away from here,* and for a moment, it worked. The Itchaian hesitated to fire. The other four Itchaian' stood waiting for him to shoot, and when he didn't, they all started grabbing for the weapons controls. They had to eliminate Bartolos and the threat he presented.

Now Bartolos was the desperate one! He told them, 'Everything is okay', but it wasn't working anymore. They were so desperate to eliminate him that his telling them everything was ok wouldn't stop them. They regained control of the weapon and pointed it at Awth's ship. Out of sheer desperation, Bartolos tried to take physical control of the Itchaian with his finger on the trigger. To his surprise, it worked! By God, somehow, he found himself entering the Itchaian's' body and taking control of it.

He forced the gunner to point the weapon away from Awth's ship. The Itchaian fired, but the yellow fire shot harmlessly into space. The other Itchaian now jumped at the weapon controls to get it pointed at Awth's ship. Bartolos found it increasingly hard to stop them. The weapon was firing, and they were missing, but it was only a matter of time before Awth's ship would be destroyed.

Suddenly, Bartolos felt a great explosion in his mind. He opened his eye, expecting to see that Awth's ship had been hit. Instead, it was the Itchaian' ship that had exploded. He had felt the explosion of their ship through their minds.

Bartolos turned to Awth. "What happened?"

"I don't know. Did you do something?"

"No," Bartolos said, turning to look back at the ship.

None of them saw what caused the Itchaian' ship to explode. The Itchaian' ship was in pieces, and the debris was floating out to the right. If another ship had shot them, that ship would have had to be to their left.

He and Awth moved up to the windshield to look for the ship, but couldn't see anything but empty space. Bartolos stepped back from the windshield, and when he did, he spotted a ship coming toward them from the right. "Look!" he said, pointing.

It was a Pellayen ship. It was approaching from the right on the other side of the Itchaian' ship's debris field. "That can't be the ship that destroyed them," Awth said. "It should be coming from the left. Besides, that ship has no weapons."

Awth turned on the earth-styled radio. "It must be one of the ships we gave to the humans," he said. The radio came alive with chatter from others engaged in battle. Awth addressed the approaching ship, but all he heard was someone asking for help to get an Itchaian off his tail. Awth tried again and heard someone talk, but it wasn't from the ship coming toward them. Bartolos tried using Mental Ability but got no answer that way either.

The other ship was still moving forward, into the Itchaian debris field. They were surprised to see the debris being pushed away without touching the ship.

"What's going on here?" Awth asked. "Am I seeing things?"

"Only if I am, too," Bartolos said. "None of that junk is hitting the ship."

Tellgus's Mental Ability told him what was happening, and he had left the quad to come forward. He saw someone inside, but couldn't make out who it was. All of them could see someone in the ship and could see he was attempting to talk on the radio, but they couldn't hear him."

They were straining so intently to see who it was that they didn't see the other Itchaian' ship coming. It was already shooting at the other Pellayen ship when they finally noticed it. Immediately, the other Pellayen ship vanished. At that same instant, the Itchaian' ship exploded. Both ships were gone. One was destroyed, but what happened to the Pellayen ship?

"What is going on?" Awth said.

Again, a Pellayen ship appeared on the other side of the debris field. It pushed its way through the debris toward them. It moved toward them, pushing debris out of the way. It was soon nose to nose with them.

"It can't be!" Awth said. "That's John Baines!"

They couldn't believe their eyes! John had been gone for close to 5 months. They had gone to his celebration of life and visited his gravestone, yet here he was right in front of them. He was alive and appeared to be attempting to talk to them on the radio. Why couldn't they hear him?

"We can hear others, so he must have problems with his radio," Bartolos said.

After a moment, they saw John lower his mic and appear to make adjustments on his dashboard. Then raised the radio mic again. "Can you hear me now?"

Bartolos was quick to respond. "Yes! We can hear you now! John, we all thought you were dead!"

"I was, and I will need to explain that, but let's do that later! Are you all okay?"

"We're all ok," Bartolos answered. "We came from Pellaya right smack into this war. We got hit by stray fire, and the ship lost power. We are adrift, but the ship is okay. John, we were attacked by two Itchaian' ships, but both of them exploded. Did you have something to do with it?" Bartolos asked.

"Yes, I destroyed them. I've been lost in space for a long time. I just got back, and the first thing I see is this battle. Then I saw your ship being attacked, so I took them out. Can you tell me what's going on here? Who's attacking Earth?"

"They're called Itchaian's, and they want your planet. We got hit by a stray shot and lost all power to our engine. Fallgonan and Awntoon are working on the problem. John, how did you destroy those ships? You don't have weapons, do you?"

John shrugged. "My whole ship has become a weapon. Some kind of shield forms around it when my Energy Drive is turned on. I just learned that radio and Metal Ability can't get through it either. That's why I couldn't hear you on the radio or in my mind. Look, you guys are sitting ducks out there. Why don't you come to my ship? You will be safe here and can tell me what's going on here."

No one realized Fallgonan and Awntoon had come into the cockpit area until they started yelling. "Hello, John! What happened to you? Where have you been?"

Startled, Awth jumped. Then turned to them, a bit annoyed. "How is the engine? Have you got it working?"

"We've almost got it running, but we wanted to see if it was true that you were talking to John, and it is. He's alive!" Fallgonan said. He paused to tell Awth that the energy bolt had burned out some wires at the power supply. "We'll be able to fix it. We have most of the repairs done. It should only be a few more minutes, and we will have it up and running."

Awth nodded. "Then I want to stay with my ship. You'd better get back to the engine. We're too close to the battle here, and Bartolos, why don't you go over to John's ship? You can tell him what we know."

Fallgonan and Awntoon nodded and went back to work. Bartolos flew a space quad over to John's ship. He was very pleased to see John and gave him a crushing bear hug. "It is so good to see you. We all thought you had been killed. Glad you're alive,"

John struggled to catch enough breath to remind Bartolos of his strength. When Bartolos had a hold of you, you knew it. When he could speak, John told Bartolos that he had just returned from a very hard and long trip. "I went through some real crap to get back here, and I still haven't had a chance to celebrate."

Bartolos put his hands on John's shoulders, "What happened to you? We all thought you were dead. Randy and Bruce saw your ship destroyed. Where have you been?"

"To heaven and hell," John said. "And yes, my ship was damaged but not destroyed. A Satellite was near my ship and got hit when they fired on me. That is probably what they saw get destroyed. I had just pushed the controls forward to go into light speed when they shot at me. I suppose my ship appeared to vanish just as the Satellite exploded. I remember seeing the Satellite explode, but that was the last thing I saw. My ship is ok. Even better than it was."

Right then, something lit up the inside of John's ship, and they saw an explosion nearby. "You better tell me what has been happening here. I've already destroyed two ships. I saw Awth's ship being attacked and reacted without thinking. Was I right to do that?" John asked.

"Yes, you did right," Bartolos said, then opened his mind to John. John learned that these Aliens had been poisoning Earth and had murdered millions of people from all around the world. Now they had come to Earth to take it for themselves.

John's anger grew as the information from Bartolos poured into his head. He looked out at the fighting going on and remembered how outclassed his ship had been before the changes. There were a lot of ships out there that he didn't recognize. He knew the Pellayen ships, and the submarines had to be from Earth, but there were other designs he didn't know. He remembered what the ship that shot at him looked like, and they weren't the one being destroyed. It was the Pellayen and Earth ships that were being destroyed.

"Okay! They want war. I'll give them war!" John snarled. "Bartolos, you better sit down and strap in. I can't sit by and watch my people get slaughtered. They want a fight! I'll give them a fight they won't forget!"

Bartolos was surprised to see John's ship go from a complete standstill to beyond light speed simply by moving the controls forward. He had never seen a Pellayen ship controlled in this way and certainly never gone faster than the speed of light. On top of that, there were no G-forces whatsoever. The maneuvers John was making were impossible with any other ship.

"Bartolos," John said. "Get ready. This is probably going to scare you, but don't worry. I know what I'm doing. Don't ask me how, but this ship has become a dangerous weapon," John said, slamming the controls all the way forward. In an instant, they were smashing through an Itchaian' ship. It happened so fast that it was over before Bartolos could raise his arms to protect himself. They were already smashing through another one just as he was lowering his arms.

"AGMA!" Bartolos had said, as they slammed through the first one. "Newnas Tasksssss!" he said as they slammed through the second.

John glanced at him. "There is some kind of shield around my ship," John said, taking a second look at Bartolos. Bartolos sat frozen in place, and it looked like he had his eyes closed. "Come on, my friend, I need you to help me, so I don't take out one of my own. You have to have your eyes open to do that," John said, punching through another ship.

Bartolos had his eyes open, but was in shock. He had never seen the carnage of War, and certainly never used a ship to smash through other ships. John's ship was moving so fast, they would smash through one ship, then almost immediately, smash through another. There was no way the Itchaian could see John coming. The Itchaian had no chance at all. Bartolos cringed every time they crashed through another ship.

Awth stood staring out his windshield, watching Itchaian ships explode for no obvious reason. He couldn't see anyone shooting at them, but they were exploding, and exploding in a continuous line. "What is going on out there? Are you doing this, John?" he wondered. He didn't quite understand what was happening, but John had said his ship had become a dangerous weapon. Could John be doing this?

Awntoon and Fallgonan came forward and reported that they had fixed the engine. When they saw what was happening outside, they too were confused. Who or what was destroying those ships?

Poor Bartolos was on the edge of his seat, cringing each time they smashed through another ship. John could see the pain and sickness on Bartolos's face. John was starting to feel the same way, but what else could he do? The Itchaians were killing his countrymen. He had a ship that could stop them. He had to continue. This was the only way to stop the Itchaians.

John attempted to ease Bartolos's mind by explaining what had changed on his ship. "When the Sperneckeens drive is on, a shield forms around my ship. As you can see, the ship becomes a Juggernaut. I have gone through Asteroids and never felt a thing.

I believe all these changes happened because of the way I replaced the engine. My ship went dead after the Aliens shot that yellow crap at me and I used one of the engines I was carrying to replace it. I cobbed it all together, and that changed things. My ship wasn't like this before the Itchaians shot me. So either that yellow crap did something or my changing the engine did."

Bartolos nodded, "Do you know if the bolts of energy from the Itchaian ship can get through the shield?" he asked, never taking his eyes off the windshield.

John shrugged his shoulders. "I'm not sure. I thought that ship that attacked me got a shot off, but I don't know if they missed, or the shield protected me."

"They did shoot you, and I thought they hit you. I didn't see what happened to your ship. It just vanished. None of us knew what happened," Bartolos said.

As he listened, John had inadvertently let the ship slow down. That allowed Bartolos to relax a bit. He sighed and turned his head away from the windshield. When he did, he spotted something in the distance. "Look! There are some very large ships over there."

John turned and spotted three large ships sitting far from the battle. "Mother Ships," John said. "That must be where all these smaller ships came from. That is probably where the invasion force will come from after they shoot down the last of our ships. I can't let that happen!" John said, pushing the ship up to full speed again.

"John, stop!" Bartolos pleaded, placing his big hand on John's chest. "Maybe there is another way. Let's go to one of those Mother Ships and try to communicate with them. I have gained great mental strength from Toc. Maybe I can do something to stop them. If that doesn't work, maybe we can show them what this ship is capable of. Your ship is moving so fast that they don't know it's you destroying their ships. They need to see what your ship can do. You should show them they can't win this war because of your ship. If we show them that, they might leave."

John brought the ship to a stop. Bartolos was right, and he did not enjoy murdering these aliens any more than Bartolos did. At first, he had been highly motivated to cause as much damage as possible, but even at such speeds, he had caught glimpses of Itchaians being crushed to death on his shield. It was a horrible sight and made his stomach turn, but if he stopped his attack, the Itchaians would win the War and take the Earth from mankind.

What Bartolos proposed was a good plan. If he could demonstrate the power of his ship, the Itchaian might break off their attack and leave. If they didn't, he would destroy the entire Itchaian fleet.

John headed for the nearest mothership. He approached the massive Ship slowly, wanting them to see him. As he got closer, several fighters the size of his own came out to meet him. He prepared to dodge their bolts of Yellow Fire, but was attacked from behind by two Itchaian ships he hadn't seen coming. They were shooting at him from point-blank range, but nothing was getting through the shield. The yellow fire splashed harmlessly on the shield. Three more Itchaian ships surrounded him and fired their weapons. Five Ships were now shooting their yellow crap at him, and still nothing was getting through. He and Bartolos were perfectly safe inside the shield.

John kept his ship in one spot, letting them shoot at him. He was hoping they would realize they weren't doing any damage to him. More ships kept coming, and before long, so many ships were shooting at him that he couldn't see through the yellow splashes hitting the shield. When he turned his Ship to look behind, he saw just enough to see that many Itchaian ships had left Earth and were coming toward him. He was drawing the enemy away from Earth, and that pleased him.

"But how long is it going to take for you to get the message? You can't hurt my ship," John mumbled. Finally, the shooting stopped. They still surrounded his ship, but were no longer shooting at him.

"Do I dare drop the shield so you can talk with them?" John asked Bartolos.

Bartolos didn't answer. John shook his head. "I don't think so. Not yet. Let's see what they do," he said.

John waited a moment longer, then moved his ship toward the Mothership very slowly. It only took one shot from one ship, and they were all firing again.

John was still angry that these Itchaian had attacked Earth, and frustrated that they weren't getting the message. He jammed the controls forward. His ship blew through the Itchaian fighters setting between him and the Mother Ship, then smashed a hole through the Mother Ship. Once through the Mother Ship, he turned to look back and see what the Itchaian would do.

He had left a large hole through the Mother Ship. Sparks flew from broken wires. Debris floated toward him, but the worst was the bodies floating toward them. Some of them were still struggling in their death throes, and some of them were children. He and Bartolos groaned. It was a sight neither of them wanted to see, and neither would forget.

"Did you get the message now?" John said, hoping they wouldn't make him continue demonstrating the power of his ship.

****

Awth had seen the Itchaian ships exploding in a line, leading his eyes to the Mother Ships. "Oh no!" he said when he spotted John's ship sitting in front of the nearest one. "OH NO!" he said louder when he saw Itchaian ships moving to meet John from the front, and more from behind. He grabbed the radio and tried to warn John, but got no answer. Then it was too late. The shooting started. So many Itchaian ships were already shooting at John, and more were leaving Earth, rushing toward him. John was a sitting duck.

Awth, Tellgus, Awntoon, and Fallgonan groaned when they saw it happen. They were convinced it was the end of John and Bartolos. Then suddenly, a hole appeared in the mother ship. Something had smashed through it! Suddenly, all the Itchaian ships around Earth headed toward that Mother Ship. "What in the world is going on?" Awth said.

****

John and Bartolos had just punched a hole through the mothership and now waited for their reaction. The ship was damaged but far from destroyed. "John," Bartolos said. "Let's try to communicate with them. We have hurt them. Maybe they will listen now."

But even as Bartolos spoke, the Itchaian fighters came around the mother ship and began shooting again.

"God! What does it take for them to learn? This is unreal!" John said.

John was again surrounded from top to bottom and side to side. "Can't they see that they aren't doing a thing to my ship?" he said, shaking his head. "Alright! Lesson number two!" he said, pushing the controls forward. Several smaller ships were destroyed as he headed toward the Mother ship.

He purposely moved his ship slowly enough that the aliens could see what he was doing. He put the shield against the Mother Ship, then started crushing through it. The outer wall buckled, and everything inside flew into space as the air escaped. He continued pressing into the ship and regretted it. He and Bartolos were sickened as they watched an entire family get crushed between the shield and the inner walls of the Mother Ship. John closed his eyes and jammed the controls forward so he wouldn't have to see the horrible carnage he was causing. Seeing whole families smeared like Jelly on his invisible shield was too much.

"I want this to end," Bartolos said.

"So do I! But I can't stop until they stop! Please stop and talk to us!" John pleaded.

It wasn't to end yet. The smaller craft came around the Mothership and started firing again.

"Damn it!" John yelled. "Okay fine. Here comes lesson number three! If this doesn't wake you up, nothing will!" he said, shoving the controls forward. He was desperate to end this war. He smashed back and forth through the mother ship until nothing was left. Then he flew toward the next Mother Ship just slow enough that the Itchaian could see where he was going. He stopped in front of the Mothership, daring them to start shooting. "Leave, or I will destroy you all," John said through clenched teeth. He was praying that the Itchaian would not attack again, and he could stop the killing.

For a moment, nothing happened. John turned his ship to look back and see what the Itchaian were doing. The Mothership he had destroyed was little more than rubble. The smaller Ships were again coming after him. John closed his eyes in despair. When he looked again, his hopes rose. The Itchaian were going around him and heading out into space. "Is it over?" he asked, turning his ship to see where they were going. The last two motherships were moving away as well! "They're leaving!" John said happily.

"I don't think so," Bartolos said, pointing into space. John looked and saw hundreds, maybe thousands more Itchaian Mother Ships heading his way.

"Oh God, please no," John said. "Don't do this. Bartolos, I don't know if I can do this. "

Bartolos understood and put a hand on John's shoulder. "You are not alone. I am here with you. We do what we are forced to do. It is not all on your shoulders, John."

What happened next was confusing. The retreating forces met the new oncoming forces. It was a shock to see them start shooting at each other. Thousands of fighters poured out of the new Motherships and engaged the retreating fighters. John and Bartolos had expected all the fighters to turn and head straight at them. The last thing they expected was for them to start fighting each other.

"What's going on?" John said.

The battle lasted for a few hours. So many fighters and one of the retreating Mother Ships were destroyed. Finally, the fighting stopped, and all the remaining fighters flew back into the Motherships. Then the whole Itchaian fleet turned and started to leave.

John and Bartolos looked at each other. "I think it's over?" John said. Bartolos only shrugged his shoulders.

All the Itchaian ships were leaving. John turned his Ship, looking for Itchaian ships that might still be around, but all he saw were Pellayen and Earth Ships coming toward him. "Earth must have sent its forces to support us," John said, then shook his head. "I don't know if I will ever get used to seeing Submarines in space." Seeing them put an odd grin on his face. "It's just wrong, but as I think about it, it makes sense. Submarines are already airtight and very solidly constructed. Put a Pellayen engine on one, and it would make a great spaceship. As long as they have an air supply, the Pellayen engine would take care of the rest."

Not seeing any Itchaian ships around, John dropped the shield and turned on the radio. Immediately, he heard someone calling, wanting to know who had driven the Itchaian away and how they had done it. When they learned it was Captain John Baines, the radio came alive with congratulations and heartfelt thanks. Then someone called through all the other voices to warn John.

"John, there's an Itchaian ship coming up behind you!"

John turned his ship and found himself facing one lone Itchaian ship. Quickly, he turned on the shield and started circling it. He wasn't about to start trusting them now. He waited for some action from the Itchaian's, but they just sat there.

"We have to try and communicate with them at some point," Bartolos said.

John nodded and dropped the shield but kept his ship moving in case they fired on him.

Bartolos reached out with his mind and found an Itchaian already trying to talk to him. "His name is Margo," Bartolos reported. "He's saying this War should never have happened. He is apologizing for what his people have done. Those responsible for the War are being dealt with. Many were killed in the battle, but most were eager to surrender.

He says their planet was dying, so they built a fleet of spaceships and evacuated to space. Several Mother Ships went missing, and they didn't know what happened to them. Then someone escaped from those missing ships, found the fleet, and reported that the Ships had slipped away on purpose. Liote was the one Itchaian responsible for everything that had happened. Liote managed to take control of three motherships and became very powerful. He controlled everyone around him. He convinced…no… he forced the rest to see things his way. Anyone who opposed him was murdered.

They found Earth and the Humans, and he forced his army to poison, then attack Earth. He got them to believe that they had the right to take Earth from the Humans.

John! They had no idea this was happening until someone escaped to tell them. Once they learn what Liote was doing, they came to stop him. Margo is here to surrender his people to the judgement of the Humans. There is a limit to what they are willing to suffer, but they wish to somehow make amends for what their people have done. They are asking for mercy."

"What?" John said incredulously. "They are willing to accept punishment and are asking for mercy?"

"That is what they are asking for. I have no say in this. What do I tell him?" Bartolos asked.

John shrugged. Bartolos, they killed millions of my people. If I take this back to Earth, they will want to put them all to death. Millions died because of their poison. Some of them could be my friends. I can't imagine the Itchaian getting much mercy from Earth."

Bartolos put a hand on John's shoulder. "But what about you, John? Can they expect mercy from you? You and your ship drew the Itchaian away from Earth and stopped the attack. If the War had continued, you and your ship would have been the ones to win the battle. And what if you took Margos' plea back to Earth, and your governments wanted blood? Would war start again, and who would have to fight that battle for them? It's you, John. So, who do you think has the right to make this decision?"

John thought about that and saw how right Bartolos was. He had ended this War, and would have, even if the new arrivals had attacked. Earth was losing the War until he arrived.

"I don't want any more killing, and I will not give up my ship so someone else can continue the killing. Tell Margo to take his people and never return. If they do, I will be here and destroy every last one of them.”

Bartolos nodded. “Adonai would be pleased,” he said, and turned his mind to Margo. Soon, the Itchaian ship started moving away. “What will you tell your people?” Bartolos asked.

“The truth,” John said. “I will explain everything Margo told us. I will tell them that Margo and his people came to stop the War and that they were truly sorry for the deaths of our people. I will not tell them about their surrender and that I let them go in peace. I will tell them, if they want to chase after them, they will do it without me and my ship. I want no more to do with this, and want to go home to my wife.”

Bartolos nodded. “You are a good man, John. You are a better Pellayen.” John liked hearing that.

They watched the Itchaian move out of sight. A few ships from Earth stayed behind to make sure the Itchaian didn’t return, while John and the rest moved back to Earth.

News of John’s return reached Earth long before he got there. The celebration that followed was grand. John and Bartolos were heroes, and the world rejoiced that the Itchaian had gone. The party would last for days, but John and Bartolos didn’t feel like heroes and wouldn’t stay to the end. They felt like criminals for what they had done. They had done what they had to, but they didn’t want to celebrate the death of so many Itchaians.

When John was asked to explain what happened with his meeting with Margo, many of them became angry that John had taken it on himself to make the decision, and said he had no authority to decide to let them leave.

John replied, "I stopped the War, and if War were to continue, I was the only one who would have fought it. I think I have every right to tell them they could go. I want nothing more to do with all this killing, and think about this. If you choose to go after them, you do it without me or my ship. I am going home."

To most of them, what John said made a lot of sense. He was solely responsible for drawing the Itchaian away from Earth and ending the War. He was also responsible for the death of so many Itchaian's. He had taken out so many fighters, and who knows how many Itchaian were killed when he destroyed the Mother Ship. He told them of the horrors he had seen when he did that, and many of those angry with him began to back off. Most agreed that he had made the right decision. They didn't like that the Itchaian got off Scott Free, but it was the right decision.

John, Bartolos, Awth, Fallgonan, and Awntoon were happy to leave the celebration and flew their ships up to the Pellayen Gate. They all went back to Pellaya and landed at Niglaie Air Carrier Center. John was surprised to see it had been renamed the 'John Baine's Air Carrier Center'. This tribute to himself only added to his joy at being home and being a Pellayen.

All John wanted now was to see Nellaynan and show her he was alive. He left the ship and ran into the building looking for her. He spotted her walking across a hallway from one room to another.

Awth had warned him that Nellaynan had taken his death very hard and wasn't herself, but he was still stunned by what he saw. Nellaynan walked with her head down and shoulders slumped. The young energetic woman he knew, appeared defeated and broken. This woman was deeply hurt, and it was on display for all to see.

John stepped forward and softly called her name. She only glanced in his direction, oblivious to everything around her. She continued walking across the hall to the other room. The other Pellayens in the hallway saw him and moved out of the way, holding their tongues and minds not wanting to interfere.

John felt so sorry when he saw the look on her face. His beautiful Nellaynan looked worn out and haggard. He stood motionless, watching this shell of a woman step through the door and out of sight. He didn't need Mental Ability to feel the world of pain this poor woman was in. Awth had warned him that she claimed she had seen him after his death, and it hurt her all the more. His death was tearing her apart.

He wondered how he should approach her because of her fragile state. He stepped toward the door just as she backed out of the doorway. She backed into the hallway and stood motionless, looking straight ahead into the room in front of her. Then she slowly turned her head and looked straight at him. She started to cry. "You're not real," she said, backing away from him.

"I am," John said, stepping toward her.

The papers Nellaynan had been holding slipped from her hands and fell to the floor. "No, you're dead! You're not real! I'm seeing things again," she said.

"Nellaynan, it's me. I'm alive."

"Nooo!" she said, and again stepped back away from him.

"Nellaynan, you are not seeing things. I am here. I am alive. I am so sorry I couldn't tell you, but I'm here now. I want so badly to hold you."

"John! It's really you?" Nellaynan asked, taking a few steps toward him. A woman stepped toward Nellaynan, and Nellaynan jerked her head toward her. The woman told her that what she was seeing and hearing was real. It was John. He was alive.

"Sweety, it's me. I'm really here," John said, moving toward her.

Nellaynan finally accepted the truth and ran to him. She threw herself at him with a force resembling that of Bartolos. John loved every breathless minute of it. Everyone in the hallway surrounded them, patting them on the shoulders and welcoming John home. Nellaynan was completely unaware of them. With her eyes closed, she clung to John like she would never let go again, and John wasn't about to complain.

CHAPTER FIFTEEN
TRACK THEM DOWN

John and Nellaynan went home to be alone, but that only lasted a few hours. The word was out that John was alive and had returned home; naturally, everyone was coming to see him. Gullaynianna was the first to knock on the door and wrap her arms around him. She was anxious to hear what had happened. "When you died," she said. "I heard you call to me. I felt you die, John, so I know you did. How is it you are here, alive?"

John nodded. "I did call out to you, and as far as I know, I should still be dead," he said. "Gail, I was in a Coma or something, and went without food or water for over a month. How is that possible? I shouldn't be here."

Gullaynianna nodded. "You might be able to survive not eating for a month, but I can't see how you could survive that long without water."

They were interrupted as a large group came to the door, all wanting John's attention. John waited until the room was full and no more people were coming before he started telling his story. He only wanted to tell the story once.

"You know I was shot by the Itchaians. Everyone thought I had been killed, and you were right. I did die. I have a clear memory of that. I felt terrible pain when I was hit, and I felt my life leave me. As I faded away, I thought of you, Gail, and how you could save me if you were there, but my last thoughts were of you, Nellaynan. If I didn't know it then, I sure know it now. I love you, girl. I certainly knew it at that moment.

After I died, I was alive again and floating up out of my body. I could see my body sitting at the controls, blood was running from my mouth and nose, and my eyes looked glazed. I could see I was dead.

Then I was pulled into darkness. I saw other people and animals of all kinds around me. Most of them were flying toward a brilliant light. Others seemed afraid to go forward.

I moved to the light as fast as I could, and when I stepped into the light, I was greeted by my parents and Eddy, my brother. They had died in a plane crash years ago. Other people I knew who had died before me were also there to greet me. Everyone I saw seemed very happy. Everyone I saw seemed to be emitting light from their very being. They wore robes that seemed to glow as well. Some brighter than others, but they were all magnificent.

Then my wife Angie came to me and stood in front of me. I remembered her, not from our time together on Earth, but from Heaven before either of us was born. We knew each other in heaven before we were born in the flesh. We had made plans to be together on Earth. She asked me why I was there and said she didn't think it was my time. She was right because I am back with you now.

Jesus himself came to me and welcomed me to heaven. I know we talked about many things, but I can't remember most of that conversation. You can imagine I had a lot of questions, but the question I remember asking was about the Pellayen gate. I wanted to know what it was. Jesus told me he would let Angie explain that for me, and asked her to show me around Heaven.

Remember, Angie died before she knew anything about the gate, but because she had come to Heaven, she had the answer for me. She told me that the Pellayen Gate, like the beginning of the Universe, and the start of Mankind, were all examples of God snapping his fingers. Scientists have the Big Bang theory to help explain the beginning of the Universe, but they can't explain exactly how it started. 'That.' She said. 'Was God snapping his fingers, and the Universe began to expand.'

Then she said the beginning of mankind was the same thing. Man has the theory of evolution, and to some extent, that theory is true, but God snapped his fingers and mankind began.

Then she finally answered my question. What is the Pellayen gate? She told me to think of two helium-filled Balloons on strings and how they rest against each other. That small area where the balloons touch is like the Pellayen gate. If you were to pass through the walls of the balloons, you would enter the space of the other balloon. You would enter a different area of space. She said, 'The balloons represent the cells of the universe. One cell contains Earth and everything in that space. The other cell contains Pellaya and everything in that space. Both cells are of the same universe, but are separated by thin walls. Energy passes from one to the other where the cells touch. When you open the Gate, you flow through with that energy to the other side.

For us, when we stand on Earth, Pellaya is incredibly far away. Traveling that far in the blink of an eye seems impossible, but the gate isn't of the physical world. It is of the spirit world. Everything that is made in the physical world is first made of spirit. The Gate is a living spirit placed there because God wants it there.'

John shook his head. "When I was in Heaven, this was so simple to understand. Now, back in the physical world, it is slipping from me. There, I could see how Pellayen ships merge with the flow of energy, which pulls us into the Pellayen cell. Pellaya is millions of light years away, but in the spirit world, Pellaya is just on the other side of the cell wall. It's that simple.

Angie told me that mankind would never understand how it worked until they understood God. The Pellayen gate works because God snapped his fingers.

I learned that everything in our lives was planned ahead of time. Jesus told me the gate was there to bring Man and Pellayen together. Before we were born, Randy and I agreed to be the first ones to survive the gate and make it back to Earth to let the existence of Pellaya be known. That amazes me."

John shook his head again. "Sadly, Jesus caused me to forget much of what I learned. I asked many questions and was amazed at the answers, but Jesus told me he couldn't allow me to remember those things. If he allowed me to remember, I would complete my Mission as fast as I could, so I could return to heaven. The results would be that others' missions would not be completed, and my mission wouldn't have as good a result as it could.

One thing I know for sure: the spiritual world is the real world. We were all there before we were born, and we all return to it. While in Heaven, we all plan our lives on Earth and Pellaya for whatever purpose we choose to come into the physical world.

Maybe to teach or to help others, but we all had a plan. I planned my life with the help of my friends in Heaven. Some of you chose to go to Earth, and some to Pellaya.

I am fully aware that the Physical world is finite and will one day pass away, but the spiritual world will live on forever. You have tried to tell me that before. Now I understand it and am thrilled to know it," John said, looking around the room. "It is amazing that we worked together to plan for this day so that each of us benefits from it. "

Everyone around him was spellbound as he told his story. They knew it was all true and were excited that he finally understood it himself.

"I know that's true," A woman said. "But what happened after you woke up from the coma. I heard you tell Gullaynianna you went without food or water for more than a month. What happened there? How did you survive that?"

John smiled. "God snapped his fingers. Just before he sent me back, Jesus said something I didn't understand. He said, 'You will need water. I will see to that need.' Now I understand that God snapped his fingers and preserved me." The woman smiled and nodded her head. She understood perfectly and asked no more of John.

John answered a few more questions, but eventually everyone thought it best to leave John and Nellaynan alone. They could see how much they wanted to be together, so they left. John and Nellaynan were finally alone. Nellaynan had been looking for the right moment to tell John her news, and this was it. She took his hand and placed it on her belly. "John, have you noticed this?"

John looked where she had placed his hand. "Notice what? I've been so preoccupied I haven't noticed much of…." There was a long pause. Then John looked up at her. "A baby?" he asked.

Nellaynans' smile could have lit up a room. John's look of surprise vanished, and was replaced with joy. He was going to be a father, and he couldn't be happier.

Early the next morning, John was up and out of the house, telling everyone he was going to be a father. He wanted to celebrate and pass out cigars, but that wasn't the custom on Pellaya. Here, families came together to pray for the health of the family and child. Everyone contributed food and drink, and there was a great feast. This was a much better practice than passing out cigars, and he enjoyed every minute of the celebration.

John was on top of the world. He had been through a lot and somehow made it back home to a woman he loved and his soon-to-be-born child. He had much to be thankful for and wanted to share his joy with his friends, which he did.

Several days later, Awth and Bartolos came to the door. As soon as John opened the door, he could see this visit was of a much more serious nature. They wanted him to help with the Chenowa. John wasn't fully aware of who the Chenowa were, or what the problem was, so Awth reminded him that the Chenowa were the little gray aliens who had been abducting people from Earth. "The Chenowa have left Earth and come to Pellaya and are now taking our people. We want this stopped. The council has created a plan to stop them, and we would like you to be involved in it."

"Why me?" John asked.

"Because of the shield protecting your ship. We understand that the shield stops thought transmissions. If that is true, it could be helpful if the Chenowa try to control our minds again," Awth said.

"Do your plans include using my ship to destroy one of theirs as a show of strength?"

"No, we have no desire to damage anything unless there is no other choice. We want peace, not War. Pellaya has never had a War, so it doesn't know how to wage War. We want to talk to them because it will benefit the Chenowa to hear what we say. Bartolos had an encounter with a Chenowa named Toc. From that encounter he learned that the Chenowa race is sick and dying. We don't know the extent of the sickness because they won't talk to us. We want to force them to talk to us, so we understand their situation. It is possible we could help them, but we can't unless they start talking to us and stop taking our people from their homes against their will!"

"Okay, how do you plan to force them to come to the table?" John said. "What is it you want from me?"

"Two things. The first is the Chenowa. Your ship is the key. Hopefully, the shield will keep them from controlling our minds and sending us away. If they start shooting at us, they could blast away all day and never do a bit of damage. If that didn't get them talking, a small demonstration of what your ship is capable of would surely get their attention. Maybe something as simple as breaking down a wall, I don't know, but we must get them talking. Bartolos thinks he knows what's happening to their race and could solve their problem."

"Really?" John said, looking at Bartolos.

Bartolos nodded. "Yes. I have discovered that they use their mental power differently than we do. If I am right, they use their mental power in a way that could deform their bodies."

"And do you know how to correct that?" John asked.

"Yes. I believe I do." Bartolos said.

"That's something to bargain with, alright," John said. "Bartolos, is it something I could understand?"

"I'm sure of it," Bartolos said. "It's fairly simple. They have been using their mental power improperly for hundreds of thousands of years. I believe they force the mental power out of themselves through their bodies. This hurts their bodies. It's like trying to force water through a sponge. The sponge prevents the water from flowing, but if the water is pushed with enough force, it can damage the sponge. I believe that is what's happening to the Chenowa. The Chenowa's mental power is incredibly strong, but they direct it out of themselves through their bodies. Do you see?"

"I do," John said.

Bartolos nodded. "We Pellayens allow our Mental Ability to leave directly from our souls. That's where the power emanates, so it never touches our bodies. The Chenowa need to understand this and stop thinking of their Mental Ability as a thing of the physical world. Mental Ability is from the spirit, not this physical world. It's that simple, but it makes a huge difference."

"Ah! I understand. And you know how to stop it, how to teach them?"

Bartolos nodded. "I do, and I will teach them if they will start talking to us.

"Well! That is a great bargaining chip, but you haven't told me how you plan to get them talking. Do you want to destroy one of their ships to get their attention?" John asked.

"No," Awth said. "We don't want to do that unless it becomes necessary. The council has debated this for two days, and we believe they must have a mother ship or base nearby. Someplace we will find someone in authority. If we go there uninvited and land, that will get them talking to us."

John nodded. "Sure. That's simple enough. My shield would protect us as long as we needed," John said. He thought a moment. "You said there were two things you wanted from me. What is the second thing?"

"Yes," Awth said. "You may not like this one. If you don't, we understand. You know the Itchaian's' planet was destroyed, and that is why that group tried to take the Earth from you. They came looking for a new home."

"Yes, I know," John said.

"I think you also know that we discovered a planet many years ago that could be inhabited. The council has agreed to offer it to the Itchaian's. We have ships looking for the Itchaian right now. When we find them, it may be necessary to use your ship to approach them. I'm sure you can understand why."

"Yeah, they might start shooting at you, and from my experience, you're right not to trust them," John said.

"We don't know what to expect," Awth said. "Bartolos tells me he saw a peaceful people in Margo's mind, but the faction that attacked Earth was intent on wiping out all humanity. It is best to proceed with caution. Hopefully, they will give us a chance to explain why we have sot them out. One way or another, we want to talk to them. Pellaya seeks peace with all her neighbors, and if we offer them this planet, that should go a long way toward that goal.

We can help the Chenowa and the Itchaian if they talk to us. Getting them what they need should start peaceful relations with them. John," Awth said, turning to face him. "We understand if you don't want to help us with the Itchaian's. They murdered millions of your people, and you might want revenge, but I have to ask. Will you help us?"

"It's true, at first I wanted to kill them all, but I saw so many of them die at my hand and in such a terrible way," John said, shaking his head. "No, I don't want to be part of any more killing. That is one reason I let them leave in peace. So yes, I will do this as a form of penance for those deaths. I will help you with the Chenowa and the Itchaian's," John said.

Awth understood. "What you did was no crime, John. You were defending your people. You did nothing wrong."

"I understand that, Awth, but I saw their bodies smear onto the shield around my ship. I did that to them. That is a picture I can't forget. I need to do this to help remove that stain. There is one more thing," John said. "You need to hear this, Awth. Many years ago, something very similar to what the Itchaian did, happened on Earth," John said, then opened his mind to show Awth Hitler and the Nazis.

"I see," Awth said, nodding. "It is very much the same, and your world forgave the German people for this?"

"It wasn't the German people that did it. It was the Nazi's, and one mans ability to use them, he force them to do his bidding. That's what happened with the Itchaians."

Awth saw it very clearly and understood John's willingness, not to forget, but to forgive. He was pleased John could put aside his need for vengeance and be part of both plans for peace. It was true he needed John's ship, but he wanted John just as much. John had become a bit of a Hero. His life seemed tragic, and yet he always came out on top.

When he and Randy were floating around Pellaya, John unknowingly called out to Bartolos, who saved them. Then, when he thought he was going insane, he discovered he had hidden Mental Ability, which he now enjoyed very much. When he was shot and killed by Itchaian's, he visited heaven where he met Jesus and learned about the Pellayen gate. When he returned, he found himself in a souped-up ship that saved Earth from the Itchaian's.

In Earthly terms, John was good luck! In Pellayen terms, John was blessed, and they wanted him with them on both the Chenowa and Itchaian missions. John was good to have around.

The Pellayens had already sent ships to search for the Itchaian fleet, but had not found them. Finding a Chenowa ship, on the other hand, was as easy as looking for one. But following their Ships was a bit harder. The Chenowa would use their minds and cause the Pellayen pilot to go away.

Finally, a Pellayen tracker spotted a Chenowa ship dropping into the Northern Ocean. The tracker followed and found several massive city-sized Ships sitting on the bottom of the ocean. The tracker watched and determined which of the ships had the most activity. That was the ship that would have someone in authority on it. Now they could put their plan to work.

While the Council made plans to enter the Chenowa ship, John took his Ship to the Southern Ocean, where he could learn to pilot his Ship underwater. He had been told that moving too fast underwater could tear a ship apart, but his Ship had a shield. How was that going to affect things? His controls were hyper-sensitive, and he could easily go too fast and tear the ship apart if the shield wasn't up. He needed to practice and experiment.

He quickly learned the danger of using the shield underwater. He entered the water with the shield up. The shield kept the water away until he turned it off. Then the water slammed into his ship with enough force to crush it if he had been deeper. They were going to the Chenowan ships, which were very deep. His Ship could go that deep without the shield, but if he had gone to that depth, then turned the shield off, his ship and everything in it would have been crushed down to the size of a softball. Now he knew he would have to leave the shield off until they were at the same depth as the Chenowa ships. Then he could turn it on to protect them from Chenowa's Mental Abilities.

He learned that if he turned the shield on while deeper in the water, then flew out of the water, the water remained inside the shield. He could carry that water out of the Ocean and into the air. When he turned the shield off, the water fell back into the Ocean. It amused him to think how valuable his ship would be in fighting forest fires.

John did one more test. With the shield up, he dove deeper and deeper, listening for anything that suggested the ship was being stressed at all. He never heard a sound. His shield had smashed through ships and asteroids, so he was sure the Ship could go all the way to the bottom, and it did. Satisfied, John left the Ocean and headed home.

When he got back, he found Awth and Bartolos looking for him. They boarded John's ship, and Awth directed John to the Ocean site where the Mothership had been spotted. They flew into the water and headed deep. The Motherships were easy to find. They were massive and had lights on that made them hard to miss. Awth pointed out the ship they intended to enter. John turned on the shield and flew underneath it.

Under the Mothership, they spotted a large opening in the bottom. The inside of their ship was well lit, and it was obvious this was where the smaller ships entered. John moved up through the opening and discovered they couldn't see because of the water contained inside the shield. He had to dump it. He turned the shield off, dumping the water, then quickly turned the shield back on. Now they could see what lay around them, and what they saw was disturbing.

"Look at this place!" Awth said. There was clutter everywhere, and everything looked dirty and run-down.

"What a mess!" John said. "They need to do some housekeeping around here."

It was not what any of them had expected. It was filthy. They couldn't see anyone around until Bartolos pointed to a doorway. "We have company." He said as a line of armed Chenowens moved out onto the dock. The Chenowens were trying to hurry and look impressive, but they looked awkward and anything but impressive.

"What's wrong with them?" John asked.

"We have their attention now," Awth said. "I hope we have put them on edge by entering their ship uninvited. It's a taste of their own medicine. They take our people without permission, so we have entered their ship without permission. That makes me feel good."

"Yeah, chew on that, Chenowa," John said playfully, mocking Awth. "And we'll stay as long as we want to! So there!"

Awth and Bartolos were grinning with amusement as they turned and looked at John. John just shrugged. But he was right. The Chenowa could do nothing to them as long as they had the shield up.

They hovered in the air, waiting to see what the Chenowa would do. They stared at each other for some time. The Chenowa weren't shooting at them, but weren't talking either. Someone had to make a move.

"Can you set us down?" Awth asked John.

"Not with the shield up. It would crush the dock."

"And if we drop the shield, we are vulnerable," Awth said. "But we need to communicate with them."

Bartolos stepped forward. "The Chenowa have never actually hurt anyone, at least that Toc knew of. They do want Pease. They are doing it this way because they are desperate to save their race. I doubt they will fire on us unless we start something. They might try to control our minds if we lower the shield, but one of us has to do something. We can't just stare at each other."

Awth turned to John. "Turn off Sperneckeens and let me try to talk to them. If you feel they are trying to control us, turn it back on."

John turned the shield off and watched as Awth and Bartolos tried to contact the Chenowa.

Even John felt anger from the Chenowa. They didn't like this intrusion into their ship. Awth's answer carried his anger back at them. *Yet you think it ok for you to take people from their homes any time you see fit. We are here giving you a taste of your own medicine. We will talk with someone today, or you will suffer the consequences. My people and I are angry that you do this. We can and will cause damage to this ship unless you talk with us! We Pellayens are willing to help you if we can, but not if you continue to treat us as your playthings.*

John saw Chenowa armed guards raise their weapons toward the ship. He immediately turned on the shield, and the mental link was broken. They waited to see what the Chenowa would do.

John looked over at Awth. "I was under the impression that you didn't know what you were going to say," he said, ribbing Awth.

"Yes, my anger did roll off my Mental tongue, didn't it."

John nodded. "Yeah, I felt it and so did they, I'm sure. What did you see?" John asked.

"Anger, surprise, and a strong desire for us to leave," Awth said.

After a few minutes, they were still waiting. The Chenowa guns were still pointed at John's ship, but no one was shooting. "Well, what do we do now?" John asked.

Bartolos had an idea, "John, we know the shield can carry water, so I'm sure I could stand inside the shield."

John shrugged his shoulders. "Yeah, I'm sure it would hold you, but I'm not sure what it would do to you. You might get an electric shock or something. Why?"

"I was thinking, it might help to be face to face with them, even if the shield is between us. And remember, they can't see the shield, so they don't know we have it. If I stand inside the shield, maybe someone will approach me and discover the shield. At least then they would know we have such a thing."

"Well, we need to do something," John said. "We can't just sit here staring at each other all day, and I'm not all that comfortable turning the shield off with them pointing their guns at us. If you go out there, Bartolos, you might draw their fire. Then they would see that we have a shield protecting us."

Bartolos looked at Awth. Awth nodded. "Go. I don't believe you will be in any danger, and maybe something will happen to get us talking."

Bartolos went to the door and extended the ramp. The Chenowa moved closer to the door, continuing to point their weapons. Bartolos walked to the end of the ramp and stood there. He knew the Chenowa didn't want war with anyone, but he couldn't understand why they were so unwilling to talk.

Bartolos looked down from the end of the ramp to the floor of the Chenowa ship. It was about fifteen feet below him. Somewhere between the end of the ramp and the floor of the Chenowa ship was the unseen shield. He sat down on the ramp, then slid off it and let himself hang off the end of it. His feet touched something solid. It could only be the shield.

He could feel that the shield was curved and very slick. His feet wanted to slide around on it. He couldn't get any traction on its surface at all. If he let go of the ramp, he would slide to the bottom, and since that was what he wanted, he let go. He slid down, coming to rest lying on the shield two feet above the floor of the Chenowa ship. *Such a graceful entrance*, he thought to himself as he got to his feet and stood before the Chenowa. It amused him that the Chenowa would see him floating above the floor. "Don't you two forget that I'm here," Bartolos said, directing his thoughts to John and Awth.

"Not happening," John answered.

All the Chenowa guns were now pointing at Bartolos. He stood looking at them, wondering what to do next. Then he noticed many Chenowa coming out onto the dock around him. Bartolos was dismayed by what he saw. Every one of them looked sickly. Many were limping and deformed, being helped by others who were not much better off. They struggled out onto the floor to look at him and the ship.

Bartolos took another look at the armed Chenowa. They were in better shape, but far from healthy. "Their dying!" he said softly.

Bartolos suddenly felt great sorrow for them. This was not at all what he expected. From Toc's mind, he knew they were a very proud and strong race suffering some kind of physical issue, but he wasn't expecting this. They had become so weak that even their Mental prowess didn't matter anymore. Every one of them was sick.

Because of his fight with Toc, and after seeing this, he could understand a little better why this proud race didn't want to talk. They had been brought low. Lower than anyone could imagine. They were too proud to be seen in such a vulnerable state. Talking to anyone would eventually expose their Mental weakness as well. It was too embarrassing for them to handle.

As he looked around, it wasn't hard to imagine that the Chenowa race wouldn't last but a few more years, and the last of them would be gone. The longer he watched, the more he understood their desperation and despair. *I can help you if you talk to me!*

Bartolos looked through the shield to the floor of the Chenowa ship. It was only about two feet below him. *Turn off the shield,* he said to John. After a moment, he dropped to the floor. With the shield gone, his head filled with warnings and other thoughts from the Chenowa. The strongest thought was that they should leave. Bartolos held up his hands and sent his thoughts to them. *Please! Send someone to talk with me. I can see what is happening to your people, and I want to help if I can, and I believe I can. We are not here to harm you; we are here to help both our races. Please, put down your weapons and send someone to talk to me.*

The armed Chenowa didn't put down their weapons, but they did relax a bit. Behind them, something was happening. Finally, an old man made his way through the crowd toward him. This Chenowa was walking with crutches and had someone on either side to support him. As he got closer, Bartolos was surprised to see he wasn't an old man at all, he just looked old because of his sickness. Bartolos looked around the area at all the clutter. *They haven't the strength or the will to clean it up! That's how sick and weak these poor people are.*

He looked back at the man on crutches, his empathy for them increasing. He longed for them to let him help them. They might have heard his thoughts because they all lowered their weapons, and the warnings stopped.

Now Bartolos felt free to move and walked to meet the Chenowa. The Chenowen introduced himself as Ellistarrau Layha. Bartolos understood that 'Ellistarrau' was the title for a high-ranking Chenowa. Layha was his actual name.

Layha was too weak to stop Bartolos from seeing his fear of a retaliatory attack from Earth or Pellaya. He also couldn't stop Bartolos from seeing his doubts that the Chenowa could defend themselves. Bartolos felt Layha's frustration, embarrassment, worry, and sorrow.

Layha stood, a broken man, humbled by what was happening. He had swallowed his pride and come forward because Bartolos had said he could help them. Layha had stepped forward for the sake of his people, and Bartolos respected that and told him so. That seemed to ease Layha's jumbled-up mind.

Layha confessed that despite their best efforts, they were unable to cure what ailed them. Early on, they had asked for help from two other races and not only had been refused, but threatened. So they stupidly stopped asking anyone for help and began taking what they wanted. Doing this angered many races, including the humans, and now the Pellayens.

"As Ellistarrau of my people," Layha said. "I have come to you because we can not afford our pride any longer. We are dying, and I heard you say you know what is wrong. Do you?" Layha said.

"I believe I do, and I will gladly do what I can to help your people, Ellistarrau Layha. We want peace with the Chenowa and with all our neighbors. My people have great knowledge of medicines and what ails the body. We will help you save your people if you let us."

Layha looked as if he were about to break down. "If it is not too late," he said. "On behalf of my people, I accept your offer to help."

As if to make the point of it being too late, a Chenowa in the distance fell to the floor. Others picked the body up and carried it off the floor. Her body was lifeless, and it looked like the end had come for her.

Bartolos sighed. He had seen enough. He didn't care that the Chenowa were taking people from Pellaya anymore. These people needed help, and a lot of it. In his mind, this mission to show force was over. It was now a mission of mercy.

Bartolos had been allowing his thoughts to go to John and Awth, and they agreed. John landed the ship, and Awth got out and stood with Bartolos. Awth's anger toward the Chenowa was gone. In a sorrowful voice, he spoke to Bartolos. "Tell them everything you know about their condition and how to stop it, and tell them we will return with more people who can help them."

Ellistarrau Layha, on his authority, agreed to move his ships out of the water and onto land so Gullaynianna and her team could go to work helping them. They had accepted the help, but it didn't seem they were all that thankful. For several days, they all seemed pensive and unwilling even to hope that their plight was coming to an end.

That changed when they saw how much the Pellayens understood about what was plaguing them. The Pellayens were very familiar with the disease and had learned how to cure it many years ago. The Pellayens called it Terrenes' disease and had struggled with it for a long time, but now knew how to cure it in its many forms. It was easy to see the relief in Ellistarrau Layha when Gullaynianna told him they knew the disease well and would be able to cure it and save his race. "The Humans are already being cured to the point that it is almost gone. They call it Cancer. We developed an organism that feeds on the Cancerous cells. It won't harm the host's body, only the cancerous cells. Once the Cancer is gone, there is nothing left for the organism to feed on. It leaves the body through normal processes. Your race will survive Layha, and it won't take as long as you might think. You will see improvement fairly quickly," Gullaynianna said.

Now, Layha couldn't thank Gullaynianna and Bartolos enough for all they were doing. Bartolos had already been teaching them how their Mental Ability had caused the Cancer in the first place. He was able to show them how to use their Mental Powers in a way that would no longer cause harm to the body.

Every Chenowa who learned to use their mental ability this way was amazed at how easily their power flowed effortlessly from them. It surprised them that Mental Power came from the spirit, not the physical brain. With this new way of using their

Mental Ability, they didn't have to push their power out of themselves. It flowed easily out from them, which greatly increased their power. The Chenowa truly had the strongest minds of all the races.

The Chenowa went from the brink of destruction to being happy and hopeful for the future. They were going to survive and had gained two new allies. The Pellayens and the humans. Both were willing to help.

Now that the Chenowa were being helped, a new plague sprang up. It was a plague of guilt for having treated the humans and Pellayens with such disrespect. It became worse because the Humans and Pellayens were so willing to help save their race in spite of what had been done to them. The Chenowa were being offered every kindness, and it made the Chenowa admit to their arrogance and their stupidity. Their view of humans, in particular, had changed. They were worth far more than the Chenowa had allowed them.

Awth, Bartolos, and John were pleased at how well everything had worked out for the Chenowa. They could only hope it would work out just as well for the Itchaians.

One of the Pellayen scout ships finally located the Itchaian fleet. They hadn't gone far because they had nowhere to go. They were still in Earth's solar system when they were found.

John approached the fleet with Awth and Bartolos aboard and the shield up. He flew into the middle of them and waited to see what the Itchaian would do. A few smaller fighters were around, but they didn't seem interested in John's ship. Nothing happened for nearly an hour. Then a small Ship approached them and stopped right in front of them.

"No weapons that I can see," John said.

"No, and I only see one being inside. Let's drop the shield and let Bartolos talk to him," Awth said.

John dropped the shield, and Bartolos made contact with the Itchaian. It was Margo, again. Margo was worried they had come looking for revenge, and let it be known that the Itchaian were willing to give what they could to appease the humans. *"It never should have happened, and we are sorry for what has been done to you. If you have come to take lives, we know we can do nothing to stop you. We will not resist you."*

Bartolos had to stop him to tell him they had not come to take lives, but to offer them peace with the Pellayen. "We know of an uninhabited planet that supports life. There is no intelligent life there, so you can go there to survive," he said and waited.

Soon, Bartolos felt great thankfulness from Margo. Then he understood Margo to say they were running out of food and supplies. He also felt Margo's unwillingness to ask for help because of what had been done to Earth. Bartolos told him the Pellayens were blessed to have an abundance of food. Pellaya would resupply the Itchaian ships with food and supplies for their journey.

Again, Margo's thankfulness filled Bartolos's head. Right after that, he felt Margo's great remorse over the attack on Earth. It haunted him that it had happened. He informed Bartolos that those responsible for the attack had been dealt with. For many, the punishment was death. He pleaded with Bartolos to understand that the forces that attacked Earth had separated themselves from the main fleet and done what never should have happened. They had found Earth and decided to take it without consulting the Authority. One man had managed to rise in power and convinced others that they had the right to take Earth from the Humans. His power over them grew until no one dared defy him. Many who followed him did so out of fear, not a desire to take Earth from the Humans. "*When we learned what they were doing, we came as quickly as we could to put a stop to it. The man responsible and those who enforced his laws have been put to death. I hope that helps ease the human's pain. We will never bother them again. We long for peace with everyone and go to great lengths to achieve it. We ask forgiveness from the Humans, but don't expect it.*"

When John heard this, he again thought of Hitler and the Nazi's. It made him feel a little better knowing it wasn't just the humans that could be coerced into doing such a thing. It also made him feel less angry at the Itchaian that survived.

The Itchaian accepted help from the Pellayens, but it was John who led their fleet back to the Pellayen Gate. Now they were faced with a new problem. How would they get a fleet of thousands of ships through the gate?

They learned quickly that any ship near the Gate, when activated, would go through. The first time through, John flew to the Council house, where Awth and Bartolos got others to help bring the rest through.

Restocking the Itchaian ship was next on the list. The Itchaian responded by teaching the Pellayens how to build what they called, 'Molecular Adhesion Devices". John and the Pellayens called them Gravity units. It was a technology built into the floor of a ship that simulated gravity. It would be hard to add to existing Ships, but it would be easily built into new ones, and the Pellayens were thankful for it.

The Itchaian fleet was soon fully supplied and ready to head toward their new home. They were told which star to follow and where the planet was supposed to be. It would take years for them to get there, so no one from Earth or Pellaya went with them to show them the way, though John considered doing so for quite a while. The Itchaian were assured they would have no trouble finding it by themselves.

The Pellayens had offered peace and friendship to the Itchaian's, but they were happy to wave goodbye to them when the time came. Itchaians were a very peaceful lot and as God fearing as the Pellayens, but they had a peculiar way about them that was hard to understand, and their language was also hard to follow. But these weren't the real reason everyone was relieved to see them go. The real reason was that members of this race had attacked Earth, intending to rid the Earth of the Human population. Because of that, they had a bad reputation that would take some time to dismiss.

Many years later, one lone Itchaian ship appeared in the Pellayen sky. On board were Margo and six other Itchaian's. They asked for representatives from Earth and the Chenowa home worlds to gather for what they hoped would become an annual meeting. When all the representatives had gathered, Margo stood before them to speak.

"We found the planet just as you said we would. I am pleased to tell you that we are prospering. Our people are happy and safe. All of us send our warmest regards to you, the Pellayen people, and to you, John of the Humans. To the Humans of Earth, we can only hope that one day you can forgive us for what our people did to you. We vow that this will never happen again. We are incredibly thankful for the mercy of the Humans and the help of the Pellayens.

We have brought technological gifts to share with you, and we welcome the Pellayens, the Humans, and the Chenowa to visit our planet as friends. We, the Itchaian's, the Humans, and the Chenowa, should be thankful to be, 'Distant Friends of Pellaya'.

THE END